PRAISE FOR BIRMINGHAM'S BOOKS

"There's no way to introduce you to all the fascinating characters [in *Words on a Plate* that] Reba has created in her new take on the war between this world and the world of magic. But I can say this: Many of her characters in both worlds just happen to be lesbian or gay, bisexual or transgender. To Reba, whatever they are makes no difference to the story. I love that. One day we may live in a world where people are just people and fairies are just fairies, but until then, Reba's writing reflects the America we all want to live in."

~**Mel White, author of** *Stranger at the Gate: To be Gay and Christian in America* **and** *Holy Terror: Lies the Christian Right Tells Us to Deny Gay Equality*

"An exciting adventure with unique characters navigating their way through fantasy and reality. . . [*Words on a Plate* is an] easy read, writing is crisp and the mystical characters are interesting with creative powers."

~**Katie Cotter, former news editor,** *The Advocate*

"From the cozy tenderness of two middle-aged lesbians spooning each other to sleep after a long day of tax preparation to an epic battle between dwarves, elves, and humans, *Floodlight* champions the magic of the ordinary and vice versa. Birmingham is the real thing, and it feels like she is just getting started. Lucky for us."

~**Patricia Loughrey, award-winning playwright and author of** *Dear Harvey* **and** *Sonata 1962*

"In this first novel in a projected fantasy series, debut novelist Birmingham's LGBTQ representation among the cast is refreshing. She parallels the fictional cult with the patriarchy, and she compares interspecies relationships in the fantasy world with LGBTQ relationships in ours."

~**Kirkus Reviews**

"I love me some wacky plots and characters, and between the thrills and chills in *Floodlight*, this book has a lot of humorous stuff in it. Besides, there are elves and griffins and dwarves—oh, my!—who could ask for anything more? If you like the funny urban fantasies of Charlaine Harris or Jim Butcher's Dresden Files, you'll likely enjoy Birmingham's new series."

~Jessie Chandler, award-winning author of The Shay O'Hanlon Caper Series

"Panda Fowler, the protagonist in the lesbian-mystery-fiction book *Floodlight*, was a nonbeliever in all things magical and supernatural, well, until her wife, Mitzi, was kidnapped. Faster than you can say Severus Snape, Fowler's world is turned on its head, and she suspends her disbelief to rescue Mitzi.... As she struggles to rescue Mitzi, Panda enlists her best friends, Juniper and Valerie Gooden, to help. Together, they battle a group of dastardly villains who practice a dark religion, Wolf Raven, that hates homosexuality."

~ QVoiceNews.com

"Likable main characters…(and) sweet elf characters. Having two lesbian married couples was refreshing to read. The balance between supportive and not supportive of lesbian relationships (was) realistic."

~Bookloverblogs.com

WORDS ON A PLATE

BOOK TWO
THE HERCYNIAN FOREST SERIES

REBA BIRMINGHAM

LAUNCH**POINT**
PRESS

Launch Point Press
Portland, Oregon

Launch Point Press
Portland, Oregon
www.LaunchPointPress.com

~

CITIZENS OF AND VISITORS TO MERRYVILLE

Alexandra Stephanovsky – Defense Attorney.

Angela - A *dezplazador de la forma* (shape shifter).

April – Young woman at New Spirit Church.

Babs – One and only employee of Fowler Tax Services.

Bill Miller – Longsuffering husband of Hortense Miller.

Bonnie Bruce, nicknamed Bon Bon – Janet's daughter, a Mavenette.

Bridgette – Of French descent, wife of socially prominent person.

Brooke Fowler – Panda's stockbroker brother in New York.

Bruno – Monk with the Wolf Raven Religion.

Brutus – Panda & Mitzi's Bengal cat.

Charlie Potts – Detective with the Merryville Police Department. Charlotte Windingle – Biggest Patron of the Merryville Museum.

Damien Simpson – Artist.

Denise McGreggor – Socialite, daughter of the late Agnes McGreggor, former member of the Merryville Horticultural Society.

Dieter – Tall German, talented with languages.

Ekkehard, a/k/a Ekk – Guardian Elf, Enrolled Agent, speaks cat.

Elsa – Guardian Elf, Special talents include shaping emotions while giving off floral fragrance.

Fernando – Panda's new Peruvian boyfriend.

Florence Dinwitter – Board member of Merryville Horticultural Society, married to Judge Dinwitter.

Hortense Miller – President of the Merryville Horticultural Society.

Janet Bruce – Board member of Merryville Horticultural Society, mother of Bonnie.

Julia - A *dezplazador de la forma* (shape shifter).

Juniper Gooden – Curator of the Merryville Museum, Valerie's partner.

Juju – Ekk's elvin cousin in Peru (Jungle Elf).

Lidia – Merryville Horticultural Society, Schoolteacher.

Linda Chicolette – Board member at the Merryville Museum.

Lucas Windingle – Young board member of the Merryville Museum.

Maribel – Exhibit Coordinator at the Merryville Museum.

Mitzi Fowler – Panda's free-spirited wife, sometimes travel agent/tour guide, half human and half griffin, apt to sprout wings in times of grave danger.

Panda Fowler – A tax preparer in Merryville, married to Mitzi.

Penelope – Artist.

Puddle Fowler – Panda's sister, recently back from an ashram in India.

Rev. Morry – Maurice, actually, Pastor at "New Spirit" Evangelical Church.

Richland Bruce – New Chairman of the Board, Merryville Museum.

Romy – A jungle elf in Peru.

Sally – Merryville Horticultural Society, wife of Jack who's owner of a large landscaping company.

Sister Lucia Reya – Nun of The Sisters of the Sun also known as Las Hermanas del Sol.

Susan Schadt – Mitzi's mother, who lives in Northern California.

Twyla – Guardian Fairy sent from the Hercynian Garden while Elsa and Ekk away.

Valerie Gooden – Home healthcare nurse, Juniper's partner.

Wolfrum – Cult Leader of the Wolf Raven Religion.

TERMS

Grunzueg – Translated as "Green Stuff," has Magical Properties, and is from the Hercynian Garden.

Moon Dog – Like a Sun Dog, but rarer.

Sun Dog - Sun dogs typically appear as two subtly-colored patches of light to the left and right of the sun. Also called phantom suns or mock suns. The etymology of sun dog largely remains a mystery. Wikipedia and the Oxford English Dictionary state it as being of obscure origin.

Zauberbuch - A grimoire or magical book containing spells and magical knowledge. Such magical books typically include astrological rules, lists of angels and demons, spells, as well as instructions for summoning magical creatures, or for the production of talismans and wretches.

~

ACKNOWLEDGMENTS

I love really busy people as beta readers, because they are interested in everything and give terrific feedback! In this short attention span world, I am ever thankful for: Verda Foster, Nikki Santisteven, Deb & Mary Love, Katie Cotter, Karina Wiechert, Jennifer Warner, Laura Bolen, Marta Mora, and Mel White. May you all be blessed for giving your precious time. A special shout out to Suzan Twilley Gridley, my Professor friend, who has such an eagle eye she is probably part griffin. Thank you also to Lori Lake for her endless patience, encouragement and editing skills.

Reba Birmingham
Long Beach, California
July 2019

∾

To Stephanie, my wife.

You saved me.

CHAPTER ONE

PROLOGUE—MAY

I glanced at my watch three times waiting for my spouse, Mitzi, then booted up our laptop to a blank page in Word and tried once more to write the story of how our world was rocked:

> *My name is Panda Fowler, and I'm a tax preparer. My wife and I live on Thistle Drive in the quiet town of Merryville, which until recently has been fairly uneventful.*

My gaze drifted to the kitchen door. Sigh, I'm always ready first.

The cursor blinked at me. "Mitzi! Hurry up," I shouted over my shoulder. She was still upstairs.

Frustrated no one would believe the story if they hadn't seen it with their own eyes, I turned back to the screen and closed the document without saving. Instead, for about the hundredth time, I Googled griffin and read that it's a legendary creature with the body, back legs, and tail of a lion, and the head and wings of an eagle. Since the lion is the king of the forest and the eagle, king of birds, it is a majestic creature—

"I'll be there in a minute!" Mitzi called from upstairs.

We recently discovered my father-in-law—Mitzi's dad—is a magical creature, a full-blooded griffin who lives in the Hercynian Garden in the Black Forest of Germany. Mitzi's mother, Susan, is fully human. So this makes my wife a . . . hybrid magical/human creature? What I do know is during times of great danger, my human-looking wife is apt to sprout wings, a development which has put stress on our relationship. Not a usual problem for Merryville couples. Neither of us is really sure about what this will mean in our future. For now, we're putting one foot in front of the other.

I escaped Wikipedia and yelled again, "Mitzi, it's time to call Puddle, come on!"

Our kitchen is small but it's the place in our home where everyone gravitates. I scooted two kitchen chairs in front of our laptop computer, making it an "office" and waited for Mitzi to join me for our first Skype call.

My sister, Puddle, is now in Peru with our two elven guardians—yes, there are elves in this story, more on that turn of events later—on a quest to find our parents. When we were kids, they were "lost." They've been missing and presumed dead for over thirty years. Puddle was recently here in Merryville. She was blown away by Mitzi's family history and new skill, but her need to find out about our parents and itchy feet to travel took her away again.

My gaze trailed around our 1950s yellow Formica table and the tea cups lined up on a shelf over our bay window. Light streamed into the kitchen through the panes of glass and bathed this scene. I drew a deep breath and smelled the fragrance of peonies coming through the partially open back door. With all the strangeness injected into our lives lately, this room, our garden and home, and our routines tethered me to reality.

Mitzi flounced in, hands spread in apology, "Sorry, babe, Brutus was on my lap."

"R-i-i-ight." Brutus is our Bengal cat. It's an unwritten rule that a woman can't move when an adorable cat is sleeping on her. He'd suffered a head injury during the "troubles" not too long ago, and we were still careful with him. I smiled and patted her chair, never able to stay irritated long.

As she sat, Mitzi observed: "The computer screen is like a magic mirror." The cursor blinked as if in agreement. She actually rubbed her hands together and said, "Another world awaits."

Unlike me, Mitzi has embraced this new magical element in our lives. I put my hand on the purple mouse and turned to her. "Ready?"

She nodded.

"Here goes!" As Mitzi and I peered into our laptop, faces scrunched up, she said, "We sure know a lot more about magic than we used to!"

I thought but didn't say, Magic, magic, magic! Give it a rest!

Aloud, I said, "This is technology, Mitzi, nothing more." I, the non-magical creature, am somewhat of a buzz kill. After all, I'm a tax preparer and don't have a griffin father. It seems to me Mitzi brings magic up constantly. My way of coping is to shut down a bit.

I double-clicked the icon of a white S on a blue background, trying out Skype to reach my nomadic sister. "You sure there aren't written directions somewhere?"

"Nope. We need a teenager." She laughed and gave me her full face. Her attention was very attractive, and I had to smile.

The computer emitted a new, to me, odd electronic beeping sound, reminding me I was actually making a telephone call.

"Aha! There it goes." We both sat up straight in our seats and leaned in. The screen opened up to show us an empty room. A ceiling fan lazily turned.

Mitzi and I shared a puzzled glance, then I spoke into what appeared to be the laptop's microphone.

"Hullo! It's Panda. Are you there, sissy?"

I peered intently, not sure if I was in front of the tiny camera, or if we'd even reached the right number.

The computer screen filled, and I mean filled, with frizzy hair, as a giggling Puddle came into view.

"Panda Bear!" Her old childhood name for me. Our parents named their three kids Panda, Puddle and Brooke. What can I say? It was the Seventies, and they were hippies.

"Puddle Pop!" I said affectionately, for turnabout was fair play. "There you are! How are you? And what happened to your dreadlocks?"

Puddle's grin was epic. "Check this out." She turned her head to show us braids on the back side of her head.

"Elsa's putting me in braids and beads, sorta like Mitzi."

I saw Elsa then, our tiny elven friend and protector, standing behind Puddle. She appeared somewhat frazzled. Puddle is a handful, and Elsa, like a good babysitter, was probably thinking up creative ways to keep her charge occupied.

"Elsa!" Mitzi moved closer to the screen, and Brutus chose that moment to hop on the keyboard. He must have stepped on the wrong button because the big picture shrank to a small square in the corner.

Elsa enthusiastically waved, probably not sure of the video call protocol either. I swatted at the cat.

"Mitzi, so good to see you!" came a harmony of voices from the screen. "Brutus too! Oh, I miss him." That last bit was from Elsa. I got their picture full screen again after pecking around on the keys.

"Um, chopped liver here wants to get in on this." I scooted back, part of our chair derby, so Mitzi, the cat, and I could all be seen by the Peruvian contingent.

I put my arm around Mitzi so she would stay put. My need to touch her was also probably a metaphor for my insecurity at her new ability to fly.

"What's it like? Where are you guys now?" Mitzi asked, repeatedly pulling Brutus down.

"Still in Lima. Ow," Puddle said, shooting a frown at the elven hands plaiting her hair.

"I think Brutus is trying to come through the glass to you, Puddle," I said. "I suspect you put pot in his cat food when you were here and he wants more."

She pointed at him on screen and said, "Brutus, dude, stick to the catnip."

Shy and somewhat crowded herself, Elsa waved again and let Puddle have the floor, or screen, as it were. I noticed Elsa's fair German skin was sunburnt.

Puddle leaned in and stage whispered: "Panda, are you sure I should talk about lookin' for Paititi on this," her eyes rolled up and then back and forth comically, "this thing-a-majigger we're using? You know, the Russians and NSA and all that."

I believed Puddle was kidding, but she did have an innate distrust of big government, ours or anyone else's.

Mitzi tensed. "Don't you feel safe? Has something happened?" and some of the merriment in the call went away. We'd been through such an ordeal in the last few weeks, what with escaping evil and all, and wanted to prolong the normalcy of having a regular call with our loved ones.

Elsa piped up from somewhere off screen. "We're fine."

"How about you sissy-in-law? Any unexpected flights?" Puddle grinned mischievously at Mitzi. We saw Puddle turn her freckled face off screen, probably to Elsa, and heard her say, "okay, okay!"

We're not supposed to talk about griffins, elves and magic and other such things to non-magical people. Elsa was probably enforcing that rule by hushing Puddle because on-line calls are not so private.

Mitzi shifted in her seat to get more comfortable. "Um, no. The last time was when Brutus here," she ruffled the fur on our cat's big spotted head, "came to the museum and let us know Elsa and Ekk were in danger." She quickly changed the subject. "Where is Ekk? Is he okay?"

Elsa, who must not have gone very far, piped up again and her pink face appeared. "Ekk is with his cousin Juju, um, checking out some things." She smiled, but I sensed tension. Ekk was Elsa's mate. She furrowed her dainty brow. "Any *visitors* yet?" She was referring to a certain missing fairy. Since Ekk and Elsa, our guardians, were in Peru, Mitzi's griffin father was supposed to have sent us a new, temporary guardian, a fairy named Twyla.

I shook my head. "Just us chickens. Any leads on mom and dad?" My sister, the wanderer, was never in one place for too long. She was very much like our parents who disappeared seeking Paititi, the legendary City of Gold.

Puddle started to speak but Elsa uncharacteristically cut her short. "I'm so glad to hear and see all of you. Ekk and I really miss Merryville. Maybe you can talk to Ekk later. He'll fill you in about that other stuff." Elsa raised her eyebrows on her rosy cherubic face with meaning.

Puddle whipped her head toward Elsa, and I saw half frizz, half braids. She giggled and said, "Elsa, don'tcha want to tell them about—"

Elsa put a tiny hand over Puddle's lips, a move I thought I would try sometime. My sister never takes a hint, and it's really hard to get her to stop talking if she's on a roll.

I got that this was not the time to have a full conversation. "Later, Puddle, just get your beads done!"

"Yes, we can be the bead sisters," Mitzi added, having two strands of beads herself framing her lovely face.

Elsa said, "Panda, you should be getting some mail soon." Her smile seemed forced, like a painted doll's face.

"Okay, no worries," I said. "Glad you're doing all right."

I was intrigued. Obviously, Elsa didn't want to say what-all was going on. It appeared it wasn't only about keeping the conversation non-magical.

I eyeballed her as intently as I could through the screen. "Tell Ekk I want to hear from him soon."

"We will," Puddle and Elsa said, with Elsa sounding more like, "Ve vill." She has quite a German accent, and it's so cute with her feminine voice.

Puddle shrugged, "Namaste."

We signed off and sat for a moment in front of the computer. Brutus, instantly bored, leapt off our laps. It made me sad to see Puddle thousands of miles away on a fool's errand. Mitzi got up and left the room.

MEANWHILE IN PERU

After Elsa braided her hair, Puddle had a smoke of her favorite marijuana, and, truth be told, Elsa didn't mind. Pot kept the newly-beaded woman calm and from peppering her with questions Elsa couldn't answer. She had to laugh as Puddle clumsily crawled into a hammock and left her watching the hummingbirds on her hotel room deck. Elsa returned to her own room to find Ekk and his Peruvian cousin, Juju, leaning over a table.

The room was small, but elves are smaller. Each man was able to swing his feet while sitting in the chairs. She loved her Ekk so and wished this was a real vacation. Peru is beautiful! Since being sent from the Hercynian Garden in Germany to watch over the girls, for that is how she now thought of Mitzi and Panda, "the girls," there had not been much time to rest.

In spite of it all, Ekk was fit and tanned, like a Brooks Brothers elf, next to the wildly unkempt Juju. Elsa hoped none of the earthy elf's jungle dirt would land on the table.

"How long have the El Chullanchaqui known about Paititi?" Ekk asked Juju.

Juju stretched his neck and scratched. He shook his wild mane, which actually had some sticks in it. "You may as well ask how long has the jungle been here?" He laughed at his own comment, then said to Elsa, "Do you have any more Chicha?"—referring to the local beer. He was acting a bit like a chauvinist, but Elsa didn't mind. Her kitchen was her sanctuary, and she didn't want his dirty mitts touching anything in there anyway.

"Where do you live when you aren't in civilization?" Elsa asked politely, really wanting to know. She got the fridge door open after jumping up to reach the handle, wrestled a beer out and brought it to Juju.

"Civilization?" Juju accepted the beer and took a long pull before answering. "I live in the most beautiful, how you say, Cathedral of green— better than your *civilization*."

Ekk was seated and his eyes and eyebrows lifted as he said to Elsa, "Chicha turns my cousin into a poet."

Juju launched from his chair, and Elsa saw he was solid muscle. "We sleep where we need to. The *selva* is our home." He stared out the window at the city below. "*This* makes me nervous. I know how to read the broken twig and follow the panther's paw print. All that concrete. I don't know how you do," he waved a dirty hand at the traffic below, "this."

"Point taken," Ekk said. "We love the forest of Germany, but when there we're more likely to live in buildings than trees. The Hercynian Garden uses *grünzueg* for everything, and it's easy to build."

"*Grünzueg*? Is that German? I don't know that language." Juju hopped into his chair again.

"Oh, it means 'Green Stuff.' It's magical. I keep some with me all the time." Ekk pulled out a tiny orb, green in color.

"You don't have much," Juju observed.

Elsa and Ekk both laughed. "Trust me, it's plenty," Ekk said as he put the green blob away. "Now, Juju, we need to make our plan." Ekk gestured from himself to Elsa. When do we get the directions to Paititi."

Now it was Juju's turn to laugh and appear insulted. "Just like that? The Jungle Guardians are going to give you a map to its most secret pearl? I don't think so." He drank again.

Elsa was frustrated and went to the kitchen to bake, her "go to" activity when she didn't know what else to do. She dragged a chair to stand on in order to better reach the cupboards.

❧

Ekk smiled affectionately at her and then turned to Juju, "We don't need a map literally, but I have people to protect, too. We need a plan."

Juju fixed a stare out the second story window toward the trees in the distance. A hummingbird zipped by.

"We've got Puddle," Ekk continued. "I want to keep her from doing something impulsive, like try to find her parents on her own." Ekk had noticed Puddle and Juju seemed to have a special connection, and he was using it.

This comment got Juju's attention. Juju grunted and mentally rejoined them, "I like her fearlessness."

"Part of the problem," Ekk said, "is how fearless she is. Now, we've got to get her sister Panda and sister-in-law Mitzi coming, and we're going to have the brother, Brooke, any minute. Meanwhile, Puddle's ready to go and find their parents *now*. I need to keep them all safe and give Puddle something to cool her jets. Brooke and Panda are also going to be hounding me for the plan."

"Sounds like we need to get Puddle in here." Juju rolled his nearly empty bottle between hairy hands and called to Elsa, "we got more Chicha?" Ekk smiled as Juju smoothed his hair.

Elsa picked up Ekk's cellular phone and carried it back to the kitchen, talking softly. In a couple of minutes, she returned. "Puddle says she's going out with Fernando for a walk." Fernando was the latest boyfriend, a Peruvian who she had met while at an Ashram in India.

"Watch him," Juju said darkly.

"Do you get a bad feeling? Elsa asked. "I don't get anything from him."

This was saying something, for to call Elsa sensitive to vibes is like saying Warren Buffet is pretty good at picking stocks. So far, Puddle's new boyfriend was a mystery. Ekk found it coincidental that Fernando was from Peru and had accompanied Puddle here from India.

Ekk said, "Elsa, it takes strong magic to mask human emanations. Usually you get something. That could be a sign in itself."

"I'll ask around," Juju said. "I don't like his smell."

Ekk stroked his chin trying to suppress a smile. "His smell?" Juju didn't exactly stink, but bathing was not high on his list. "I think you're just jealous."

Juju responded with an exasperated expression. "There is a smell like perfume—man perfume. It puts me on edge. It's not real. Make sure he's not a *dezplazador de la forma*, a—"

"A what?" Elsa asked.

"A shapeshifter?" Ekk squeaked, his brow furrowed.

"Si." Juju's face was totally serious, unlike his usual smiling self.

"Have you been smoking some funny stuff with Puddle again?" Elsa popped a pan of *galletas* into the oven and put her hand on her hip. Juju and Ekk made meaningful eye contact and broke up laughing.

∾

CHAPTER TWO

BACK IN MERRYVILLE

I studied my reflection in the bathroom mirror, trying to see if I had grown a whisker, a new and disturbing thing in my life. Observing my face close up, it was impossible to tell I had been part of rescuing my wife from an evil villain in another country a few weeks ago. Still "fluffy" and with my cowlick, I would never be mistaken for Wonder Woman. Honestly, I could never understand why someone as beautiful as Mitzi gave me the time of day. Now she was Magic Mitzi, with wings. Would she stay with her boring old tax preparer?

Mitzi popped up unexpectedly behind me and said, "Let me show you something." I put down the tweezers and let her take my hand. She led me to her "travel office" in our humble home. I didn't mind. Anything was better than obsessing about whiskers or my insecurities. In her "office," usually there were many posters of far flung destinations. Her favorites were "Three Pearls of Italy" and "Greece is Paradise." She had taken those down.

In their place, she had put up maps of Peru to keep track of Puddle's progress. The whole wall was pretty much full of pictures, articles, and flight schedules having to do with Lima and its proximity to the legendary lost city of Paititi. There were bits of yarn stretching from places on the map to dates and even pictures of expeditions.

I knew she was interested in where Puddle and our elves were, but this was way more than casual interest. "Babe, are you tracking a serial killer?"

She hates my cop shows but knew what I meant. She ignored my funny comment, and stood before the wall, checking her work. "We need to join Puddle in Peru."

I instantly shut down.

"Listen, I wouldn't bring up the subject of Peru, or your parents, lightly." She glanced at me, then back to the wall. "I hope you know that, Panda." I got the full face again—those eyes! "I wouldn't unless I had something important to say."

I stayed silent and tried to stave off the resistance coursing through me. "I know it's painful for you."

My gaze went to the ceiling, tears welling. "Yes, having one's parents permanently disappear when you're a kid is painful, to say the least." I must have frozen physically, thinking of this.

She gently touched my arm, "Um, why don't you get comfortable."

I sighed and resisted plopping in the bean bag chair, ironically one of the only tangible pieces I had of my parents' past. They weren't materialistic. All my sister and brother and I split among us were some tapestries, books, and this bean bag chair.

I watched Mitzi take a deep breath, sensing she'd been working in earnest. A little background here. My parents were hippies, always chasing utopian communities. As a child, I had lived on a farm and in a VW bus, and been to more music festivals than you could shake a stick at. Being the "baby of the family," I was so young when they disappeared in Peru my memories of them were blurry. The family story was that they left to find "Paititi," also known as the "City of Gold" in Peru, and never returned.

Puddle and Brooke, my older siblings, had more stories about mom and daddy, and most were good. I was probably the most judgmental of the three of us—traipsing off to get killed in a jungle seemed an extremely irresponsible thing to do when you had small children. Thank God our folks had the sense to leave us three kids with our aunt and uncle while they gallivanted around. Mitzi's voice snapped me out of my reverie.

"Earth to Panda." I focused and she continued. "Okay, these red pins are where Elsa, Ekk and Puddle landed. I put these blue ones to mark where they've been staying and met up with Juju. I think they must be on to something because you can see they were here," she pointed to an area by Lima, "then abruptly moved to here," she tapped a place on the map, "the highest city in Peru, Cuzco."

"What's the green pin?" My heart sank. "Oh, yeah, that's where they were last seen." There was a spot a few kilometers east of the Andes with a lonely pin in it. Mitzi gave me her stern face. Clearly, I was being negative.

"Does it matter where they are? We both know this is crazy. I only hope Ekk and Elsa can talk Puddle out of going into the jungle. Our parents' disappearance was a long time ago and no one, even experts, have been able to find this lost city or a trace of them."

"You haven't even heard what I have to say yet."

But I was on a roll. "Face it, Mitz, it's just a sad story, and Puddle can't stay in one place after the childhood we had. She recently spent six months in an Ashram in India. She won't be in Peru long. She met that Fernando guy in India, and it's as much as chasing him back to his country as anything else. He's from Peru."

Mitzi put a finger to my lips. "Hush. I love you, Panda, but we've lived with this elephant in the living room for too long. Your parents' disappearance is a huge deal in your life. It's an unhealed place. You never want to talk about it, but don't you see?" She put my hair behind my ear. "You have to face it sometime and there'll never be a better time!"

Peering at the map, she gestured with one of her arms, like Vanna White: "If we use all our American Airlines miles, we could do this for not a whole lot of money."

I sharpened my voice. "Mitzi, we're not going to Peru." Better to nip these things in the bud. I didn't want to sound harsh, but even talking about it made me angry. As Doctor Tina, our occasional therapist, says, I have abandonment issues the size of the Grand Canyon.

"Panda, your sister is there now. This is the best chance we have of finding out what really happened to your mom and dad. Think about it! Elsa and Ekk are a magical resource, and Ekk even has a cousin who's connected to the jungle where they disappeared! How often will these things all line up?"

I completely shut down again. "Puddle is chasing a pipe dream. She, she smokes too much pot!" I folded my arms over my chest again.

"About a month ago, you didn't believe in the 'pipe dream' of magic elves and ravens working for and against an evil empire, or that your half-griffin wife could fly either."

Uh oh, Mitzi's brown eyes were heating up like embers. She rarely got angry, but I could tell she was getting there.

I kept my arms folded and kind of actually harrumphed, not liking this conversation at all. I wanted my normal life back. I shut my eyes. But Mitzi, being the dynamic creature she is, will not be shut out. Truthfully, it's one reason I love her so much. She physically unwrapped my arms. I started to leave.

"Hear me out!" Mitzi gave me a playful push, and I landed on my butt on one of the last true bean bag chairs in the world. "You promised to take me somewhere after tax season. Well guess what? Tax season's over!"

I squirmed awkwardly in the bean bag chair, fished out a couple of Brutus' fake mice from underneath me, and settled in. She had gotten my attention. "Okay, babe, what else you got?" I love her with all my heart, which was the only thing helping me to face this and listen.

She cleared her throat, like a school teacher, and actually picked up a pen to use as a pointer. "Your parents disappeared seeking the lost city of Paititi, east of the Andes mountains in the southeastern part of the rainforest." Her pen landed on what I assumed was a color blow up of the area.

"And never returned. Yes," I said, "I know." The story was still painful, and I crossed my arms again. Puddle was the only one who still believed they could be out there somewhere. Brooke, a New York stockbroker, had isolated himself from the family with work and wouldn't even talk about it.

Mitzi continued, "I'm interested in this for my own reasons too."

"Yeah, you like to travel." A smile tugged at my lips. "You're a travel agent."

She wagged her pen at me. "Don't piss me off. Do you want to hear me or not?" I finally shut up.

"Did you know in 1600 a missionary actually found Paititi, the "City of Gold," and wrote back to the Vatican about it? And he's not the only one. There were others, but Puddle told me your parents followed one explorer in particular: Carlos Neuenschwander Landa, who literally wrote the book in *Paititi in the Mists of History*."

Puddle's recent visit had yielded opportunities for her to talk with Mitzi about the past. She knew more about this than I did.

"And, as recently as 2014, a French explorer came really close to finding it. The next expedition is set for the Valley of Lacco this summer. So, yes, there is reason to believe it truly exists."

I tried to make a stone face like the statues on Easter Island. My final argument. "Even if Paititi exists, it's too dangerous."

"We have magic elves to guide us." She folded herself into a comfortable lotus in front of me.

"Yeah, a couple of European Elves to guide us through a *tropical* rain forest. I don't want to die, Mitz, not for some stupid quest that caught my parents' eye. And I hope you don't think they're still alive because they're not." There, I said it—the thing I never wanted confirmed.

We stared at each other a moment, a battle of wills.

"You could also have a heart attack working yourself to death. We haven't been on a vacation in a long time."

"True, unless you count the Black Forest last month." Score one for me, snap.

"That was different. I was a hostage and you had to come rescue me."

I cracked a smile. That adventure was what brought out my wife's heretofore unknown magical ability. "You would do the same for me. This sounds a lot like that, Mitz, trudging around a jungle, seeking something that no one has been able to find. Except in Peru there are poisonous frogs and snakes and spiders the size of your head." I unfolded and started petting her arm. "Why can't we go to Cancun like normal people?"

She leapt forward, "Because we're not normal people! Not anymore."

She landed on me, smooshing the chair into smithereens as the old cracked vinyl finally gave way under both our weights.

We sat laughing in a pile of old dry beans and tiny flecks of Styrofoam. I blew my bangs up in the air, feeling ridiculous. We hugged and I gave in.

Mitzi could be formidable, even without her wings extended. I guessed it was a good time, if there is ever a good time, to chase old dreams. I'd rather risk my life to giant snakes and spiders than face the possibility of a divorce from Mitzi Fowler. Brutus came in the room chasing elusive floating Styrofoam, a fitting metaphor for our upcoming adventure.

∾

OUTSIDE THE FOWLERS HOUSE ON THISTLE DRIVE

Bill Miller, the longsuffering spouse of Hortense, pulled to the end of the Fowler's block on Thistle Drive, his van full of "Merryville Mavens."

Hortense disembarked with Lidia, Janet, Sally and Sylvia in tow. After Bill took off rather more quickly than what was required, the women surveyed the modest neighborhood, recently considered an eyesore in this growing town. In front of the tiny estrogen pack was Hortense, whose clipboard clacked against her glasses, on a chain hanging around her sturdy neck as she walked. Her companions, ladies of similar social strata, accompanied her down Thistle Drive in Merryville, California. They were there to take stock of the neighborhood flora and to point out any weeds.

Hortense was chairwoman of the Merryville Horticultural Society, her name a seeming prediction of her lofty status as leader because, as every biography in every program they ever printed says, Hortense means "gardener" in Latin.

The first three houses had minor offenses.

Sally, Hortense's devotee, peered at her through thick glasses. "What's next?" Sally was attired in the dress she always wore for neighborhood surveys, a yellow sundress with big pockets. It was somewhat girlish and had silhouettes of a watering can and a spade on the pockets. The others forgave her for this, as her husband owned the largest landscaping company in the county and gave generously to their cause.

Hortense frowned. "This next house, number nine, is a two-bedroom, upstairs and down, part of an older development, but not quite old enough to be historical. Quite unremarkable but for the thistle problem. However, you may remember it from the scandal a few weeks ago having to do with a body in the backyard." She said this last with relish, offering a short detour from the high-minded mission they were on.

Three of the four women accompanying Hortense gave sharp intakes of breath. Sally was very sensitive, which befitted her practically magical abilities to grow roses. She had grown up sheltered somewhere in the "Outer Banks," wherever that was, and was generally nervous. Janet, who also gasped, but with drama, was a trust fund baby who had way too much time on her hands. She engaged enthusiastically, "This was the house? I remember that!" Janet actually clutched her pearls as her eyes widened in a "tell me more" pose. Lidia, an older semi-retired teacher, clucked and shook her head.

Sylvia, the only woman of color among the five, commented. "Come on, there was no body, and no one was convicted or even charged with anything that I know of." The attractive, fortyish woman, other than being upper middle class, didn't fit the demographic of her group, which was white and a bit older. She flashed a radiant smile at the surprised eyes gazing upon her, adding, "Just saying." She laughed alone.

Hortense shot her a glance. She was still studying the pretty Latina. The Society was very careful about who could call themselves a Merryville Maven. The Mavens were responsible for most of the beautification of the medians around town and had singlehandedly rooted out non- indigenous weeds from city premises. They were a big favorite of the Mayor, who allowed use of the public warehouse for one dollar for their annual flower show. Add to that their regular mention in the Merryville Bee, and Merryville's social climbers were lined up to join. Lidia narrowed her eyes at Sylvia and then shot a private "I told you so" look at Hortense.

No way Sylvia's membership could have been rejected, Hortense thought for the hundredth time. Sylvia applied to the group because she said she loved beautiful things, a very acceptable stated motive. She also was willing to pay the rather hefty membership fee.

There was something about the woman, however, that set Hortense's teeth on edge. Miriam, the librarian, was Hortense's "go to" for intel on Merryville residents and had confirmed Sylvia was part of an old Spanish family that had been in Merryville since it was known as Merida. Still.

Hortense sniffed, hating to have her drama watered down, "I've sure never been arrested for anything, and, you know, where there's smoke . . ." They walked in silence for a beat, and then Lidia, a huge suck-up to Hortense, said quickly to Sylvia, "Just because they didn't find any dead bodies doesn't mean something unsavory wasn't going on."

"But—"

Hortense stopped and cut off Sylvia, gesturing to the house with her clipboard. "I'm sorry, those lesbians are shady. One of them disappeared, then they got arrested at the museum with that woman who runs it." Her eyes narrowed at that last bit. "And, Sylvia, in case you forgot," Hortense gave Sylvia the gimlet eye, "it was Juniper Gooden, another lesbian, whose right-hand man killed the Board Chair at the museum! Now I understand you want to put her up for membership in the Mavens? Please."

Sally, Janet and Lidia cackled on cue.

Sylvia kept her voice even, "It's her wife, Valerie, not Juniper, whose name I put in."

The older woman waved her hand as if warding off a bad smell. "Bad press for whatever reason isn't good for Merryville. To be fair, I said we would give her a chance." Hortense and Lidia shared a smirk.

Sylvia effectively changed the subject as she squatted down and placed a bloom between her fingers. "What are all these purple flowers?"

Janet spoke up. "The thistles! Something that has to go! "She adjusted her glasses up her nose and brought a paper she held in her chapped hands so close it almost touched the glass. It's on our hit list."

"Thistle Drive has the only actual thistle bushes left in Merryville," Hortense added, "a remnant of one Scottish family decades ago who let them take root and seed. Scots are partial to the weed it seems," she said, as if that were crazy. "They're tough to get rid of, but we need to keep it from spreading to the other parts of the development."

Sally, who gazed as if hypnotized by the purple thistles, quietly said, "the color, its soothing somehow." She was unpredictable, and apt to comment randomly. Upon receiving stink eye from Hortense she added, "But if they need to go—"

Hortense recited a Mother Goose poem in a sing song voice:
"Cut thistles in May, they'll grow in a day,
Cut them in June, that is too soon,
Cut them in July, then they will die."

"Lovely little poem, that," Janet complimented as the women moved on to the next house. "I guess we'll be back in July."

Sylvia compressed her lips but kept silent. As they moved on, the door to the infamous house opened, and she saw a pudgy woman pick up the newspaper on her front porch.

❧

NUMBER 9 THISTLE DRIVE

I brought in the paper and then left Mitzi to plot and plan the air miles and schedules for our trip. I hate figuring details like that and was glad Juniper, my bestie and curator of the Merryville museum, had asked me to lunch, one of my favorite things. I was early, so I took a detour to the beach to think.

Being somewhat OCD, I like touchstones for marking time. I use the calendar for that. April Fifteenth is a big marker in my world, when all the taxes have to be filed, or at least extensions sent out. It lets me know where I am and makes sense of my world. Mitzi and I also like to do bonfires on Fall and Spring Equinox and Winter and Summer Solstice. I wondered if that would change now. Would these simple rituals be enough to keep her interest in our home in Merryville?

So far, this year has been, to say the least, challenging. Everything I know about pretty much anything has been turned on its head. It was only the beginning of April when I met Ekk, my first elf, and got hauled into an adventure that took me, Mitzi, and our bestie Juniper to the Black Forest in Germany. Since coming back, I've been putting one foot in front of the other and kind of compartmentalizing the surreal. Mitzi and I have been under pressure because of it, and the stress is showing. On top of that, our temporary fairy guardian, Twyla, hasn't shown up. Sometimes I wonder if I imagined it all—very unsettling.

I parked my Smart car, Sweetpea, in a spot near the museum where I could watch the ocean waves, one of my favorite things to do when overwhelmed. The sea is bigger than me and has many moods. As a water sign, I find it calming.

My therapist, Tina, would probably say I had not even begun to process being married to a half-magical creature. I say probably because I hadn't had the nerve to call Tina. How would I explain the tale of the past couple of months?

It would go something like this: Ahem, Doctor Tina, I was working late one night and saw an elf named Ekk, who has become one of our closest friends. No, let me start over. My wife was kidnapped by an evil being named "Wolfrum" who heads up a crazy religion called "Wolf Raven" centered in a magical forest in Germany. His goal is to subjugate the entire world, and, oh yeah, this whole thing is invisible to regular humans. What's that you say? Stand by while you call in the men with the white coats?

Through my windshield I saw skateboarders, people walking dogs, and a couple of surfer chicks with boards on their heads. It all seemed so normal, just another Spring in Merryville. Except it wasn't. Puddle was in Peru chasing our long-lost parents, and now Mitzi and I were, apparently, going to join her. Killing time, I cleaned the trash out of my car and opened the back hatch to fix my sunscreen that had snagged on part of the convertible mechanism. While jiggling the plastic piece and trying not to break it, a slender ebony hand reached by me. I'm usually easily startled, but this time I was relaxed because I immediately knew I was in the presence of a magical being.

"Let me."

I turned to see one of the most beautiful faces I have seen outside of a fashion magazine. I stood back, speechless. You would think by now I could not be shocked, but until that moment my mind had been trying to rationalize all that had happened. Maybe we exaggerated some of it, I thought, maybe Mitzi and I got confused and had a mass hallucination. But, confronted by this new creature, my final defenses dropped.

"Twyla?" The fairy guardian we had been promised.

The woman didn't answer. She faced the snag in my car and fixed it quickly but turned to me at her name. She was slender and dressed in yoga pants.

"I was watching you. You need to be more aware of your surroundings." Her voice was sensual and drew me in.

"You were watching me?" My voice fairly squeaked from disuse.

"Yes, that's my mission. Ehrenhardt sent me weeks ago, and this seemed a decent time to—to make contact."

I was flabbergasted. Ehrenhardt, Mitzi's griffin father in Germany, King of the Hercynian Forest creatures. "But why not come to our house? You're our guardian fairy, right? Ekk told us you'd be coming."

She laughed, which was quite musical, and shifted her yoga pad under her arm. "I've been establishing myself locally. You and Mitzi have become a wee bit lax in the security department, and I needed to see if anyone else was stalking you. We've been giving you some space to recover from your first contact with the Garden."

I felt pudgy and fully imperfectly human in her presence. "The garden? You mean the Hercynian Garden? In the Black Forest? Of Germany?" I was babbling.

The laugh again. Her smile and the rolling of her eyes belonged to an old soul. "Uncle Ehren calls it that. Anyone under a hundred calls it the Garden. In fact, that's the name of my yoga studio!"

"Oh, my God, the one Mitzi's been going to?" Head smack. "She didn't tell me how beautiful you were."

A sly grin. "Suggestion? Be more aware of your surroundings."

I stood there like an awkward twelve-year-old. "I will."

Twyla turned and waved at a group of yoga-mat people. "I'll be right there!"

I stood there, processing, and said, "Yoga on the beach?"

A shrug, "That's me!" Again, the toothy grin before she dashed off to join her group.

I snapped the back hatch of Sweetpea shut and wondered if there was anything else Mitzi hadn't shared with me.

It was a short walk to the museum, and I saw my best friend and curator of the museum, Juniper, immediately. She was out in front, talking with a deliveryman holding a very large box. There were several more still on the truck.

Juniper was directing, "Easy, easy! It's china and extremely breakable!" This must be something to do with the new installation. Valerie, had mentioned she was working on one.

I smiled. Today Juniper wore all white and sandals with leather tassels. She was always, kind of like, her own mini show. Her hair was expertly coiffed, and she reached for me with manicured nails for a hug while keeping her eyes glued on the UPS man. "Panda, hurray, I need some sane conversation." To the man, "put them all in the small hall." Then she smiled her best curator smile at him and said, "Come see the show in a few weeks." He grunted something unintelligible and grumpy sounding, then nodded and headed off to the smaller of the two museum installation spaces.

"New show?"

"Yes, in this business you're only as good as your last five minutes in the newspaper. After the unfortunate death of our board chair, we're rebranding everything and keeping the focus on art."

"Oh, yeah, huh."

We were both silent for a beat. Neither of us had liked Dick Mortimer, but we didn't want him to die either. He'd been killed during a confrontation by Juniper's former assistant, Garcia, who had discovered he was Dick's illegitimate son. It was an accident, apparently, and there were good people working on getting Garcia out of jail. Even without magic, Merryville could be interesting.

"Any news on Garcia?"

"You know how these things go. Alexandra Stephanovsky is working on it, but it could take a while to sort out what happens to him. Poor lad."

The UPS man came back for another box, and right about then my stomach rumbled loudly enough for Juniper to hear. We both laughed as I rubbed my belly.

We turned toward the large Craftsman home that serves as the entrance to the museum and Juniper said, "I'll tell you more later. Let's eat! I asked Clarisse to make something healthy for us."

I inwardly cringed. Clarisse was the chef for Origin, the new gluten free, organic, totally hipster café housed at the Merryville museum.

"Um, I was thinking we could hit that cute Mexican restaurant down the street."

"Nonsense! Wait 'til you try her reimagined meatloaf. I know you'll like that." Juniper was excited, and I love seeing my good friend happy, but she knows I'm vegetarian.

"Meatloaf?" My eyebrows raised as I followed her down the remodeled hallway in the old Craftsman style building to a small, bright place with incandescent bulbs hanging from cords wrapped around planks attached to the ceiling. It still smelled a bit like wood stain. A chalkboard on the wall touted today's "charcuterie" selections, and White Stripes blared from hidden speakers. She led me to a table with a Scrabble board holder on it with the tiles spelling out the word RESERVED. "Don't worry my salad eater, it's "meat" in quotation marks. This whole café is vegetarian!"

"Awesome." Hmm, good move, I thought. Garden to table vegetarian hipster meatloaf fit in nicely with the relaunch of the Merryville Museum.

No one would confuse it with the old one, that's for sure. The former chairman of the board, God rest his soul, had opposed any change to bring the museum, or the café, into the modern world. We never would have eaten at the previous restaurant as it was very meat and potatoes.

I plunked my bag on a chair and immediately launched into what had happened at the beach minutes before. "So, there I was at the shore just a block from here, messing with this screen cover that got stuck in the back of my car, and this fairy woman appears and helps me. Remember I told you Ekk said someone would be sent to watch over us?"

A twenty something server floated over to the table and we gave her our drink orders. Juniper's green eyes lit up like opening night on one of her shows. "Oh, my God! A fairy? I love this! Was she like Tinkerbell? What did she say?"

I sipped my water and gathered my thoughts. "Not much, except she had been here a while establishing herself, whatever that means. She was very beautiful, and you know how sometimes you just know you're in the presence of magic? I felt it, Juniper. And you're not going to believe who she is."

Juniper glanced over my shoulder. "Incoming, hold that thought," she called out: "Charlotte!"

I turned to see Charlotte Windingle, of the illustrious Merryville Windingles, edging her way toward our table. I was used to seeing her in the paper, and she was no less impressive in person. She had a sour-faced woman in tow, and I could see they were on a mission.

Juniper said in her best sorority sister voice, "Join us!"

Cringe. I'm not exactly anti-social, but this was going to seriously cut into my bestie time. Who else could I speak to about going to Peru and about Twyla the fairy?

I felt my presence register on the woman who was accompanying Merryville's largest museum patron. The ol' sourpuss companion gave me a look that was hard to define. I felt a bit self-conscious and wondered if my t-shirt was too informal for the setting. Mitzi would have thought so. I had ducked out of the house without her approval. She hated my faded *I Heart Taxes* t shirt. Mrs. Windingle nodded and reached out her bejeweled hand to Juniper saying, "Juniper!" then turned to me, "and I don't think we've met."

Juniper was in high social mode. "This is Panda Fowler, who keeps Merryvillians out of trouble with the IRS."

"Hi," I said lamely.

Juniper started to say more but Mrs. Windingle cut her off by addressing me. "Oh, yes! Nice to meet you, dear." She turned back to Juniper.

Actually, I'd been introduced to her at least twice before and, obviously, hadn't made much of an impression.

Interestingly, everything slowed down then like it does those few seconds before a car accident. There are those moments in time you just know something is about to change. My skin actually prickled. This had happened to me more frequently since encountering the magical world, and I wasn't sure yet if it was my imagination or something else.

Mrs. Windingle went on to introduce her companion and time resumed. "Juniper, Panda, this is Hortense Miller of the Merryville Horticultural Society?"

Juniper stood. "So pleased to meet you, Ms. Miller. Valerie, my wife, loves the Society's annual flower show. In fact, she's quite a genius with orchids herself and has applied to join!"

She seemed to recede a little at the word, wife, but said, "In that case, I should like to meet her, and call me Hortense, please." Hortense's mouth twisted into a not very convincing smile.

Mrs. Windingle continued, "We're not staying for lunch. Mona at the front desk told me you were here. Can we have a word?" Then to me, "Will you excuse us a moment?"

"Sure." I wasn't feeling very masterful in the speaking department today.

Juniper nodded and said "*Certainement.*" Juniper often reverted to French in hoity-toity situations. Then to me with a smile, "Order me the crème of corn soup, please." She left to join the women on the deck of the restaurant, out of my hearing.

While she was gone, I did order the reimagined "meat" loaf and her soup. Through the window I saw Hortense doing most of the talking. I saw Juniper fold her arms, never a good sign, and Mrs. Windingle shrug and bestow her beaming gaze on Hortense. They all laughed and waved goodbye to each other like they'd had the most marvelous time, but when Juniper came inside, she was steaming.

"What was that all about?"

"Give me a minute." She swallowed some water and made a visible attempt to control herself. After a pause she said, "Hortense Miller wants half my museum space for her flower show."

"What?"

"Well, not exactly half, but apparently Charlotte just loves her, and they have some ideas. She thinks her flowers are . . . God's art"—Juniper did air quotes—"and should be equal to my art exhibition."

"Why not simply plant flowers outside like everybody else, like, in a garden?"

"It's more *avant garde* and a very annoying trend. They are partnering all over town to landscape Windingle properties and do, out-of-the-box things with plants. They've already done the Mayor's new City Hall project."

"I remember seeing that in the paper. The ivy all over the front of City

Hall isn't bad, but that woman *Horse tense* really likes roses too much."
Mocking Hortense's name was juvenile, I know, but my friend was upset.

"I know, right? Roses are so yesterday. She's trying to turn this place into
grandma's house." She sighed dramatically and made me laugh.

I said in an exaggerated voice since she was being so distracted, "Anyway,
I met this *fairy* at the beach who's teaching Mitzi yoga!" This brought her
back to our original conversation. On hearing this, a male gay couple
returning from the salad bar paused by us on the way to their table.

"Excuse me? We couldn't help but overhear. I find the word fairy
offensive."

I was stunned. "Oh, my God, that wasn't how it was meant."

"It never is, darling. Please don't use it anymore, okay?" He left, and
Juniper and I giggled. If he only knew we both have wives. "Maybe we should
talk later. Can you and Val come by the house tomorrow night for dinner?
We need to talk to you about our upcoming trip to Peru." I said that
nonchalantly, as our server put a cupcake sized "meat" loaf in front of me.

Juniper lifted her eyebrows and nodded. "Val and I were wondering when
you two would be leaving."

I guess I'm the only one who didn't know Mitzi and I would be going to
Peru.

ભ

When I got home, Mitzi was in the backyard, surveying the work to be
done. Our humble home and grounds were certainly a work in progress.
There were unfilled holes, purple thistle had kind of gone crazy in many
areas, and our really big cathouse was shoved in the corner by a fence.

I hugged her, feeling insecure.

Mitzi returned the hug distractedly. "How was lunch?" Her beautiful face
was framed by long braids with colored beads. I was impressed by how they
always matched her outfits.

"Fine." I gave her my most beguiling smile.

"You wore that?" She took off a green garden glove and pointed to my
chest. I loved my t-shirt but had to admit it had seen better days.

"Yes, I most certainly did." Defiant. "How goes the gardening?"

"About the only thing I like about our back yard is the old tree."

If I were really honest, I was afraid there were a lot of things she no longer
liked in our boring old house, including me. How can living on Thistle Drive
compare to literally flying into epic battles against evil? But all I said was.
"Me too. I wish we were Home Depot lesbians. We'd have this fixed up in a
jiffy."

That got a smile out of her. We linked arms and gazed up at our Oak tree.

I went on, "And maybe go on one of those shows, like, HGTV?"

The tree predated our house by at least fifty years. The base was very thick and the limbs were strong and gnarly, covered in green leaves. It truly was majestic.

Her mood softened. She let go of me, knelt down and touched the dirt as if trying to find answers there. "Yeah, sure. And you know what else? I don't feel the same about the yard after the crime lab dug through it expecting to find a body—mine in fact." She was referring to an over-zealous detective named Potts who had the Merryville Crime Lab dig up the yard when Mitzi went missing. She stood, dusting off her hands. Before I could respond she said, "We also need to figure out what to do with Brutus' cat condo."

An old argument, tension again. Both our heads swiveled to the overly large structure, a gift from a former flame of mine who did construction. It was too big for the yard but was really solidly built. To me, it was a well-crafted piece. To Mitzi, it was a reminder of my former girlfriend.

It made me tired just thinking about the work to be done. I was about to say something else when, a dark bird shocked the heck out of me by swooping near us. A familiar green-wrapped package flew at us from sharp talons.

Mitzi leapt on it and cried, "A message raven!" She was nimbler than I and soon had the small package in her hand.

"I thought it was a crow." Feeling crabby, I watched the bird fly away. "I don't know how you tell the difference."

Without taking her eyes off it, she said, "Ravens are shinier and don't caw. Do you think this is a dagger?"

As she ripped open the green covering, I recalled the last time we got a magical message, a ruby set in a dagger you could move and receive a 3D holographic message. This time it was a thumb drive.

She laughed. "I guess Ekk is getting pretty used to the non-magical world!"

"He still had a raven deliver it. That seems pretty magical." I picked up bits of the green packaging material on the grass and put them in my pocket.

Mitzi was already headed to the computer, and I followed her yoga toned butt, which reminded me I wanted to ask her about Twyla but was still stung she hadn't shared that bit of info on her own. It seemed to me that she was taking ownership of everything magical—and keeping secrets. Was I jealous?

Back in the kitchen, Mitzi put the thumb drive in our laptop and we waited through the machine's warm up routine, staring at a spinning hourglass.

An eternity and a double click later, we saw Ekk, our elven guardian, smiling at us from the computer screen. "Oh, I wish this was Skype. I want to talk to him," Mitzi said. Like his girlfriend Elsa, Ekk was newly tanned and his linen sleeves were rolled up. It must be hot in Peru.

"Me too." I scooched my chair closer to her.

It was a video. "Panda, Mitzi, watch this alone, then destroy it please. I had to send a message this way because it's very important for us not to use magic here. Not to scare you, but there may be someone on our tail. My second cousin, Juju, is part of *El Chullanchaqui*, guardians of the Amazon forest, and what he told me I must tell you now." He patted his sweaty forehead with a cloth.

"They think they know where the village called Paititi is located, but he's not sharing it with me yet. Puddle wants to go now, but I have a bad feeling. Elsa and I are trying to change her mind, but she's champing at the bit to find your parents." Ekk paused and swatted at some invisible bug. "We have no idea where they are or even if there's a chance they could still be alive."

I felt a dull ache roiling in my stomach, and for once, it wasn't hunger.

"But the other day Fernando received a message from someone claiming to have been to Paititi and saying they've seen Americans there. This fact Puddle is taking as proof of life." He mopped his brow again. "We plan to go to where El Chullanchaqui indicate by the next full moon. I think you should come." He frowned. "I'm also worried. No one from the Hercynian Garden has heard from Twyla, who was supposed to arrive at your house in Merryville within hours of our departure. That can't be good. As fluid as the situation is, we should probably all be together. It may even be safer. Come to Peru."

Mitzi whispered, "Told you."

"Oh, and Panda, call your brother, he needs to be here too. For some reason the three of you are part of this thing with Wolfrum. I don't know why."

My eyes went to Mitzi whose expression mirrored my surprise. The mention of Wolfrum sent a shiver of fear down my spine. Ekk went on.

"Maybe they see you as a family with Mitzi, and, therefore, you're all a threat." He held his hands palms up in that 'who knows?' gesture. "The Hercynian Garden scholars are working on it. Puddle seems unaware of the danger you're all in, so we must stay with her for her own good. We are at the Principe hotel in Cuzco—come now. And, ladies, trust no one."

The screen went dark.

I yanked out the thumb drive and Mitzi scolded me for not doing "safe eject." I gave her the Duh look. "Ekk said to destroy it, Mitz."

"Oh, yeah, huh."

I took it to the garage and hammered the sucker into bits of plastic and metal. "That ought to do it." I left a message for Brooke and grabbed our suitcases, taking them back into the house. Now that those tasks were done, it was time to deal with my beach experience.

"I have a question, Mitzi. Today I met Twyla, who runs The Garden yoga studio on Pine. Isn't that where you go?"

"Yes." Mitzi suddenly became interested in making sure we had tags on our bags.

I actually put my hands on my hips. "Why didn't you tell me Twyla was your yoga teacher?"

"She said not to." She still didn't meet my eyes.

"Mitzi, is there anything else you're not telling me? This feels really weird. We don't keep things from each other. How long has this been going on?" I moved closer.

She pushed the bag away and turned toward the stairs. "Going on? God, you make it sound like we're having an affair!"

"I didn't say that. I hate being kept out of the loop like this. Letting me know our guardian fairy is here was important."

Silence.

"So what were you thinking?" I padded over to her.

Mitzi turned to me and uncharacteristically exploded. "You know what I was thinking?" She spread her arms dramatically, "Yes, okay, I kept a secret. It was wrong. But put yourself in my shoes. Here is someone who understands what it's like to be magical. My body that I always thought was just mine," she hugged herself, "partly belongs in some other world. How could you know how I feel about that? It's not like you're apt to sprout wings."

"Mitzi."

She was on a roll, "I've got wings, what's next, an eagle head in my old age?"

I shook my head. "Babe, I don't have to be magical to get that flying is a huge deal, or that there's a lot more to know. Twyla's not the only one you have to talk to. You've got me."

She stayed unimpressed.

"We can talk to Elsa and Ekk about this when we get to Peru."

Mitzi paused, and her slender hand went to her left shoulder, a move she'd been making more often lately. "But it's not your body." Her eyes had a faraway focus, as if she was trying to see all the way to the Hercynian Garden. "I know you love me, and I know you would do anything for me, but you can't know what I'm going through. Twyla understands. She was born in The Garden, and she flies!" She softened her voice, finally looked at me and tried to change the mood. "I have questions, dontcha know."

"Like what?"

Mitzi shrugged. "Why do my wings spring out only in times of danger? Will there ever be a time we're sitting watching television or stuck on an airplane and they blow up like an airbag? How do I control this thing?" She started to cry.

I hugged her, not knowing what to say. This half-griffin thing was all still so new. "I'm tired and I bet you are, too."

She melted into me, calmer and moist-eyed, and a sense of relief rushed through me as strong as a gust of wind.

"Let's lie down." I took her hand and we walked upstairs. Our bed has always been a no argument zone, but my need to have the last word took over. "I still don't like secrets." We moved Brutus from the exact center of our bed and lay down together.

The house was so quiet, I could hear the grandfather clock downstairs chime. Mitzi picked up the thread of conversation.

"Neither do I."

I flipped over and faced her. "What?"

"I don't like secrets either, but I trust Twyla." She rested her head on her hand, elbow bent.

A beat. I ventured, "By the way, what have you told her? Ekk said trust no one. And what about Ekk saying Twyla didn't show up?"

She shrugged again. "Put your butt in my gut." She turned me back the way I'm supposed to go, and I complied in a maneuver honed by years of habit. "Maybe he didn't know. She said she was keeping a low profile."

"She told me that, too." I snugged her arm around me tightly and tried to shut out my fears. "Forget about her for now. We're alone, let's savor that."

Mitzi asked quietly, "Do you think Puddle will be okay? Does she really think she can find what your parents couldn't?"

"She'll be okay, maybe a tad depressed when the trail goes cold is all. She gets sidetracked by men and new surroundings. She has that Fernando guy she met in India to get to know better. I'm thinking she'll be just fine." I closed my eyes, "If she doesn't get herself killed in the jungle first."

Our bedroom was quiet for a few minutes, and I started to drift off.

Mitzi was still awake. "What about all that other stuff. You know, our new enemy." I felt her body shiver and was sympathetic. She had been taken captive and almost raped by the crazy cult of Wolf Ravens as part of a scheme to "re-educate" her. Any upset with my wife about secrets was gone.

"She'll be okay. Puddle's a survivor and she's got guardians." I kissed the part of her arm I could reach. "And we'll be okay too, babe. You got me."

"And Twyla." She snugged me tighter.

My eyes popped open.

Reflecting back on how our lives had changed, after a couple of minutes I said "Funny, I kind of miss Ekk and Elsa already. They're such a part of our lives now."

"I know," she mumbled sleepily. "Him and his popcorn and movies. I'm sorry it's not working out for them where they rented." And with that, she fell asleep. I stared at the ceiling, now wide awake, wondering what she was talking about. I remembered he mentioned something about that before leaving. And that response "and Twyla" when I had said "you got me"? I decided to find out more about this mysterious yoga fairy.

❧

CHAPTER THREE

FERNANDO AND PUDDLE IN PERU

Fernando was lean and handsome. He lifted Puddle's hand to kiss it. She met his soft brown greenish eyes with hers as he gently held her hand. Puddle let him be the Latin lover, for now, and said, "This seems a lot less frantic than Bangalore. I kind of like it."

"I like your new outfit." She loved her local purchases, from her white cotton blouse, carefully stitched with colorful thread, to her huaraches. She would have passed for a native if not for her fair coloring and height. "Tell me about growing up here, Fernando."

They strolled along cobbled streets in Cuzco and met the occasional llama or alpaca being led by indigenous people. "In Spanish or English?" he asked humorously.

"English please. I'm tired of working so hard." She fanned herself. Puddle had a broad face with freckles, which had multiplied exponentially under so much sun. Her pale blue eyes peered at Fernando under blond eyelashes. It was their private joke. Puddle wasn't good with languages, and he knew it. Her Hindi sucked too.

Answering her original question, Fernando said, "We were better off than many. My parents owned a store and sold sweaters."

"Sweaters?"

At Puddle's surprised response, he added, "Seems funny now in the warmth of the sun, but it really gets cold here in the mountains. There is nothing like an alpaca hair sweater to keep you warm and, how you say, toasty." He touched her nose affectionately.

"Will I get to meet them? Your parents? Are they in Cuzco?"

"Hopefully in time and, not anymore." Fernando became hard to read. Puddle changed conversational direction because he seemed to be uncomfortable.

"Tell me again, how did you end up in India?"

"That is a long story, maybe different from what you think." They stopped walking and he pointed at various parts of the city. "There's the Cathedral, also known as Temple of the Sun, there's a St. Mary's church, and the

Catholic school is down this road here."

"So, you were Catholic?" Puddle asked mischievously, playing Captain Obvious.

"Yes, I was Catholic." He shook his head. "It was never a choice. When I went to college, there was so much to know. I wanted to see the world." He picked Puddle up and spun her around. "Just like you."

"But you came back. What brought you back?"

He put his arm around her waist. "Maybe I went away to find the woman of my dreams, so I could share all this." He gestured with his free arm at the city. "With her and her little elves."

Puddle stopped walking. They were in a fairly quiet place on a short bridge and sat down on a stone bench. "How do you know about my elves?"

He sputtered, "You told me, remember?"

"I would remember that." Puddle thought about all the warnings from her sister about going to Peru.

"You were," he made swirling motions with his arms while trying to find his words, something she used to think was charming, "smoking the pot."

"Sorry, dude, not buying it." She studied him. "I want to go back to the hotel now." Puddle crossed her arms.

Fernando seemed stricken. "What do you mean? I thought we were sympatico."

She focused on the Cathedral of the Sun below. "When I met you in India you were so intense, and, honestly, I think I was ready to leave the Ashram. I told you about my parents, but then it became your quest, too, which is kind of weird."

"But I'm from Peru. It is natural."

"No, it's weird. What gives?"

Fernando actually deflated like a balloon. His brown/green eyes almost glittered, and it appeared he was making a decision. He dropped her hand gently. "Okay, okay. I can't introduce you to my parents because they disappeared before I went to India. In fact, that is why I went to India."

Her jaw dropped. Puddle was aware of the sounds of the city, as she really saw him for the first time. "What do you mean that's why you went to India?"

A vein worked in his neck. "My parents are missing, too. A . . . well, someone told me our parents might have met the same fate." His face was stone.

"You're only telling me now? After you let me go on and on about my parents? How can I trust you anymore?" She pushed him away, feeling like a character in a *telenovela*.

He grabbed her arm, more forcefully than was usual and said, "Follow me, there is someone I want you to meet."

"Ow. Let me go!" Puddle was not one to go for abuse of any kind.

He immediately said, *"Lo siento,"* and took Puddle's elbow, guiding her down an alley off one of the main drags. "You want answers? You must come."

Puddle was frightened but curious. "Where are we going?"

"Los Ciudad Perdida." I want you to meet a friend of mine, actually, a few of them."

Sensing she really had no choice, Puddle said, "Do they have *tapas*? I'm getting kind of hungry."

"Si. I like a woman with appetite." They giggled at that, and then Fernando went back to being intense and focused. They went this way and that, and each cobblestone alleyway resembled the last. After walking what seemed like an hour, they came upon a door-shaped hole in a wall with a steep staircase leading down and away from the Peruvian sun.

The doorway arch was stone and classically Incan. Puddle noticed there was no sign saying *Los Ciudad Perdida*.

"Here? Are you sure?" Puddle again felt serious trepidation.

His eyes were intense. "I am sure, my Puddle. Follow me, it's time."

"Why should I follow you? You lied to me."

His face was a poster for sincerity. "Not telling everything is not lying. Do you want to know what happened to your parents or not?" And with that, he turned and went down the stairs. Well, he did trust her to follow, and she didn't have handcuffs on her.

"Hang on a sec," she called after him. Puddle texted Ekk that she was at Los Ciudad Perdida and followed Fernando into the dark.

༄

INTO THE JUNGLE

Puddle descended the granite steps behind Fernando. She felt unsure and off center but also excited that finally, maybe, she would meet someone who could tell her what happened to her parents. Her Hindu training served to calm her nerves as she breathed and quietly mouthed *"om mani padme hum"* over and over.

The sun had been hot, and she felt an actual chill as she passed from sun into shadow. The stair corridor was narrow, and her hands brushed the sides of the rough stone wall. Finally, she followed Fernando into an underground chamber, dimly lit by naked bulbs hanging from a beam in the rock ceiling. An old man sat hunched over a wooden table, as if he'd been waiting. "Puddle, meet Jose Luis. He's going to be our guide to the Lost City, Paititi."

"Oh. You said you had a friend you wanted me to meet. Is this him?" She gestured at the old Indian, who had ancient cards displayed on the table. The man didn't seem hardy enough to make a journey through the jungle.

To Puddle, he said in his best Ricardo Mantalban voice, Mister Suave. "Appearances can be deceiving. Sit, please." To Jose Luis, "Do you have anything to eat?"

The old man snapped his fingers and from a dark corner a woman in native garb entered with two drinks of water, ice clinking, and some *galletas*. Puddle stared. "Whoa, where did you come from?"

The woman either did not understand English or simply chose not to answer and smiled as she set the water and sweet in front of Puddle and Fernando. Jose Luis nodded to the woman who left, seemingly disappearing into a dark corner. As her eyes adjusted, Puddle saw several small openings leading to . . . other places? As Fernando picked up his drink, he said, "Welcome to the Lost City."

"Is that the name of this bar? If that's what it is."

"Actually, we are at the opening of a portal to Paititi." He turned to his friend, Jose Luis, "it's time to tell her."

Puddle picked up her drink and swallowed cool water. It felt glorious to her parched throat after walking in the sun. The sweating glass had left a ring on the scarred wooden table.

Jose Luis slowly fanned the cards on the table, then gathered them in his cracked, papery hands and offered the pack to Puddle. "Pick."

"What?" She was so confused.

The old man gestured the pack toward her "Pick card."

Fernando sat staring at her with an odd expression on his face. His voice had a hint of an edge. "Take a card, Puddle."

"What is this? Oh, okay." Puddle chose a card as everything turned to black.

❧

The next morning Mitzi bounded out of bed at seven a.m. and went straight to the shower. When she walked out of the bathroom toweling herself dry, I was sitting on the bed in shorts and a t-shirt.

She did a double take. "You're up early." She opened a drawer and rummaged for shorts.

"Yep. I'm going with you to yoga."

She paused, still damp, and sort of snorted. "Okaaay."

"What's that supposed to mean?"

She sighed. "I've been asking you for a year to come with me and you always say no. I finally stopped asking." A beat. "This is so you can mad dog Twyla, isn't it?"

"No." I stood and patted my belly. "It's time to get into shape. Last one in the car is a rotten egg." I gave her what I hoped was an endearing smile.

She laughed in spite of herself as she opened the linen closet and threw a beach towel at me. I caught it clumsily. "What's this for?"

Mitzi waved her rolled up yoga mat around like a wand, pointing it in my general direction. "This is your yoga mat."

"I don't have one?"

"You used it to line the cat condo in the backyard—remember?" Boy did I. Years ago my ex, the woodworker, tried to rekindle the old flame. When I ran into her and mentioned Brutus was very doglike, she took it upon herself to gift me with a very large "cat" house. I couldn't get past how well built it was, which is why it was still in our yard. The yoga mat fit the entrance perfectly, and it made a padded floor. Well, it seemed like a good idea at the time. We called it Brutus' summer house. The thing had sat in the yard for years.

"Don't start." I knew she was going to ask when we were going to get rid of the thing. It took up a lot of space.

We jumped in Sweetpea and went the three or four blocks to beach parking. So much for exercise. I wished I'd brought my coffee, but then there didn't seem to be many places to pee.

There was Twyla, lithe and catlike, speaking with several adoring students prior to the class. She gave Mitzi and I a wave. She was even prettier than I remembered.

As we got out of the car, I asked, "So how do we do this?" I perused the limber athletic yoga regulars and knew I was in way over my head.

"Panda, listen carefully and do what she says. Twyla is a very good teacher."

"I'm sure." I gave what I hoped was a nice smile. Mitzi smiled, too.

The sand was clean, and we found spots next to each other. Everyone else was stretching, so I did, too. I thought this might not be so bad.

Then the torture started.

We went through corpse pose—my personal favorite—lunges, happy baby, down dog, and I can't remember what else, but they were impossible poses for my northern European body style. Mitzi did them easily after having come to class fairly regularly for the last year. As I grunted and groaned, Twyla moved in between the lines of yoga students, randomly giving out positive advice such as, "At the point you're ready to give up, that's when transformation happens," and "This is where you decide who you are to be."

I still didn't know why I insisted on coming, but some things still bugged me about Twyla.

Then something weird happened. Toward the last part of the hour-long class I was lying on my back and breathing deeply, pondering the sky. I became aware my body was tingling all over. At the same time, the day became cold and dark, and . . . I was alone. I lifted my head and saw there was a void of life except for a figure moving near the shoreline. I sat up, goose bumps up and down my arm in time to see a panther, black, sleek and deadly racing toward me, teeth bared and yellow eyes on me.

"Panda, you fell asleep!" Mitzi was shaking me and seemed embarrassed. Most of the yoga class was in the process of picking up their mats and casually conversing. Twyla stared at me from about fifteen feet away. Her head was cocked like an animal, her gaze odd. I shook my head and knew that something about her was more than "off." Before I could say anything, Mitzi ran up to her, and they had a quick conversation while I shook out my towel. I had my car keys in hand and walked up to them, feeling like I was interrupting. "Ready?"

"Panda, I think I want to stay and have coffee with Twyla."

"Then so do I." Where did that come from? I stood my ground. Mitzi was chewing the inside of her cheek, a habit for when she gets nervous. She said to Twyla, "Give us a minute?"

When she got me some distance away, and Twyla was talking to some others, Mitzi said to me: "God, Panda, we talked about this. You have no reason to be jealous."

"I'm not. It's a feeling I have, Mitz. I also had a night, or rather a *day*mare in class so give me a break." I sighed. "Let me take you out to breakfast. Ask your buddy to come. We can ask her questions." I sort of massaged her shoulder as I said that.

For a moment she seemed torn. After a beat, she yelled over to Twyla, "We're going to catch some breakfast. Wanna come?"

My intuition told me the woman would rather eat sand. "No thanks, love, I'll see you tomorrow."

I waved and we started walking back to the car, but Twyla's use of "love" in referring to my wife was eating at me. Something was going on and it didn't sit right with me.

We were rather sullen sitting at the café, and I knew that I'd rained on Mitzi's parade. She really enjoyed her yoga classes and had wanted to meet with Twyla some more. Was that so bad?

The server put my plate in front of me, a rather plain spinach omelet. Mitzi's bacon and eggs actually were more appetizing to me.

Mitzi raised her eyebrows, then broke the ice. "Did you enjoy yoga?"

"Loved it." I shook salt and pepper on my breakfast.

"What were you dreaming about?"

I put my fork down and said, "A panther was going to eat me."

"I'm worried about you, baby. A panther? It's a metaphor for your fear. Trust me, Twyla is not a threat," finally referring to the elephant in the café.

"Mitzi, she's asking you to keep secrets!" I put my fork down like a gavel. There it was.

"Panda, you're paranoid. I would have told you eventually."

We ate in silence. I hate not getting along.

Mitzi buttered her English Muffin and finally spoke. "Are you coming to yoga tomorrow?"

"I don't know. I have to pack for Peru." I said it in a hurt voice, a cheap trick. I knew any reference to packing for travel would get her attention.

Mitzi immediately brightened. "That's right. Okay, let's go shopping for some things first. We need jungle things." She chewed slower and swallowed. "I kind of like it when you come to yoga. It was funny seeing you try to do down dog."

I groaned. "I almost bit her leg. Ruff."

"Panda!" She was happily scandalized.

"Okay, okay. I probably won't go every day, but we are leaving for Peru soon." I scooched closer to her in the over padded booth. "I don't want to let you out of my sight with everything going on."

"Mmm-hmm."

"I'll go shopping with you," I said in a sing-songy voice. This was the deal closer as Mitzi loves to shop. She punched my arm seeing right through me, but not minding, and I felt much better. The rest of breakfast was more peaceful. I started thinking. If the dream meant something, and Twyla was into some kind of dark magic, Ekk needed to know. It also possibly could have been a dream and my subconscious was projecting my jealousy on to the whole deal, who knows? Whichever, I didn't like the effect this woman, or fairy, or whatever she was, was having on Mitzi and suspected I was about to get in shape.

∾

THE MERRYVILLE HORTICULTURAL SOCIETY
REGULAR MAY MEETING

Sylvia and Valerie got to the Merryville Horticultural Society in time to hear Hortense rap the gavel. "This meeting is now called to order!"

The friends sat in the back row and whispered to each other as the nearly twenty members present settled in. Valerie leaned close to Sylvia's ear, "Hortense could do a spot-on imitation of Dame Judy Dench."

Out of the side of her mouth Sylvia said, sotto voice, "If she had a sense of humor."

Valerie added, insecure, "Are you sure it's okay I'm here?"

Sylvia shushed her before saying, "Yes. This is an open meeting."

Hortense straightened some papers at the podium before looking up to say, "Welcome, Merryville Mavens!"

Valerie and Sylvia exchanged grins. This was it!

"We have many exciting projects coming to full bloom," polite titters, "and an annual flower show next March to plan. But here we find ourselves in May, which is going to be very busy. We also have, ahem, some housekeeping matters to discuss in closed session and action items on corrective issues in Merryville."

The women murmured in excited whispers as Hortense continued. "You all know my husband Bill. I've asked him to assist us today. Janet and I have put together a power point presentation for the action item portion of our agenda." Everyone turned to see old long-suffering Bill, sitting primly next to a vintage projector that probably had come from the Millers' attic. He waved a half wave. A glass with amber liquid sat next to his tea cup.

Sylvia glanced at Janet Bruce-Pippin, who she knew would take a bullet for Hortense. She suspected Janet had done the entire technical part of the presentation to come.

"So, let's get started! I'll now turn the gavel over to Lidia for an update on Climate Change." The crowd hushed. Valerie was impressed. They should be talking about climate change.

Lidia, a seventy-nine-year-old science teacher with a pronounced hump on her back approached the mike, which squealed as she asked in her wavery voice, "Is this thing on?"

"Some of you have noticed the early Spring we experienced this year and are worried about the causes. We are also in for a hot summer," she smiled at Hortense, "very hot. I have made some handouts." She nodded to a Junior Maven, Janet's daughter Bonnie, who handed out sheets of paper with a picture of a sun on top and some bullet points.

"The bottom line, ladies, is don't worry. I've been a science teacher for over forty years and have seen this kind of hysteria before." She pushed her cat glasses up her nose and leaned into the microphone. "News flash, sometimes it's hotter than at other times. It's a natural process." Laughter. "Gardeners, be sure to water more, conservatively of course, and use your sunscreen. This too shall pass." She sat down to clapping and laughter.

Valerie caught Sylvia's gaze and waved the flyer. Sylvia put up her hand in a "wait" sign. Valerie read the sheet very carefully and saw it was provided by Tillercon Oil Refinery. She pointed that out to Sylvia, who gave her the "wait" sign again, and added a shhh finger to her lips.

Next up was Sally Johnson, who gave a nearly incomprehensible report on roses. They all clapped because, well, she's Sally, and sweet, and her husband donates heavily to the Mavens. Finally, Hortense took the podium again and said, "Now, we must discuss our action items." There was a murmur among the women, who all knew this was the best part of the meeting. This is where you got to see which of Merryville's citizens were on the "hit list."

"Lights please."

Bonnie raced to the switch ahead of Bill. He swatted his hand at the air in her general direction and sat back down.

A picture of the Merryville Bluffs filled the screen. "I thought we would start here. Ever since the, ah, unfortunate events at the museum last month, the overgrown state of the bluffs has been at the top of our list." She clicked and several angles appeared, each more unkempt than the last, with garbage and food bowls for the feral cats intermixed with weeds. "The cats are mostly gone, which is what we've been waiting for, and the homeless man was relocated." Small clapping here.

"Thanks to our partnership with the city, soon an army of city landscapers will remove all the bushes except for a few approved types that we need to prevent erosion. This is the artist's rendering of what it will look like when we are finished." She clicked and the group murmured approvingly as the tidy hand drawn color sketch appeared. Valerie couldn't wait to tell Juniper as it was her wife's Floodlight exhibit that started the whole thing.

Hortense next turned to the Westernmost side of Merryville, a tired section near the refinery. She showed some slides of several homes in the area, literally, on the wrong side of the tracks. Pictures of the Junior Mavens with shovels helping Merryville's less fortunate clean up their yards were shown. There were approving "awes" as the girls, wearing their bright pink polo shirts, posed with an elderly resident and her dog.

"So, for those of you who are new, you can see we are a powerful force for good in Merryville. The Mayor credits us with an increase in tourism and neighborhood pride of ownership. With the fun we have there is also great responsibility, however." A hush fell over the room.

"Unfortunately, there are some who thumb their noses at our community." She clicked and a picture of a house with nothing but dirt in the front yard appeared. "Sometimes it's because they need guidance." A click to a yard with household appliances rusting in the weeds. "Sometimes it's a mental health issue. This next series is dedicated to a new threat, the Scottish Thistle issue, Latin name *Onopordum acanthium*." A picture of the purple flower filled the screen.

Hortense let the picture have its effect. "Pretty, yes? Well, see what you think of this!" Hortense clicked her clicker and a color rendering of the entire town choked in thistle filled the screen. "Ladies, I give you Scottish thistle unchecked."

A collective gasp. Sylvia and Valerie exchanged a "wow." A hand went up. "What can be done?" a nervous woman in the front row asked. Valerie almost laughed out loud. Seriously? These girls were sheltered.

Hortense adopted the tone of the patient teacher. "I'm glad you asked. There's only one way to stop it—in its tracks." Hortense leaned into the mic.

"First we ask nicely, by sending a letter. Then we get the City Prosecutor involved." She clicked through images of small patches of the weed that were, not surprisingly, mostly to be found along Thistle Drive.

"Sometimes it's hard to literally nip it in the bud." Titters from the audience. "This time, we know who the responsible parties are for ground zero." Valerie was stunned when a picture of Mitzi and Panda Fowler's home appeared on the screen, complete with address. She turned to Sylvia, mouth open. Hortense continued. "Not six blocks from this very location, thistle is back, and it threatens to spread exponentially. We have notified these homeowners that either they remove it, or come July, we will. So far we've heard nothing. City Prosecutors have been notified."

"Why would anyone do that?" a woman in the middle of the pack cried.

"The house was on TV," came another comment.

Hortense gave a pained smile and shook her head. "I might mention this is not the first time they've been in the papers, but we don't name names at meetings."

Janet leaned forward and spoke regretfully into her mic. "The executive session is where we deal with that level of detail." The women in the audience nodded.

It was all Valerie could do not to race out of the meeting and call her friends. Social niceties, however, required she sit through the rest of the meeting, and through several introductions to bland ladies before being edged out to the patio. After a suitable period, when Valerie had Sylvia alone, she asked, "Did you know about the picture of Mitzi and Panda Fowler's house being on the hit list?"

"I did not, although I knew we sent them a letter. At least they didn't mention names."

Valerie was blunt. "The house number showed up quite nicely in the power point presentation."

Sylvia waited a beat, then went on. "Val, I'm new on the board. This is actually my first executive session. I can find out more." Valerie pulled back and Sylvia placed a hand on her arm as if to stop her. "We're going to talk about membership applications today."

Valerie was still upset. She crossed her arms. "I'm not so sure I want to join now."

"Valerie," Sylvia said, "I—we need you. I joined, but we need more reasonable, rational women, like us, to really make this thing great." Valerie was still listening. She'd been so excited to join and showcase her orchids. "Let me also repeat something I learned a long time ago, Valerie: keep your friends close, and your enemies closer. Now, do I go to bat for you or not?"

After a beat, Valerie nodded. During the conversation they had moved outside. It didn't hurt Sylvia's argument to join the garden club to be standing in a beautiful garden filled with incredible flowers.

"Good choice. I'll only be a half an hour or so. Do you want to sit here and finish your tea in the garden?"

"No, I have a lot to think about." Valerie left as Hortense went around to gather her executive board for closed session.

The Horticultural Society had one of the plumb pieces of real estate in town and a charming old two-story house that had belonged to Virginia Merry, for whom the town was renamed in the late 1800s. Valerie was torn as she left the historical site that until now as a non-member was only open to her on special days. If they accepted her membership, she could bring Juniper and sit in the garden any time.

Other than her wife, Juniper, and work as a home healthcare nurse, Valerie's greatest passion was raising orchids. She had all kinds and colors and could bring almost dead ones back to life. When she and Juniper went to the annual flower show, she always stared wistfully at the beautiful displays and wanted to share her love of the unique flowers with others who knew the difference between a Oncidium and Maltonia.

She opened the wrought iron gate and walked outside, her Skechers silent on the sidewalk. On one hand, she could really bring something to the table of the Merryville Mavens. On the other hand, she and Sylvia were the only two women of color, and now her best friends were on the Merryville Maven hit list. Maybe working from the inside was the way to go.

She strolled on and saw a group on an upcoming corner advertising "free water." Clean-cut young people handed out chilled water bottles while a handsome slightly older man distributed flyers. Valerie took one to be polite and accepted a water. After a thank you and smile, she continued home, her mind turning back to the Merryville Mavens.

She had made her decision to keep her "frenemies" close, but, truthfully, they might not even accept her application to join. She nodded to a neighbor and climbed the old wooden steps to her front porch. Conversation tonight at the Fowlers would be interesting for sure.

❧

CHAPTER FOUR
CUSCO HOTEL

Juju folded the map and stood to visit the *baño* when Ekk's phone gave a "you have a text message" ping.

While Ekk cleared away empty bottles of chicha, he asked, "Is it Puddle?"

Elsa took off her oven mitt and picked up the phone. "She's at a bar."

"Which one?" This from Juju.

"It says: W/Fernando at bar Los Ciudad Perdida."

He and Ekk exchanged a glance.

Ekk said, "She's in trouble."

Elsa didn't speak Spanish. "Why?"

Juju said to Elsa, "It's not a bar. Los Ciudad Perdida means literally—The Lost City"

A knock on the door made Elsa jump. "Maybe that's her." She climbed down from her chair and went to the hotel room door.

Ekk and Juju were up and behind her before her hand touched the knob. She opened the door, and they all raised their faces to a very tall man, dressed in a suit.

The man, impeccably dressed, 40ish with a short haircut, looked down at them and blurted out, "What the hell?"

"Are you Brooke Fowler?" Ekk asked. Three serious little people fixed their eyes on him.

The man laughed. He dropped his bags. Holding his sides, he didn't stop shaking until tears rolled down his pale cheeks.

When the unexpected laughter passed, Brooke rubbed his eyes and said, "I'm so sorry, it's—I wasn't expecting—" He appeared uncomfortable, as well as tired and disheveled.

"Little People?" Wiry and small, Juju still cut a fierce figure.

Elsa remembered her manners and reached up to Brooke. "Come on in. You must be tired."

"I am. Hey, guys" he patted Elsa's hand, "and little gal, I have questions." He wiped a tear from his eye.

Juju moved past the tall man to drag his many bags inside. Brooke stepped in, and Juju quickly closed the door. "*Avanzan aquí permanentemente*? (Are you moving here permanently?) This last question was said as more of a sarcastic grunt, under his breath.

Brooke turned and sharply replied, "No, señor, this was kind of an unexpected detour from New York. Now what's going on?"

Juju stopped dragging a bag almost as big as he was. "You speak Spanish," he said, clearly startled.

Brooke put his glasses on. "I did a semester abroad in Spain. Now what's going on?"

Ekk snapped out of his momentary pause and took control of the situation. "Since you're here you know some of the story. We'll fill you in on the rest. But first, would you mind telling us who got you on the plane?" Elsa moved to the kitchen while Juju moved to peer out the window. Ekk sat down at the table, inviting Brooke to join him.

Brooke pulled up a chair, and Elsa put a glass of water in front of him. He gulped from it greedily before speaking. "I got off the subway in Manhattan when two guys asked me if I'd heard about New Spirit and would I go to a meeting with them. They were weird and were more trying to take me somewhere then take my wallet. My gut told me to run but there was no obvious threat." He paused, and looked embarrassed, "You're not going to believe this." He gave a nervous laugh and gazed around at the faces in the room. "Or maybe you will. The platform filled up with ravens which chased them away."

"Go on," Ekk said.

"I thought at first maybe I was having a hallucination, a breakdown. Then a woman approached me and said there was something I needed to know. She apologized for breaking into my reality—she actually said that. By the way, she was the most beautiful woman I've ever seen."

Elsa and Ekk caught each other's gaze. They knew exactly the type of woman the Hercynian Garden had sent, a creature with powers to mesmerize, and it was a good choice.

"Anyway, we talked for hours about my parents, my sisters and unfinished business. I realized I hadn't seen my sisters in years. Suddenly I wanted to leave so badly. The woman gave me the plane ticket and said all my questions would be answered once I arrived. And now I'm here."

Ekk said, "Thank you, Brooke. Elsa and I are Panda and Mitzi's guardians. We live near them in Merryville, California. Puddle is here. We came with her to make sure she was safe."

His head jerked up. "Where is she? I want to see her."

Ekk studied his shoes.

Juju returned from staring out the window. "That's a problem right now. She's been kidnapped."

ᐷ

DINNER AT THE FOWLERS

Our doorbell is unusual, which is par for the course in our lives. It was installed by the former owner and plays the first few notes of "Scotland the Brave." I secretly vowed for the thousandth time to change it to a simple ding-dong.

"I'll get the door." Brutus and I raced each other to the door to let in Juniper and Valerie. After hugs and friendly cheek pecks and pets for the cat, we all talked merrily into the kitchen, where Mitzi was cooking.

Mitzi couldn't leave her station in front of the stove, where she was stirring gravy, but called out, "How wonderful to see you guys! How are you?"

Juniper carefully sat on a chair at the kitchen table, making sure her tunic was smoothly draped. "Crazy. Putting on a new show called *Words on a Plate*. It's totally different than anything I've done before."

I plopped down on a chair. "How so?" I held up my index finger. "Let me guess, it's not oil paintings of people who died hundreds of years ago." The reference was sarcastic. The museum, under Juniper's watch, had become a place for exciting installations.

Juniper laughed. "You are correct. It's an interactive artistic representation of an internal process." We all stared at her blankly, and she continued. "You know how sometimes you have these conversations, and they're stilted and awkward in some way. Maybe you're confronting someone or have to admit something, or saying truth or lies. Artists have pictured these words, literally, on a plate. It's been super fun matching up china with the dialogue."

"Yeah, super fun," Valerie, who had been volunteered to help, said dryly.

Juniper kissed her hand. To Mitzi and me she said, "You'll have to see it for yourselves."

"What's it called?" My head was tilted, trying to get the image.

Juniper held out her hands like jazz hands and a big smile stretched across her pretty face. "Words on a Plate."

"Intriguing" offered Mitzi, "Can't wait to see it. What about you Val?"

Valerie was hovering near Mitzi and had picked up a dish towel to help with a tiny spill, "I've been in between clients and working on my orchids. I—"

Juniper butted in, fixing me with her penetrating eyes, "Did you know you're on the Horticultural Society hit list for your thorns out front?"

Valerie swatted her with a dish towel. "Thistles, Juniper. Scottish Thistles, and you're stealing my thunder."

My gut leapt. "What? Oh my God! We got a letter from them and I forgot to read it!" I dashed out of the kitchen and up the stairs to the clothes hamper. I dug down to my jeans and reached in the pocket. I found the letter, but it was half consumed by the green stuff Ekk's thumb drive had been wrapped in. I carried the whole thing downstairs and showed everyone.

Mitzi said, "Is that what I think it is?"

Valerie said, "What?"

"You probably haven't seen it, Val, but, Juniper, do you remember this substance? It was what practically the whole of the Hercynian Garden was made out of." Mitzi had a good eye for detail.

Juniper's eyes lit up, "Yes! Gruen-something. Where did this come from?"

"Ekk sent us a package from Lima, and this was the wrapping. Apparently, it consumes paper because the Horticultural Society letter was in the same pocket and now you can't read it." I was trying to remember if there were other properties I should know about. It would probably ruin our clothes.

Mitzi said, "Throw it out. You don't know what it's going to do."

I got up, and Juniper followed me into the backyard. I was squishing the green blob like Play-Doh and tossing it from hand to hand. "They actually build with this," referring to our time in the Hercynian Garden in Germany.

"I know, I remember," Juniper said, fascinated. "You can't just throw it away—it's magic."

"Okay, let me see if it sticks to wood." I walked over to Brutus' summer palace and smeared the green stuff over the front panel, hoping it would make that disappear like it did the letter. Surprisingly, the green stuff seemed to love the wood and gradually spread itself over the entire front panel evenly like some sort of thick paint. I faced Juniper with a surprised expression. "It ate the letter, which came from a tree, but apparently it loves wood, which paper is made from. Trippy."

Juniper was thoughtful, chin between thumb and index finger, "Ask Ekk or Elsa about it when you get a chance."

"Totally. Let's go see what's for dinner." I rinsed my hands under a faucet before we walked through the sliding glass door in the den and back into the kitchen. Valerie stood next to Mitzi cutting a sunchoke. Mitzi said over her shoulder, "Panda, Valerie tells me our Scottish Thistles are on the Maven's hit list—our house was actually in a slide show today." She scooped up a bunch of the vegetable and put it in a hot pan. "Remember when I told you about those ladies walking around with clipboards? That's never good."

"Yes, dear." Then to my friend, "Our letter's gone, but you're going to join the old biddy committee and argue on our behalf, right, Val?" My head nodded yes, exaggeratedly. I made the universal pleading gesture with my hands.

She reddened. "I've put in for membership, but, honestly, if you don't think I should. I mean, they might not even accept me."

"With your talent for orchids? Pa-lease!" Juniper put up her hand as if this was the last word.

"Do you have any friends on the board?" I knew that being connected politically helped.

"Sylvia Arviso. I met her when I took care of her dad before he made his transition." Valerie smiled sadly. "She's really nice. And really, really rich, which doesn't hurt."

"Yes," Juniper said. "I may have to take out a second on our house to pay the membership fee, but it's worth it." She hugged Valerie, who mouthed "sorry" then smiled endearingly. We all laughed.

"Panda darling, what are we going to do about our out of control yard?" Mitzi put an appetizer on the table.

Honestly, yard work was pretty low on my list. Since tax season and what we had begun to call "the recent events," finding out Mitzi was a half magical creature and going to Europe and back, I'd hardly given it a thought. "It has grown a lot more in the last few weeks. Maybe I should take a whack at getting it cut back." I wondered where my clippers had gotten to.

Juniper jumped in, "Tell us about Peru! When do you leave?"

The rest of the evening was spent catching up and making plans for the girls to come by and check on Brutus and the thistles. They would also make a point to go by and meet our erstwhile guardian, Twyla, at The Garden Yoga Studio.

After Valerie and Juniper were gone, Mitzi and I sat on our couch with the cat and watched a couple of taped Jeopardy shows for about an hour and then went to bed. It was hard to shut off my mind, but eventually we slept. At about six a.m. the famed Panda stomach decided I needed a snack to stop the rumbling.

I need breakfast, snacks, lunch and dinner or I get "hangry." I could smell garlic and other spices as I extracted myself from my wife's loving arms and descended the stairs, almost stepping on Brutus. Funny, the smell from the kitchen didn't jive with what we had for dinner last night. Our Bengal cat had taken to sleeping at the top of the stairs, presumably to see threats coming at us. Poor boy! Since April, right before taxes, his world had been turned upside down, too. He meowed indignantly as I walked by but did not seem alarmed by anything.

I was wearing sweatpants and a t-shirt, and my bed hair was probably sticking up crazily. It felt good to be at home barefoot, not caring what anybody thought, on Thistle Drive, in our humble abode—finally alone, at least for a couple more days. I stretched as I entered the semi-dark kitchen. We had lived here for about ten years, and our house was a work in progress, but it was ours. I shook my head to clear it as I hunted for a big spoon, thinking that only weeks ago I had flown to Germany to rescue Mitzi.

We needed this time to get used to the new normal, but here we were ready to take off again to Peru, and we were fighting. Odd, the stove was hot. I lifted the lid to the pan, and delicious smells of homemade vegetable soup filled my nostrils, although I noticed there wasn't very much left. I used my right hand to stir up the steam and get a better whiff. I almost jumped out of my skin when a voice from the kitchen table spoke, "Oh, goody, you're up!"

I turned, lid in hand, to see a small red-haired woman sitting at our yellow retro kitchenette. It was quite a picture, even in the semi-dark. "Who are you?"

"Twyla! You must be Panda— your hair is funny!" She put her small white hand over her mouth and stifled a giggle.

It is rare that I have an instant dislike for a person, but this might be one of those occasions. I flipped on the light to get a better gander. "How did you get in?"

She rolled her large eyes. "A *nithling* could have figured it out." Without waiting for my question about what was a *nithling*, she kept talking as my mouth hung open. "Go ahead and eat. I read in my notes you like to do that."

As the shock wore off, I replied, "Would you like some soup?"

"Already had some."

"I can see that," I said, noticing the diminished soup and her detritus on the table.

"So, you know I'm here to protect you."

My wheels were turning, who was she? "Uh-huh."

I got myself a bowl of soup, and sat down—not a usual breakfast, but it was food. "When did you arrive?" I could see that Twyla had left most of her soup in her bowl and had also opened some crackers, which were all over the table.

It took a while to see this because, frankly, she was one of the most striking creatures I'd ever seen. She was a small woman but could pass as normal human size, with white, almost translucent skin and curly red hair. Her large eyes were hazel to green. The overall effect was like a big porcelain doll you wanted to put on a shelf.

Trying not to stare I said, "I thought fairies were tiny, like Tinkerbell."

She gave an almost musical laugh. "Some are. My mother is fully human, like Mitzi's. I can't wait to meet her—we're related!"

I hadn't taken my eyes off her and was forming a plan in my mind to find my pepper spray. "She's sleeping."

"It's morning! I've been sitting here for what seems like days! Let's wake her up!"

Fairies. Now I knew what Ekk was referring to when he said I would see for myself what they were like.

I got angry. "No, she needs her rest. It's been quite a strain on both of us these last few weeks. Besides, there are some things we need to clear up."

"There you are!" She said, eyes sparkling. She looked past me, craning her slender neck to see Mitzi.

Mitzi was up, great. I wondered if pepper spray even worked on magical folk.

"Who are you?" Mitzi said in wonder from the kitchen door. She was wearing cut offs and a t-shirt and rockin' it. Her beaded braids framed her lovely face, which was soft from sleep. She rubbed her face. "I thought I heard talking down here."

The fairy's face fell. "Didn't Ekk tell you to expect me?"

I took control and said, "Sorry, babe, yes, this is *Twyla*." I hoped she'd wake up more and realize we now had two Twylas.

The diminutive fairy sprang up gracefully and ran toward Mitzi. She held Mitzi at arm's length and exclaimed "You and I are related! My uncle and your dad were married! I'm also a half-magical creature. This makes us family!" She hugged Mitzi close. Mitzi's eyes found mine over Twyla's shoulder. She had a "what the?" expression.

The grandfather clock in the living room struck six-fifteen, and I opened the blinds, any hope of a return to bed having evaporated. "Well, why don't we all sit down and get to know each other. We have some questions for you."

Twyla reluctantly let Mitzi go and sat at our kitchen table, leaving her mess next to her. I silently counted to ten and cleaned up her bowl and wiped crumbs off the table while Mitzi settled in next to her and to ask questions.

"Ekk and Elsa left weeks ago. Why didn't you come before?"

At that, the ginger fairy reddened. "Um, I got sidetracked?"

I'd had enough. "Do you have identification?"

"How many fairies you were expecting have shown up?"

I turned around from the sink and rested my hands on the counter behind me. "Well, actually, two."

"Uh oh, I knew I shouldn't have stopped in New York." The fiery visiting fairy actually started to glow a bit. "I got a message to check on your brother—"

In unison, Mitzi and I said, "Brooke?"

She was hesitant, "Unless you have two of those, too?"

"No, only one brother," I said. "What did he say? How is he? I left him a message, but he hasn't called back." I hadn't seen my brother since before last Christmas.

She lowered her big fairy eyes. "I got detoured going to New York and missed him." She pinned me with her gaze, and I felt a shimmer of energy. "He's already on his way to Peru. I think." She made what I surmised was a worried fairy face. "I'm pretty sure."

"What? I need coffee." Now I was concerned. Mitzi moved to the Krups and filled it with water.

I tried to impart how this was nothing to joke about, and my expression was probably fierce. I used my hand like a karate chop in the air. "Twyla, Explain." I was also getting one of those hard to describe feelings I had lately, where everything was more than what was said.

She stood and said, "I hate all this serious talk. It makes me nervous." Without further ado, she lifted about six inches off the kitchen floor, translucent wings humming they moved so fast. "Sorry," she reddened, "this happens sometimes."

Now Mitzi turned, coffee cup in hand, her eyes glued on the fairy floating near the kitchen ceiling in our humble home on Thistle Drive.

Twyla continued speaking, zipping back and forth over the linoleum. "I got a message at the ticket counter in Germany, saying to go to New York first. Ehrenhardt said Wolfrum is going after both of you, actually all three of Panda's siblings, or is that just both." She was puzzled. "I'm not sure how Brooke knew to go to Peru. They may have gotten to him first."

I thought about Brooke, my stone serious stock broker brother on Wall Street meeting up with the magical. I would have laughed if the implications weren't so serious.

"How do you know that's where he went?" Mitzi asked.

"And who is *they*?" I almost shouted. Mitzi gave me a "calm down" glare.

Twyla was indignant. "I can read a scene: his luggage was gone and his computer showed directions to the hotel from the airport." She turned to the friendlier Mitzi and said, "he arrives in Lima today," then scratched her head. "I'm pretty sure." Twyla turned back to me. "And, Panda, this is evil with a big E. It's Wolf Raven in Germany, but it pops up under different names elsewhere. Can we simply say the bad guys?"

I started to feel sorry for her. She was only the messenger.

"But why me, and my sister and brother? Mitzi is the only half griffin here. How could Puddle and Brooke possibly pose a threat? And why would Wolfrum want us all in Peru? That's where Ekk wants us to go." I sat down hard, confused.

Twyla slowly lowered her dainty feet to the linoleum and took a deep breath.

"After the ritual you both performed here in Merryville, the shift of power from evil to mostly good is kind of spotty, like your wireless coverage." She laughed at this. "Ehem, sorry. Panda, you were part of that."

Mitzi snorted, "But my wife isn't magical."

I stood up again and addressed the ceiling, already irritated. "Nooo, I don't understand anything about anything because I'm a boring human." This was part of the fight from the night before.

Twyla got an "uh oh" expression on her face.

Mitzi said, as if she were not there, "Well, to me you are magic, darling, but come on—you don't have wings, okay?" We both turned to Twyla, who was following us back and forth like a tennis match.

She took that pause to jump in. "The analogy to wireless coverage is not a joke—it's, it's all energy. Apparently, the other side sees an opportunity to beef up Wolfrum's power, which to us is all evil magic, through the South American portal, which is in flux."

"Another Sun Dog?" I was getting knowledgeable about this portal stuff. The ritual Twyla referred to was conducted a few weeks ago at the local museum through a portal connected to a Sun Dog in another place. The outcome was supposed to increase the balance of either good or evil in the world, depending on which side won, but it was a draw.

"Kind of, but this one is a portal to Paititi, which contains ancient Incan magic. One is due to be opened in Peru soon and the Wolf Ravens need whatever it is to attack again."

"Seriously, a portal to a magic city?" I made a big sigh. "Why us?" I lifted my hands up and appealed to the ceiling.

Twyla went to the fridge and acted sulky, "Hey, don't kill the messenger. Why are you talking to the ceiling?" She got philosophical. "Maybe if the bad guys can get all of you out of the way, it makes their plans to establish themselves here in Merryville easier. You see, magic attracts magic."

I sat down and tried to focus. "I'm still confused." I leaned forward on the table, tired. "Why Merryville, and why the Fowler adult children?"

Twyla turned to us with the fridge door still open, chomping on a celery stick: "Merryville sits on the biggest portal of all. And, oh, yeah, Panda, your parents? They were magic."

Mitzi's jaw literally dropped. My brow furrowed.

"What? My parents were hippies." As if being a hippie and being magical were mutually exclusive.

Now Twyla laughed heartily. "The hippie movement attracted lots of magical people. We resonate to peace, love and music." Her facial expression was comically expressive.

"Wait a minute, what kind of magic did they have?"

"It was of a kind that probably you and maybe your siblings have." My eyes got larger. "No flying," she added quickly. "It's more like, have you ever had a moment when you knew that something was happening that was more than the surface would indicate?"

"Y-yes." That was the feeling. Mitzi gaped at me. I added, "Sometimes."

"Well, that can be developed. You have sensing magic, like you knew I was magic right away."

"Duh, you're a fairy."

"And someone else might see me as a small woman with red hair."

Then I thought about it. "I knew the other Twyla was magic, too." Mitzi studied me with a tilt to her head. "Instantly." I got excited "What else can I do?"

Twyla smiled, "I'm not sure what all you can do, if anything. Your bloodline is quite diluted, no offense. But your strain of magic, however buried or faint, is probably why you were attracted to Mitzi in the first place and why you're being sought by the bad guys."

The feeling we had discussed was upon me now. The kitchen felt bigger and each detail more vibrant. "I met Mitzi at a dance."

"Who invited you?" Twyla spoke softly and moved to about a foot from my face.

"I, I don't know. It was a long time ago."

"It was Beth." Mitzi put a coffee cup in my hand, fixed as I like it.

"Beth. Hmm, whatever happened to her?" With her interrogation, Twyla reminded me of a police investigator I met recently.

"I dunno, that was fifteen years ago."

"Hmmmm," Twyla said. "Can I try coffee? It smells good."

I wouldn't be distracted. "Are you saying this Beth was magical? That she introduced us for a purpose? If that's true, why am I only hearing about it now?" Mitzi handed Twyla a smaller cup than mine, filled with black coffee.

"I don't know everything, only that the Hercynian Garden researchers have been working around the clock on your ancestry. I'm guessing about how you met. I like to help." She smiled her goofy smile.

I sipped my coffee, my lifeline to normalcy. "Well, Mitz, what do you say about that?

She put her arm around me and her head on my shoulder. "Magic, no magic, you're my Panda Bear and I love you."

"Awww," Twyla said, then "Uh oh."

Mitzi and I broke up our love fest to see Twyla quickly put her coffee down and take flight again. "There was something in there—a drug!"

Now it was Mitzi and my turn to laugh. "Yes, it's called caffeine."

"Okay, as long as it's normal. I mean I don't feel normal. Why can't I stop talking?" Twyla continued. "I'm worried about that woman claiming to be me. I want to meet her."

Mitzi said, "Well, yoga starts in about an hour. Shall we all go?"

My aching body from yesterday said no, but I wanted answers. "Absolutely."

CHAPTER FIVE

Meanwhile at Valerie and Juniper Gooden's household, Valerie was straightening up the house and happened across the flyer she was given the day before.

A NEW SPIRIT IS BLOWING THROUGH MERRYVILLE
COME TO OUR NEW SPIRIT GATHERING SUNDAY
AND HEAR THE TRUTH ABOUT GOD AND HIS KINGDOM
IN THE CENTRAL GREENSPACE OF MERRYVILLE.

The flyer showed a picture of the park, and there were more than a few shiny black birds in it. No, it couldn't be, she thought. Juniper had told her of the role ravens played in the evil religion they had battled a few weeks ago. Come to think of it, she saw some of the birds herself during that crazy time.

WE WELCOME ALL—ESPECIALLY
THIEVES, LIARS, DRUNKARDS AND HOMOSEXUALS—
WHO WISH TO TURN THEIR LIVES AROUND.
11:00 A.M. EVERY SUNDAY THROUGH JULY.

"Great," she said as she crumpled up the paper and tossed it in the recycling, thinking, what is wrong with people? Whatever happened to live and let live. She shook her head with its sleek blue-black hair. The Gooden home was old, and the floorboards creaked as Valerie entered the kitchen and kicked off her clogs near the back door that was open an inch. She felt hairs prickle on the back of her neck and her right hand automatically slid into her pocket to feel for her cell phone. She always locked that door before leaving. She peered out the window to the backyard and didn't see Layla, their old hound dog. After listening and finding it too quiet, Valerie padded back to the bathroom she had turned into her greenhouse to see if the old dog was sleeping in there. From the door she stopped as if running into an invisible wall and let out a wail. "The Rothschilds!" Someone or something had broken her two most rare and beautiful orchids and left them there to die. As if that were not enough, there was a note by their pot: "People are fragile like flowers."

A new chill went down her spine.

PERU

Puddle gradually became aware of vibrations and rumbling and something hard on her side. She opened her eyes to see she was in a tunnel, being pushed along in a coal cart. She saw Jose Luis, moving ahead with surprising speed, and she could smell Fernando's aftershave. He was the one pulling the cart. Her mind spun; where were they taking her? She wasn't tied up and still didn't know what to make of the situation.

"I think she's awake."

"Good. We need her on foot."

Fernando reached into the coal cart that had come to the end of its tracks. "Sorry for the dramatics. We couldn't risk you coming back on your own."

At that, Puddle relaxed. It was nice to hear she would be on her own at some point in the future. "Drugging me is not cool," she said. She shook out her arms and legs and smoothed down her beads. "Ever!"

Jose Luis was up ahead and turned impatiently, "Hurry, we're almost there." His English was suddenly pretty darn good.

Fernando turned to her, and his eyes bored into hers. "Puddle, trust me, please."

Sylvia entered the sunroom off the main Merryville house to join her new board. Janet and Lidia were already seated on either side of Hortense, like Chinese Foo Lions. She smiled and strolled slowly to her chair, one of only two empty seats at the table. Sally was doodling on the agenda, and the others seemed sharp and ready for duty. She stifled a giggle at the image of the Mavens as a military organization.

Hortense wrapped the gavel. "Now that we're all here, let's get started. Report!"

Lidia cleared her throat. "We have secured city permission to hold next year's flower show at the arena, same arrangement as before, one dollar. It helped a great deal to have the Windingle Foundation to underwrite the insurance."

Among "very goods" and "good job," Lidia went on a bit about details related to the event. Sylvia couldn't help but think she could have hit "save as" from the year before. Mavens weren't known for radical departures from the past.

Sally was next and gave a rambling report about seed supplies. They all knew her husband, Jack, handled the whole thing, but she got a hearty round of applause anyway.

After a couple more reports, Hortense again had the floor. "Time to go over new applications. First, we have Denise McGreggor. She is from the Smith-McGreggors, and we've been expecting her to join now that she's back from Europe."

"I vote in." This from Janet.

"Fine," Lidia added.

"Wait," Sylvia said. What are her qualifications?"

Exasperated, Lidia said, "Her people have always been part of the Society. It's tradition to honor legacy memberships."

Sylvia would not let it go. "Have you actually met her?"

"She's been living abroad." Hortense gave an amused smile. "I knew her mother, Agnes, for ages. She was a member for thirty years before her death, God rest her soul." The gavel came down.

"Next." Hortense perused the applications. "The only other application is Valerie Gooden."

"I vote in." Sylvia interjected. If Janet could do it, so could she.

"Wait a minute, wait a minute, not so fast," Lidia said. "I'm still reading." She had a copy of Valerie's application in her spidery hands. "I don't see any previous awards. Oh wait, there's one, but it's from Hanford."

Janet tittered. "What does she bring to the table?"

Hortense got up and poured herself a cup of tea. "Well, you know, she's in with those lesbians with the Scottish Thistle problem. Do we really want to go there?"

"Guilt by association, really? Is that we do?" The voice came from the door, as Florence Dinwitter came in late and slung her Louis Vuitton bag on the remaining empty chair. Florence was the wife of Judge Dinwitter and the only women of sufficient social stature to threaten Hortense.

"Flo, nice of you to join us." Hortense smiled, but it didn't reach her eyes.

"Sorry, ladies, the Judicial luncheon went on longer than we hoped. Willard got Judicial officer of the year—*again*." She shook her head, laughing like it was just the craziest thing, all this winning. Sylvia smiled. She might like this woman, if for no other reason than she could make Hortense nervous.

"To catch you up, we have the arena for our March flower show, and remember Agnes?"

Florence put her hand in the general vicinity of her brooch. "Bless, what a wonderful woman she was." The two older women displayed dopey smiles, remembering the sainted Agnes.

"Her daughter's moving back to Merryville. She's put in her application."

"Outstanding! I approve. Anyone else?" Florence took her seat. She peeled off her gloves and warmed to the agenda.

"Yes," Sylvia spoke up "Valerie Gooden—she's a whiz with orchids."

"Who are her people?" Florence actually said this with a straight face.

Hortense looked directly at Sylvia and flashed a malicious smile. "You put her up for membership. Defend her."

Sylvia found her spine. "She's married to Juniper Gooden, Curator of the Merryville Museum. This will help us with our plans to redo the landscaping there."

"Don't need her," Lidia said. "Charlotte Windingle is all in."

Sylvia felt like she was being stalked by triangulating cats. She glanced at Sally, who was still doodling. "Sally, you've met Valerie, and what about your comment when you came in, Mrs. Dinwitter? Guilty until proven innocent, or something? Ladies, she's grown Rothschild Slippers, and they're the rarest flower in Merryville! Maybe even California! Last meeting you all admitted we were weak in the orchid area. Here's our chance to fix that."

Lots of darting eye contact and studying of agendas followed her brave speech.

Hortense broke the tension. "Yes, it was very ambitious of you to seek her out. Next time, it would be good to have a meet and confer first—that's how we usually do it."

Sylvia took the chastisement silently.

Hortense cleared her throat. "That being said, I propose we give Miss Gooden a chance." Immediate low discussion ensued. "But! She will be on probation until we can see these miraculous orchids and make sure she won't defend the Scottish Thistles in her friend's yard."

Florence nodded. Hortense surveyed her troops, and, of course, they all fell behind her. Sylvia felt she had made a difference. The rest would be up to Valerie.

Meanwhile, back at Valerie and Juniper Gooden's house, Valerie scrolled through her cell phone until she found the number for Inspector Potts. He had actually arrested her some weeks ago at the museum, another complex story, but he was a changed man now that he was dating her old defense attorney, Alex Stefanovsky. Now she believed he was the best choice to call. Funny how much things could change in a few weeks.

He picked up on the first ring: "Potts."

"Detective? This is Valerie Gooden. I-I don't know if you'll remember me."

"Valerie Gooden—as if—what's up? This is my private line."

"I know, you said only use it in case of emergency."

"Where are you?"

"My home, two twenty-nine Lemon Avenue."

"On my way."

"Don't you want to know—" she began, but he had already hung up. She thought about calling Juniper, but that dear woman had enough to think about with her big art show coming up. Next, she steeled herself and went out into the back yard. As she descended the wooden steps, the front doorbell rang, but it was too fast to be Detective Potts. She went to answer it. A neighborhood boy from down the street grasped Layla's collar with both hands. The aging dog, completely white on her muzzle, seemed frazzled.

"Dougie, where was she?"

Dougie was a rarity these days, a child who was actually outside throwing a ball or riding his bike instead of sitting in front of a computer. "Our house. Somebody left your gate open, and she was eating our cat food."

Valerie took the animal with a sigh of relief. She reached in her pocket for a bill and gave the boy a dollar. "Thanks, Dougie."

"No problem, Mrs. Gooden."

Valerie turned her attention to the old dog, who was straining to get back into the house and, no doubt, to her spot on the cool linoleum floor in the kitchen. "I do wish you could talk, old girl," she said, giving Layla's big neck a hug and rubbing her ears.

A black Chrysler 300 pulled up in front of the house, and the now semi-retired Detective Potts eased his big frame out of the driver's seat.

Valerie, feeling somewhat better now, called out "Thanks for coming, I hope I didn't alarm you unnecessarily."

"So'kay. Truth be told, things are slow at the precinct. Alexandra's off saving some criminal's hide up north. What's up?"

BACK ON THISTLE DRIVE

"Well, if we're going to yoga, we better get ready," I said, always the practical one.

Mitzi put her hand out to the fairy. "Twyla, we have a guest room, let me show you. Do you have a bag?" Mitzi was such a gracious host.

Twyla responded like a kid who had a secret "Umm, actually, I kind of like outdoors?"

"Okay. We have a tent in the garage." I felt better thinking of her outside, actually, until we really knew what was going on.

"Not necessary. Come on, I got here hours ago. Come see." With that, Twyla jumped up and gaily walked out of the kitchen into the back yard.

"You first," I said, motioning with my hand. Mitzi raised her eyebrows, took a deep breath and followed the fairy.

Not having any idea what to expect, I was nonetheless very surprised to see Brutus' Summer Palace—up in the tree. "What the?"

"I saw you had *grünzueg* and used it to finish the treehouse."

"*Grünzueg*?" Mitzi echoed.

"Treehouse?" I said.

"Yes, the green stuff we use in the Hercynian Garden. I had some too for fixing things, and it turned out pretty good."

Pretty good was an understatement. The green "treehouse" blended in nicely with the old tree foliage and cleared up space on the ground, which was still pretty rough in spots. "How do you get up there?" I asked, before thinking.

She put out her arms and kind of floated up to a small platform leading into the treehouse. "And I can watch for intruders from here. Pretty neat, huh?"

She was fishing for a compliment. It never occurred to me that fairies were so insecure. "Amazing."

"I can't believe you got it up there," Mitzi said. "Never mind, I have to shower." She turned and went into the house, shaking her head but smiling.

Twyla floated down. I was hoping none of the neighbors saw her. "Um, people don't do too much floating around here. Can you put in a rope or a ladder or something?

She laughed her tinkling laugh. "Sure." With that she whistled, and a rope ladder fell. "I forget sometimes. This is my first trip to your world."

"Find a towel. This is about to get very interesting. You know what yoga is, right?"

Twyla nodded.

I gave her my biggest smile. "Okay, let me get my stuff, and we'll go in my car." I turned to her halfway across the yard. "No flying, no magic, no nothing like that, okay?"

She nodded, but I didn't trust her, what with all the floating and whistling and childlike energy about her. A treehouse—of course, she would live in a treehouse. A thought occurred to me. "Are there different kinds of fairies? Are you a tree fairy?"

"See," she replied, "you *are* a sensing person—that's exactly what I am." She ran up impulsively, put her arm around me as if we were the best of friends, and walked me inside. "I'm going to like it here."

My mind screamed, how long are you staying? But I wanted to wait for that conversation until we sorted out who the real guardian was. So far, I was tipping towards her, scary as that thought was.

Pretty soon the three of us were in my Smart car. If Twyla had been any bigger, we would have had to Uber it. Mitzi had a two-seater Miata, so it's not like we could take the other car. As it was, the diminutive fairy sat in the back and gracefully folded herself into the storage compartment as if this was the most normal thing in the world.

We pulled up to *The Garden*, which is where today's yoga class was. A gathering of mostly women were milling around the front door, which was locked. We overheard, "She said 'I'll see you tomorrow.' Does anyone have a phone number for Twyla?" and similar comments. A few more people arrived and left, and the general consensus was there would be no yoga class today.

"Told ja. She was probably a shapeshifter," our Twyla commented. "Pretty gutsy naming the place *The Garden*."

The window was down. I heard a jangle of keys from the inside of the yoga studio and the door opened. There she stood, the beautiful, sleek yoga instructor from the beach. "Sorry folks, got hung up on the way in. Welcome." She looked, it seemed, straight at us, or maybe straight at Mitzi, with her golden eyes. Was that a smirk?

I almost fell over myself getting out of the car, not really sure how to proceed. Mitzi got out, as if entranced, and made for the front door. I let redhaired Twyla out of the back.

I said quietly, "What do you think?" My magic senses, or whatever they were, buzzed like never before.

Twyla, oblivious, said, "I think we should do yoga!"

I grabbed my towel. If this kept up, I'd need my own mat. I followed the rest of the herd into the medium-sized room. Otherworldly Enya-type music was playing, and I felt out of my comfort zone as I lay my towel between Mitzi and the Twyla we brought with us.

"Okay, class, we're going to warm up with our Sukshma Vyayama poses." We stood and did minor stretches while the *other* Twyla walked, panther-like, between rows of students trying their best not to fall, and to look cool while holding hard poses. Mitzi was silent and gave nothing away, seemingly untroubled by the appearance of a second guardian fairy.

I sighed, my thighs still screaming from the day before, almost as if they knew the exercise was only going to get tougher.

Redhaired Twyla was as bendable as a Gumby doll, and keeping up quite nicely with the teacher. Adopting a "when in Rome" attitude, I did my best to follow directions and waited for something to happen. I don't know what I expected really, a screaming match? A standoff of some kind, magical sparks flying? Falling asleep? Whatever it was, it wasn't this. Nothing but more yoga poses I couldn't do, and that same hypnotic voice that seemed even more so in this warm crowded studio.

"That's right, when you think you can't go any further, let go of that monkey thought. Let your body reach through," was the last thing I heard.

BROOKE IN CUSCO WITH THE ELVES

Brooke's face turned to granite, all the wonder at his strange journey gone. "Facts. Now. Why are we here, where is Puddle and what do you know?" His demanding speech and size were intimidating.

Juju got defensive, "It was that Fernando, the boyfriend—"

But Brooke was having none of it. "You *say* you're my sister's guardian—but she was taken on your watch. By whom—this Fernando?" The hotel room seemed small with the big man in it.

Elsa could tell things were spinning out of control. Juju's fists were tightening. She concentrated on peaceful flowers. The room calmed down a bit and started to smell of lavender.

Ekk put a restraining arm on Juju's chest. "Maybe, Brooke. There are two stories to tell first. You must hear them both before we search for Puddle. The first is that there are two worlds—the one you grew up in and live in now and the world of myths and magic. Your first conscious intersection with the magical one was in the subway."

Brooke said, "Go on." There was an edge to his voice.

Ekk continued, "We all know there is good and evil in this world—"

"And lots of grey in between," Brooke interrupted. "Let's cut the fairy tale short and tell me who took Puddle? Has there been a ransom demand? I can pay it."

"No ransom, but you need to know everything. I think you need a beer for this."

"Getting me drunk won't find my sister."

Juju went to the fridge and got a round for everyone. Elsa was happy to see he didn't expect her to wait on him all the time.

Ekk went on, "We'll find her, but first you must understand. This world is not the only one."

"You said that. Where's the other one?"

"Hard to explain. It's kind of side by side to this reality. That may be a conversation for later. Suffice it to say there are intersections or portals, places where one can enter the other, places where good and bad can slip through. Your sister Panda and her wife and their friend Juniper entered the magical world a few weeks ago through the Black Forest in Germany." Brooke's head jerked up.

"That's where we have our headquarters, if you will. Panda's okay—she's in Merryville again, a story for later." Ekk jumped up to pace. "There are many portals." He stopped and faced Brooke directly: "Peru has one connected with Incan magic."

"But why me? I'm not religious. Why Puddle? She wouldn't hurt a fly?

Why would someone want to kidnap her? I thought this was about some lost city!"

"This brings me to the second part." Ekk opened his mouth to speak, but Juju jumped in.

"The same reason anybody kidnaps anybody—leverage. Your parents were magical, Señor Fowler."

Elsa and Ekk turned to Brooke and smiled encouragingly.

"Okay. Joke's over. This is too crazy." Brooke was shutting down, his arms crossed tight.

After a pointed look at Juju, Ekk turned again to Brooke. "They were part of the Big Battle."

"Yes, they were," Juju said defensively, then to Ekk. "We need to speed this up. Here's the short version, Señor Brooke. Your folks were on a mission when they disappeared. Even with all our magical resources, no one really knows what happened to them."

Despite himself, it appeared Brooke was curious. "What kind of magic? Are there different kinds?"

Ekk took over the explanation again. "They were very strong sensing people. Mostly human but with incredible intuition. It takes time to find humans with this diluted magical blood. Ehrenhardt, our leader, sent them to find Paititi because he didn't want fully magical people moving in this world, your world. He wanted this whole thing below the radar, so to speak, and convinced the Fowlers to work for good in this way." Ekk spoke softly. "He wants to know what happened to them, too, and feels very badly your parents disappeared."

Brooke clenched his jaw, and Ekk was concerned he would hit someone.

"They were searching for Paititi," Elsa said, cutting in, "because it's a very powerful city that contains ancient information that may tip the scales of Good against the Wolf Ravens."

"Wolf Ravens?" Brooke ran a hand through his hair, clearly on overload, but managed a sharp laugh. "Sounds like a boy scout troop."

Ekk tried again. "The wolf is a predator. Ravens are often harbingers of change. This religion, an ideology of war and violence, has chosen these two creatures as their symbol. Wherever you see people in this world organizing in hate, Wolf Raven is in there somewhere."

"Like ISIS?" Brooke was trying to make sense of it. He drew deeply on his beer.

"Yes, I believe so," Ekk said, "and others like it. Hitler's Nazis, Ghengis Kahn and the Mongol Hordes—"

"So," Brooke rubbed his hand over his face, "my parents were on a mission, they were magic, then what?"

Ekk put his hand on Brooke's resting arm gently. "Then nothing. People disappear for non-magical reasons, too. The cover story for you kids was that there was a bus accident. As far as we know, that may be true."

"Except the other side sure thinks you three know something." This was from Juju, who seemed intent on keeping things stirred up.

Ekk wanted to swat Juju. "Anyway, when was the last time you spoke to Puddle?"

Now it was Brooke's turn to study his shoes guiltily. "It's been a while. She was still in India."

Ekk continued. "While she was in India, she met a guy named Fernando, who was from here—Peru. He convinced her to come back with him to search for Paititi."

"That's crazy. But Puddle was always the one who was most like our parents. If I find this Fernando, I'll—" Brooke's fist slammed on the table, and the elves jumped.

Ekk looked at Juju, as if expecting him to take over again. "We don't even know what his role is. The only clue we have is that your sister called about a half hour ago from her cell phone and said she was at a bar, *The Lost City*—there is no such bar."

Brooke jumped up and ran for his bag. "She called from her cell?" He let out a bark of a laugh. "I put her on my iPhone account years ago. What's the Wi-Fi passcode here?"

Ekk gave it to him, and soon Brooke was doing a search for the phone. "I put a special tracker on Puddle's phone because," his eyes watered, "I knew she was apt to be anywhere on the planet at any given time and is far too trusting." The three elves watched him work with surprise.

Reading their expressions, he said, "I won't apologize for violating her privacy if this works. I love my sister. She's different from me. Both my sisters are." Elsa turned off the stove and put away the food on the counter. Brooke had something of his world to do, which made him clearly in command. "Who knows their way around here? Juju?"

The jungle elf nodded, "Si," and jumped to his feet, ready to go.

Elsa pointed to the New Yorker's hard leather footwear, "Brooke do you have other shoes?"

Brooke studied his dress shoes and quickly abandoned them for sneakers the size of boats.

"Good catch, Elsa." Ekk nodded approvingly.

Brooke read Juju an address while changing his business jacket for a windbreaker. "Let's go." Elsa made a move to leave with them, but Ekk turned and asked her to stay. "Please call Panda, and let her know what's happening. I'll keep in touch." He kissed her gently. "I promise." Juju and Brooke were already out the door, and Ekk had to run to keep up with them.

"Be safe!" Elsa called, and then went to find her phone.

CHAPTER SIX

AT THE MUSEUM

A white exhibition tent, part of "Words on a Plate—A Special Installation," was filled with tables lined up end to end. Juniper, the curator, walked them like a general, a small assembly waiting for the verdict. Her beautiful assistant Maribel, of the green hair, was stock still. She knew when to be quiet. I'd describe her getup as punk rockabilly, but always tidy. Several artists and volunteers stood around. The air was tense.

Even without the words, the overall effect of the exhibit was of a mad hatter's dinner, with hundreds of place settings. Some of the plates were fine china, some were chipped, many were colorful, and all had dialogue, one, two or many words that made up a communication. For example, a picture of a silent couple facing each other stubbornly was paired with a plate that said, "You First."

A painting of a battered woman with a bandage over her mouth was paired with a plate that said in blood red, "you'll never leave." There were more, the messages paired with paintings which creatively invited the observer to internalize what the "words on a plate" really meant. It was very interactive. The topics were intentionally provocative: sex, religion, relationships, ennui, immigration. It was a very different show that would either flop or be another feather in Juniper's cap.

Juniper was in a white pantsuit and had her hair up in a chignon. She turned and addressed the waiting group with a straight face. "Three words. Not. Edgy. Enough."

After a pause, the group burst into applause. Those were the three words on the last plate paired with a picture of Kathy Griffin holding up a manikin head.

"Good work, people." The tension broke and Juniper grabbed Damien, the chief artist, to discuss minor adjustments to the presentation.

"I hope people get it." This from one of Maribel's younger volunteers. Maribel turned her attention to the chubby volunteer. Bonnie Bruce-Pippin was an over eager girl, always on Maribel's heel. After moving tables and other physical work, today her overall affect was sweaty.

"Whether they get it or not," Maribel lifted the program in her hand and read from it: "Words on a Plate will challenge perceptions and, hopefully inspire." Maribel smiled and turned to leave, thinking about preparations still needed for the *avant garde* show.

Bonnie wasn't finished. "I hear the tent can't be here much longer. How are you going to move all this stuff?"

Maribel stopped in her tracks. "Heard this from whom?"

"Oh, never mind." Bonnie's hands twitched, and she put them behind her back to hide her nervousness, but Maribel could see a malicious light in her eyes. She knew something. Her listless brown hair kept falling out of her large butterfly-shaped hair clip, and she had chewed her nails to the quick.

Maribel read over the "Thank You" section in the program she held in her hand. Bonnie Bruce-Pippin's mother was listed as a patron. "Your family is quite involved in art I see."

"Yes, I want to be a curator like Juniper," she practically whispered.

"Have you been to Origins yet?"

Bonnie nodded yes one more time.

Maribel made a decision. "Let me buy you a coke and some fries and we can talk about that."

YOGA

I opened my eyes and this time was the only one awake. Mitzi to my left was frozen in a down dog as was the red-headed Twyla to my right. Some guardian, was my first thought before panic seized me. "Bad" Twyla was barking orders, no longer using her sensuous yoga voice. "Put the fat one in the van. The plane leaves in an hour."

I was still somewhat groggy, kicking myself for not being more prepared or for not losing those ten, okay fifteen, pounds. My limbs felt as if they had lead garments on them. I wondered if this is how Mitzi felt when kidnapped weeks ago and taken on a plane to Germany. I couldn't run or even speak, and my overall feeling was that I was slipping into a coma.

Two yoga participants, obviously enchanted somehow, wordlessly grabbed both my arms and led me to the back of the studio where a gaily colored van awaited. The evil yoga instructor locked up the back door as if it were a normal day and got behind the wheel. She was actually humming.

I tried yelling but didn't seem to have energy for anything more than basic thought. After doing the instructor's bidding, the two helper dudes sat down outside the studio and slipped wordlessly into a lovely lotus position with unfocused eyes. The driver laughed wickedly. "Don't worry, Panda Fowler, your wifey will be fine. In an hour or two."

I wanted to ask who she really was and where we were going, but sleep sounded so good.

THE GOODENS' HOUSE

Valerie and Potts walked back to the kitchen, and Valerie told him everything that had happened culminating in her discovery of the broken orchids. At that he relaxed and, truthfully, seemed a bit annoyed. He screwed up his face and closed an eye, which was a mannerism she was becoming familiar with, "You called me because you have broken flowers?"

Valerie was kind, usually the soother and healer as was her profession of nursing, but Potts needed some schooling. She flipped her black silky pony tail, which Juniper would have recognized as a warning sign, and gestured to her orchids. "Let me tell you about these flowers."

She lovingly and gently lifted a broken orchid. "This one is a Rothschild Slipper Orchid, market price five thousand dollars." Her voice wavered. "Juniper and I brought seeds back from Sabah."

At his quizzical expression, she added, "It's in Malaysia."

"This one, too." They were still beautiful, even as they were dying.

"So that's ten thousand dollars for two flowers?"

"Yes, but to me, it isn't even the money. It's the fact that they're extremely rare. Its almost unheard of, to grow these here, but I've done it."

His tone grew more respectful. "So what about these others. What are they worth?"

"To me? Everything. I take care of people who eventually die. That's the nature of hospice. These other flowers are excellent specimens but not too expensive." Her eyes were watery. Until now she'd been shocked and angry. Now she was simply sad. "This orchid garden represents healing and growth. It renews me. Oh, and there was a note." She bent to pick up a torn piece of paper that had fallen to the floor.

No! Stop!" Potts bent over with a grunt, and actually picked the small note up with some tweezers pulled from his pocket. He read it before carefully putting it in an envelope. "I'm getting some uniforms over here to take a report. Don't touch nothing."

❧

FERNANDO AND PUDDLE

It was obvious that the tunnel led directly to the jungle, but Puddle had no point of reference after that. "What now?"

Fernando was sweating. Jose Luis had led the way, finally stopping in a clearing. Fernando ran his hand through his black hair, nervously. "We're supposed to meet people who will take us to my, maybe our, parents."

"It sounds like yours disappeared only a while ago. Mine either died or were taken decades ago—it's not the same thing. How did you meet these people?" She swatted a mosquito. "And, why not go by yourself?"

His face was full of guilt. "They said if I didn't bring you, they would cut off my parents' heads."

Puddle was disgusted, "I'm leaving."

Fernando collapsed on his knees and started crying. "Oh, Puddle, what have I done? I was crazy with worry and grief when I went all the way to the Ashram. My parents are everything. Please don't go."

She stood there like a stone. This selfish jerk had used her in a terrible way.

"But then I met you, and, and, I have feelings!" His big brown eyes must have worked on his mama when he was a boy—he was sure using them now.

Puddle was unmoved. "You never believed my parents were alive, did you?"

"I don't know, I don't know." He sniffed.

Jose Luis rolled his eyes and handed Fernando a rag from his pocket and said, "I go now."

"Well, do what you want Fernando, but I 'go now' too." Puddle started to follow Jose Luis back the way they came.

"Puddle, wait!" Fernando ran after her "If you leave, you'll never really know what happened to your mother and father!"

"And I might get killed, you selfish jerk!" She started moving faster as the reality of her situation hit. She'd been so mad before that she wasn't afraid. Now she thought about people who would cut other people's heads off.

She almost ran into Jose Luis' backside because he had abruptly stopped. The canopy cast a green glow over the scene as she soon saw creatures with spears poking at her guide.

"*Ay Dios mio!*" Jose Luis backed up and crossed himself.

There were six of them, short colorful men wearing masks designed like cows' faces. Each man had very dark skin and spears with feathers and shells dangling from their sharpened tips. They moved fast and herded Jose Luis and Puddle back to where Fernando stood. Instinctively, Fernando, Jose Luis and Puddle put their backs together and the warriors circled them.

"Lo siento! Lo siento!" (I'm sorry!) "Puddle and Jose Luis! I will give myself to them for your release!" Fernando put his left and right arm back behind him, presumably to shield those he had caused to be with him in the jungle. The air was stifling with humidity, and Puddle's new clothes stuck to her skin.

The men circled and occasionally jabbed a spear at the three, cutting off any idea of escape. They occasionally shouted something, but it wasn't Spanish. There were yips and clicks! And some guttural call from deep in their throats. Puddle heard drums somewhere in the distance and almost laughed thinking this was not the way she thought she would go someday.

ॐ

THE GARDEN YOGA STUDIO

Twyla of the red hair stood and shook out her limbs. Holding position when she was not really magically paralyzed was exhausting. She looked around at all the others, who still held poses, and went to Mitzi, frozen in down dog. After a gentle shake, Mitzi awoke as if from a deep sleep.

"What's going on? Where's Panda?"

"Listen to me very carefully." Her hazel eyes were really large. She reminded Mitzi of a cartoon. Panda's been taken by the Yoga teacher." Twyla watched Mitzi's face as she wrapped her brain around what she was being told and took in the others who were magically paralyzed.

"And you let her get taken? Where did they go?" Mitzi lunged at Twyla, then put her hands up and said, "Aaagh!" She made a sudden beeline for the door.

"They left by van a few minutes ago, so you won't catch them that way." Twyla took Mitzi's hand and spoke to her, slowly. "Since I could hear them, I know she's taking her to a plane, to fly to Peru."

"This can't be happening."

"It is, Mitzi."

"Why didn't my wings spring out? I should be flying after them right now!" She shouted.

Twyla spoke calmly. "Your wings stayed where they are because you were under a spell of some kind, dark magic. The immediate danger has passed. I guess you've noticed you can't make yourself fly when you want to."

Frustrated, Mitzi's nostrils flared. She was fierce. "You're supposed to be our guardian. How could you let this happen?"

Twyla took a couple steps back but held her composure. "I ran through my options, and this was the safest for both of you—and these other people. This person who was pretending to be me is not a person at all—she's a thing." Mitzi felt a chill to her bare feet. Panda was taken by a "thing." "Now let's get you home to pack and on a plane to Lima. I'm sure you can get a flight into Cusco from there. I, ah, I might find someone to fly with you."

Always the travel agent, Mitzi said "There is a direct flight to Cusco. I've been checking it out already. What about all these people?"

"Please get in the car. I'll handle it. They'll probably be fine on their own in time, but there are some things I know how to do to help. Go. I'm right behind you."

Mitzi ran to the door, then back for her mat, having recently been in a trance and not knowing what to do first. Her opinion of Twyla improved when she stopped at the Yoga room door. Twyla was walking person to person and putting her hand on their foreheads. She then went to the front of the room and took out what appeared to be a white carrot.

"All of you have had the most wonderful yoga experience today. You leave fresh and revived, knowing the studio will be closing. It was a great day. Now you want spin classes."

Twyla rushed to the door as people woke up, smiling. "Let's go."

Thankfully, Mitzi had a set of keys to the car in her purse that was in the back of the yoga room with Panda's cell phone and other personal items. After noticing a message from Elsa on Panda's phone, she used her thumb to hit keys and retrieve the message.

Elsa's voice was an octave higher than normal, a sign of stress: "Panda, Ekk, Juju and your brother left to rescue Puddle, I'm afraid the other side has her. Please call me. I think you need to come now."

Then to Twyla, Mitzi repeated, "That was a message from Elsa, Wolf Raven has Puddle."

Mitzi hit return and was shortly connected with the distraught elf. "Elsa?"

"Oh, Mitzi, I called Panda. Are you with her? Wait, you're on Panda's phone."

"They've got Panda, too."

"*Gott in Himmel!*" (God in Heaven.)

"What?"

"Never mind. I'm sure it's going to be okay—we'll fix this. Did Twyla, ever show up?"

"Which one?"

It was Elsa's turn to say, "What?"

"She's here. Twyla's here. There were two Twylas, and one was my yoga teacher, who turned out not to be a person at all. Oh, I'll explain when I get there. I'm on my way. Are you still at the Principe in Cusco?"

"Yes." Elsa gave a few more directions and their room number and promised to wait.

Twyla was in the shotgun seat of Sweetpea and was all business. She was staring out the window, talking to herself.

"Hello, earth to Twyla."

"Oh, sorry, the elders at the Hercynian Garden gave me this Unicorn horn right before I left. It's really powerful, and it worked."

"Are you really that new at this?" Mitzi shook her head and hit the accelerator. "I get the feeling things aren't quite as organized as you would like them to be in your magical headquarters."

"It's like your world in a way. Magical creatures are flawed, but we do our best."

Mitzi hadn't really expected an answer to her rhetorical question, but it made sense.

Panda's phone rang again, and this time it went to Bluetooth over the car's radio.

Elsa's voice came through. "Is Twyla with you?"

"Yes, it's me, Elsa." Twyla held on to the door frame as Mitzi took a corner like a Grand Prix driver. "I really am going to take care of anything you need, I—"

Elsa cut her off with a barrage of German. Mitzi understood it! "Listen up, guardian fairy, you need to stay in Merryville and actually *guard* Panda and Mitzi's home as well as Brutus, and keep an eye on the others who were involved in the Sundog Ritual, Valerie and Juniper. Ekk and I will take it from here." She didn't sound exactly angry, but maybe a little cross. "I don't want to talk too much on the cell phone, but you and I will need to talk later, hopefully, when we all get back to Merryville."

"Elsa, I—"

"Let me finish. I'm disappointed you let Panda be taken." Twyla's red hair started to flame redder.

"Well, that's the pot calling the kettle black! Didn't Puddle get taken, too?"

Mitzi pulled into her driveway. Some guardians, she was thinking, now they were blaming each other.

There was silence on the other end from Peru. "True, but by all the Hercynian Garden holds dear, we are going to get her back."

Twyla sat up straight and said clearly, this time in English, "We're getting Panda back, too. I coated her Fitbit with *grünzueg*."

Mitzi and Twyla heard Elsa's musical laughter. "Maybe there's hope for you, Twyla. Great idea. That will help a lot." She soon rang off.

"What was that about?" Mitzi enquired as they entered the garage to the house.

"*Grünzueg* has many interesting magical properties, but the main use is building material. I had the idea to coat Panda's Fitbit with it because both were green."

"And?" Mitzi paused to listen.

"And it gives off a low-grade magic signature that can be detected by Hercynian Forest citizens. It's undetectable to the other side."

Mitzi hugged Twyla impulsively. "Thank you."

ॐ

Maribel and Bonnie went to Origins and were quickly seated at a table. After the fries and coke were ordered, Maribel asked questions.

"What made you volunteer for the museum this summer?"

"My mom. She makes me volunteer for something all the time. I told her I was tired of being a Mavenette and wearing those stupid pink polos."

Maribel laughed. The Mavenettes' uniform was a bit precious for a girl going through what appeared to be a difficult puberty.

"So, you want to be a curator?"

"Yes, like Juniper Gooden."

The fries arrived, and Bonnie pounced. Maribel put a maple-bacon sweet potato fry in her mouth and pondered what she'd heard.

"Why Juniper? Your mom is Janet Bruce-Pippin, right? One of the original Mavens or something?"

Bonnie echoed some of her mother's pretentiousness. "Oh, no, we joined second generation. The first was the Smiths. Then when my grandfather moved here from the Midwest, he said we needed to bring some culture to the Mexicans." She squeezed ketchup on the potatoes. "Oops, not supposed to say that. They were Indigenous People."

"Oh, I see. Does your mom like Juniper?" Maribel said this with a sweet smile. It was amazing what she could get out of people with some tasty food and her youthful green hair.

Bonnie laughed and spit out bits of food. "Sorry. No, Mom hates Juniper. They all do." She brushed back her bangs, and Maribel saw a rather large zit forming.

"Why?"

"I dunno. She's different. Our church says she's going to hell." In the way of young teens, Bonnie abruptly changed topics. "Didn't the guy who used to have your job kill somebody?"

"Yes, his name was Garcia. It was an accident." She wasn't going to lose track of why they were here having a nosh. "So, what's this about moving the exhibition?"

A shadow fell across Bonnie's face. She knew she'd said too much. "Um, I don't know why I said that. Thanks for inviting me to lunch." She gave Maribel a syrupy smile and got up to leave, brushing her as she went by.

Uh oh. Maribel suddenly suspected why Bonnie was acting so weird but kept it to herself.

LATER THAT DAY

The phone rang, and Valerie answered with a tentative "Hello?"

"It's Sylvia."

Valerie felt her stomach drop. "And?"

"You're in."

"Oh, my God! Serious?" Val sat down on a kitchen chair. "I guess it didn't really dawn on me I would be accepted. Let me tell you, though, about something that happened today—"

"In a sec. The Executive Committee of the Mavens want to see those tricky orchids you found on the highest peaks of Tibet or wherever. Isn't this great?"

"Malaysia. The orchids were from Malaysia. When are they coming?"

"Today at two o'clock. I hope that's okay."

Valerie tried not to scream. "I need to talk to you first. Something's happened."

"Oops, later Val, my name is being called for tennis doubles, I'm at the club. *Ciao!*" Valerie sat with the phone in her hand, pondering several questions:

Who would hate her and Juniper enough to break the stems of her Rothschilds?

Why would fate allow her to be accepted to the Merryville Mavens, only to snatch the opportunity away hours later? Was Juniper in danger?

What would she tell Sylvia? Hortense? She sat thinking a while, absently shaking her head. Pictures of the Rothschilds would have to do, she thought. Layla, the ten-year-old hound dog, plodded over to her and put her graying muzzle on Valerie's lap. They sighed in unison.

THE LITTLE HOUSE ON THISTLE DRIVE

"You have lots of bags," Twyla observed. "I'll help you. Do you want me to drive you to the airport?

"Do you even know how to drive?" Mitzi asked.

"Not yet, but I can learn really fast. I watched you drive earlier." Twyla was serious.

"Um, that would be no. I like your spirit, but driving takes some training—and a driver's license." Mitzi gave a mirthless laugh.

Twyla cocked her head. "Driver's license?"

"Never mind. Juniper's picking me up. Now, please repeat all the things I told you."

"First rule, no magic." Twyla frowned. This had been a big conversation. Apparently, Ehren himself had laid down the law.

"Right." Mitzi gave her the gimlet eye. "Nothing that will endanger anybody. This is from Ehrenhardt. And?"

Twyla ticked off the items on her thin fingers. "Clip the thistles in the front yard."

"Yes, those Mavens from the Horticultural Society are on our butts." Mitzi watched out the window as she spoke, eyeing the overgrown thistles. "Next?"

"Feed the cat every day. As if I could forget! Brutus won't shut up when he's hungry. He's always like—purple bag, purple bag.'"

"You understand cat?"

"Oh, yeah, it was one of my first languages in Kindergarten."

"Kindergarten? I thought you would call it something else, like baby fairy school, I guess."

A honk outside made Mitzi gather her things.

"We invented the word, you know. Kindergarten. It's German." She had a point.

The front door burst open and Juniper called "Hello, Mitzi! Hellooo." She tried to pick up a bag. Her tapered nails made it comical as well as impossible.

"Twyla stepped forward and reached for the bag, "Let me."

Twyla was tiny but grabbed two big bags and lugged them to the car without too much trouble.

"Was that?" Juniper's eyes were large, and she pointed a rainbow painted nail in Twyla's direction, mouthing, "your fairy?"

As tense as she was, Mitzi had to laugh. "Yes, that's Twyla. Let's go."

Juniper could be frustrating sometimes. This was one of them. Mitzi wanted nothing more than to get going to her flight, but Juniper prevailed: "Mitzi, we have time, your plane won't leave any faster if we get there super early. I've got to go by the house to check on Valerie. Something's happened."

Forgetting her own troubles for a moment, Mitzi said, "What happened? Is she okay?"

"She's had a bit of a shock. Someone broke in our house and destroyed her two prized orchids and left a note implying she and I could be similarly harmed."

"Oh, no!" Mitzi covered her mouth, and truth be told, felt a pang of guilt. "I have to leave, but you need protection."

"I'll be here, don't forget!" Twyla practically saluted. "You're Juniper. I recognize your hair and nails."

Juniper shushed Mitzi, smiled, and bent over to shake Twyla's hand.

"Pleased to meet you, Twyla. Now let's go to my house for a minute on the way to the airport."

All three beings piled into Juniper's Citroen and raced the two or three blocks to Juniper and Valerie's house.

Juniper pulled into her driveway, jumped out of the car and was first to hit the porch. "Valerie, honey?"

Valerie opened the front door with red eyes. She fell into Juniper's arms.

Twyla and Mitzi followed, as Valerie took Juniper into the kitchen.

"Are you okay, Valerie?" Mitzi had rarely seen her friend in this shape. The American Indian woman was so strong and usually the one comforting everyone else. "Did the Mavens reject your membership?"

"I got accepted to the Merryville M-M-Mavens today." She sniffed and waved her hand in front of her face as she tried to compose herself. "They, they don't know yet."

Mitzi was puzzled. "Oh, man, when do you have to tell them?"

Juniper said, "They're coming *today*, at two o'clock."

"Crap, that's in fifteen minutes."

Valerie waved them to the back to see the damage. The two beautiful orchids were broken in the middle of their delicate stems, enough to drain the life from them slowly. "I can't bring myself to throw them away."

Mitzi sucked in her breath. The Rothschild Orchids had been a long-time topic of conversation. Aside from being worth thousands of dollars, they were Valerie's triumph and crown jewel of her orchid garden.

Mitzi skedaddled back toward the kitchen, "Let me put on some Chamomile for you, Val. Have you called the police?" Mitzi moved to the kettle while Juniper held her distraught wife. In the midst of all the comforting of Valerie, Twyla slipped away.

Valerie said, "Yes, but we need to change the locks. I don't feel safe here anymore. I called Lulu, but she won't be here 'til later today—I can't leave."

"Can I do anything for you?" Juniper said. "I'm so sorry. We have to get Mitzi to the airport for her flight to Peru."

Sniff. "No, I've got to meet with Sylvia and figure out what to tell the club. Oh my God, here I am worried about some dying flowers, and Panda was kidnapped?"

Mitzi nodded, "Puddle too, and their brother is there." There was a momentary pause as all the women pondered the situation. Mitzi went on in a wavery voice, "My yoga teacher kidnapped her—of all people. I feel so bad I didn't listen to Panda."

Valerie put her arm around Mitzi and said, "It's not your fault."

Now it was Mitzi's turn to cry. Twyla returned and watched the woman be mushy.

Juniper kissed Valerie and gave her a final hug. "I wish we could stay, but we need to leave for the airport. I'll be back soon. Keep the door locked!"

The diminutive fairy, until now, had been staying out of the conversation. After circling the "greenhouse" and petting the dog, she stood on the periphery and said, "I'll stay with Valerie." Twyla stood by the beautiful but sad woman, who had her dreams of joining the club realized, only to be dashed. She lifted her slender arm to open cupboards. "Where are the tea cups? There's no caffeine in this Chamomile, is there?"

Mitzi laughed and quickly told the story about Twyla's first coffee.

"Actually, tea would be nice," Valerie said, "and it would be great if you stayed with me, too. How do I introduce you to Sylvia?"

"You can tell her I'm Mitzi's cousin." Twyla and Mitzi were not exactly twins, but it was a plausible story. They *were* related. Mitzi was warming to the ditzy guardian, who was trying very hard to be useful.

Valerie followed Mitzi and Juniper to the car. "Call us." Before Juniper left to take Mitzi to the airport, Valerie hugged Mitzi hard. "You'll get Panda back."

Mitzi stepped back, and said firmly, "I will. There's no other acceptable outcome."

"That's my girl. Don't worry about us here. Twyla and I can handle anything, right Twyla?"

Twyla walked up then with two cups of tea. The girls saw the tea bags had been put in the water with their plastic coverings still on. She smiled engagingly.

Mitzi did a face palm and then waved goodbye as Valerie explained to Twyla how tea was steeped. She called out the window, "Me and the elves and, I guess, my brother-in-law will be at the Principe hotel in Cusco. You have Elsa's number and Ekk's too, right?"

"I've got all that. Now go get Panda and Puddle back!"

Valerie and Twyla waved as the Citroen pulled out of the driveway and raced to the Merryville airport.

The distance wasn't far, but Merryville had been "discovered" and traffic was increasing. "Come on!" Mitzi was starting to boil. Juniper gave her a sideways glance but didn't say anything.

When Mitzi was about to go through security and they had to part, Juniper handed Mitzi a copy of *Eat, Pray, Love*. Mitzi was puzzled. "What's this?"

"Give it to Panda when you see her. It'll make her laugh—and it wouldn't hurt you to read it. Hey, try to make it back by the grand opening of our new show!"

Mitzi hugged her very positive friend and tucked the book in her carry on. There were many miles to go to find her wife, and nothing would keep her from doing exactly that.

∾

IN THE JUNGLE

Puddle, Jose Luis and Fernando were preparing to meet their maker when a change occurred. The jungle people settled down a bit, and a path opened for a tall, gangly man in safari gear holding a machete. He had brown hair and was quite sunburnt and kept slapping mosquito bites on his neck area with his free hand. He was accompanied by a medium sized panther that moved sinuously beside him. The two made a very odd pair. Although the sharp spear points were still directed at the three, the masked assailants were obviously distracted by the new arrivals and turned slightly toward them.

In a German accent, the man said, "Part the way, they must come with me." Almost as if he had forgotten which language to use, he then said something guttural with the same tonal quality as the yips and clicks used by the painted native captors.

The fierce, masked warriors took the lanky man's measure and seemed indecisive over whether to do what he said or to include him in the tight prisoner zone at the end of their spears.

Then the panther roared frighteningly. It was a truly scary sound, and the jungle warriors parted to make a way for the three to follow the man. Puddle was at the head of the single file, with Fernando in the middle. Thankfully, he had finally stopped crying and apologizing. Puddle found it ironic: Fernando, who had gotten them in this situation, was now somewhat protected in the middle of the pack.

"Follow me," the German accent guy said to the three.

"Who are you?" Puddle asked.

"You can call me Brother Dieter." The man's expression was hard to read. He was trying hard to sound commanding, but his fogged-up wire frames made him less of an Indiana Jones and more like an out-of-place academic.

They made a strange parade, panther walking beside and sometimes in front of this Dieter guy and the trio of prisoners in a single file. Some warriors melted into the jungle. Three or four walked behind to cut off escape.

The ground was covered with vines, and they moved slowly through the deafening sounds of the jungle. How had she missed how noisy it was? Puddle's shirt was pasted to her with the almost one hundred percent humidity. Jose Luis was breathing heavily. She heard him along with the whistles, clicks, whoops, and calls of a million birds and insects.

Puddle noted Dieter was alternately slapping his mosquito bites and scratching them. She thought Dieter could've used some Deet, and this made her giggle unexpectedly.

The panther turned and made a low growl, and the entire procession stopped. The beautiful but deadly animal fixed its amber eyes on Puddle and let out another cat roar. Dieter appeared shaken and said to her, not unkindly, "Be quiet if you want to stay alive."

Puddle simmered down, and the group marched on for miles. Try as she might to memorize the location, there were so many cliff sides, waterfalls, big rocks, clearings and fallen trees the scenes were too similar. After a couple of hours, Jose Luis called out something in Spanish and they all stopped.

Dieter unstrapped his canteen and went back to the old man, who drank from it but appeared not to be doing well. A sheen of sweat gleamed on his face, and his breathing was ragged. The panther seemed to communicate with the German, the man cocking his own head like an animal when the panther growled. Dieter spoke to the warriors in their own strange tongue. One of the guards in the back put the shaft of his spear on Jose Luis' shoulder, keeping him seated. When Puddle and Fernando were encouraged to get moving at the tip of a spear, it was clear the old man was to be left behind with a warrior.

Fernando spoke in Spanish with Dieter, pleading actually. Although Puddle knew little Spanish, it was clear he was pleading for the old man. Tears ran down his eyes. Again, the panther fixed her amber eyes on the three, but this time she sprang to Jose Luis without further warning and pinned his heaving chest with her claws digging in. Puddle and Fernando lunged forward but crossed spears stopped them. The panther made sure she had an audience, then, mouth open, teeth bared, it quite deliberately lifted a heavy claw as if to deliver a final, fatal blow. Jose Luis kept saying "*Dios mio, Dios mio.*"

Instead of killing him outright, the panther actually smiled and let up on the man. Puddle and Fernando were pushed roughly from behind and the entire group moved on, leaving the old man behind. Puddle knew the bloody wounds would attract predators. All in all, it was much crueler than killing Jose Luis outright.

~

CHAPTER SEVEN

A DANGEROUS TREK

Juju and Ekk had a difficult time keeping up with Brooke and his gigantic strides, but they did it. Adrenaline fueled the search party as they followed the signal from Puddle's iPhone through the streets of Cusco. The sun had gone down, and the skies were mostly dark. Occasionally, Juju had to get them back on track with his exceptional vision. Soon, the three stood before a whitewashed wall with an opening showing the top of steep stairs.

"This is it?" Ekk plastered himself against the wall and attempted to peer into the darkness, as if bullets might fly out. Brooke said, "The phone stopped transmitting here—probably no signal inside."

Juju, not as cautious, raced ahead of the two and bolted down the stairs. Ekk shrugged and followed Brooke in the rear. Brooke was so tall his head bonked the ceiling in a couple of places.

In the stygian darkness at the bottom of the stairs, Brooke spoke first, "Crap, didn't think to bring a flashlight." Ekk and Brooke felt their way along a rough wall. Juju crossed the room and flipped on the overhead bulbs, hanging by exposed cords.

"How?" Brooke was surprised.

"He is El Chullanchaqui," Ekk replied with pride. "Guardian of the forest—their night vision is preternatural."

The jungle elf rubbed his slightly dirty chin and seemed to be pondering the many possibilities. There were seven dark openings, leading to unknown places.

"I don't see how we can figure out where they went." Brooke sat at the rough table. "Wait, her phone!" He picked up Puddle's iPhone, which was on the floor in shadow. "She must have dropped it while sitting at this same table."

"So, we know this is right." Ekk stared at the phone as if it could tell them where she went.

"Get up!" Juju yelled at Brooke and ran over to the seat.

Brooke jumped up, "Snake?"

Instead of answering, Juju knelt down and sniffed the seat Brooke had vacated.

Brooke raised his eyebrows and looked at Ekk, who shrugged.

Juju was single minded. "Give me the phone." Brooke handed it over without delay.

Juju closed his eyes and sniffed and actually licked it.

Brooke now appeared somewhat appalled. "What's he doing?"

"Shhhh, watch." Ekk pointed to the jungle elf who was now sniffing at each of the openings.

He pointed a dirty fingernail down a dark corridor with railroad tracks. "Here, it's this one."

"How can you be sure?" Brooke was really out of his element.

The look Juju gave Brooke would have withered a lesser man. He was animal-like and feral in his element and very serious. When he bolted down the path chosen, Ekk and Brooke followed.

∾

CHAPTER EIGHT

SYLVIA GOES TO THE GOODENS

Valerie was nervous about leaving the unpredictable fairy in the kitchen so she could dress for Sylvia and the Horticultural Committee's imminent arrival. Things had been so wonderful the day before. Now Panda was missing, her prize orchids dead, and she and Juniper had been threatened. She held up one outfit after another and none seemed right. How does one dress for what promised to be a very short stint on a Horticultural club?

Finally, she put on a simple polo shirt over white pants, choosing to dress "yachty." Valerie appraised her appearance in the mirror and wondered if, as an indigenous person, she was trying too hard to fit in with the white girls? What next: would she downplay her relationship with Juniper, act straight—to be accepted? More tears rolled as she followed this train of thought, interspersed with images of her broken Rothschilds.

The front door bell rang, and she dabbed her eyes dry, calling out, "Give me a minute!"

"Don't worry, I'll get it." came the cheery fairy's voice from downstairs.

At least someone's happy, she thought, squaring her shoulders and descending the stairs with a final dab at her eyes. Huh, Sylvia was not in the entry parlor, and Valerie continued on to the kitchen. It was funny. She and Juniper had a living room and the parlor, but people always ended up in the kitchen. She rehearsed how she would tell Sylvia about the broken flowers, squared her shoulders and entered the room, which was empty save for Layla. Valerie was surprised, and then angry. Twyla had apparently already taken Sylvia back to the bathroom, repurposed as her greenhouse. It was for Valerie to face the music, no one else.

She quickened her pace and walked in the sunny room to see Sylvia's face absolutely lit up in admiration. "Valerie, they're even more beautiful than you said! The pictures didn't do them justice." Sylvia and Twyla stood before the Rothschilds.

Twyla had donned the role of Valerie's assistant. Over her clothes she wore an apron and a smile and stood with her hands clasped behind her back, nodding toward the previously damaged flowers. Valerie approached slowly, and it was good Sylvia's attention was entirely on the flowers because her face showed her shock and amazement. Gobsmacked is how the British might have described it.

There they were in all their glory, her twin beauties, her actual Rothschilds, grown from seeds from Malaysia and brimming with life. Was this a trick? Valerie peered closely at the orchids, then back at Twyla. Other than a slight addition of some organic material on the stems, they appeared to be whole. She moved to brush it off, but Twyla stopped her saying, "Remember you decided to let the organic moss grow."

Valerie was dying to ask questions but simply dropped her hand, still not believing her eyes.

Sylvia said, "The others will be here soon. Well done. Do you have another ladies room? I see this one's being used, and quite well I might add!"

Still rather stunned, Valerie smiled weakly, pointed down the hall and said, "yes, by the front door."

"I'll show her, ma'am." Twyla was acting like someone she probably saw on the TV show *Downton Abbey*. Sylvia, used to being pampered, smiled and followed her to the other restroom.

When Twyla returned, Valerie actually grabbed her, "Is it a trick? Are the orchids really alive? And what's that green stuff?"

"They never really died, but it was close. Thank goddess I got here before that happened or there would have been no chance of saving them—that would be creating life not rescuing it. As for the green stuff, it'll absorb. Give it a minute or two."

"How did you do it?" Valerie was ready to pinch herself, almost afraid to ask, "Will the flowers last?"

"They should last like they normally do. The green stuff is from the Hercynian Garden. I'm a tree fairy and this is in my area." Valerie watched as Twyla frowned which was followed by an expression of worry. "But please don't tell Mitzi. She said not to use magic."

Tears again stung her eyes, and Valerie impulsively hugged Twyla. "Thank you. It'll be our secret."

The front doorbell rang as Sylvia reappeared in the entryway. Valerie turned to Sylvia, smiling. "Shall we?"

ON THE PLANE

Mitzi was beyond agitated. Everything went so slowly at the airport and people were acting stupidly. She tried Starbucks, but the line went beyond the normal limits and people seemed frozen in time. After that, she went to Häagen Dazs, not for ice cream, but at least for some potato chips for the plane. Only one couple stood at the register. She waited as the nimrod clerk pulled out change and laboriously counted. Coins? Seriously? She put the chips back and decided to hit the bathroom before the flight.

All stalls were full except for one that was being cleaned, and there was a line. The bathroom cleaner seemed to take her sweet time cleaning the one empty stall. Mitzi finally got to go into the stall and spent her time peeing and crying. Drying her eyes with the heel of her hand she got out and had to wait again for one of the two small sinks to open up. One of the women washed and washed and got more soap and stood admiring herself at the same time. Finally, Mitzi snapped, "You're not doing surgery, for God's sakes!" The woman said "sheesh" under her breath but gave up the sink.

At least she had a priority ticket and had been able to zoom through security. Even though the travel industry was all but a memory due to the internet, she still knew some tricks. The only flight at the last minute was a cattle-call flight out of Merryville, and she was lucky to get that. Mitzi made her way to row 11 and settled in the middle seat, wondering who would be sent to help her. She hoped it was a couple of strong warriors like Heloisa from the Hercynian Garden.

Instead, two nuns in full habit made their way down the aisle and sat on either side of her.

Fabulous, she thought. I actually deserve this, letting my wife get kidnapped. Not particularly religious, she sometimes joined Panda at St. John's, her Episcopal Church, but these appeared to be Roman Catholic nuns. The one on the aisle was as old as East Saint Louis, and the young one by the window smiled, opened a Spanish prayer book, and started reading. Good, she thought, I don't want to talk to anybody right now. Elsa must have been wrong about hooking her up with magical folk.

Earbuds in, Mitzi sat rigid as the flight attendant went through her spiel about what to do in case of emergency. When she got to the part about never inflating the life vest for water landings inside the plane, Mitzi got nervous. What if her wings burst out?

She had shouted at Panda not two days before about the scenario of her wings sprouting on a plane of their own accord. She wished she could take all of that back now. Dammit! She let that bitch of a yoga teacher put doubts in her head. Hot tears rolled down her eyes again in the cramped space and she wiped her eyes with the back of her hand. The nun to her right handed her a tissue. "Thanks."

The elder nun was snoring already, and her chubby arm took up the whole armrest. Searching for some music, Mitzi at first was blessedly distracted, but then came unglued with "You Saved Me" by Will Young. Panda always said it was their song.

In fact, almost every morning Panda would open up her laptop and play some You Tube thing or another, and they would cuddle. Sometimes Panda would lip sync and dance and make them both laugh. Had she really appreciated the time they'd already spent together? Would they ever listen to silly songs together again? Mitzi rummaged in her seatback for a napkin she had stowed there. The nun on the right stole glances at her and finally turned to ask, "Are you okay?"

 confused

PANDA IN PERU

I was still drowsy, letting myself be helped out of the van, put in a wheelchair, coming to briefly to walk through security. My companion was dressed like a nurse and was very beautiful. People seemed to do her bidding cheerfully as she accompanied me through the aisle. Outside there were puffy clouds, and I felt I was floating in them.

The next thing I clearly remember was having cold water splashed in my face and the hot humid climate. My wrists hurt. I lowered my eyes and saw them tied together with thick rope. I lifted my head and saw Twyla, the yoga teacher, and several short, dark men. We appeared to be near a boat dock, on what had to be the Amazon. She didn't address me, saying something in Spanish to the men. My hands were swollen, and I had to pee like an Arabian mule.

She noticed I was awake and said: "Oh, you're awake. Good, my *pollo poco*." Little chicken—the men laughed at that.

"Who are you?"

"Your tour guide to Paititi. I'm going to do you a favor. Get in the boat and my men will take you to meet your family." Twyla went to the van, and climbed inside, still in her nurse's uniform.

"What? You kidnapped me! You're one of them, the Wolf Ravens!"

At the name Wolf Ravens, the men stared at me with fear. It must be some of the only English words they knew.

The ebony Twyla shortly emerged from the van, dressed in comfortable clothes. She fairly hissed, "If you don't want more sleeping medicine, get your ass in the boat. I don't mind putting you at risk of overdose, but for some reason Julia wants you alive."

There were four swarthy guys helping fake Twyla, and I tried to shake off the feeling of stupor so I could attempt an escape.

As if she could read my mind, she said, "You were terrible at yoga, and you're no match for these men." She then spoke in Spanish again, and pointed at me and the boat. After a nod, two of the men grabbed me on either side and walked me toward the brown water.

"Can I at least go to the bathroom?" It wasn't a trick.

She checked her watch, shook it, and huffed, finally removing it and flinging it into the jungle. "If you must." After speaking in Spanish, which mentioned pollo again, one especially burly guard took me to a tree.

"I can't pull down my pants with my hands tied."

Insolently, the woman walked over and removed a very sharp serrated knife from somewhere on her person. She cut the binding around my hands and said, "Nice watch. Now, no trouble or I'll deliver your corpse. We have your brother and sister. Two out of three alive's not bad."

She laughed again and moved to turn away. As if on second thought, she turned back. "Give me that." She took my Fitbit and strapped it to her wrist. "Pretty color."

A kidnapper and a thief, great.

Shit! They had Brooke and Puddle, if she could be believed. I said a prayer of gratitude for the unseen Julia, who wanted me alive. The guard was so close I could smell his sweat. He stared at me, making sure I wouldn't bolt. I tried to remember my high school Spanish and said, "Pardon?" then "*Privacidad*?" That worked.

The man turned away and I started to pee. Without warning and in midstream, someone snatched me upward. Two very strong arms had hold of me as a hordes of elves, slightly larger than Ekk and Elsa, dropped from the sky.

Jungle elves! The El Chullanchaqui! On a branch, a dirty elf made a hurry-up sign, and whoever gripped me let go. I pulled up my pants, too shocked to be embarrassed about the wet splash down one leg.

Instead of fighting, my captor ran to the boat and leapt in with the grace of, well, a yoga girl. One of her henchmen was already there by the motor, and they took no time leaving the dock of boards stuck in the mud. Her Spanish-speaking guards ran for the hills at the sight of the jungle elves. The El Calvary hooted at the retreating men and beat their chests like gorillas. It was surreal.

I must have some magic in me because this was one of those times I inwardly knew to relax, that my rescuers were not evil. "Are you the El Chullanchaqui?" Strong arms lowered me to the ground. My senses were buzzing like crazy.

"We're part of their coalition, but you don't add *the*, it's Chullanchaqui, or Chock. Call me Remy. I'm the only English speaker here. The others stood around and, with a nod and a few words from Remy, went down to the dock area. A particularly shaggy Chock whistled like a bird and a rustic canoe like thing was brought to the dock.

"Are we going to chase that woman?" I was so happy to be rescued, the idea of getting in harm's way so soon again was unappealing.

"She's our map to Paititi. No time to discuss. Now get in."

Now that the immediate danger passed, I became fully aware of my surroundings. The buzzing was insects, probably mosquitos, and I was standing in the middle of a jungle, in peed-upon yoga pants. Stupidly, I asked, "Are we in Peru?"

In heavily-accented but plain English, the elf said, "*Jes*, now will you get in? This is the Amazon, no good to stand around."

My need to speak to Mitzi was overwhelming. "I need to call someone. Do you have a phone?" I said, stepping carefully over the wiggly boards and into the equally unstable canoe.

"Later. No cell service here. Now you will hold on to sides."

As I sat in the canoe with Remy up front and one elf in the back paddling, my head started to clear. I was, apparently, going to Paititi and might find out what happened to my parents. I needed to know why my yoga teacher had kidnapped me. Remy informed me that not only was I kidnapped, but he had heard from his group that another was kidnapped too, maybe my sister. Puddle!

About forty-five minutes rolled by and, since I could do nothing else, I observed the fauna on either side of the vast river. My mind wandered. Mitzi would have loved it. I trailed my finger in the water. Still, we didn't come upon the fake Twyla.

The boat slowed. Remy shook his head, and I could tell the chase was over.

"Can we talk now? Who was that woman?"

"She goes by many names. No one knows her real name. She is whatever the Lobosnegro want her to be."

"Lobosnegro?"

"Blackwolf, and don't drag hands in water like that—piranhas."

I pulled my hand out of the water fast. "They're called wolf ravens in Germany. Hey, they referred to me as a pollo, a chicken, back there. Why?"

Remy grunted and showed extraordinarily white teeth for a jungle elf. "Chickens get their heads cut off." Dejected, he said, "We lost her. This boat was no match, but it's all we had."

"What now?"

"We'll take you to the hotel in Cusco."

"What about my sister?"

He shrugged with a sad smile and turned the boat around.

Post-drugged and overwhelmed, I decided to save my questions for Elsa and Ekk.

Juniper returned to the museum after dropping Mitzi at the airport and ran into Linda Chicolett on the stairs, saying goodbye to Charlotte

Windingle. "Charlotte! Long time no see," Juniper said. Charlotte gave her a half hug and said, "Linda was showing me all the space you have under the small hall."

"Oh?" Juniper was smiling, but she would have loved to kick Linda in the shins. The woman had been trying to undermine her since she came to the museum.

Linda seemed to have the good grace to at least be honest, or maybe with Charlotte there she couldn't lie. "Yes, well, we were thinking your latest installation would fit down there."

Juniper's eyes got wide and she squeaked, "In the basement?" She openly stared at Charlotte who quickly said, "Well, it's one idea we discussed. Hortense Miller, the woman I was here with the other day? She asked for space to show her flowers as art. It's pretty incredible really."

Juniper echoed, "Flowers as art?" Her eyebrows rose higher. "Isn't that what the annual flower show is for?"

Linda said in her reasonable tone, ignoring the warning signs from Juniper. "It's really only an extension of the landscaping that's already been started. We were thinking—"

"You were thinking what? That you're the curator now?" Juniper pressed her lips and shook her head at Linda. She turned to Charlotte. "I'm sorry, Charlotte, but Linda is not the art director here. I'm happy to meet with you and this Hortense."

"I don't want to get in the middle of anything," Charlotte said, "When Mister Bruce called me personally…well, let me know when you all get these things straightened out." Her eyes went from Linda to Juniper as she spoke. Her driver pulled up at that moment, and she gave air kisses. "Got to go, ladies." Then to Juniper, who she grabbed lightly and fixed a meaningful gaze upon, "Let's go to the club soon, Juniper."

When Charlotte's car pulled out, Linda tried to escape, but Juniper put out a bangled arm to stop her. "Oh, no you don't. What was that all about?"

"Juniper, you think you've won, don't you? Words on a Plate, Really? What's next, Graffiti art?" A gaggle of tourists walked by, and they both automatically stopped talking and smiled.

The swords were out. Juniper was hot. "We all know your love of the avant guard stops at Hello Kitty, Linda. That's not what this is about. Who is this *Mister Bruce*, and why is he calling our biggest financial supporter directly?"

Linda pointed at Juniper's chest. "If you read your mail more often, you'd know. Rick Bruce is joining the board from the Cleveland Museum. He's got some great ideas."

Juniper let out a laugh. "Oh, *that* Mister Bruce. Richland Bruce. The one who was chased out of the California Artists for Equality because he pulled the Ohio Honors Stonewall Exhibit at COMA?"

"Don't call it that. You know it's Cleveland Museum of Art, CMOA." Linda tapped her foot, and her arms were crossed. Juniper was getting to her. "That's the problem with you, Juniper. You see everything as Gay, Gay, Gay, and more Gay!"

"Is that what you think?" Juniper's voice had gotten very measured. "Tell me more."

"This is a large community. Your narrow obsession is your problem, Juniper, not the museum's. Most people don't care about LGBTQ all the time. I reached out to Richland."

The two women stared at each other for a beat.

"You homophobic back stabber," Juniper said. "You called Richland Bruce. Nice to know how you really feel."

Linda's face drained of color. "What I meant to say was," she took a deep breath before continuing, "the museum needs more balance."

Juniper's lips pressed together so hard the blood left them. She pointed an index finger with a rainbow-colored nail and lifted it in an exaggerated, wait-a- moment gesture.

Linda opened her mouth to continue speaking.

"Nope. Stop talking." Juniper shook her head. "Linda, thank you for saying out loud what you've meant to say for a while." Her eyes were blazing. An observer would have seen her pulled upright, giving Linda the gimlet eye.

Linda was losing steam. "But—"

"To be clear. I am the curator. Not you. My space is my space to do with what I will. Period. The reason I'm here is because Merryville has a significant LGBTQ population, and, oh yes, all the awards I've won for my work with battered women, youth and emerging Latinx artists. If you'll notice, Words on a Plate addresses many issues. Perhaps it's only you who sees Gay, Gay, Gay whenever you view my work. Or me."

In a softer voice Linda said, "Juniper, there is also a significant evangelical population growing in Merryville. This is their museum, too!"

Still steaming, Juniper's eyes flashed as she appraised the shorter woman. "Maybe you should take some time with the exhibit and then ask yourself why you're so bent on destroying what I'm trying to create." She walked away from Linda, and then turned dramatically before going in the museum. "And stay away from Charlotte Windingle!"

CHAPTER NINE

Puddle was beyond tired. She had given up wondering how Fernando was. She was so angry at his betrayal of both her and Jose Luis, who was now probably dead. Perhaps Fernando had been duped, perhaps he loved his parents. She didn't care. He was now tied up, facing her, his eyes closed. His lips moved as if in prayer. Good. He had a lot to answer for.

Dieter had stationed them close to a cliff's edge and was now standing at the actual edge with the panther. Puddle heard running water below. Their jungle guard, after being given instruction in clicks and their own guttural language, seemed to relax their weapons and sat down in a ring around their prisoners. Even in despair, it was impossible not to notice how beautiful the area was. The heat was still oppressive, and an ant was making a beeline toward her ankle. Puddle was thirsty and hungry and tired. Her wrists were numb, and she realized in TV fiction that people could escape from being tied up—but she was no MacGyver. She kept her eyes on Dieter and his animal and the cliff, not thinking anything else.

Her first awareness of something new was that the panther's silhouette was changing. Dieter stayed the same, gangly and sunburnt. The panther was un-becoming a panther and becoming a woman. Its—her—limbs lengthened, and she stood upright. The guards were silent as they watched the transformation. Dieter appeared shaken.

As soon as the transformation was complete, the panther/woman was handed a robe to wear by one of the guards who approached the cliff's edge for that purpose. Dieter and whatever it was continued their conversation, which was drowned out by the sound of rushing water. They pointed down and appeared to come to some sort of agreement. The two walked back to the small opening in the jungle where Fernando and Puddle were being kept.

Dieter said, "We camp here tonight."

Puddle's would-be rescuers were a motley group. Brooke, a stock broker from New York, Ekk, an elf from the Black Forest of Germany, and Juju. Of the three, Juju was far and away most able to handle the terrain as they came out of the underground tunnel and burst into the *selva*. As for Brooke, he was frightened in a way he had never been before.

First, it was hot. Not muggy hot like summers in NYC but a cloying, oppressive hot which takes your breath away. He had run several marathons before hanging that up due to a knee problem, but he still kept in shape at the gym. Nevertheless, the treadmill at his sports club was no match for this alien world. There were roots and vines all over the floor, and he watched his large feet as he followed the two elves nimbly navigating them. He was grateful the female elf, Elsa, had insisted he change shoes.

Juju was in the lead, obviously, and was fascinating to watch. He moved so fast Brooke was afraid he would lose him but then would catch up as Juju sniffed an area, sometimes going down on all fours. There was no talking. For one thing, he didn't have the breath. Each time they stopped, Brooke put his big hands on his hips and bent over, trying to stretch.

Ekk came up behind him. "What are you doing?"

"It's called stretching. Don't little people stretch?"

Ekk frowned.

"Sorry, that was rude." His mother, if she were still alive, would tell him to stop being so cranky, a habit still with him. He saw the other small guy's face go red.

Ekk restrained his cousin and responded, "Actually, Juju and Elsa and I are elves."

"Ha ha, like Keebler elves," Brooke said.

Neither Juju or Ekk laughed and both stared at Brooke. Ekk moved his hair to show his pointed ears.

"Oh." Indeed, Brooke's mouth formed a perfect O.

Juju was surly. "Can we get back to saving your sister?"

Brooke tried to sound rational again. "Where do you think we are?"

Ekk was the most level-headed of the bunch. "No idea. My cousin will tell us in a minute. Are you holding up okay?"

"Yes, but I'm really thirsty." Brooke always had a water bottle with him, and he turned it upside down to show it was empty. "I should probably fill it up in the stream."

Juju stopped sniffing. "Stream? What stream?"

Brooke looked puzzled. "Over there. Don't you hear it?"

The jungle is not quiet. It's always a symphony of caws, roars, a million birds, snorts, rustles and other unidentifiable sounds. But there it was, the sound of running water.

Juju was mad. "I can't believe I missed that. Wait here." He disappeared into the jungle. While they were waiting, Ekk smiled at Brooke and said, "I think I know why you and your sisters are wanted by the Wolf Ravens, or Lobos Negros as they are known here."

Brooke made the universal sign of impatience. Ekk continued, "Your parents were on a mission for Paititi? I'm thinking the enemy believes one of you knows where it is."

CHAPTER TEN

MERRYVILLE

Bonnie went in the back door of her house and flung her Museum ID lanyard on the kitchen counter. "Mom? Mom, I'm home."

Bonnie Bruce-Pippin lived with her parents in the affluent part of Merryville and was kept very busy between school, the Mavenettes, and now the Museum. Bonnie wondered why her mother didn't care for her volunteering at the Museum until now.

"Bonnie? Can you come in here, sweetie?" Uh oh, whenever her mother got that tone there was an audience. When she entered, her mom was seated on the sofa with Bonnie's least favorite relative. There were cookies out with the good tea set in use on the shiny coffee table. She smiled at that, tea on the coffee table.

"What are you grinning about, young woman? Come over here and give your Uncle a hug." She cringed, "Hi, Uncle Ricky."

"Richland's moving back to Merryville!" Her mother actually clapped.

Richland Bruce was a slight man with a goatee. His fingers were covered in turquoise and he wore a bolo tie. His clothes had turned decidedly western since moving to Ohio. "Well, most likely. I have to see if the museum and I are a fit for each other." Was that a drawl?

"Oh, Ricky, how could you not be? You're big time now!"

He sipped his tea. "Um, Janet, no more Ricky. It's Richland or Rich. Rick's okay too, I guess."

Bonnie eyed the cookies. "Don't even think it, Bon Bon. You're bursting out of your Mavenette polo already." At that slight, Janet and Uncle Ricky had a laugh.

"I think she's pretty in her pink." Richland stroked her shoulder. Bonnie made a maneuver like a cat that didn't want to be petted. His hand wilted like a flower.

"I'm going to study. Nice to see you, Uncle Richland."

"Oh, my, that does sound formal, now doesn't it?" Janet and her brother laughed again. Bonnie went up to her room thinking it was weird for a sister to get out the good china for her brother. On the way up the stairs, she heard

Richland say in conspiratorial tones, "Wait 'til that Juniper Gooden finds out about the changes a-coming. I've already asked Reverend Morry to" His voice reduced to whisper something Bonnie couldn't make out.

Janet squealed with laughter in response and helped herself to a cookie.

ↄ

Mitzi was miserable. She felt guilty and frustrated and, if she were honest, hopeless. It was much easier to be rescued than to be a rescuer. "I'm sorry. I'm going through some stuff," She replied to the Latina nun.

The nun calmly placed her prayer book down and her eyes met Mitzi's. Her round face and brown eyes were open and warm. She was about thirty and wore a navy coif with a crisp white lining. She smelled of Dove soap. "I have time. My name is Sister Lucia Reya."

"I-I'm not very religious," Mitzi stammered. "Besides, you would never believe what I have to say and," she wanted to nip this in the bud, "I'm a lesbian so we don't have much in common." Mitzi closed her eyes to shut out the kind woman's sure to be disappointed response.

There was silence, and Mitzi wondered if the woman understood her. She opened one eye and slightly turned. The woman was still staring at her, face beaming. "God loves all his children. Now what wouldn't I believe?" The woman got more comfy as if ready to hear an epic story.

The flight attendant was coming down the aisle, and Mitzi asked for a glass of wine. Sister Lucia spoke in rapid Spanish to the attendant, and soon she and Mitzi had lots of miniature bottles of red wine and some cookies. "It'll help you relax since it's a nine-hour flight."

Mitzi buckled up and downed two drinks, realizing she hadn't had much to eat.

"Until I was forty-three years old, I had a normal life, with a mom, my father passed away—well not my bio dad. Anyway, I thought my maiden name was Schadt. Fifteen years ago, I met a woman named Panda, and we fell in love and got married. I'm a travel agent. Well, sometimes. My wife Panda does taxes. We had such a nice quiet life in Merryville, until—"

"Merryville, California?" The woman was already on her second cookie.

Mitzi nodded. "Yes, so ordinary. Then, one day, our lives were changed—just like that." She snapped her fingers. The old nun to her left snorted in her sleep, and both she and Sister Lucia laughed. It felt good to laugh. She picked up a cookie.

"It's good you're talking about it, whatever it is. Maybe you would feel better if you knew I'm a licensed psychotherapist. There is nothing you could say I haven't heard before."

Mitzi softly laughed. "Oh, I think that'll change today. My story involves evil and a kidnapping."

Sister Lucia sipped her wine. "And? Elsa didn't tell you help was coming?"

Mitzi's eyes got big. "You?" She laughed in spite of the circumstances. After this moment of realization, Mitzi tentatively started telling her story. "Last March Panda was working, and I was helping out at the tax office. A weird handwritten invitation was delivered to her office that talked about the Hercynian Forest."

At mention of the Hercynian Forest, Mitzi saw her new friend's first spontaneous reaction. "As in *selva negra* in Germany? Oops, I mean the Black Forest?" Her eyes were very alert.

"Yes. How much do you know?" Mitzi's stomach gave a twist. The topic still scared her.

"Sorry, there wasn't much time to talk to your guardian. Sister and I were going back to Peru and can be of help. Our order is the Sisters of the Sun or *Hermanas del Hijo*. We devote our lives to increasing the good in the world and fighting against darkness. We know about the Hercynian Forest. If that's the evil you are fighting, we have the same enemy, although it goes by other names. Tell me more."

Mitzi paused, wanting to feel not so alone, but almost unable to take in what she was hearing.

"So, we're for sure on the same side?"

The young nun nodded.

"My wife is in danger and her sister and brother are too."

Over the next eight hours of the flight, Mitzi proceeded to tell Sister Lucia about everything. Her own kidnapping and rescue, the new mission to find Paititi. Maybe it was the wine talking, but it was easier to tell the nun about the fantastical things than it was to admit she and Panda were having some trouble with their relationship. They spent the last hour talking about Mitzi's partial griffin DNA and the fact that she could fly in certain circumstances. The woman was rapt and never seemed to doubt.

"Our cloister is up in the mountains of Cusco. As a therapist, I am privy to many things I can't share. Give me a dollar."

"What?"

"Let me call you my client so we can keep this between us legally." Sister Lucia was so sincere and, apparently, knew of the evil Mitzi had faced. She dug through her pocket and produced a neatly folded bill. She put it in the young nun's hands and said, "This is a dream come true. I didn't realize how badly I needed someone other than Panda to talk with about this." She closed her eyes. "Poor Panda."

"I need to hear more about that, but all this wine is killing my bladder."

After a bathroom break, the women resettled. The ancient sister had hardly moved a muscle. On their return, before climbing over the inert nun, Mitzi asked, half kiddingly, "Is she still with us?"

Sister Lucia climbed over her companion and said simply, "Ambien."

Once settled, Mitzi made her confession of sorts. "The worst thing about all of this is that I realize I've been taking out my frustration on my wife. She's always there for me. Yes, she snores and hates exercise, doesn't cut the front lawn, and works too much, but she's mine and I love her. I know she's worried about me right now, even though she's God knows where." Tears streaked Mitzi's face again. "If I keep this up, we're all going to be waterlogged."

Sister Lucia put her hand on Mitzi's and said, "I've heard enough of some of the old sisters' stories about living in the jungle to know anything is possible, although they would never admit it outside of our sessions. We focus on doing the good we can for the local people and try to get them to be humane with one another. Every once in a while, we work with the elven people. There are many in the forest. In fact, you can't be too careful with so much superstition right now, probably always. Do you know a tribe in Peru burned a village woman as a witch?" She gazed out the window at clouds, and her face turned sad. "Seriously."

Mitzi wiped her eyes. "What can I do?"

"Well, two things. First, we pray." Mitzi pulled her head back like a turtle but nodded.

"Then, I give you our address. If things get tough, or if you want to talk, come find us. We'll give you refuge."

Sister Lucia said a simple prayer, and then the overhead speaker announced that the flight attendants were to prepare for landing. Mitzi felt better than she had in weeks. The challenge of getting Panda back was still in front of her, but she was in a much better frame of mind to do it.

∾

Valerie opened her front door to the Mavens. There they were: Hortense, Florence, Lidia, Janet and Sally, on the porch, smiling. "Ladies, please do come in."

The living room was tidied within an inch of its life, and sun streamed through the antique glass windows. Hortense gave an almost imperceptible nod and the ladies all sat. "Well, I suppose you've heard the good news?"

"I have, indeed." Valerie's smile was larger than usual. Why did she want this so badly?

Sylvia interjected, "I've seen the Rothschilds. They're exquisite."

Hortense brushed some cat fur off the couch, "Er, yes, we need to see those. From Malaysia, yes?

"Yes. Thank you for getting it right. So many people don't know that. Would you like to see them now?" She was babbling.

"In a moment." Hortense held her purse in her lap. All were quiet while she collected her thoughts. She picked a piece of dog hair off the couch and theatrically placed it in a decorative dish on the living room table. "You understand that being part of the Merryville Horticultural Society is a very big responsibility?"

"Ye-es." Valerie silently cursed Layla and drew out her yes and cocked her head as if to say, what?

"It has not escaped our notice that you are very friendly with those Fowler women with the thistle problem—remember from our slide show?"

"Ye-es." Another careful yes. How could she forget?

"Before we finalize your membership, we need assurances you will assist us in eradicating the thistle problem in this town. Starting with those friends of yours."

"I'm sure she can do it," Sylvia said.

Florence gave an amused smile.

Valerie was dumbstruck at how bold this challenge was.

The tension in the room was thick. Valerie was actually getting pissed that Panda was so lazy with her clippers, but they'd all been pretty busy lately. She opened her mouth to answer, and at that moment Twyla zipped into the room with a laden tray. "Ladies, I have your tea and cookies." Valerie was pleased that the plastic tea bag covers had been removed.

Twyla continued, "I overheard you talking about those thistles. Let me tell you, Miss Valerie hates those thistles, and has put me in charge of getting rid of them." They all looked surprised, none more so than Valerie.

Hortense picked up a cookie. "That's exactly the attitude we wanted. Now, let's see those Orchids!"

Valerie had to weigh in. "Wait. I need to say that I'm very glad to be accepted into the Horticultural Society. I also need to say that we may need a few weeks to deal with the thistles because the Fowlers are currently out of the country."

Hortense narrowed her eyes. "Then it's a good thing you have," she turned to the fairy, "what is your name, dear?"

"Twyla," she shared her fairy smile with the room, "Twyla Green, ma'am." She actually curtsied.

This show of servitude pleased the older woman, who said to Twyla, "You have until May thirtieth to get rid of those weeds." Then turning back to her hostess, "Ms. Gooden's membership depends on it."

Without further ado, the mavens walked to the greenhouse, tea in hand. Sally put cookies in her big pocket for later. The sun streamed through the windowpanes in the makeshift greenhouse, and the effect was spectacular. A moment of silent reverence was observed.

Hortense spoke first, "Valerie, you have indeed accomplished something rare and important. I am hopeful your membership will become permanent at our next meeting in June. Young Twyla Green here might even make a good Mavenette." The tension broke, and the next forty-five minutes or so were more like victory laps. Twyla beamed but hovered protectively near the Orchids.

Sylvia hugged Valerie, and the group turned its attention to the Mayor's latest proclamation for the ladies. Florence took full credit for that, with her husband having been appointed by the mayor, and Valerie noted they all seemed to have their predestined roles. She wondered what hers would be and hoped it was simply Valerie the "orchid lady."

When everyone left, Valerie turned to Twyla, eyebrows lifted, and said, "Really, *Miss Valerie*?"

The fairy smiled sweetly and said, "Downton Abbey—the Council made me watch it to prepare. I'm so glad this went well for you. I'll get those thistles out, don't you worry." She shoved a cookie in her mouth and spoke around it, "What's a Mavenette?"

Valerie opened her mouth to say something but then decided to let things take their course.

༄

Twyla had saved the day with the orchids, served tea and been generally adorable at the Gooden's house. She felt quite good about herself and only left after a locksmith named Lulu arrived. Valerie seemed to know the enormous woman with a tool belt, and it felt right to leave as Lulu was there to secure the house.

Upon getting back to the Fowler's house, Twyla felt she was on a roll. She opened the front door and found Brutus waiting for her.

"Hi, Brutus, how are you, big kitty boy?" She plopped on the couch and patted the cushion next to her. He jumped up.

"Meow."

"You're lonely? Your mommas aren't going to be gone that long. I hope. Besides, you have me!"

"Meow."

"I hear you." She moved the big Bengal close to her and petted him, looking out the front window at the overgrown thistles. "We'll talk to your people about getting you a friend when they get back."

"Meow."

"You met someone? How cool! When can I meet, um, is it a girl or boy?"

"Meow."

"A girl. Is she pretty?"

At that Brutus got up and headed toward the kitchen. Twyla took no offense. Cats have short attention spans. She said under her breath, "Your momma, Panda, eats when she's feeling emotions, too." She tapped her foot on the carpet. The thistles were going to be a problem, she could see that. Two trees stood tall and majestic in the front yard, and the hearty bush had grown around the base of each.

She went to the garage to get the clippers, figuring there was no time like the present to tackle the job. Carefully closing the front door, she went to the largest bush and stuck her arm in to cut the prickly plant at the base. "Ouch!" A ribbon of blood ran down her arm. She'd been pricked at the tender part, a couple of inches in the tender flesh above her elbow. "I can see why these things need to go."

She had overheard the tall Maven, with the Julia Child's sounding voice, going on and on about the Fowler's weeds. Valerie's membership depended upon their being gone. She knew that no one wanted her to use magic, but this manual labor was so inefficient. She decided to wait until dark and see if there wasn't a teeny bit of tree fairy magic that might make the job easier.

~

CHAPTER ELEVEN

Juju led Brooke and Ekk to a cliff with water below.

Ekk said, "It's getting dark. We should either go back or stop for the night." Ekk may be an elf, but he was unaccustomed to the jungle.

Brooke was miserable and didn't disagree. He was bone tired and slapped his exposed leg between his pants and the top of his socks. "These mosquitos are eating me alive."

Juju still had not said anything. He was right up to the edge of the cliff, staring down at something, then said distractedly, "We lose too much time by going back now, and it'll be dark soon." He put up his muscled left arm and waved the other two to join him. Below, they saw a river of boiling water with steam coming up in plumes.

"The boiling water of Mayantuyacu. I read about this in National Geographic!" Excited, Brooke momentarily forgot his discomfort and turned to Juju. "What does it mean?"

"It means we're close. I'll go down and get the water. Then we need to protect ourselves for the night."

While Juju was so engaged, Brooke said to Ekk, "We should think about going back to the hotel. How does the Mayantuyucu let him know we're close? I thought nobody knew where Paititi was?"

"He's a jungle Elf. This is his element."

Brooke opened his mouth to argue, but Ekk said quietly, "Trust Juju, Brooke. We'll lose too much time if we go back now, and I don't want to be wandering in the dark, do you?"

The New York city dweller said to no one in particular, "I wish I had a Satellite phone" as he waved away no-see-ums.

The Chullanchaqui nimbly navigated the handholds on the cliff, and soon returned with hot water. "It's clean. The river is probably ninety-three degrees."

Brooke was about to put his canteen to his lips, but Ekk stopped him. "That's Celsius, not Fahrenheit. It's about two hundred degrees—not so soothing. Let's wait a bit." Then, reacting to Brooke's frustrated expression, "We'll find Puddle tomorrow." Ekk surveyed the darkening jungle as a cat roared in the not too distant greenery. "Let's get off this jungle floor. It's dangerous at night."

"Now for our jungle hotel." Juju shimmied up a nearby tree and disappeared for a moment.

The sun was rapidly disappearing, and Brooke was getting visibly nervous. Leaves rustled, and Juju's head popped out from above, he actually looked happy. "This'll do!"

It took some doing but, between Ekk and Juju helping, Brooke laboriously moved his big frame into the tree chosen by Juju. There were ants and Juju had to dispatch a snake, but finally they were able to string the one hammock brought by Juju from one limb to another. It was small but sturdy, and Brooke curled up and tried to trust in the smelly netting. Juju swore it would hold an elephant. Ekk and Juju were able to fit in the Y of the tree and lay on Ekk's cloak. Brooke was beyond tired and went to sleep immediately.

Juju and Ekk talked into the night about possibilities. Ekk knew he probably wouldn't get a straight answer but needed to know, "Do you actually know where Paititi is? And don't give me some poetry about the *selva*."

Juju opened his mouth to say something. "No. No one does. Well, there are rumors, but our leaders say the city entrance moves. It's protected by strong magic, but it's near the boiling river."

"What are the chances we'll find Puddle?"

Juju regained some of his old bravado. "We'll find Puddle. I have an idea." And with that, the jungle elf closed his eyes and fell to sleep.

Ekk stayed awake for a while, trying to see in the dark, frightened by the unfamiliar sounds. There were so many bugs, which crawled on Juju or maybe from Juju. Ekk was a tax preparer and had grown up in the Hercynian Forest Garden, not a rough place like this. He wished Panda was there to talk to, having grown quite fond of her. This outdoor "bed" reminded him of the two weeks he spent living in bushes scoping out Panda Fowler before they met in March. As he pondered these things, sleep finally overtook him.

CHAPTER TWELVE

Things at the museum were not getting any better. Juniper had hardly spoken a word to Linda since their heated tête-à-tête. She stopped at the front desk, and Mona handed her a rather large stack of mail and some phone messages. As expected, the minutes of last month's board meeting were there, a meeting she'd missed due to a quick trip to the Hercynian Garden in Germany.

As if on cue, the front door opened and Richland Bruce himself walked in making a beeline for Juniper. He stroked his goatee. Today he was dressed in a vest and cigarette leg pants over boots. He looked like an ironic version of a cowboy. His hair spilled over his collar, and his appearance made her wonder how anyone who dressed so unintentionally gay could be such a homophobic dick.

"How wonderful, Juniper Gooden!" He reached with both hands as if to take hers in an embrace. She stiffened, and then her inner good hostess appeared. After all, the museum was "her house," and she would defend it.

"Richard Bruce! It's been years."

"Ahem, Richland, actually, but Rick is fine."

"Rick then. Say, have—"

He cut her off. "Do you mind, I'm starving! Let's go to the café. Origins is it? And have a burger. We can talk there."

Juniper tittered. "Well, come on then. We do have a faux burger made with soy. It's on the meatless munchie list." She walked ahead and motioned to the hostess for the table with the best view.

Richland followed her and sat on the carefully varnished bench seat, making a show of dubiously scanning the decor. "Oh, that's got to change, Juniper. Not everyone shares the California, Vegan, airy-fairy sensibility." Then surveying the menu, "Are there at least real potatoes here?" He smiled, but it had the effect of a crossed sword to the seasoned curator.

She ignored the burger comment. "Really, Rick, already changing the menu? The maple bacon fries are to die for." She waved at the server, dressed in hemp over jeans. "Cynthia, can you get us a plate of fries to share?" Her eyes narrowed. "And bring one of our fabulous burgers!"

Cynthia Snively ignored Juniper and fawned over Richland Bruce. "Mister Bruce, I'm a big fan of yours. My family is from Cleveland, and I got to visit the museum when you were curating it. The series on Buckeye Trees and their curative powers was fabulous!"

The foppish man smiled humbly. "Most people don't know about the miraculous powers of the Buckeye. Glad you liked it."

"Liked it! My mother's Rheumatism has been improved because of it. Now, did I hear you say fries? I'll get it. Sorry about the burger." She shot a rebellious glance at Juniper. "I love a good burger, too, but that's not what Origins is all about." She said this last with relish and then disappeared into the kitchen.

Juniper was getting depressed, but the artist in her was intrigued. "Tell me more about these Rheumatism trees."

"Oh, that was actually a minor series we had when I first joined that museum. Really, it was nothing. The artist that brought it to us was later accused of stretching the facts. I would rather talk about the morale issues you seem to be having, and vegetarian food?"

"Rick, you haven't been in California ten minutes, and already you're criticizing? It's a serious food movement to not only help our bodies but to also reduce global warming." Juniper was glad she'd been preached to by Panda for years.

Richland was not convinced. "I bet we get a lot of visitors from the Midwest. I wonder how much the bottom line could be improved by *beefing* up the menu?" He smiled at his own pun. Juniper inwardly cringed at the use of "we" when Richland spoke about the museum. Cynthia put a larger than usual plate of fries in front of her rival and pranced away insolently. Maybe he did have a point about morale.

The woman was jolted to her toes when Valerie Gooden led them to her Rothschilds. How had she done it? Was there green tape? Were there more than two of the accursed flowers? She was sure the orchids were broken in a way that was quite fatal to them. Of course, she thought as she gathered her purse and keys, she wasn't done yet.

She smiled inwardly at Valerie's deadline to get rid of the thistles. "Cut them in May, they'll grow in a day. Cut them in June, it is too soon." Oh yes, there was plenty of time.

Remy had felt sorry for me and loaned me a phone which I used to access my cell phone messages. I punched keys from the back seat of the cab as we road down *Avenida Cultura Prolongacion*, on my way to the hotel. The first message was Elsa's recorded voice telling me of Puddle's kidnap, which I already knew. Next, I heard my beloved's messages to me.

The first one was an explosive apology. She was sorry. She didn't even know if I would ever get the message, but she was so effing sorry. She loved me, she was getting on the first plane and would find me if she had to tear the effing jungle apart. The last message Mitzi left was calmer, and I knew that her resolve was like steel. She was coming to get me.

I called my home phone, but Twyla didn't pick up. Did she even understand how land lines worked? Frustrated, I called Valerie and left a message for her and Juniper that I was safe. Even though I was alone in the back seat, I felt embraced by Mitzi's words. She loved me and that felt good. I leaned forward and watched the colorful world speeding by.

Not knowing Mitzi was in the air, I left a babbling message and then called Elsa.

"Oh, Panda! This is the first good news I've gotten since your brother left to find Puddle! He and—"

"My brother was there?"

"Ja. Come to the hotel. We have lots to talk about. Mitzi's on her way."

My driver pulled into a grand plaza and drove around the huge fountain in the center. The hotel had a beautiful colonial visage that was bathed by the waning sun. Well-dressed pedestrians entered and exited, and I was all too aware of my own sniffy, dirty outfit.

The driver had been prepaid, and I had no luggage. I got out and paused a moment to take in the majestic hotel.

"Panda!" I turned to see Mitzi running toward me with bags on both arms.

"Mitzi!" I imagined running toward her in slow motion, but we collided rather quickly.

"Are you okay?" She dropped the bags and took both my hands in hers. I grinned and said, "Yes, now I am. Oh my God, Mitzi." I put my hand behind her head and drew her close.

"I want to know everything. How did—uh, babe, you need a bath, whew!"

She laughed, and I realized I'd gotten used to my peed upon yoga pants smell. "I don't have anything to change into."

"I brought you some clothes." She lifted the bags again. I tried to peek into one with a drawstring, but she smiled and swatted my hand. Ahhh, marriage.

We walked then, plastered together, through the lobby and into the elevator. There were probably some strange looks, either because we were two women who would not let each other go or because I smelled like a goat, but we didn't care. Mitzi babbled about meeting a nun on the plane, and I asked if she had any news about Brooke and Puddle. Elsa had the door open before we even got to the room. I smelled cinnamon and baking.

Elsa practically pounced on me. "Panda, thank God you're all right. Come in and—" Her sensitive nose twitched. "You need a bath, *liebchen*."

"Okay, you two, I get the picture." In the bathroom, I turned on the water in the tub. Mitzi came in with some lavender salts. For that, she got another kiss. "You think of everything."

She held her nose and said, "see you in a few." I stripped off my clothes and, after only a moment's pause, put them in the trash. The bathroom was bright yellow and the bath inviting. I put my foot in, then my other leg, then lowered my bum into the delicious liquid. The door opened again, and Mitzi stuck in her head. "Want some company?"

"If you take out the trash." I eyed her lasciviously. "Won't we make Elsa blush?"

She grabbed the trash can and returned shortly, locking the door. "Move over." I knew we still had some things to work out, but, for now, we were together.

Detective Charlie Potts was getting ready to retire. After thirty-six years on the Merryville PD, he'd earned it. As a result, not many cases were piled on his beat-up metal desk. After a remodel of the department, he managed to convince his superiors that the desk was important to his "process." His Lieutenant already told him it was going home with him.

He mused about his recent relationship with Alexandra Stephanovsky, a high-profile and very beautiful defense attorney. Who would have thunk it? When it seemed his life was over, it had begun again. He put his feet on the desk and leaned back in the chair where he'd solved so many cases. It would be good to have one more big case, but—

"Potts."

"Hey, Jimmy." He put his boots back on the floor as the young Crime Scene Investigator appeared at the opening in his cubicle.

"Check this out." Jimmy handed him a stack of papers.

"What am I looking at, Jim?" He picked up his cheaters from the desktop and stuck them on his nose. "Ahhh, The Great Flower Heist." He did a stretch in his chair, which emitted a rusty squeal.

"We got a hit, well, a familial hit. There was a smudged print on the note left at the victim's house."

"And?" Potts made a "go on" motion.

"Well, it's weird. We apparently arrested a relative of whoever left the print back in the Seventies, but his or her report is missing—I've got records digging."

Charlie's investigative senses tingled. "Sit down and tell me everything."

Puddle had fallen asleep. She woke to see Dieter's face in front of her making the universal "shhh" sign with his index finger. She chanced a quick glance around and saw everyone sleeping. The panther was nowhere to be seen. Fernando was already standing without his binding. It took her only a nanosecond to assess this new scenario, and she was all in.

The three made their way through the jungle and away from the cliff's edge. Puddle wanted to ask questions but knew how dangerous their situation was. Dieter was tall and geeky but pretty athletic. She followed, after giving Fernando a withering glance. They followed the sound of the water and finally stopped when daylight began peeking through the canopy. "Dieter, why?"

Fernando started to speak then, but Puddle turned on him. "I don't want to hear a word out of you. If we get out of this well, ugh, just shut up." Fernando slumped to the ground and put his head in his hands.

Dieter's face was drawn. He was sunburnt, skinny and tired. "I'm from Schwartzwald, in the Black Forest. I have been," at this he looked at the ground, "a follower of Wolf Raven." He looked up directly into Puddle's eyes. "I was wrong."

She whispered furiously, arms folded. "What are you now, Baptist, agnostic?" She dropped her arms to her sides. "I do want to hear this story but not now. Can you get us back to Cusco?"

Dieter nodded. "I was chosen for this mission because I've studied the ways of the forest and the local dialects. This will help us."

"So what now?"

"There are guardians of the forest called Chullanchaqui. It is said they will come if you know how to call them."

"Do it." Puddle was still whispering. Fernando lifted his head and nodded.

Dieter closed his eyes for a moment and then let out a trill that sounded like some kind of bird. It was eerie, but Puddle had no choice but to trust the strange German.

The sounds in the jungle paused for a brief moment, then began again. The physical sensation was like that of a small concussion of air. Dieter put a small set of binoculars to his eyes, straining to see into the forest. "Now we wait. The ancient books say it can take a while, but, if they're around, Chullanchaqui will answer."

High up in the tree, Juju was already awake planning their next move. For whatever reason, his tracking wasn't working like it usually did. It really bothered him that Brooke was the first one to hear the rushing water. What was wrong with him? Ekk was curled up like a kitten in the fold of the tree branches, and Brooke snored softly through his hammock netting. Juju didn't really know what to do next and was startled to hear and feel the call for El Chullanchaqui. He shook Ekk awake. "I've got to go. You and Brooke stay here."

Ekk nodded solemnly. This was Juju's territory. He brushed himself off as Juju shimmied down the tree.

Twyla climbed up to her treehouse and rummaged through her meager things. She had one extra set of clothes, the yoga mat Panda had added to the house, and her kit of magical things. A lantern she'd found in the garage lit her cozy home. She nibbled on Ritz crackers from the house and thought. She always felt more herself in the trees, as one would expect of a tree fairy, and tried to give herself good advice.

Before she left the Hercynian Garden, Ehrenhardt warned her not to use magic in this non-magical world. He said magical works would attract the attention of the enemy. She was always being warned about one thing or another—don't get sidetracked, can't you follow directions for once? It had taken her eons to get out of fairy school. This attitude was irritating. Hadn't she proven herself? So what if she'd missed Brooke in New York. Apparently, someone else had directed him to Peru.

It wasn't her fault some other Twyla had shown up in the meantime in Merryville, but she'd probably be blamed for that too. Well, the Garden had trusted her to come here, and now she had seen real evil in that shapeshifting yoga teacher. There were big things at stake, and Ekk and Elsa were handling them. She had used barely a touch of magic to fix those flowers and look what good had come of it! Surely a skosh more magic couldn't hurt? Not for something like this. Ehren couldn't have meant for a tree fairy not to use tree-magic. She actually made herself laugh at that.

She ran her fingers over her inner arm and along the red scratch she got from trying to clip the thistles the conventional way. Her main goal here was to protect the Merryville people, Panda, Mitzi, Juniper and Valerie. Wasn't part of that to protect them from domestic enemies? That Hortense woman was a domestic enemy if she ever saw one.

She rooted through her kit and pulled out a tome, labeled *Zauberbuch*, and paged through to find a proper spell. It had been ages since she'd followed a spell recipe, but knew if she followed it exactly, nothing could go wrong.

Her tiny home had a glassless window, and a squirrel appeared in it, curious to see what its inhabitant was doing. Twyla sat cross-legged on the wooden floor, big book in her lap, and tried to remember how to speak to the rodent world.

✐

CHAPTER THIRTEEN

Juju ran through the forest. In all his years, he'd only heard the cry for El Chullanchaqui a handful of times. Not many knew the call, and it always meant someone was in grave danger. The morning light was filtering through the trees, and the air was still cool. This was Juju's favorite time of day. The fogginess of yesterday seemed to burn away as his tracking was clear as a bell. Instinct had him jump over this clump of bushes, duck under that mossy limb. He carefully avoided the tripping hazards. Sensing a clearing ahead, Juju slowed and then crept to a place where he could see what, or who, was there before they saw him.

There was Puddle! The beads in her hair glinted in the sun. She was with two men. One was that Fernando, the other a tall, white man. All three were very out of place in the jungle. He circled them to make sure there were no hostiles around before making himself known. At the same time he broke cover, Remy and his fellow Chullanchaqui also came into the opening. Remy nodded to Juju and held back as Puddle ran to Juju and bent to give him a hug.

Dieter brightened at the eight or so who had answered the call. He went to Juju and haltingly spoke in ancient Chullanchaqui. "We are needing to escape this place to city."

Juju said quietly, "I speak English." Then to Puddle, who he pulled aside, "Can we trust them?"

She glanced back at her two sorry companions. "I think so. That's Dieter, he helped us escape. Fernando's an idiot." Despite the circumstances, Juju smiled.

Puddle went on, "But, Juju, the old dude who was with us in the jungle was left wounded. We need to find him now." She shot an "if looks could kill" glance at Fernando. Fernando started to say something . . . then closed his mouth.

Remy joined them, and Juju and his fellow tree elf talked quietly. Puddle, Remy and Juju returned to Dieter and Fernando, and Remy asked what they knew about where Luis had been left. After discussion, in which the tree elves kept watch, a decision was made.

"Follow me." Juju took Dieter, Puddle and Fernando back the way he had come. Soon they met up with Ekk and Brooke at the base of the tree in which they had slept the night before. Brooke's hair was a tangle, and he was dirty from being in the hammock. Puddle was unused to seeing Brooke in anything but a suit and had not laid eyes him in a year or more. He rushed toward Puddle and embraced her. "Thank God you're alive."

"Yeah, yeah, I'm alive alright. By the grace of Vishnu."

"What the hell—how'd you get into this mess?" Brooke asked. "How did *I* get dragged in this mess?"

"Long story."

"Start at the beginning."

"Bro, we have a lot of catching up, but there's a man dying out there, and we need to go find him first."

Brooke reddened. "Okay then, but aren't you people starving? How're you going to organize a search party if everyone's fainting with hunger?"

"Sounds like you're the one fainting with hunger."

Juju rummaged around in his sack and came up with a couple of Kapok fruits he broke and handed all around.

Brooke narrowed his eyes, clearly suspicious of the green cucumber-looking thing. "What's this?"

"Jungle food. You need it for energy." Juju chewed with his mouth open. "Go ahead. Eat. Won't kill you."

Brooke reluctantly accepted the fruit. After the first bite, he snarfed it down like a wild dog.

Still standing, they quickly partook and drank the now-cooled water from the boiling river below.

"Not so bad, huh?" Puddle asked. "Better?"

Brooke wiped his mouth against his shoulder. "Strangely filling. Now, how do we find this old man?"

Fernando finally spoke. "Jose Luis. I will find him. It's my fault he was with us."

No one disagreed.

Juju puffed up his chest and said, "*Pendejo.*" He spat. "You couldn't find your city butt in the jungle."

Fernando turned aside, his face flushed with color. "Not stupid. Maybe just unlucky."

Puddle nodded solemnly. A strange bird cry punctuated the silence.

"I can help you find him," Dieter said in his heavily-accented English.

"Ha!" Juju made a dismissive wave with his hands at the skinny German. "You're no better. It'll be hard, but my tracking skills and Remy's help—"

"Wait." Ekk had kept his calm blue eyes on Dieter. "Let's hear him out."

Dieter seemed relieved at the intervention and went on somewhat nervously. "With all due respect, Wolf Raven has extensive maps of the area.

I marked where we were when we left the old man."

Juju was still mad. "We need to get Puddle and Brooke out of the jungle now. The *dezplazador de la forma* are the second best trackers around. They'll be here soon."

Ekk put a restraining hand on the excited man's arm.

Remy nodded in agreement. Everyone knew who Juju thought was number one.

Dieter reached in his shirt. "I have maps of the area and can show you pretty close to where the old man was left." He said this sadly as he unfolded a damp sheath of paper from beneath his pocket area.

Juju, face red, wrenched his arm away from his elven cousin and grabbed the map, shaking it in Dieter's face. "You stole this from the *Chullanchaqui.* You or your *Lobos Negro* killed to get this."

Dieter slapped a no-see-um on his neck. He studied the jungle floor. "I don't know where it came from to be honest, I didn't ask. Wolf Raven—*Lobos Negro*—they gave it to me so I could help with navigation. Now can we get out of here?"

The Jungle heat was becoming oppressive, and the insects merciless. A roar from afar gave them all renewed energy to part.

In the end, it was decided that Juju would take Fernando to find Jose Luis, Ekk would take Dieter, Brooke and Puddle back to town, with Remy leading the way. Not wanting to leave his human friends, Juju huffed and gave Fernando an unnecessary push in the direction Dieter's map had indicated. Puddle gave her ex-boyfriend one last look, sadness in her eyes, then followed Remy, Ekk and her brother back to the hotel.

✺

After Mitzi and I bathed, I sat at the table in Ekk and Elsa's room, full of *galletas.* When the cherry-cheeked elf approached with more, I said, "No, Elsa, I'm good." Mitzi was sitting next to me and had regaled me with all that had happened back in Merryville. The broken orchids at the Gooden's. The note warning that it could happen to them was worrisome.

"So are Valerie and Juniper in any danger? That note sounds scary."

"Valerie called Detective Potts. Remember our old friend?" We both laughed.

"How could I forget? You were my cellie, *Orange is the New Black,* baby," I said, putting my arm on her shoulders. Detective Potts had arrested us about a month ago after a ritual we performed at the Merryville museum, and at one time thought our friend, Valerie, a possible murderer. How fast things can change.

"Oh, yes, having a defense attorney for a girlfriend has really mellowed him out." We both laughed again. "And Valerie was having their locks changed when I left. They'll be okay. She called Lulu."

Lulu was the security guard at the strip mall where I worked. She was good people.

"Well, that's good. She's awesome. I'm glad she's making some money on the side. What about our guardian fairy?" I used air quotes. It seemed to me she had not done much guarding.

"At least we know she's on our side and is the real Twyla." Mitzi touched my cheek. "Oh, honey, I'm so sorry."

She had already apologized. This was overkill. I didn't blame Mitzi for anything really, except liking her magical yoga teacher who turned out to be evil. It felt good to have my gut response to the situation validated. "Stop saying that. I think the bad Twyla put a spell on you."

Mitzi opened her mouth and sighed and squeezed my hand.

From the kitchen, Elsa added, "Its highly likely she did put a spell on you, Mitzi. Don't feel bad. Her magic is really strong. I understand even Remy felt it."

"Oh, yeah. I told Elsa she was ordering those Peruvian men around like nothing, and they were scared of her." The thought of that sobered me a bit. "Why didn't the Chock come and rescue Puddle?"

Elsa was quiet for a minute. "I don't know. We'll have to find out more when Juju gets back."

Mitzi was curious. "What I don't get is how a patriarchal religion like Wolf Raven, or Lobos Negros, or whatever the hell they call themselves, would allow a woman, even a woman panther, to run things down here. I mean, talk about an oppressive regime."

Elsa put a protein plate down and I helped myself, having eaten dessert first. "Good point, Mitzi."

Elsa joined us at the table. "Wolfrum is a user and an opportunist. Remember, he used his sister to get to you, Mitzi. He'll use men, women, or creatures to achieve his goals. But make no mistake, he's calling the shots."

"What the hell does he really want?" I said. "He has a castle in Schwartzvald and lots of followers." I was clean and fed and with my darling. I was feeling a little spicy, then felt guilty to feel so good with my siblings still in danger.

Elsa finally sat down, her feet swinging in huaraches. "He wants more, more of everything. Isn't that what all power mad people want? His goal is only cloaked in religion."

"Thank God he's across the pond and we live in Merryville."

"Don't be so sure about that," Elsa said. "Evil jumps from heart to heart if you're not careful, like fire. He caused that City Councilman to try to cut me and Ekk's heads off, remember? That was in Merryville—at your house!"

"I'm sorry, you're so right. We've all been through it." I sighed deeply.

Elsa's cell phone rang, and she leapt on it. "Ekk!" she fairly squeaked. She covered the phone with her hand and after a beat announced to us, "He's on his way back with your brother and sister and someone else." I loved the way she said brother. It sounded like "brudder."

"Hurry!" she giggled into the phone, "I'll get some more *Chicha*." Now it really was starting to feel like a party.

Juniper was irritated, a state more and more common lately since Richland Bruce had arrived at the Merryville museum. She left Origins and went in search of Maribel, her very reliable and rational assistant. Juniper found her in the Words on a Plate exhibit tent, making sure the trifold brochure explaining the exhibit was placed strategically around the room. Juniper watched the slender young woman with the green hair and couldn't help but smile.

"Juniper! Hi. I didn't see you there." Maribel had been with the museum for four years, after completing her degree in Fine Art. "I think we're ready for Saturday."

"Good. Now, will you give me some honest feedback?" Juniper walked to the South facing windows and stared out over the ocean.

"Of course. Is anything wrong? I could put out special holders for the—"

"No. It's not about the exhibit. Not directly. It's about me, here," she turned to Maribel, "at this museum. I had lunch with Richland."

"Oh, him. He's a piece of work."

Juniper was wearing a blue suit that matched her Aquamarine earrings and, as usual, looked stunning. "It's that—you know I've been involved in things outside the museum this year."

"Yes, and you were arrested at the museum after doing a ritual. People are still talking." At least Maribel was honest. She chewed her lip as if thinking, "The general consensus is they think you're a witch."

"Fabulous." After a beat, Juniper added, "Oh, and my last assistant is currently sitting in jail while they sort out the death of our old chairman. God. It's too much." She rubbed her neck, shaking her head. "At least he's getting out soon."

Maribel responded. "It's true, the whole Floodlight exhibit put the museum through stress, and there are those who don't like the direction you're taking the art, but it's not everybody."

"Thanks, Maribel, but let me finish." Her energy waning, Juniper sat heavily onto a chair.

"Let's be honest. Linda would throw a party if I quit, Richland is champing at the bit to take my job, and even that awful woman at the local Horticultural Society wants to replace this exhibit hall with roses. Roses!" She started to sob, and Maribel moved to her and put an arm around her shoulders.

Both women turned their heads as Bonnie dropped a box of trifold brochures noisily on the floor and stomped out.

"What was that all about? More morale issues?" Juniper asked.

"Nothing, well, nothing to do with you. I'll tell you about that later. Listen to me." Maribel squatted with youthful ease to meet Juniper's eyes. "I've been here a while and have to say that this museum is necessary for the cultural and mental health of Merryville. A younger crowd and people from the University come now. That never happened before. Mrs. Windingle even hangs out more often. Art should be challenging, and under your direction— it is. What you're experiencing is probably the last gasp of the old guard. They're losing power, and it's hard for people to change."

"Well, I've always thought so, but it's getting toxic. I can't even have lunch without Cynthia Snively giving me evil looks. Maybe it would be better if I quit."

Maribel laughed. "She's no better serving fries than she was in Human Resources." In a soft voice she continued, "Hey, you're the only reason I'm still here. Sounds like you need some time."

"That's part of the problem apparently. Time. I took time to go to Germany. Ever since I've come back there seems to be a target on my back. I'm sorry. I'm usually not so snively." She wiped her eyes, her manicured nails carefully holding a tissue. Juniper stood and tucked away her emotions. "Well, let's get through Saturday and see what Merryville thinks. My future is up to them."

Maribel opened her mouth to speak, but Juniper stopped her. "No. I think that makes sense. If Words on a Plate isn't a big hit, I'm done, and that's okay." The vulnerable Juniper was gone, replaced by The Curator with a capital C.

"You don't have to do that!" Maribel paused a moment. "I'll quit, too!"

Juniper took her hand. "No, dear. You have a great future here. In fact, I'm sorry I haven't seen it sooner—you really should be putting your own exhibits together. One more thing, Maribel. Do me a favor and keep this conversation under your hat."

"Whatever you need, but it makes me sad to think about you leaving. I'm confident this exhibit will be well received." The two women were very professional again and strolled along the curated tables with their plates and paired paintings. It was challenging and colorful and would probably piss off a lot of people. But still, it was good.

Juniper was thoughtful and, as if a light bulb went off over her head, snapped her fingers. "I want to call a meeting with some of the artists."

Maribel pulled out her iPhone, already on it. "We only have a couple of nights. Do you want them to meet here?"

"No, not here. Get me this artist," she pointed to a painting on domestic violence, "and this one," indicating the Not Edgy Enough plate. "And call Phillip from the newspaper. Tell them I'm having a meeting at my house seven p.m. tonight." Juniper smiled mysteriously.

∾

The trip back didn't seem to take nearly as long as the original rescue mission. It's amazing what a tiny battalion of Jungle Elves can do. Ekk is an elf, too, but more comfortable doing taxes than trekking through a sea of green. He was definitely a city elf.

They stopped for a moment to get their bearings. Dieter appeared nervous and said to Brooke and Puddle, "I'm sorry for my part in this. I was wrong."

Disgust all over his face, Brooke hissed, "So you say."

No sympathy there.

Puddle looked at her brother. "Brooke, if not for Dieter, I'd still be with that Panther and the Pygmies."

"Sounds like a band," Dieter deadpanned, and Puddle giggled.

They hadn't had time for idle conversation, and Brooke eyed the stranger while he drank from his canteen. "Let's be clear. I appreciate what you did, but don't expect a parade."

Puddle tilted her head and spoke to Dieter, "Where will you go now?"

Dieter met her eyes. "I have relatives here, in South America. I'll be okay." Then to Puddle and Brooke, "I want to tell you what I know about *Lobos Negros* plans before we part. You two and Panda are in a great deal of danger."

Ekk, having spoken to Elsa, closed his phone and said, "Good idea. Come with us to the hotel."

"Then he'll know exactly where we are!" Brooke was not a trusting soul. Remy had stopped up ahead and made an impatient sign to us, arms raised in question.

Ekk put his hands on his hips. "We can't stay here, and everyone else is there anyway. We need a place to debrief him." Referring to Dieter.

Brooke turned obstinate. "How can we trust him? He kidnapped Puddle!"

Ekk's voice was soothing. "And he helped Puddle escape. Come on, Brooke, we can cut him loose afterwards."

Remy appeared out of the jungle leaves and looked pointedly at Ekk, "*Disculpa por romper tu fiesta. No es Seguro.*" Remy moved back to the path and motioned to the path with his hand, showing impatience.

Ekk translated for Puddle. "He says he's sorry to break up the party, but it's not safe."

They were a motley crew as they tromped through the final piece of the trail and found themselves at the edge of the city. Remy and Ekk spoke quietly off to the side, and Remy waved before turning back to the forest.

"I'm so tired and hungry." Puddle was also out of pot.

"It's up here, come on." Ekk got them back to the Hotel, their little troop garnering more than a few stares from tourists and locals alike.

CHAPTER FOURTEEN

Elsa and I opened the door and fell over our new arrivals, hugging and crying. I had not seen Brooke in years, and we held each other tightly. He had not come to Mitzi's and my wedding, but right now was not the time to open old wounds. I was not sure Mitzi felt the same way as she stood clear of the love fest.

Questions were shouted as people talked over one another. "Where's Juju? What happened to Fernando? Are you okay?" Through this reunion, Dieter stood there awkwardly. Elsa grabbed him by his boney hand and dragged him into the now crowded room. She spoke to him in German and soon he was laughing. I suspected she'd thrown some lavender into the room, but it was hard to tell over the baking smells.

Even with everything going on, Puddle appeared to notice Dieter was not unattractive when his face wasn't so drawn and gloomy. She handed him a *Chicha* before sitting down next to him at the table to tell her story. I sat on the other side of her with Mitzi scooted up close to me at the small table. Brooke leaned against the wall. It felt good to finally have us all in one place.

"We were walking, and Fernando started getting weird," Puddle said. We listened raptly as her story unfolded.

Ekk was amused. "I'm surprised Juju didn't strangle Fernando when he caught up with you. He was really pissed."

Puddle went on, "Juju heard Dieter's special call. What a long strange trip it's been."

Mitzi quipped, "To quote Jerry Garcia."

Dieter focused on Puddle and pushed his dusty glasses up his skinny nose. "You like the Grateful Dead?" It was the first thing he'd said in the hotel that wasn't in German.

"Um, like yes, who doesn't?" Puddle turned to me, while peeling the label off her bottle of beer. She was blushing underneath her sunburn. "What about you, Panda Bear? I hear you got snatched too."

"I got kidnapped by Mitzi's yoga teacher." They all laughed. "She had guards too, but they weren't pygmies. I was rescued by *El Chulla*, well, the Chock?"

"*Chullanchaqui*," Ekk corrected.

"Whatever, Remy said Chock was fine. Don't be a school marmy elf." We all had a good laugh and many small details were shared. I left out the part about being rescued mid pee.

Puddle got quiet. "Sis, wait. Did the yoga teacher shape-change?"

Now all side conversations ceased, and eyes were on me and on Puddle. This was indeed a startling question.

"I saw that in a dream. But no, she put a spell on me during yoga class. I was frozen in down dog." My story was being trumped, but I didn't mind.

Ekk asked what happened.

"Dude," Puddle said, "this lady started out as a panther, then him," she pointed to Dieter, "and she went to the edge of the cliff and she, like morphed into a woman."

"This is indeed serious," Ekk said to Dieter. "A *dezplazador de la forma.*"

Dieter nodded. "Wolfrum uses them, but it's an uneasy alliance. He has followers everywhere."

Puddle turned to Brooke and Ekk, with brow furrowed. "How did you guys find me anyway?"

Sensing Brooke's discomfort, Ekk jumped in. "Modern technology. If it weren't for Brooke, we may not have found you in time."

Brooke knew he couldn't avoid answering. "Sis, I had a tracker put on your iPhone before I sent it to you."

Her expression was fierce, "I knew I shouldn't trust you! Talk about geeks bearing gifts! Were you listening in on my life? I hate this. Good thing I lost it in the jungle, I think."

"Nope, got it right here." Ekk pulled the iPhone out of his pocket and put it on the table. "It got us to the place you were snatched, or led, away. Juju picked up your scent, and we followed you into the jungle. We would have found you eventually, but your friend here," he nodded to the kitchen where Dieter and Elsa had moved and were speaking German, "put out the emergency call to *Chullanchaqui.*"

"Can we call them Jungle Elves?" I was serious, but no one paid any attention.

"Puddle, I'm sorry, but you know how you are." When Brooke said this in his best fatherly tone, my gut said, Uh oh.

I knew my brother and sister. These were fighting words.

"How would you know how I am, Brooksie?" The use of his childhood name was meant to be inflammatory. "I haven't seen you in probably what, six years? Everybody thinks they know me—Oh, Puddle is so crazy, now she's joined an Ashram, oh Puddle is so paranoid, she doesn't trust technology or the government, oh, Puddle smokes pot. Okay, that's true, but I don't need you worrying about me. I do fine."

Brooke pulled on his beer. "Oh, so you didn't get kidnapped by a new boyfriend you followed to Peru all the way from India? Do you even have any money left from our parent's insurance?"

Ekk got up and left us siblings to work it out. I was tempted to follow. Instead, I picked up a spoon and rapped it on my teacup. Brooke and Puddle turned to me, and I remembered my role as peacemaker and clown in our childhood. Mitzi wisely stayed quiet. "Kids, this is fun and all, but we're sitting here in Peru, South America, and some pretty bad people and, um, *things* are apparently after us."

Mitzi nodded.

"And they say New Yorkers are crazy," Brooke said to no one in particular.

Puddle needled him again. "You only moved there ten years ago after college. You were born in California."

"Really? What, so I'm not a New Yorker? I'm a poseur. Jeesh, well, now that you're all back and safe I should be going back to New York with my poser friends." He stood up. "This nutty stunt may have cost me my job. I left without notice, Puddle Pop, to save you. You're welcome. You don't leave without notice when you're a licensed stock broker."

"Like I wanted to be kidnapped!" She held her hands in supplication and looked around the room. "I didn't ask you to come." She folded her arms across her chest. "It was Dieter who rescued me."

Ekk came back to the conversation with some sandwiches. "It's true. No one asked for this. You were all kind of swept into this battle. Brooke, it must seem crazy to you, but the last thing we need right now is to fight each other."

"Crazy? Yes, an elf told me to stop arguing with my sister, and I probably lost my job because of all of you." Boy, he could be a butthead, but I detected a faint smile.

Ekk continued, "I don't blame you for wanting to leave, but until we finish whatever it was your parents' started, I don't think you'll be safe in New York or anywhere."

Brooke spread his hands in frustration. "And what was that? What did they begin? The last I heard, we don't even know how they died, or apparently even *if* they died."

"I think you should hear what Dieter has to say before he goes," Elsa said.

Everyone had forgotten about the tall German in the chaos of old arguments.

My wife was angry. "Well, I for one am dying to hear this. You may have helped today but you're still the enemy." She probably had PTSD from her experience a couple of weeks before in Germany. Dieter's old boss Wolfrum was going to have her "reeducated" by sexual assault to cure her lesbianism. Although Juniper and I got there in time to avoid that, she was not about to let him off the hook.

"I'm sorry," Dieter said quietly.

Mitzi wasn't finished. She stood and pointed as she spoke. "Your comrades took me to Schwartzvald Castle. I think I even saw you there." I tried to keep my arm around her, hoping her wings wouldn't sprout.

The man took a deep breath. "You did see me. I was a monk in, um, well, in Wolfrum's cult."

"Why did you join those guys if you knew they were bad? Huh?" She was relentless. We all watched the verbal volleys like a tennis match as this played out.

"Mitzi, I was an orphan. Becoming a brother with the Wolf Raven monastery was the first family I knew. The castle was my home."

Mitzi moved from the table and walked to the balcony area. "I'll play a tiny violin for you."

Ekk pulled out a chair and sat. "It's a fair question, Dieter. How did you rationalize all the violence? Kidnapping, beheading?"

The skinny German warily took in his audience. "First of all, I *personally* never beheaded anyone. We were told that we were the future, the true spirit of the Wolf and the Raven, the world needed us to save it. Everyone out there in your world was a sinner, especially people like you," he looked at me, then Mitzi, "the same-sex people. But I studied and read about things that were forbidden. I had access to the library, and then I got on the internet. It was my awakening."

"Why did they send you to Peru?" Puddle put her hands on each side of her freckled face with her elbows on the table. "You're not exactly Indiana Jones."

"I speak dozens of languages. That's my job with the castle. I'm not much of a fighter but have a knack for learning foreign tongues. We get recruits from all over the world, and someone must teach them German." He looked at Ekk. "Some are from California. After a while, I realized that these young men were like me. They needed food and a job. Wolfrum gave them a cause to fight for. Most were willing to give their loyalty to a strong leader who would send money home to their families. Others had nowhere else to go."

"Why should we trust anything you tell us?" Brooke had an edge to his voice.

"Believe what you want." He paused and put his chin in his hand in resignation. "I'm done with it. It was already in the back of my mind to get out and coming here was an opportunity to get away. I've seen too much. Enough about me. Listen, tomorrow night the window is closing for Wolfrum to find Paititi before it moves. Something's there, something magic that he needs."

"We need more evil in the world?" Mitzi sounded sad now. I went to her.

He continued. "Once he gets there, well, it would be awful for everyone.

Wolfrums' ticket in was the three of you." He stood. "I was not going to let that happen."

"Thank you," I said and meant it.

Dieter stared out the window, his face sad.

Puddle got up and walked to him, touching his arm, "No, really. What's going to happen to you?" Puddle inquired. Brooke rolled his eyes.

"I'll find my distant relatives. All that time studying, I spent some of it researching the family tree."

Brooke was disgusted. "How do we know this isn't another plot? I suppose you know where we're supposed to go?"

Dieter responded as if the question had been asked nicely. "As a matter of fact, I do have one more map." As he dug his hand in his pocket, Brooke grabbed his arm to make sure he wasn't going for a weapon. Dieter slowly pulled out nothing more lethal than a folded-up map. "It's the last one."

He spread it on the table, and they all turned their heads this way and that to get a good idea of where we needed to go. The map was old and yellow and hard to read.

Ekk said, "I wish Juju was here."

"There's someone at the door," Elsa said.

"But I didn't hear—" Brooke started to say. Then the knock came. He looked at Elsa in wonder.

I got up because neither Elsa nor Ekk was tall enough to look out the peephole. No one was there, and, too late, I had one of those moments when I sensed danger. Someone—or something—battered the door from the other side. I stepped back and shouted, "Get out!"

♄

Bonnie had walked into the exhibition tent in time to see Maribel embrace Juniper. It made her mad, but she didn't know why. She threw down the trifold programs and stormed out. Everything was awful. She couldn't go home or be at the museum, which had been her retreat lately, without running into Uncle Ricky. She was always hungry but was busting out of her clothes. Why couldn't she be a pretty girl like Maribel. She tried to dye her hair blue once, but it looked stupid on her.

Bonnie felt she needed to do something drastic to change her life. Maybe go down to the park and be alone. She walked the several blocks to the town center and saw that she was far from alone. A banner across the entrance welcomed one and all to "A New Spirit." A band was setting up on stage, and clean-cut youth were manning tables with literature. There was free lemonade and cookies and Bonnie took one. A very pretty, young woman came up to her and said, "Hi, did you come for the concert?" The girl was slender and tall, her hair the color of wheat. A gentle breeze blew the wisps around her face.

"I didn't even know there was one. I actually came to be alone, kind of." She felt vulnerable and shy, and something else, undefinable.

"Well, come on, my name's April. I'm with the New Spirit revival." With that, the young woman motioned with her arm at the carnival-like setting and beamed a huge smile on Bonnie.

Bonnie had no idea what she was getting into but, for some reason, felt she might follow April anywhere.

ᘒ

Valerie felt safer after the locks had been changed on the house and was spritzing her reanimated orchids and ogling them for the hundredth time when the phone rang.

"Hello?"

"Hello, my love."

"Juniper! Panda called!"

"Oh, hallelujah, is she okay? Well, she must be if she called."

"Yes, she left a short message. Apparently, she's on her way back to the hotel in Cuzco. She was rescued by those jungle elves. I'm not sure Mitzi even knows yet.

"Now that that's settled, can I complicate your life?"

Valerie laughed. "It's not complicated enough? I keep staring at these orchids—still can't get over it. What's up?"

"We're having a meeting at our house tonight. Can you put some food together?"

"Sure, who are you having?" Valerie put her water spritzer down and walked into the kitchen.

"Artists," Juniper gave a throaty laugh, "and press."

"Okay—"

"I'm tweaking the exhibit."

"Oh? Isn't the opening, like, in two days?"

"Yup."

Valerie put the receiver between her shoulder and ear so she had a free hand to open the fridge. "Well, if wontons and veggies and dip are enough, you're good. How many are you having?"

"Only two or three." Juniper was being mysterious. "And have wine, lots of wine."

"Anything I should know?"

A beat on the other side. "Mmm. I feel under attack at the museum. They brought in Richland Bruce from the Cleveland, Ohio Museum, and then I've got your Hortense Miller wanting to take my space for her flowers."

Valerie laughed. "She's not *my* Hortense. So, are you planning a coup?"

"Something like that."

"Is Twyla still with you?"

"No. She left when Lulu came to change the locks."

"Good. I'll be home soon, my love."

"You're not going to tell me what you're up to, are you?"

"The less you know the better. Plausible deniability."

"Okaaay. See you tonight."

"Ciao."

Hortense rapped the gavel. Other than herself, there were only four in attendance, so the formality was a bit of overkill. "Okay, Janet, report."

"I spoke to my brother, Richland. He says once he's in, we can have whatever hall we want."

"Good. Flo?"

"The Judge doesn't know anything about this." Florence leaned forward, confidentially.

Hortense sighed. In all the years she had known Florence, she still didn't refer to her husband by name. "Naturally."

Florence went on. "When the City Council votes on the thistle ordinance, you can be sure it will have teeth. Those pictures you showed at our meeting were scary." She scanned the other women for support. "We're all tired of scofflaws."

Lidia piped up in her papery voice, "Let's run those lesbians out of town."

Hortense cleared her throat and gave Flo a nod before turning back to respond, "Lidia, you know it's not about that. In fact, the Merryville Horticultural Society recently accepted its first openly homosexual member, Valerie Gooden."

Janet said, "That's right, we did."

Their leader went on, "And, of course, Sylvia Arviso is a Mexican." Hortense's smile was lizard-like. She went on. "We don't have a problem with *diversity*. The real problem is that our quality of life in Merryville is declining. It's getting crowded with tourists, immigrants and, yes, this gay element who want to change the face of our city. The gay men aren't so bad. They at least buy the old houses and fix them up. But the women! Have you seen what they wear in public? It's common."

Janet got comfortable and exchanged a look with Flo. Hortense actually stood and paced. She was on a roll, "Coffeehouses abound, parking is impossible, and there is no respect for the law. Trash everywhere! I was talking to Mayor Reed the other day, and he's on board." She turned toward her board dramatically. "We need to show people we mean business, starting with those weeds."

Sally spoke up for the first time. "Jack says we can't turn back time." Her voice was wavery. Sally's husband Jack was very generous with the Society. Hortense couldn't lose her support. "Jack's right. We might as well accept it will never be exactly like it was, but it can be better."

Florence said, "We need to vote, but shouldn't Sylvia be here? She's also on the executive committee, isn't she?"

Lidia said, "This is her tennis day. She couldn't make the meeting." She appeared slightly guilty.

Hortense took Sally's hand and said, "What's your favorite flower dear, roses?"

"Actually, peonies."

"I was thinking, Sally, we could have" Hortense gestured as if to a vision she was seeing, "a whole *section* of peonies as people walk into the museum, and you could design it."

Sally was easily distracted. She perked up and smiled. "I would need some help."

"Our wandering legacy member, Denise McGreggor, gets here soon. I'm sure this would make a good first project for her."

Everyone nodded, and Hortense rapped her gavel. "Done. Let's get to work cleaning up our town!"

Richland Bruce was feeling pretty good. He straightened his Master of Fine Arts certificate on his wall in the small office, knowing it was only temporary. The Curator's job was in sight. In his mind, Juniper had one foot out the door and another on a banana peel. Good thing. Ohio was getting small. People like him need to grow, and Merryville was the place to do that. He looked out his office window at the expanse of lawn between the main Craftsman Museum that housed the administrative offices and connected the large tent exhibit on the property. He put his feet on the desk and hands behind his head. He saw his niece running out from the exhibit hall toward the parking lot. What the heck was that about? He hoped she wouldn't complicate his plans at the museum but noted at least she was getting some exercise.

Linda Chicolet appeared at his door with an armful of trifolds.

He smiled and put his Cole Haan loafers back on the floor. "Did you get them all?"

"Yup, these new ones will certainly give things a stir Saturday." She smiled maliciously as Richland took one and opened it up, covering his smiling mouth.

Twyla was ready—those weeds were as good as gone. She had read and re-read the spell in her *Zauberbuch* many times and even chatted with the Squirrel about it. She climbed down from her treehouse and smiled, thinking about the animal chatter. Squirrels were such gossips. She crossed the yard, noting it was going to be dark in minutes. She opened the sliding glass door to the Fowler's home and met Brutus, who, big surprise, wanted to be fed. He had a large head and almost human expressions. Even without speaking "cat" it wasn't too hard to figure out what he wanted as he herded her to the kitchen.

"Yes, Brutus, I live to serve you, Brutus." She giggled at her own speech. "By the way, I heard about your new friend from Mister Squirrel. She should be coming out soon. It's dark."

Brutus paused only a moment as if embarrassed. Twyla wondered if he was blushing under his dense fur.

"Don't worry. Your new 'possum pal will be our pinkie swear secret." Twyla tried to find a place on Brutus' paw and settled for linking her pinkie finger with his tail.

After the big cat made quick work of his soft food, he scooted out the back door in the way of cats, probably going to find his friend. Twyla cracked her knuckles, a determined expression on her face. Now it was time to deal with those pesky Scottish Thistles!

CHAPTER FIFTEEN

DANGER IN PERU

To their credit, Ekk, Brooke, Dieter, Puddle and Mitzi jumped up from their seats without questioning me. Ekk shouted to us by the door and pointed "To the balcony!"

Brooke focused his fear and rage at Dieter. "You led them here, you Nazi bastard!" He socked him squarely in the eye, and then he turned to the door and stood at the ready. Dieter stayed on his feet like one of those punch balloons that bends way back but then pops back up. He winced and touched his check near his eye responding, "No I didn't! I swear!"

"Then help me fight whatever this is!" Brooke's courage was impressive.

"Panda!" My wife yelled for me, eyes open as wide as they could go, and I got scared. Nodules were already forming on Mitzi's shoulders. Her wings! I ran to her and pushed and pulled her towards the open door on the balcony, I had never seen her "get her wings" inside before. The balcony door was open, and I yelled "I love you" with tears in my eyes as she looked from one shoulder to the other, mouth open. I wanted to hold her. It still had to be an overwhelming thing to get her head around. Would we even make it through this? The Ravens had formed a blockade along the railing, and the front door to our room showed dents and cracks in its middle. I imagined shapeshifters trying to get in and said a quick prayer.

Elsa stood perfectly still, and, as she had done before, a smattering of lavender petals materialized, and the scene slowed down for a few seconds. My own senses were singing out, danger! If only there were a warning before all this hell broke loose. Mitzi made it to the balcony when Whoosh! Her blazing white wings simply exploded from her body, and she took flight. The ravens were so stunned they smashed into each other in confusion, phalanx broken. Mitzi's eyes were fierce, dare I say eagle or hawk like? This was almost more frightening to me than anything else. "Get Puddle," she called to me, and I did. Puddle stood there frozen in fear. She let me lead her out of the hotel room to the balcony. Mitzi swooped down. I could actually feel the wind from her wings as she picked up my sister, carrying her over the balcony and beyond my sight.

Meanwhile, Dieter and Brooke moved furniture to the front door, while we heard the fiercest thumping and scratching and roaring from beyond. I was terrified. My whole body went weak. "Ekk was saying something to Brooke when Mitzi returned and said, "Panda, come here, you next!" I was torn, wanting to protect everyone and also wanting to escape.

I made a decision. "Take, Elsa!" Ekk pushed Elsa toward Mitzi, who clasped on to her with arms that now bulged with sinew. What was happening to my wife? There was no time to think further as she carried the diminutive elf to safety.

The door cracked and would soon break. Brooke stood ready with a chair in hand. I had no weapons and wished for some kind of magic or talisman. I was crystal clear that my brother and I were of one mind in this. Brooke looked as surprised as me, and I knew he felt it, too. While Dieter ran to the kitchen to get knives and Ekk fended off ravens on the balcony, he said "We can do this." It was a bonding moment in the midst of pandemonium.

Mitzi soon returned, and I yelled, "Ekk! Go!"

He hesitated and one of the ravens tried to take a chunk out of his neck.

"*Shutzen die Madchen!*" Dieter shouted, then in English said, "Protect the girls."

That was enough for Ekk to let himself be taken. Now it was Brooke, Dieter, and me present as the door completely gave way, and the angry creature burst through the door and leapt over our barricade.

A *dezplazador de la forma* has all the characteristics of the animal it assumes. Panthers crouch then spring, talons flashing. The only thing we had going for us was that it was no longer a surprise. Dieter, Brooke and I did something as if we had planned it ahead of time. The room was fairly small, but we managed to make a triangle with the panther in the middle.

The monster's teeth were yellow and big and especially noticeable because of all the roaring.

"She's furious I betrayed her! This is my fight." Dieter lunged forward with a knife that clattered to the ground with one swipe of her big paw. Dieter pressed one hand over his wrist to stanch the bleeding.

The panther growled low and toyed with him, watching his blood drip on the floor before what I thought might be his certain death.

Mitzi chose this moment to land on the balcony. The distraction was enough for Brooke to get a chair upside the big cat's head. I picked up the nearest thing, which was a cutting board of heavy wood, and brought it crashing down on the animal's neck with force. The ferocious yowl and twist of its body told us we had injured it.

Mitzi couldn't enter the room because of the size of her wings but threw something to Dieter, who was casting around for a weapon.

He caught it with his one good hand. "*Grunzeug*? Brilliant." He leapt forward in a courageous lunge and slapped it on the animal's face. The substance quickly encased its whole head, and we watched in fascination as the creature struggled first with paws, then with transformed human hands to remove it from its face. I hoped we didn't have to see it suffocate. Even though it was the enemy, such a death would be nauseating.

Brooke pulled the curtain down off its rod, while the ravens quickly departed, knowing their protector was subdued. The creature's haunches turned into legs, and Brooke tied them with the cord from the window covering.

"She'll suffocate!" I screamed.

Mitzi's wings were deflating, and I knew the greatest danger had passed.

Dieter hugged his injured arm to his body but moved forward gingerly to make a hole for the woman to breath. "We are not like you, Maria. You don't have to die today."

Brooke finished hog tying her, wrists behind her back to her ankle ties.

"Maria?" It was strange to think of that thing as a woman.

"Part of the coalition with Lobos Negro. She'll be fine in a while. Let's go." Dieter was holding his wrist. His right eye was starting to swell.

"Shouldn't we call the authorities?" Brooke said. He was such a boy scout.

I nailed my brother with the same look I used to give him when we were kids and he said something stupid, "And tell them what? We subdued a panther who turned into a woman?"

"Leave her on the bed," Mitzi said. "Maybe when they find her, they'll think it was some kinky sex thing gone wrong."

I was overjoyed to see her return to me as herself, even though she was rattled. "Good idea, Mitz, but what about the door? We need time to escape and that's more than ordinary wear and tear. Now that your wings are gone, we need to walk out."

We all took a moment to study the motel door that now had a large hole in the middle and many scratch marks. It was a testament to Peruvian wood and craftsmanship that there was any door left at all.

Dieter took the piece of *grünzueg* he had torn off to make a breathing hole for "Maria" and smeared it on the door. The three of us watched, fascinated, as it took the form of the old door, and the hole shrank to nothing. The door was now mostly green, but it appeared as if someone had repaired and painted it.

"Okay," I said approvingly. "I want to invest in that stuff when this is all over." I got a towel from the bathroom, cut it into strips, with Mitzi's help, and tied it as tight as I could around Dieter's wrist.

Brooke and Dieter then lifted the furious woman, who was struggling against her ties. Brooke grunted, "I wish we could question her."

Dieter said, "She won't talk. There is nothing we could do would scare her into it. And she's not even the strongest one. More are coming. We must go."

I looked at the hogtied woman on the bed. She was actually pitiful now that she had transitioned. "Will she be all right? How will she get that green stuff off her head?"

Dieter replied, "Don't worry, the effects don't last forever in your world. Now let's go."

"There's nowhere to go!" Brooke was still amped. "They know where we are!"

"Don't worry," Mitzi said confidently, "we have somewhere to go. Come on."

ペ

Potts had put the great flower destruction caper on the back burner, but eventually it made its way to the top of his "to do" list. It was morning, and he hoisted his heavy frame from his desk chair onto his black leather shoes and made his way to the Merryville police parking lot and his Chrysler 300. Truth be told, checking in on the Goodens was as much a chance to smoke as anything else.

He drove through Merryville, cigarette hanging out the window. He realized this was his best year ever. Funny what being in love would do. Alexandra, Alex, his girlfriend, would be back this weekend and he couldn't wait. He was taking her to "Words on a Plate," another wacky art show led by Juniper Gooden.

The last big museum exhibit was Floodlight. The events from opening night had exploded across the city and led to newspaper headlines, arrests and the death of the museum's Chairman of the Board, Dick Mortimer. He had arrested Valerie Gooden. Alexandra had defended Valerie and gotten the Fowlers out of the clink for acting like witches on the lawn of the museum. What a way to meet.

Women were crazy. Lesbians maybe double that, but it sure did make life interesting. He shook his head and took another drag, chuckling.

The kid accused of killing Dick Mortimer, Garcia, was being released tonight. Potts instincts tingled. Maybe it was the cop in him, but he had a feeling there was another shoe to drop somewhere.

This flower and note thing at the Gooden's house had to be connected. He mused over his girlfriend Alex's comment that law enforcement personnel were probably all adrenaline junkies. Maybe he was bored and trying to make something out of nothing. Besides, Garcia couldn't have left the note. He was still in lock up when that happened. But this new DNA hit was puzzling.

These were his thoughts as he pulled up in front of the Gooden house. He threw the gear into park and walked heavily to the front door of the old craftsman. Juniper herself answered the door. It was early, so she was wearing a pink robe over her pajamas with matching fluffy slippers. Her red hair was wrapped in a silk scarf. He smiled in spite of himself. She always dressed like she was ready for her fashion shoot, kind of like his Alex, but more flamboyant.

"Detective Potts!"

"Ms. Gooden."

"Come in. Any news? Actually, we have some."

Suddenly, Valerie appeared at the door to the kitchen and motioned for Juniper to join her. Potts rocked on his heels while he tried to decipher the furious whispering in the other room. Juniper backed out, squeezing both her wife's hands. Valerie had obviously been crying.

"You first, what's your news?" Potts cop senses were tingling. Maybe they were fighting?

Juniper gave him her professional smile. "I personally wanted to make sure you knew you and your plus one invited as our guests Saturday night for the Words on a Plate opening."

The old detective had the distinct sense Juniper had lied, and that was not what she was going to say before the interruption by Valerie, but why?

"Great, I'll bring Alexandra. And, thought you'd want to know, Garcia's being released tonight. That's pretty big news."

"Fantastic!" Juniper brightened considerably. "We need to get this out to the public." She turned to find her purse with her cell phone in it.

Potts sat down on the couch, "There's something else." Juniper stopped to listen. "Actually, we've made some progress on your case." Both women appeared puzzled. "The flowers and note?" Something was up.

"Oh, yes, of course!" Juniper smiled her practiced curator smile. Valerie tucked a tissue in her jeans pocket. Juniper sat down and fixed the Detective with her piercing green eyes. "Do tell."

He hesitated, then said, "Ladies, did something else happen?" Juniper and Valerie shook their heads in comical unison. He leaned from his position on the couch as if to see if someone was holding the ladies hostage and hiding in the kitchen.

"Do you have a suspect?" Juniper was rapt.

"Look, if this was only about flowers—"

Valerie flipped her black hair, appalled.

"Sorry," Potts continued, "I would just give you a name," he tapped his pencil on his knee, "but there was a threat, remember?"

"How could we forget!" Valerie's tone was getting edgy.

"We got a hit on a partial fingerprint from the note."

"Oh, my God! Who was it?" Valerie sat next to Juniper silent. Their grandfather clock ticked in the background.

He shifted in his seat again and pulled out a three-inch spiral notebook. He chewed on his pencil as if trying to make up his mind.

"Well, who?" Juniper was impatient. What a diva.

Potts listened to his gut. "You gotta understand, it's a partial, and they lifted some DNA. Oh, well, the lab guys could describe it better, but what we got is a hit from a relative of whoever left that note."

"Don't make me shake your lapels, detective. Who the hell was it?" Juniper was so intense he stood.

Maybe it was their "hinky" behavior, but Potts snapped his old school notebook shut.

"I'm going to ask you to be patient a few days longer while I investigate. The reason I told you this is to warn you to be very careful. At home and at work."

"What?"

"Someone at the museum?" Juniper threw her hands up and Potts put up his hands in defense. Even Valerie put her hand on Juniper's arm.

He walked toward the door, notebook back in pocket. "I can't. Not 'til we're sure. I'm coming around when the museum opens tomorrow. Have you told anybody about the break in?"

Juniper and Valerie shared a look he couldn't decipher. Almost again in unison they said, "No."

"Well, don't. As far as anyone knows, if I show up at the museum, I'm an art lover, okay?" He stood up to go.

Juniper dialed it down a notch. "Maybe you should buy a black turtle neck."

"Seriously?" Potts always felt like he was treading water and couldn't touch bottom with these two.

Juniper stuck out her lower lip in a pout. Valerie took the detective's arm and led him to the door. Layla grunted and accompanied them. "She's just being catty. Juniper hates being left in the dark."

Potts repeated his warning before the door closed. "Keep it locked."

"Will do, Detective."

Once the door closed, Valerie led Juniper back to see the dying Rothschilds orchids.

∾

LATER THAT NIGHT.

Juniper opened the door while Valerie put *hors d' oeuvres* on vintage plates. Artists Penelope Pop!, Damian (no last name), and Phillip from the Merryville Bee were there in a pile.

"Come in! Come in!" Layla, the old hound dog, had gotten up to accompany Juniper to the door and gave a friendly ruff. Now that her duties were done, she plopped herself by the fireplace in the living room.

Penelope was known for her purpleness. It's all she wore, and her cut-to-the-chase style of speaking. "I'm super busy but glad you called. What the hell is going on at your museum?"

Juniper air kissed her. "Nice to see you too, Penelope. Have a seat, folks, and I'll tell you what this is all about."

Damien was silent and made some sort of obscure hand wave, as was his way—artists—and draped himself over an overstuffed chair like a cheap scarf. At least Phillip was more socially normal. He spoke first.

"Juniper, thanks for the invite. I can't stay more than a minute or two—deadlines, but knew you wouldn't have called this meeting on short notice unless you had a scoop?"

"Calm down, Jimmy Olson." She laughed, showing her white teeth. "But as a matter of fact, I do."

Valerie entered the room, carrying a tray of wontons, raw vegetables and wine. She almost giggled at the difference between this gathering and the uptight Horticultural Society a few days before. It's one of the things she loved about being married to Juniper.

"Thank you, darling." Juniper took a glass of white wine and sat on a hearth pillow next to Layla. "I invited you here because I'm afraid these last few weeks have been stressful for you. Dick's death, my absence, the Floodlight exhibit, and I want to hear your thoughts about this weekend's show."

"That's it?" Penelope pulled her head back, turtle like on her neck. Tonight, she was wearing a flowing purple caftan with black ballet slippers. Her hair was done up in a paisley scarf.

"Well, that and I wanted to tell you the charges against Garcia have been dismissed."

Phillip sputtered wine. "When?" The Merryville Bee had carried the story from the beginning, when Dick Mortimer had either been pushed or fallen off the cliff on the bluffs.

"I heard through a back channel. He's being released tonight but it's okay to tell you, Phillip. Apparently, the death was ruled a tragic accident."

"I better get over to the jail. You say he's being released now?"

"Tonight."

"Sorry, kids, I'll see you at the opening Saturday. Gotta go."

Phillip zoomed out, and Juniper was left alone with her artists.

"Well, that was dramatic." Penelope drained her glass.

"You're not hiring him back, are you?" Damien asked. He put the back of his hand to his forehead like a handkerchief and said in his best Scarlett O'Hara voice, "It's been hard being an artist for the woman who destroyed the museum." His humor was dry.

Juniper ignored Damien's joke and answered, "Who, Garcia? Maybe, haven't decided. Maribel's doing a great job, and we haven't yet talked. He may not even want to come back. What do you think?"

Penelope sounded bored. "That's museum business, a big *whatever*. That's for pencil people and bean counters. I *create*, but okay. I'm glad I'm here because I feel like this whole," she moved her splayed hand around in a circle, "*Words on a Plate* thing has been all wrong."

Juniper sputtered, "What? Why?" The shift from talking about her former assistant to the exhibit was unexpected. Juniper leaned forward, her gold ring and the white wine catching the light.

Penelope took a breath and then said, "Oh, I like *my* stuff, but honestly I think you sold out by including the safe plates to balance the message out for your board." Then, "Since the controversies, it's something I've gotten used to. That's why I put the plate out: Not Edgy Enough."

Juniper laughed. "So you were speaking words on a plate . . . to me."

Penelope smiled her lopsided grin. "Exactly."

Now Juniper turned to Damien. "Do you feel like you've been stifled as an artist in any way?"

He smoothed the silk on his black vest and picked at imaginary lint. "I'd rather not answer. I'm glad Garcia got cleared—nice kid."

Now he had the attention of both women. Juniper waited him out.

Damien continued, picking up his wine glass. "I got a call from Ricky Bruce, excuse me, Richland Bruce, a week ago. He and I go way back."

"And?" This was like pulling teeth.

"He asked me what it was like to work with you."

"I see. And you said?"

Damien popped a wonton in his mouth and talked while chewing. "I told him I had rainbows and unicorns coming out my ass." Then he barked a laugh.

Penelope asked, "So why did you really call us here? I mean, yay about your old assistant. It kind of helps with the gossip around the museum, but what does it have to do with the installation?"

Juniper stood up to pace. Her crepe pants swished in a frothy movement as she gathered her thoughts.

"I think I've been too safe. I actually agree with you, Penelope. Damien, you two are here because I think of you as the leaders of this exhibit. Let's make it all it could be. Do you have time to mix it up a little?"

CHAPTER SIXTEEN

Twyla stood in the dark, unicorn horn wand in hand. She had read in her spell book that a touch of *grünzueg* would make the whole thing have an even greater impact than the spell alone. She was, after all, a tree fairy, and this was in her wheelhouse. What could go wrong? She touched the wand to the thorny bush where she had cut herself. Take that, you prickly thing! The thistles magically receded. Success!

She went from bush to bush, keeping an eye on the street for anyone who might see her. Nope, the coast was clear. Brutus joined her on the lawn—another small breach in the rules, but she barely noticed him in her thrall.

Thistles off the fence, poof!

Thistles off the tree, poof!

Thistles off the grass, poof!

Thistles off the porch, poof! Oh, this was fun. The yard was shaping up. In her joy, she started to levitate but stopped herself, not wanting to go too far. Soon the yard was tidied within an inch of its life. Take that, Horticultural Committee! she thought, as she sheathed her wand like a pistol. "Let's go inside Brutus. Oh, is this your new friend?"

Brutus went inside, followed by a portly 'possum, and headed for his kibble.

Brooke, Mitzi, a black-eyed and bandaged Dieter, and I joined the rest of our group gathered down the street from our hotel in Cusco. Ekk had arranged transportation for us and put out a short arm to pull me up on the back of a truck filled with bales of hay and a cage full of live chickens. Puddle, the nature lover, was enjoying her perch on a bale of hay, while Elsa had taken out a scarf from somewhere and put it under her bum to shield herself from the prickly stuff. Mitzi's wings had completely retracted, and she called out to Brooke to sit next to her to share the maps. The old wagon groaned as Brooke lifted his heavy frame onto the truck. Dieter gave him a wide berth as he climbed on and sat next to me.

Elsa rapped the window to the cab with her knuckles, and we took off with a jerk. The heavy bales were stacked and tied, swaying with the truck. The rusty truck bed groaned under the weight. It felt to me like we narrowly escaped a panther attack only to be done in riding this contraption, but I digress.

Puddle glanced at Dieter and frowned. "What happened to Dieter?" She studied the rest of us. "Are you guys okay?"

I answered grumpily. "Yes. We're okay, for now." I looked dubiously at the hay. "Where are we going?" I directed this last question to Mitzi, who had announced so confidently that we had somewhere to go.

"You'll see." She opened the window to the cab of the truck, map in hand, and Ekk spoke in Spanish to the driver.

"No need for the map. Our driver knows the way. Everyone, do your best to keep out of sight."

We were all tired, and the late afternoon sun was doing its work on us. The transformation to wings and back must be exhausting for my darling. Soon, I was cradling a sleeping Mitzi and watching my brother glower at Dieter in between watching the road behind us. The truck bounced down a dirt road and took us back into the jungle. Puddle shivered, and I knew it had to be scary for her—as a former captive. I also shared the fear. The jungle was dangerous. I wondered where Juju was and if Juan Luis had made it. This was a strange and dangerous world.

Hours later we were dropped in front of an ancient structure with an inscription in Spanish above the arched door. The tableau was like a ruin before the final pieces had fallen off. Ekk paid the driver who raced away as fast as the old truck would take him.

℘

Black clad nuns spilled out of the opening, and soon we all knew we were at *Hermanas del Hijo*, or "Sisters of the Sun." Sister Lucia Reya warmly hugged Mitzi and hurried us all behind the walls of the old convent.

My wife, uncharacteristically, took the lead. "Sister Lucia, thank you for welcoming us. I'll be honest. This is what we talked about on the plane, and we're in danger. This was the only place I could think of." I had never known Mitzi to show such deference to religious folk and was pleased she had made this connection. I was praying inside that we were in a safe place and kept checking Elsa, our very own energy reader, to see how she reacted.

Sister Lucia came to me and gave me a hug. "I'm glad you're okay. Your wife was very worried." I mooned at Mitzi but then was startled out of my reverie.

The old nun from the plane who had slept next to Mitzi wasn't pleased to see us. "For goodness sakes, come in and out of sight." Her accent was American, and she made no effort to smile. She glanced worriedly at the jungle as she waved us into the convent, as if counting heads.

Inside first, Elsa walked around slowly, taking in the candle holders, portraits on the wall and tapestries. She gave me the "ok" sign and nodded. Did she know what I'd been thinking? That I had wondered if we were in a safe space? These elves of ours, there was so much depth to them. It would take years to really know all they were capable of.

The older nun and Sister Lucia conversed in rapid Spanish. Sister Lucia smoothed the front of her habit and said, "Let's give you a very quick tour, for safety, and then see you to your rooms. I must report to Mother Superior. We can likely hide you here for a few days, but Sister Beatrice," she looked at the one I was coming to think of as the "mean" nun, "is worried about collateral danger for our charges."

As if on cue, several nuns came through, herding a group of children. The noise was happy, if chaotic, a mixture of laughs and admonishments in Spanish. Lucia continued, "One of our missions here is to run an orphanage. The kids are finishing up their studies and are about to be unleashed on the yard." Brooke, who had never married and didn't have kids, had a strange look on his face. He was such a fish out of water here.

Mitzi was flummoxed. "I'm so sorry. I didn't mean to put anyone in danger."

"The children will be fine. We have a duty to protect everyone." She frowned at Sister Beatrice. "Now, let's do the tour so you can escape if needed." Wow, this was a practical nun.

The space was large, if run down. Walls were beautiful but crumbly. Nuns openly stared at our group, and Sister Lucia spoke to them in Spanish. The jewel of the place was a large chapel with a stained-glass window picturing a sun. It faced east, and Lucia explained that the sun poured through in the morning and bathed the worshipers in warm light. Sadly, some of the smaller pieces of colored glass had been broken out.

"Are you a Catholic order?" This was from Puddle.

"Actually, sort of. We are Catholic in the Universal sense, but not Roman. Kind of like Episcopalians, but a South American version." The young woman laughed.

I noticed Brooke was again staring at her and wondered what he was thinking.

When we went outside, the kids were corralled in a space that was mostly dirt. The fence was broken down in places, and the jungle was doing its best to reclaim the space. Sister Lucia commented, "It's a constant battle to keep this place clear of the jungle. We're so far out from the city, we don't get much help."

Brooke finally asked a question. "Who funds you guys?"

"Funds?" Sister Lucia laughed. "Donations, chickens, what we can get from working in the city. We feed ourselves from our own garden."

"You need a patron. If you're a nonprofit, we could probably find some programs and grants."

"Señor Fowler, thank you, but we treasure our independence. If you take money from others, they have a say in how you run things. See those children? They live here for a time and periodically rotate to the city and our other orphanage. They get what they need here and learn about the country and its jungle." She turned to us. "Now, I bet you're all tired. Let's get you to your rooms. Dinner is at six."

After being settled in, I knocked on Ekk and Elsa's door. Elsa was napping. Ekk and I went back to our room. Mitzi, Ekk and I sat on the beds and talked.

"What's next, Ekk?"

Puddle popped out of our bathroom. The tiny cell was now very crowded. "We can't go home yet."

Brooke eased his large frame through the door and leaned against a wall. "And where would your home be anyway, Puddle? India? California?"

Before they could start fighting, I jumped in. "Puddle's right. Dieter said the *Lobos Negro* people were going to do their own ritual and needed the three of us for a sacrifice. They're not going to just give up." I couldn't believe the words that came out of my mouth. I do taxes in California, but here I was talking about the human sacrifice of me and my siblings in another country.

Elsa, done napping, joined us in the cell. "We do need direction. The other side has been too quiet. I'm also worried about the children if they attack us here." Elsa was always one to worry about others.

"True," I commented. We were all quiet. "But thank you, Mitzi, for giving us a resting place." I put my hand over hers. I didn't want her contribution lost in the shuffle.

"Elsa did it, not me. She found out who was flying last minute." She put her arm around the elf with affection, "Thank you, Elsa."

Elsa laughed. "Juju has a connection here, as long as we're giving credit."

A knock came on the door and all our heads swiveled as Mitzi hopped up to open it. Sister Lucia stood there in her black and white habit. She giggled, covering her mouth. I'm sure there had never been this many folk in a small cell before.

"Mother Superior wishes to see you now, before dinner."

Twyla felt pretty full of herself. She was tired after all her spellin' and had taken a nap. Upon awaking, she discovered she was famished. Something was wrong. Her treehouse was tilted. A squirrel appeared in the window and chittered at her.

"What?" Then she became alarmed.

After carefully navigating the rocking floor, she made it to the door and took stock of the treehouse. All the *grünzueg* was gone! As if it had never been there! The cat house was back to its original color, kind of a faded wood, and the green supports had simply vanished, thus the instability. "Uh oh." The squirrel disappeared, laughing its chittery laugh. She frowned at the petty creature's *schadenfreude*.

Not to worry, she thought. Being a tree fairy, Twyla knew how to do proper wood working. She laboriously climbed down the tree and went in search of human tools. Her mind was furiously turning over the facts. She had done the treehouse with green stuff only a few days ago and now it was gone! The potting shed was unlocked, and she squatted down rooting for a hammer and nails in Mitzi's gardening mess. Did that mean magic didn't work here? Or maybe it was only temporary? At that her eyes got very wide. The Thistles! Uh oh, indeed.

Back at the convent, Ekk, Elsa, Mitzi, my siblings and I all shambled down cool tile halls following Sister Lucia. The adobe walls were thick and managed to keep the inside of the convent considerably cooler than outside, a real relief. Dieter was made to wait in a cell, and I noted a formidable sister was posted outside his door. I wouldn't want to cross her. We all knew Dieter may be repentant, but he still was not to be completely trusted. Judging by the guard-nun's wooden cudgel and muscled stance, the skinny German would be wise not to test her resolve.

We were led past the chapel and down a hallway of dark, heavy wooden doors. Each one had the name, I assumed, of a Saint. Sconces with actual flickering oil lamps lighted the way. Santa Sol, Santa Luna, Santa Estrella, and other celestial beings were referenced. I resolved to learn Spanish upon my return to Merryville, if we should be so lucky to resume our normal lives. Mitzi spoke more Spanish than I, enough to be a tour guide. I wondered what she was thinking as she loves to travel. It was easy to think funny, random thoughts. Easier than dealing with what was actually going on. The big door at the end of the hall was open, and Elsa and Ekk were the first to make it through. Nothing could have prepared me for what I saw.

Behind the big desk was an elf in a nun's all white habit. She was so cute I wanted to squeeze her, but her wizened face showed great dignity and made me keep my distance and my mouth shut.

Mother Superior's office was, no surprise, of Spanish design. The mission white walls were supported by dark beams and the furniture was sparse. A small child-sized desk was near a window, and I suspected that's where she mostly did her work. The big desk was probably for formal visits such as ours appeared to be. She had a brown face, her size slightly larger than Elsa, her features delicate. She appeared to be standing on her chair to address us over her desk. Brooke was acclimating and this time did not burst out laughing, his go-to reaction for the unexpected.

"Please sit," she said in heavily accented English. "Sister Lucia Reya has told me why you are here. We must prepare."

Ekk bowed deferentially and indicated Mitzi and I should sit. He stood next to Elsa while Brooke leaned against the wall in the back. Puddle dropped into lotus position on a woven rug. Sister Lucia said something in rapid Spanish, and a younger nun left the room and soon returned with a couple more chairs. They were old and fragile, and I worried they might collapse even under their elven weight. Brooke wisely stayed on his feet. Puddle said she was good where she was.

Ekk took the lead. "Thank you for giving us shelter. Elsa and I are from the Hercynian Garden in the Black Forest of Germany. I understand we have the same enemy."

Mother Superior waited until one of the novices left and closed the door before responding.

"Yes, Sister Lucia told me. In fact, since Lucia returned from the flight where she met Ms. Fowler, we have had several reports of unusual activity near our orphanage. It seems your visit has stirred things up. We want to help but must be mindful of our young charges."

I had to ask, "Are you an—"

Elsa put her hand on my arm in warning. "She is wondering if we're related."

Again with the mind reading.

Mother Superior smiled. "In a sense, yes. I understand Juju has been helping you. He is a *sobrino*, a nephew."

Brooke, Mitzi and I shared a quick glance. Puddle appeared to be meditating.

"Do you know anything about us, about our parents?" This was from Brooke.

"*Poco*. Not much. There are so many who have disappeared chasing the lost city of Paititi. I understand your parents made that unfortunate journey. We live in this jungle, and it has many secrets. Our order is part of the balance of good and evil, obviously working for the good. We teach the children about the sun, moon and stars, and those who are called to learn more join us eventually. Even the smallest child here knows there are treasures of the jungle and forces, dark organizations, who seek to exploit them."

Mitzi and I had taken part in a ritual when a portal was opened in Merryville. We were experts now. These portals were windows between the magical and so-called normal world. They allowed energy, good and evil, to travel from one world to the other. The balance is apparently a very tricky thing to maintain. "Are you talking of the portal?"

The elven nun's eyes opened a wider. Clearly, she didn't expect this.

Sister Lucia jumped in. "She already knows too much about the portal, Lobos Negro, and the *dezplazador de la forma*." Apparently, Lucia had not told her Mother Superior the extent of Mitzi's and her conversation.

The older nun's face barely hid her alarm. "I see."

"I was kidnapped by one," I added. "A *desplazador de*—you know, a shapeshifter. And so was my sister Puddle here. We aren't looking for trouble, really, or even our parents at this point. We're in over our heads."

"I'm still looking for our parents," Puddle said stubbornly. I rolled my eyes.

Mother Superior had the most interesting green-grey eyes and fixed them on us. "My advice is for you to go home as soon as possible."

Puddle shook her head. "Nope." I notice she had lost some of her beads during our recent adventure. Part of her frizz was breaking through.

I was frustrated. It was Puddle who had gotten us in this mess. And now she wasn't ready to leave.

Puddle seemed unperturbed and actually shrugged. "I met this guy in India. His name was Fernando and he was from here, Peru. He said he wanted to help me find my parents or find out what happened to them."

Mother gave her a knowing smile. "He lured you here. Otherwise, you would have stayed in India."

"Yeah, until I met him, this thing that happened, us losing our parents, was just a story. It didn't have any energy to it." She turned to me and Brooke. "Then, amazingly, there was a way, like, a lead to follow. You know?"

My heart softened a bit. I did get it.

"Okay. This is what you're going to do. You all need to go home." Mother Superior's tone brooked no opposition. "Sister, feed them dinner. They will spend the night. But first, show them the way to the airport—safely."

At that Sister Lucia moved behind the big desk and took up a gaff that had been leaning against the wall, using it to lower a huge map of the surrounding area. Mitzi loved maps and stood to inspect it. Lucia handed Mother Superior the pointer.

Before she could speak, Brooke interjected, "I want to find our parents, too." I stared at him like he had two heads. Now both of the Fowler siblings were barking mad in my book.

Mother Superior put the pointer down and said, "You have no idea of what you're up against. We have no way to keep you safe on this journey."

Ekk said, "With all due respect, they do know about the danger. Mitzi was kidnapped by minions of Wolfrum and taken to his castle in Germany—Panda led a successful rescue."

Both nuns swiveled their heads towards me, incredulous, my pudgy self hardly the stuff of lesbian romance novels. "Don't judge a book by its cover," was all I could think to say, and it sounded a bit defensive. Mitzi squeezed my hand.

Mother continued. "There are rituals having to do with the celestial movements of sun, planets and stars. You couldn't possibly understand. Our order has been studying this since before all of you were even thought of. It's not child's play. If things go wrong, everyone is affected." She looked kindly at Puddle and Brooke. "Everyone, even the children." She went on, "The chances of your parents still being alive is so small, and the chance things will go wrong, for all of us, *esta muy grande.*" She picked up the pointer and tapped the glass on a photo taken outside the convent. There must have been fifty kids in the portrait. "Think of the children who have not yet even had a good start in life or—"

This was not going well, and we were all surprised when Elsa spoke up. "Mother Superior, Sister Lucia, there are times when logic doesn't apply. These three," then she corrected herself and pointed at Mitzi, "four, have a mission. Sometimes we simply have to trust. Ekk and I are with them. We were sent here by Ehrenhardt himself, and I think we have to go on." She then smiled her beautiful smile, and I smelled roses in the room, although they would never in a million years grow here in this climate.

Ekk glanced gratefully at his Elsa and picked up where she left off. "There is, I understand, a lost city Paititi, and something there that Wolfrum needs. Panda and Mitzi already have taken part in a Sundog ritual back in California. They can handle this. Since they're here, we need to use the opportunity to make sure Wolfrum, and any other creatures bent on evil, don't gain access to any more power."

The diminutive nun sighed and appeared to relent. "You stay here tonight. We have several of us on guard. I will send for Juju. Our astronomers tell us you will have twenty-four hours to either find Paititi or it disappears again. Either way, you go home, yes?"

This time even Puddle nodded.

ى

CHAPTER SEVENTEEN

As soon as Detective Potts left, Juniper and Valerie turned to each other. Juniper put her hand on Val's shoulder. "What the Fudge, Val? What happened? Did someone break in again?"

Valerie shook her head and closed her eyes. "I don't know. All I know is I came back here to make sure my," she sniffled and opened her moist dark green eyes again and continued "babies were misted. Wait, Twyla would know. She's the one who," Val did air quotes, "fixed them."

Both women walked back to the greenhouse and stood before the now very dead orchids. "There's something off about that fairy. If she did this on purpose, I'll—"

"Oh, you know she didn't. She was trying to help, but she's a hot mess. What am I going to tell the Horticultural Society?"

"Nothing. Flowers die. Let's give them a decent burial." Juniper reached for the rare orchids.

"I can't." Valerie started to cry again.

"I'll do it, baby, go lay down."

Juniper went to the back yard and found a spade. She was unaccustomed to gardening, but this was different. She dug a hole about six inches down and turned the soil over the Rothschild Slipper Orchids, shedding a tear. She went to lie down with Val and hold her.

ى

Bonnie swayed to the music of the New Spirit Revival and dropped her chocolate ice cream on the center of her t-shirt. "Uh oh." She looked at April, who laughed.

"Don't worry about that. Here, take my water." The lovely young blonde handed Bonnie her Arrowhead and a napkin, and Bonnie dabbed at the blob, wetting the entire front of her shirt.

"Here, let me." April took the napkin and removed the spot, perilously close to Bonnie's breast. A warm sensation overcame her.

"I've gotta go." Bonnie blushed and fairly ran from the park. April started after her, but then a handsome young man called to her, and she returned to the bandstand. Bonnie was frantic. She felt awkward and confused. She kept running until she reached the gate to her back yard. She leaned against the wall, trying to catch her breath. Her old dog Chipper snuffled at her through the gate. She sank to the ground and let him lick her ear. She felt like she wanted to die and didn't know why. She was lost in her thoughts and closed her eyes, trying to squeeze in tears, burying her face in Chipper's thick coat.

"Hello, Bonnie, is it?"

She took her face out of Chipper's fur and saw April and the young man standing there seeing her with snot running down her nose. "I'm Adam. Are you okay?" He seemed so nice and held out his hand to her.

She wiped her face and struggled to get up. "Yeah. Sorry about running off there."

"It's okay. The spirit moves people in many different ways." April leaned over the fence and petted Chipper's head. "Who's this guy?"

"Chipper, my dog." She said unnecessarily. All she wanted was for a big hole to open up and swallow her.

The young man wasn't much older than Bonnie and April, but was dressed conservatively in black pants and white shirt. "We're having a prayer meeting tonight. Maybe you'd like to come?" He handed her a flyer.

WE WELCOME ALL, ESPECIALLY THIEVES, LIARS, DRUNKARDS AND HOMOSEXUALS WHO WISH TO TURN THEIR LIVES AROUND. 11:00 A.M. EVERY SUNDAY THROUGH AUGUST.

On it he, or someone, had handwritten: *Prayer meeting every night in the park at 7:00 p.m.*

"We have a bonfire. It's really cool." April smiled as if she really wanted Bonnie to come.

"Okay, maybe I'll see you there."

"Great! Are you sure you're okay? Anything we can do for you?" Adam smiled, but it didn't quite reach his eyes. Bonnie wondered if he and April were a thing.

"No, I'm good. I need to get going, uh, thanks." She fumbled with the gate and her stupid dog kept getting in the way. Would this day never end?

"Okay, I'm looking forward to seeing you!" April called as Adam took her arm and they turned to walk down the alley.

Once inside her house, Bonnie flung herself on the bed with Chipper. She squeezed his furry head so tight he yelped before they found the right cuddle position. She surveyed her room. Her walls had posters of Harry Potter and the Princess Bride. Her old stuffed animals, mostly pink, stared back at her from shelves. She felt like her room was more fitting for a five-year-old than who she was becoming—whoever that was. Why was her world suddenly such a strange place? She wished she was at the museum. Maribel would know what to say.

Daybreak was coming, and Mitzi and I, Ekk, Elsa, Dieter and my brother and sister were all eating oatmeal in the Convent kitchen. Good Peruvian coffee was perking us all up. Our spirits were lifted even further by the arrival of Juju. He was a tough nut, very brown and full of energy. "Friends! We get to meet again!" He gave a rakish smile at Puddle, who grinned. I was introduced to him by my sister. The two seemed to have a special chemistry.

Ekk hugged him. "What happened with Fernando? Did you find Jose Luis?"

Juju's smile dimmed a bit. "Yes, but it was too late. Even jungle magic is not enough to stop a heart attack. I made sure Fernando dug him a deep grave."

"Where is Fernando?" Brooke asked, his expression dark.

"I left him in Cuzco at his parent's shop. He wanted to come, but I told him no."

Brooke nodded. "Do you think he's in contact with Lobos Negro?"

"Not after this. He's hiding out." Juju grabbed toast and dug in. "He doesn't really know anything, anyway."

We were all silent for a moment. Sister Lucia came in and greeted him. "Señor Juju!" She turned to the group. "We're about to have morning prayer. Are you leaving now?"

Dieter had barely eaten but now stood. "I'm ready."

Juju said between bites of toast, "We need to get going—better before it's light."

"Wait." We all turned to see Mother Superior enter the room. When she was not standing on a chair, it was very apparent she was an elf. The nun's habit had been cut down to her size but didn't hang well. Her head piece also was overly large and emphasized her smallness. It was her personality and the way she carried herself that made her large and in charge.

Juju did a courtly bow.

"Nephew, come for a blessing." He went to her and did another little bow. I was amazed to see the jungle savage exhibit such manners.

Elsa closed her eyes and the room smelled faintly of roses. I felt that shift that I was increasingly recognizing as a harbinger of sorts.

Mother Superior belted out in her sweet voice: "May the God of Suns, Moons and Stars bless and keep you all." The nuns in the room and Juju responded, "May you always turn toward the light." Mother turned to leave and a nun standing behind her handed each of them what appeared to be a Hawaiian lei. Instead of pikake, there were orchids, heliconia and even a lily. Elsa's eyes got big, and she smiled hugely.

"These have special properties. We have been praying over them all night.

Don't take them off until you are finished with this journey."

"Oh, ve von't," the excited Elsa said as Lucia placed a ring of flowers around her neck.

"Thank you, Mother Superior," Mitzi and I said almost in unison, as Puddle said something similar. Brooke and Dieter smiled and put on their "leis," but I could tell they treated it more as showing respect to old lady eccentricity than a solemn rite. The same nun that handed out the leis gave us provisions for the journey. There were dried fruits, water and flashlights. We quickly said our thanks and goodbyes.

Once outside, Dieter tried to remove his lei and pack it in his backpack.

Juju said, "Do as she says. These are powerful magic." Elsa nodded vigorously.

Dieter shrugged and put it back on. "I feel like I'm going on vacation in Hawaii."

Mine made my neck tingle. I remembered the feeling I used to get when I wore my magic pendant and hoped these were equally powerful. "Mitzi, do you have your pendant on?"

She lifted the chain from her blouse and nodded. "And the lei. I'm not taking any chances."

Puddle laughed, "We are on vacation." Dieter and Puddle shared a smile, and I thought, uh oh, there she goes again. Brooke shook his head and followed Juju into our uncertain future in the forest. When the convent was nearly invisible through the forest, I caught Brooke taking one last wistful look back.

❦

Things at the museum were in high gear awaiting the opening of "Words on a Plate" on Saturday night. Bonnie arrived in time to catch a dramatic face-off between Linda Chicolet and Juniper. The two stood in front of the exhibit tent, and Juniper was literally blocking her from entering.

"What do you mean I can't go in there? I'm on the board!"

"And I'm Curator. Back off!"

"We'll see about this." With that Linda turned on her heel and stomped off toward the Craftsman house where the administrative offices, including Richland Bruce's office, were located.

As Juniper turned back to enter the exhibition tent, Bonnie wanted to approach her, but Juniper was unapproachable with her red hair practically aflame. Bonnie decided instead to go around the tent to a spot she found a few weeks before that allowed her to see into the tent without being seen. Inside, two of the artists were unloading boxes with new art! She struggled with her duty to tell her uncle Ricky versus her duty to her idol, the Curator. What to do. Maybe she should talk to Maribel.

❧

When Linda got back to the Museum offices, she made a beeline for Richland. She knocked on his door, and he opened it while letting Hortense Miller and another woman out.

"Do keep me posted, Richland!" Hortense said, all smiles. A smaller woman with her clutched her handbag strap with both hands, a large watering can silhouette on her dress pocket.

"Will do, Hortense." Richland beamed "Linda! Come on in."

"Hello, Mrs. Miller. I'm looking forward to seeing your beautiful flowers soon!" A casual observer would have no idea of the argument Linda had been in with Juniper. Everyone was all smiles.

"It's an honor to dress Merryville in roses." Hortense Miller stood holding her Coach satchel which was full of pamphlets.

"And thank you, Miss Sally, you're very generous indeed." This was Richland Bruce at his most charming. He actually bent and kissed her hand. A thick lock of brown hair brushed over his face, and he flipped it back with a toss of the head.

When the ladies had gone, Richland motioned Linda to a wooden chair and then sat, as was his custom, with one butt cheek on the desk and the other connected to his leg touching the floor. He appeared relaxed and in charge. "You seem breathless, Lind. What's up?"

"I don't know. I've gotten several messages from Phillip, that annoying reporter? He's asking about the Words on a Plate show. I went over to the exhibit tent because there were people going in and out, but Juniper Gooden wouldn't let me enter. We need to go over there and find out what's going on. I don't want to read it in the paper first. You weren't here for that Floodlight fiasco. The museum is still reeling from that. You don't know what she's capable of."

"Calm down, Linda, you forget," he held up his keys. "I'll go in tonight and check it out." Then he smirked. "By the way, Auntie Horse Face took enough of our new pamphlets to choke a horse." He laughed at his own unkind joke.

"You're not worried about Juniper?"

He stood and went behind her chair to massage her shoulders. "Nope. Linda, I know what I'm up against. In Cleveland, we were picketed by the Gays every time we had a new exhibit, or the Jews, or somebody. I know how to play this game. Whatever she's doing is a desperate attempt to draw attention to herself."

Linda relaxed, "Ooh, I'll give you twenty minutes to cut that out!" He fixed the tag to her blouse and moved to the window and looked across the expanse of lawn. Indeed, there was stepped up activity at the tent, which was scheduled to open Saturday to a big crowd.

"Don't worry, Linda. I'm giving Juniper all the rope she needs to hang herself."

❦

Valerie had a horticultural meeting to go to and made a point to drive by her friends' house on Thistle Drive. She wanted to see if Twyla had made any progress on the overgrown thistles. It might be time for her to suck it up and hire somebody. The good news was, she and Juniper had received a call from Elsa saying everyone was safe, and, with any luck, they would be home soon.

Truth be told, Valerie was feeling a little irritated. She was the only one in her world, seemingly, who wasn't causing drama, yet she was always getting caught up in other people's. Her own wife contributed Lord knows.

Then there were her friends, Mitzi and Panda. Damn. Now that she was getting into her orchid club, there they were with their damn thistle problem. She made the turn onto Thistle Drive and stopped in shock in front of the Fowler's house. It was pristine. The thistle bushes were so cut back she could barely see them behind the white picket fence. Finally, a change of luck. She got on the phone to talk to Sylvia and raved about the cleanup.

Twyla had come through! Her mood brightened as she gunned it to the Horticultural Society. Take that, Hortense!

❦

IN THE JUNGLE

The panther paced back and forth on the big sunlit rock. She was joined by another beautiful feline, and quickly they morphed into human women. Both of them were naked. Julia, the slightly older, larger woman growled, "Maria lost them at the hotel."

"I should never have sent her to retrieve the three sacrifices in Cuzco," Angela said. The ersatz yoga teacher hung her head in shame.

"That was bad, Angel, but Dieter betrayed us by helping them escape. For that he will die."

Angela put her hands on her hips. "I'm getting sick of all this running around and kidnapping. By the way, for what? For some . . . *man* six thousand miles away giving orders."

Julia's eyes darkened dangerously. "Don't talk like that. Someone will hear you. We need his protection."

"Do we? I mean, really. Do we?"

Julia turned toward the jungle and gestured. "We have a truce for the first time among all those who hunt us. Do you want to be killed in your sleep? Now that the legend of the *Dezplazador de la formas* is out, young men want to be the one who killed the mighty panther! We're finally in a place where we can build our own kingdom and live in peace. It's a compromise to be sure, but I'm getting old, Angela. This is a better way."

Angela moved to put her arm around Julia. "I'm sorry, it won't happen again."

Julia pushed her away. "The jungle has eyes. You know how *Lobos Negros* thinks about women who don't want men. Come, the portal will close soon, and Wolfrum will not stand for failure." Julia whistled and pygmies came from seemingly nowhere, bearing their human clothing. The men were surly interacting with the women, and Angela snarled at them. Only Julia and Angela's ability to transform into creatures with claw and fang made them obey.

"If we called the Amazons, this wouldn't even be an issue," Angela commented as she pulled on her blouse.

"Angela, your mouth is going to get us killed. *Callate la boca.* Shut up. Besides, the Amazons would never work with them."

Angela sighed and snapped on Panda's stolen Fitbit. "At least they haven't sold their souls. All right. We have the maps, or at least the map we need to find the portal before it moves again. Let's go."

As the rain forest does, the sky cracked open and a deluge drenched the two women and their entourage. Julia hoped they had chosen the right side. Things had not gone too well so far.

Angela fell in line behind Julia and the troop trudged toward their destiny as far flung allies of *Lobos Negro*, distant mercenaries for the Wolf Raven cult.

☙

DESTINATION: PAITITI

The day had been stressful and hot. The tension was high as my brother, the human alpha male, vied to show he was as useful as the elves, an impossible task under any circumstance. Puddle was out of pot and everyone was tired, so we finally stopped for our evening meal. We all knew there was no time to set up camp and have a proper rest, but Mitzi and I held each other and closed our eyes for a minute.

I must have dozed off and opened my eyes to loud male voices arguing. Elsa and Juju ran to the jungle edge with Mitzi where Dieter and Brooke were having a tête-à-tête over how to read the map. "Put that thing away," Juju said breathlessly. "We don't need it."

Brooke flicked the paper in irritation. "Um, I'm in awe of your jungle tracking skills, Juju, but we need to find this portal thing fast. I'm a New Yorker. We ask for directions."

"No, you don't need to ask," Juju said, chest puffing.

Elsa took a deep breath and bellowed, "Boys." She cleared her throat. "Tell them, Mitzi."

She did. "After Panda was kidnapped, Twyla told me she put *grünzueg* on her Fitbit."

Brooke was confused. "Whose Fitbit?"

I jumped in, shaking off my fatigue. "Mine! I was wearing it when that yoga bitch kidnapped me and then she stole it."

"She stole your Fitbit? Wait, *grünzueg*? Whoever this Twyla is, she's a genius. Let's go!" Dieter turned toward the jungle path.

"Hold up, I'm not following." Brooke was obstinate. "What are you saying?" He turned to Ekk and me. "Why didn't you tell us before?"

Ekk explained, "We magical creatures have a link to our home country, the Hercynian Garden, through this *grünzueg* or green stuff, actually—we use it to build and do certain low-level magic tasks."

Brooke kept his arms crossed.

"Think of duct tape, but it has even more uses." Ekk's patience always amazed me. "And, I didn't feel it near before now. Mitzi reminded me about Twyla putting the *grünzueg* on the watch thingy and then I felt it."

"My Fitbit!" I shouted.

Brooke still didn't follow.

Ekk continued. "Now that we're close enough, it means we can easily track the Panther yoga lady to wherever she is, and where she is—is going to be where the portal is."

All of us waited while Brooke processed this information. He tucked the map in his back pocket and said, as if we were the ones holding things up, "Well, let's go then."

We dusted ourselves off, and soon Ekk and Juju led our pack, followed closely by Dieter, Puddle, Mitzi, Elsa and me pulling up the rear with Brooke. My brother wasn't totally comfortable with me and Mitzi's relationship, but I saw an "aha" in his eyes. I had no time to analyze if his attitude was really changing, but I had a feeling we would all be different after this adventure.

I noticed Puddle was un-raveling her hair as we went, dropping colorful beads here and there as we walked along. When she saw me noticing, she smiled and said, "I'm doing my part."

I remembered the story our parents read us and commented, "Hansel and Gretel?"

Dieter turned around and said, "Good German band that."

"New York. They're from New York." Brooke said harshly.

"Sorry, my bad." Dieter was being deferential to Brooke after the black eye my brother had given him.

Puddle laughed girlishly and grabbed Dieter's arm. I wondered what was happening between those two.

She replied to Dieter, "Not the band, that's Hanzel und G R E T Y L, spelled differently. Too dark for me. I'm dropping bread crumbs like the kids did in that story." We all smiled at her. Puddle operated on a different bandwave than the rest of us.

Ekk smiled. "Ah, then it's a good Danish children's tale. The Brothers Grimm, much better than some band."

The air was hot and wet, even with a tall canopy of green to protect us from the late afternoon sun. Juju made markings on the map as we went, hopefully marking our return, although he joked we had the beads if needed. The merriment was needed and all too short lived as I had no idea what to expect when we reached our rendezvous.

CHAPTER EIGHTEEN

Back in Germany, Wolfrum sat silently in the garden with his sister, Odilia.

She spoke after a full minute. "Have you heard from ground forces in Peru?"

Wolfrum sat there, with a thousand-mile stare on his white, drawn face. "I have. There is no more time. Julia and her pathetic panthers have failed to hold on to the three sacrifices."

"Oh, brother! I'm so sorry. Shall I make the usual preparations for the ritual?"

He turned to Odilia and asked an uncharacteristically honest question. "How is it these queer people have so much power? Their blood is corrupt and only holds a small amount of magic. And Dieter too."

"You have their pendant. And the relics of Paititi will soon be yours."

Wolfrum's eyes were hard. "The pendant is a fake."

Odilia was nervous and her old voice waivered. "But this mission, in Peru. Surely this will fix things."

He continued speaking as if he hadn't even heard her. "I let myself be swayed by a traitor. I treated Dieter like a son, took him in when he had no one."

"I know, brother, your mercy is great." Odilia was trying to understand.

He stood. "Now I hear Dieter has betrayed us." He looked through Odilia, furious. "For this he will die." His eyes narrowed. "This is what happens when our faith is corrupted by weak men and women in trusted positions! At least I have a new man where those women live in the other world. California."

"Wolfrum." Odilia was alarmed, never having seen her brother so upset. She felt the garden around them start to tremble. The pond nearby sloshed and a few faces in monk hoods peered out windows.

When he opened his mouth next, his voice came out in sepulchral tones, as if an amplifier had been inserted in his vocal cords. She knew he was speaking magically beyond the castle. He lifted his staff and shouted, seemingly to the trees, "Portal Open!"

Odilia jumped to her feet, was he crazy? "This is not the way!"

He turned to her, eyes a glowing red, not fully human. "Silence." With one flick of his wrist she was flung backwards and fell over the bench. Odilia felt something snap as she hit a tree trunk.

Monks came streaming out of the castle and formed a circle around Wolfrum. They were nothing if not loyal. The chant began.

"Wolves are always followed by Ravens"

"Scavenging for the Kill"

"Eat fast ravening Wolf"

"Ravens follow five and twenty"

"Cleansing the world of unworthy prey"

"Taking out the weak"

"Consuming the meek"

"Wolf Raven Cycles this world to the next"

ॐ

Instantly, across the world, Mitzi was the first to notice. "Oh, my God, the ravens! Look!"

As our motley trail of trekkers looked up, seemingly thousands of ravens descended upon us. Several things happened at once. Elsa became still and closed her eyes. Dieter's eyes went wide in terror and he threw his body over Puddle. Brooke picked up a fallen limb and waved it at the hordes of black bodies pelting us. I instinctively turned toward Mitzi, who was rapidly growing wings. Juju pulled a dagger from its sheath and jumped on a fallen log to gain more height. Ekk shouted, "Don't let them stop us, we're almost there!" Then to me, "Let Mitzi handle this!"

I felt helpless as my wife took flight. The awesome experience of seeing her muscular wings unfold still stunned me, aaaaaand there went another blouse. Thank God she had on a sports bra. Ekk put his arm around Elsa and urged her along, muttering something to her in German I couldn't understand. I went to Dieter and Puddle and urged them to keep moving. Puddle was crying.

Up ahead about fifty feet, a portal was opening. We had participated in a Sundog Ritual back in Merryville, so, oddly, I did have experience with this sort of thing. This phenomenon was supposed to be the entry to Paititi, and the timing was critical. Mitzi's wing expansion and quick ascension momentarily disrupted the birds and gave us the cover we needed to surge toward the focus of jungle activity.

The air thickened then, and as we drew closer to the portal it was as if a great wind was blowing to keep us away. The air turned cold and froze the sweat on my arms. The moon was clear and had a ring around it, making it similar to a target in the night sky. The last and only such ritual I had experienced was nothing like this. Where was Ehrenhardt and the Hercynian Forest? It felt chaotic and dangerous.

I saw two women, surrounded by short indigenous people, standing right inside the edge of the portal. Were these indigenous people the "pygmies" referred to by everyone? Were they Wolf Raven or Lobos Negro? If so, we needed an army. Mitzi flew directly into the portal, now chased by hundreds of ravens. She was so brave. I ran after her toward the chaos on this seeming suicide mission, yelling "Mitzi!"

Denise McGreggor surveyed the old McGreggor mansion. Since her mother had died, she felt safe returning from abroad, where she'd lived summers in Scotland and winters in the South of France with her then new girlfriend. Merryville movers were busy unloading pieces of furniture she'd shipped half way around the world. Denise's wife, Bridget, popped out of the parlor and back into the great room. "*Magnifique!*"

Denise instructed her major domo, Fergus, to handle the move while she lifted Bridget's chin and gave her a kiss. "This is ours, my love. Welcome to California."

The two stood, watching the busy crew at work. "Come, let me show you around." Denise took Bridget by the hand, and they walked through the dining room hall with its many windows overlooking the garden and then out to the garden.

"Ohhh, beautiful."

"Yes, my mother put her heart and soul into the garden. I've had it kept up while away." A tear collected in the corner of her eye.

"This makes you sad, no?" Bridget's beautiful face scrunched in worry.

"A bit. Agnes, mommy dearest, loved her garden. More than me at times. I haven't been here since, well, since we fought. I always hoped we could reconcile before she died. She would have loved you."

Bridget faced her squarely. "But no more sadness. That's not the way this is going to be. We shall make it ours."

"The house, absolutely." Denise smiled mysteriously. "The garden, well, I do need to make an appearance at mummy's horticultural society. I've already been given a legacy membership!"

Bridget laughed and picked up a cutting from the damp walkway. Denise mused, she was so beautiful.

The two women walked back into their new home and thought about new beginnings.

Juniper was worried. She didn't know who broke into their house and threatened them. On top of that, Linda and Richland were up to something, and she still had an art show to put on. There was only one magical creature she knew, and this idea would not leave her alone. Juniper got into her Citroen and drove over to Panda and Mitzi's place, hoping to find Twyla. As far as she knew, Twyla didn't have a cell phone, and she certainly wasn't answering Mitzi and Panda's house phone.

On the way, she went to pick up Valerie but found she had already left for her garden club. Damn. Things felt existential and she wanted answers. Why did the Rothchild's Slippers die? Why was everybody being kidnapped? Who had threatened them? She felt powerless and didn't like it at all. If they were all together in Merryville, somehow her strange family of choice would work it out. Panda would be praying, Mitzi would get busy with travel to distract herself, and Valerie would be making them all a cup of tea. Juniper was alone and needed some solid info.

As she pulled into the driveway on Thistle drive, she gave a low whistle. The house had never looked so good. The normally unruly thistles that had gotten her friends in so much hot water were all trimmed back to practically nothing. Well done, little fairy, she thought, but you still have some answering to do about the orchids.

Juniper marched up to the front door. When Twyla didn't answer her knock and the Scotland the Brave doorbell, she went around to the yard, remembering the tree fairy had moved into the new treehouse.

"Twyla!"

She caught Twyla coming out of the Fowler's shed, loaded down with tools. "Um, hi, Ms. Gooden." Her face was red and swollen as if she'd been crying.

"What's the matter, dear? I hope this isn't a bad time. Oh, by the way, the front yard is stunning!" She took in the back yard. Juniper was wearing a white suit and staring at all the dirt piles. "Is there a place we can sit down?"

"I ahh, need to get gardening and do some repair on my house."

"Well, the front garden has never been tidier." Juniper looked up and saw the treehouse was tilted. "What happened to that?"

Twyla dropped her tools and burst into tears. "The *grünzueg*— it doesn't work here like it did in the Hercynian Forest! Or, it did at first, but no more."

"Oh? Well, that explains the orchids. I'm afraid they're quite dead."

Twyla's wet face jerked up. "Oh, no! The orchids, too? I'm so sorry. Maybe I can fix it. I—" Tears streamed down her slender face.

Juniper did something close to jazz hands. With her thin fingers and decorated nails, it was quite dramatic. "No more fixing! Not 'til we find out what's what. I have questions." The distraught expression on Twyla's face made her soften her tone. "Come here, Twyla. Let's go get a drink of something and talk a minute." Juniper put her arm around Twyla and led her to the sliding glass door. "Tell me what happened."

Twyla went into the kitchen, got a glass of water, and sat down at the kitchenette. Between gulping for air, sipping water and crying, she got her story out. "I know I'm not supposed to use magic. That's the last thing Ekk and Mitzi said to me, but Valerie was so sad. I thought it was fine, but then I woke up and my house was broken. I was getting ready to fix it when you arrived. Ekk sent a raven, and I got a message that Panda and Mitzi are coming back." Her eyes widened at this. "They're going to kill me."

"I know what you did, but what about this green stuff? Did you get a bad batch? The front yard is beautiful."

This made Twyla cry harder.

"Deep breath, Twyla. What?"

She hiccupped. "If the orchids and my treehouse . . ."

Brutus came in and swirled around her feet. "Meow."

Twyla cocked her head at Brutus as if he'd said something she could understand. "*Ach Nein*, the front yard!" With those words, she dashed to the front door with Juniper following. She swung open the front door only to find the yard returned to its former overgrown self that, if anything, was worse than before.

"Oh, nooo!" She put her hands on both sides of her face, reminding Juniper of *The Scream* by Edvard Munch. Juniper peered over her head and gave a deep sigh. She pulled out her cell phone and left a message for Maribel that she would be late. She rolled up her sleeves. "Doesn't Panda have a t-shirt somewhere I could put on?"

 ❧

CHAPTER NINETEEN

PAITITI

Time was suspended and then seemed to go forward in slow motion as I entered the portal. Instead of an orderly entry, like previously when Ekk had us standing on certain directional points, all was chaos.

Through the portal I saw a village, but it was miragelike and wouldn't come into focus. There were people there, waving. I tried to wave back but the wind was so strong.

I scanned the sky for Mitzi and instead saw an image of Wolfrum, somehow ported in from thousands of miles away in Germany. I saw Mitzi then, battling a host of flying ravens by flapping her powerful wings and disrupting them. Brooke's face wore a stunned expression as he grabbed Puddle while making his way to me. I heard one of the panther-women yell, "Get them!" and felt great fear as they morphed into fearsome panthers and sprang at us. As if this weren't enough, the small warriors, I guessed they were the pygmies, came running our way also, spears at the ready. We were going to die.

Ekk and Elsa made their way to us through the maelstrom and once together, we did a tight group hug. Juju and Dieter were doing their best to protect us, but only had sticks and rocks they had picked up from the ground. It was hard to hear with the celestial wind blowing, but Ekk and Elsa appeared to be chanting and praying. Ekk stopped briefly to tell us all to touch our necklaces given to us by Mother Superior. We didn't need to be asked twice. No one had time to think. I squeezed mine and said my own prayers.

"Look!" Juju pointed at Mitzi. The ravens had left, and she was floating on an air or energy current. She reached out her arms and appeared to be speaking to someone, or something, but there was no one there. The village image came into focus, then blurred into nonexistence.

Chanting of another kind, the Wolf Raven chant, bounced off the contours of whatever force held together the portal to Paititi. Then the shift happened. It was as if all that had come before was trying to tune into a radio station.

Ehrenhardt's voice called out clearly, "You have broken our treaty! The balance was set at the last Sundog—for the sake of the world, you must stop this now. It's too much for the non-magical world to take—it's ripping the fabric of time and place! You know this!"

Wolfrum shouted back, "You come late to this ritual. Treaties are for fools! But you are here in time to watch your favorite pets die and bow down to the one true power, you filthy abomination!"

The ground shook, and Ehrenhardt tried once more. "I see you recruit women for this mission. Isn't that a breach of your religion? Are you admitting you need females to fight for you? Who is the abomination now, Wolfrum?"

At this point, I thought: is now really the time for a theological argument? I said out loud, "What the hell, Ekk?"

Ekk held us tighter and kept up the strange guttural chant he and Elsa were doing. I could sense Elsa was working her magic, but every time I smelled a floral scent the weird wind would whip it away. My feet felt the vibrations in the earth, as if a great hole were about to be rend in the surface. A palm tree crashed to the ground, narrowly missing us.

Whatever Ehrenhardt meant to do with his words, he only enraged Wolfrum further. "These women are not important. They're ants in the eternal struggle, and even these lowly and unworthy creatures revere the one true religion. Like Christ said, if every voice were silent the rocks would cry out! I am the power! You are finished and so is your corruption. We are changing the world." Then he laughed his evil laugh. "Merryville is already mine."

I tried to keep my eyes on Mitzi, but there was so much to see and hear and wonder about. Those words stopped me: *Merryville is already mine?* I fiercely wanted to go home. The ravens had fled, and Mitzi now turned her attention to the spear wielding attackers. She swooped down and actually carried one off into the jungle and dropped him into a nearby body of water. It may have seemed more humane to her than killing them, but this was a numbers game. For everyone that she picked up, there were three more on the ground.

Juju and Dieter were fighting valiantly but couldn't hold them off forever. Juju picked up a shield dropped by one of the pygmies and used it to stop the spears. There were already three sticking out of the shield, and I'm sure it was getting too heavy to hold.

One of the panthers turned back into a woman. Naked, she roared at the deities in the sky, "Ants? You think we're ants? Find your own way to Paititi!"

Immediately, the larger panther turned back into her naked self and screamed, "Angel, do you know what you've done?" The woman had fear on her face as she appealed to the younger woman.

Angel yelled back, "Yes, we're stopping this alliance right now. Hey, Wolfrum, let me show you what a pissed off lowly ant can do, you *mujer odia!*" And with that, she turned back to a panther and pounced on the pygmies. The older woman followed suit, morphed back into a panther, and soon made short work of those nearest us. After a few eviscerations, the rest of the army fled into the jungle. Mitzi slowly lowered to the ground, and the wind returned to a normal breeze. I saw no trace of Wolfrum, Ehrenhardt, Paititi, or any heavenly voices. The night sky was again filled with stars and moon.

The panthers stood for a moment at the edge of the battlefield, yellow eyes fixed on us, then shot into the forest.

Alone, we collapsed in a heap on the jungle floor. Mitzi made her way to me, and I held her as her wings retracted. Her hair was settling down, but mine was standing on end with static electricity. She smoothed it down but did not speak. "Are you okay? Who were you talking to up there?"

Mitzi peered deep into my eyes, gasped for breath, and said, "Please give me a minute."

Ekk shook his head. "We found it, but now it's over. The portal closed. It was all wrong." Elsa continued her prayer/chant, eyes closed.

Dieter appeared dumbfounded and said to no one in particular, "It was real."

Brooke was pale and shaken and kept looking up at the sky, then at Mitzi. Nothing in his frame of reference had prepared him for this. At least Mitzi and I had been through a Sundog ritual before.

Speaking of Mitzi, I pulled her closer and asked again. "You were talking to someone up there. Was it Ehrenhardt?"

She shook her head and whispered, "not now."

Juju breathed heavily. He'd taken a hit and blood trickled down his arm and dripped to the ground, but that tough little nut laughed. "Did you hear her? *Mujer odia*, woman hater!'

Puddle got the canteen and went to him. "I saw it! I saw Paititi! Man, can we figure out where it went?"

Dieter didn't look so great, either. He still sported the bloody rag around his earlier panther injury and was rather pale. "No, the location is lost again. Maybe for the best."

"What just happened?" Brooke sounded confused.

"This was a portal opening," Ekk said. "Very rare and few humans have ever witnessed it. We almost got to the lost village of Paititi, but there was too much bad energy. Puddle and Mitzi took part in a portal opening that was like a walk in the park compared to this. Something must have gone wrong. Nothing was accomplished except to put the entire magical/ non-magical world at risk of implosion. Wolfrum must be desperate. Thank God we had these. He lifted his lei and let it fall onto his chest."

"Oh, something happened all right." Dieter smiled. "He was betrayed not only by me, but by those *Dezplazador de la formas*, the panther women. I guess he found out the depth of their loyalty wasn't so much."

"Why did the panthers leave?" Brooke asked. "They went away! Did you see that?" He gazed at the jungle where the two frightening beasts entered the almost impenetrable green.

Mitzi walked to Brooke and put her hand on his back. He was so tall she had to bend her head back to address him. "I guess this was no longer their fight. It was a stupid mistake for Wolfrum to call them lowly unworthy creatures."

Elsa smiled. "Yes, I think we witnessed Wolfrum lose his hold over this area."

Juju laughed heartily. "Yeah, and jungle chicks don't like being called ants!" Everyone laughed but Dieter, who threw a broken spear from their path. "He's not finished yet. Don't underestimate him."

I added, "Yeah, did you hear him say he had Merryville?"

The Merryville Museum was closed. The last of the cleaning crew locked the door and loaded their van. Richland Bruce smiled as he pulled back into the parking lot, ready to see what Juniper was up to with her "Words on a Plate" nonsense. He wore all black, a nod to the dramatic, even though as a board member he had a perfect right to go to the museum at any time. He had keys.

His BMW nosed into Juniper's reserved space, and this made him giggle. It would be his soon enough. The grass was wet as he made his way across the green expanse toward the exhibit tent, new trifold brochures in his man purse. A banner announced, "This Saturday, WORDS ON A PLATE." He shook his head and thought Juniper Gooden would sink on her own without any help from him, but the trifolds he would swap out would nail the coffin shut. Words on a plate, indeed. Even so, he was always one to remove risk.

Richland reached into his pocket for keys, but was startled when a gravelly voice said, "Hold it right there." He almost peed his pants. His head jerked up and he saw an overweight, older man in a crumpled suit. It was dark, but the man soon lit a cigarette.

"What are you doing here! This is private property. I'm—"

"I know who you are."

The man's quiet certainty rattled him. "You need to leave. I don't know who you think you are but —"

The older man flipped open his wallet, clearly showing a shield. "Potts. Detective Potts of the Merryville P.D. What are you doing here at," he checked the watch on his meaty wrist, "eleven-thirty p.m. after the museum is closed?"

"None of your business! I don't have to explain myself, I'm the Curator—I mean, the acting Board Chair. Now if you'll excuse me." Richland put the key in the lock, his hands shaking.

"You grew up here, didn't you? I've been doing a little research. You see, some friends of mine were left a note that was rather threatening. You wouldn't know anything about that would you?"

Richland pulled a cell phone from his pocket. "I'm calling 9-1-1. You're threatening me!" The lock opened, and the slender man slipped inside and zipped the door closed behind him. "Hello, Merryville P.D.?"

"Goodnight, Mister Bruce, glad you're okay." Potts said loudly through the tent. He heard the hysterical man complaining to the emergency operator and demanding a black and white be sent. Potts got in his Chrysler 300 and pulled from the parking lot toward home, smiling.

Behind the closed and locked exhibit door, Richland's heart was beating hard. After making the call, for which he now felt stupid, his original mission still lay before him. He switched on the regular light and saw the same tables as before.

Richland walked around, seeking to find out what Juniper's mysterious behavior was all about in trying to keep Linda out. The big tent light was at the other end of the hall. He picked up trifold brochures as he went along, replacing them with the ones in his bag.

He came to the end of the first row and nearly had a heart attack when Damien stepped in front of him from the shadows and said, "Boo!"

"Jesus, Damien! What are you doing here?" Damien was dressed in his usual artist togs, black on black.

"I could ask you the same question. Nice outfit, by the way."

Since stealth was no longer an issue, Richland walked to the light switch by the back wall and flipped it on. "Oh. My. Gawd."

The "Words on a Plate" exhibit was still there, but greatly enhanced. Now there were enormous artifacts dangling from the ceiling, creating the effect of an upside-down dining hall, complete with papier-mâché family. They were conservative tropes, stilted, except for the centerpiece, a platter serving up a colorful headless elephant. Richland made a sound that died in his throat. Penelope had been given free reign also, and some of her plates leaned toward mocking religion.

"Oh, don't clutch your pearls, princess, this is art." Damien slung his own bag over his shoulder. "I remember when you used to know what that was. Hey, what's in the bag?"

"You can't talk to me that way!" Richland pulled himself up to his full five-feet, eight-inches and actually tossed his hair. "And this isn't art—this is perversion! Merryville will not stand for this. Why, a decapitated animal at dinner? It's . . . it's ugly."

Damien put his hands on Richland's shoulders and tried to make the man stay still and look at him. "It's the proverbial elephant in the living room. Which brings me to you and me. Don't you find the symbolism ironic?"

"Get out. I can have you thrown out. I," he sputtered his words, "and you know I'm not gay anymore."

"I know who you've reinvented yourself to be, sweetheart, but you're still little Ricky to me." Damien, all in black, appeared completely relaxed. "What's in your bag?"

"That was a long time ago, Damien. You have no right! Why I—"

Damien put his finger to Richland's lips, their bodies close. With his other hand, Damien picked up a trifold and shook it open to read. "Why, you slimy son of a bitch!"

Richland shouted, "Give me that!" In a panic, he shoved Damien with both hands. He fell backwards, hitting his head on the edge of a table. Ironically, the plate that said "You can't hide" flipped off the table and smashed. Blood went everywhere. Richland stood there, transfixed in horror. A rap on the door snapped him out of it. "Police! Open up! We got a 9-1-1 call."

❧

Back in the jungles of Peru, our group made a bee line for the city. With the portal closed, there was no longer any need to stay. Juju was in the lead, with the lanky Dieter pumping his legs to keep up with the agile elf. Puddle joyfully pointed out a bead on the jungle floor each time she saw one, which made us all laugh. She painstakingly picked them up and put them in her pocket as we went along. We finally had to stop and catch our breath.

"All I want is to hold Brutus." Mitzi said.

I leaned against a rock to shake out my shoe. "I want our normal life back. Babs at the tax office must be ready to send out a search posse." I gazed at my brother, who'd been strangely quiet. "Brooke, what's going to happen with you?"

He knelt on the ground and rearranged his backpack. "I guess I'll call my firm and see if I still have a job."

I'd never seen Brooke humbled. This was new.

Ekk took over, "Mitzi, can you make arrangements to get us all home?"

"Absolutely." She grinned. "I'm loving these air miles."

It warmed my heart to hear Mitzi speak of the mundane. She was herself again.

"We can spend the night at the convent before heading out tomorrow." Elsa said. "We all need showers and rest." With that we moved back toward the convent as silently as we could, not wanting to tempt the luck we had against hostile forces.

∿

HORTICULTURAL SOCIETY MEETING

It was Friday, the day before the *Words on a Plate* exhibit was to open. Juniper arrived late and picked up a program at the front table. She headed toward Valerie, who smiled and gave hugs to her new group. Juniper took the time to attend with Valerie because this was a special occasion. This showed a lot of love, given this was also Juniper's big weekend.

Hortense rapped her gavel and called the Merryville Horticultural Society Meeting to order. The crowd was more boisterous than usual. Everyone loved to see new members inducted. Hortense was in, well, full Hortense mode, holding court at the front table. Sylvia, Lidia, Flo and Sally were nearby, as usual. Janet was out in front of the building greeting people distractedly, scanning the crowd for someone. Hortense's husband, Bill, was there and appeared to be sober, but it was still early. He nodded at the women as they filed in and acted as a sort of usher, handing out programs. Valerie wondered where Janet's daughter Bonnie was. Handing out programs was usually her job.

Seated near the front was the new celebrity joining the Merryville Mavens, the legacy member, Denise McGreggor. Everything about her said High Society. Valerie had heard a hundred times how wonderful her mother, Agnes, had been. Denise was dressed in a frilly colorful summer dress and had a gorgeous woman with an updo sitting next to her, probably another prospective member. Valerie inwardly compared herself to the woman, newly returned from Europe, and felt diminished. This wasn't helped when Juniper said, "Why does it say provisional next to your name?"

Valerie snapped her head over to look. "What?" Sure enough, the names of the two members being inducted were Denise McGreggor and Valerie Gooden, with *Provisional* typed neatly to the side of her name. She immediately searched for Sylvia who met her eyes and shrugged as the meeting started. They would definitely talk about this later. Valerie had to shush Juniper when she said, "Richland Bruce, Keynote Speaker?" as Hortense rapped her gavel again.

"Welcome, Welcome, Welcome to the Installation meeting of the Merryville Horticultural Society!" Hortense beamed. "Today we have a special treat! A field trip! Bill?"

Valerie and Juniper hadn't noticed Hortense's' husband Bill leaving, but now a loud honk made all their heads swivel. Hortense clapped her hands. "Ladies! We're going on a garden tour!" Excited voices talked over each other as Janet returned and said, "Everyone on the bus!" She then went to the corner and got on her cell phone. Something was up. What about the keynote speaker?

Sylvia ran up to Valerie and said, "I didn't have time to call you. Hortense added this tour just now. We've had a change in the program. I hoped you'd get here earlier." She looked meaningfully at Juniper.

"My fault. It's the day before Words on a Plate is revealed. People kept calling." Juniper looked contrite. She didn't offer that the most important call had been from Panda and Mitzi, who were on their way home from Peru. "What's going on, dear?"

"At the last minute our speaker, Richland Bruce, canceled." Sylvia said. "He was to announce some special thing with the museum." Juniper's eyebrows raised. "I guess he didn't show. I'm not even sure he called. Janet's been worried. Hortense said she'd promised everyone something special, so she got Lidia to call the school and get the bus at the last minute." She grinned at Valerie. "We're going to drive to see your Rothschilds. Isn't that great? Then visit some other Horticultural places of interest before coming back here for the installation."

Charlotte Windingle, who loved surprises, said loudly, "Let's get on the bus. Come on, Denise!"

The newly arrived blue blood took her friend's hand and they made their way to the street, regular members falling in line like lemmings.

The blood drained from Valerie's face. "No, this is not great. Sylvia, you can't—" She was about to explain what happened to the orchids when Janet screamed and dropped her phone. Bill, who was oblivious, kept honking the bus horn as some of the women were still milling around in front. Hortense came back in the meeting room to see what the fuss was about.

Hortense scowled as if Janet screamed only to inconvenience her. "Janet, we need to go."

"It's her brother," Lidia said, and then fanned Janet with a program.

Hortense moved in close, "What happened?"

"Not with her here." Janet pointed a pudgy finger at Juniper.

"Moi?" Juniper was the picture of innocence. "Okay, fine. But our house is off limits. You didn't ask first and—"

Valerie stepped in front of her. "Someone destroyed the Rothschilds."

Hortense gasped. She may not like lesbians particularly, but she loved those flowers. "What happened!" Then to the room, "Will somebody tell me what the hell is going on?" Another honk from outside made Hortense yell, "Stop honking, Bill!" Then, "Sylvia, Lidia, Sally, go ahead with the bus tour. We have some things to straighten out."

Lidia looked reluctant and sat next to Janet. "I'm staying."

"I can see this is a family matter," Valerie said, "and it might be a good idea if we go home. By the way, where else is the bus going?"

Hortense looked somewhat crumpled. "To the tidied-up houses by the tire factory and then by the house on Thistle Drive."

Valerie said, "That's great!" At the same time Juniper said, "Not a good idea."

Juniper had arrived home earlier, dirty and disheveled. They didn't have time to talk about her visit with Twyla while she showered and threw on clean clothes.

"Glad to hear it," Hortense said. "Now, if you'll excuse us, I need to see if Janet's all right."

Juniper led Valerie out the front door and almost ran smack into Bonnie, Janet's daughter. "Is my mom still here?"

"Yes, dear. What happened? Is everything okay?"

"Yes, I mean no. Uncle Ricky's missing!"

Juniper gave Valerie a look and then said to Bonnie, "Go inside darling. Take care of your mom."

Bonnie hesitated, "Can I bring a friend to the opening tomorrow?"

"Of course, child, and let me know if there's anything we can do." Valerie and Juniper walked to the Citroen trying to process this information.

"Call Potts," Juniper whispered. Juniper was behind the wheel as Valerie dialed their detective friend to get the scoop.

Valerie put her hand over the speaker, "I have to leave a message. What was that all about, saying: not a good idea."

Juniper said, "You know what, let the damn bus go to the Fowler's house. It's not perfect, but it will have to do. The same thing happened to the yard as happened to your orchids."

"Oh, no! Is that where you've been?"

Juniper pulled up her sleeve to reveal thin red scratches. "Panda and Mitzi owe us big time."

Valerie put her hand on Juniper's shoulder. "I love you so much."

With a gleam in her eye, Juniper said, "Now call Phillip! Maybe he knows what's going on with Mister Bruce."

CHAPTER TWENTY

The plane ride back to Merryville took ages and two Ubers to return Ekk, Elsa, Brooke, me, Mitzi, and Puddle back to our house. We were all tired and sad to have left Juju and Dieter behind in Peru.

When we pulled into the driveway, Mitzi exclaimed, "Wow! What happened to our yard?" The bushes were cut back, but still a little funky, well, a lot funky. All the lights were on. Twyla opened the door and ran out to help with our luggage.

I looked at Mitzi, setting my lips in a firm line. "I don't know what the heck happened, but I know who we can ask."

We all piled into the house, which was fairly tidy. "Welcome to Casa Fowler," Mitzi said to Brooke. I couldn't remember the last time he was there. Brooke avoided her eyes and said he needed to lay down until dinner. Brutus tried to ignore us for leaving him, but that didn't last but a half a minute. Puddle sat on the hearth of the fireplace, and he eagerly climbed onto her lap to be petted.

Ekk and Elsa went into the kitchen and left Mitzi and I to our own devices. I took off my shoes and put my feet on the ottoman. "It sure feels good to be home."

Mitzi was silent.

I said, "I'm ordering pizza." Mitzi was still quiet, and I worried, again, that things would never be normal between us. "Mitzi?"

She seemed a thousand miles away, her expression sad. Finally, she focused her gaze on me and said, "Uh, babe, after dinner we need to talk." She got up and went toward her travel room, presumably to take down her pins and maps.

I caught her hand. "Are you okay? Are we okay?"

She forced a smile. "Yeah, sure. Tell Brooke and Puddle they should hear what I have to say, too. I don't want any pizza." My heart sank. Was she going to announce she wanted a divorce in front of my family?

Twyla entered the room, and it was only then I noticed how scratched up she was. "Hey, did you lose a fight?"

She sat on the hearth next to Puddle and said, "No, silly," and laughed. It was nice to hear someone semi-cheerful. "Juniper and I were working on the yard."

I only commented, "Uh huh."

She picked up Brutus, hugged him and buried her face in his fur. "Please don't get mad. I need to tell you what happened while you were gone."

THE MERRYVILLE MUSEUM

Juniper dropped Valerie at home and was frantic to find out what happened to Richland Bruce. Potts had not called her back, nor had Phillip, who was probably out chasing scoops for the Merryville Bee. Curiosity was killing her. As she pulled into the museum lot, she noticed Richland's car in the Curator spot. Pissed, she parked next to it and restrained the urge to key it with her diamond ring as she walked by. She was in no mood for bullshit.

Maribel came out of the front door and asked, "Where have you been? We've been trying to call you all day." Juniper studied her phone and noticed several missed calls. She'd left it inside the Fowler's house while cutting weeds and then turned the ringer off at the Horticultural meeting.

Still seething, she asked, "Where is Richland Bruce?"

"I-I don't know. But Damien's in the hospital in an induced coma."

Detective Potts didn't call Juniper back because not only was he busy, he was also unsure how to proceed. The night before a patrol officer arrived at the museum on a 9-1-1 call. He discovered Richland Bruce babbling and one of the artists on the floor. What was going on at that museum! It was Déjà vu all over again, his favorite Yogiism.

He wanted to brainstorm and luckily his favorite brain was about to land. The airport was busy, so he flung his shield on the dashboard of his car and left it running. After a nod to airport security, he was good to go. Alexandra, already outside of baggage claim, met his gaze. He ran to her, picked her up and spun her around. The petite defense attorney laughed and said, "Why somebody would think you've missed me!"

He threw her bags in the trunk and started the drive back to Merryville. After some small talk, she said, "I heard Garcia's been released."

He nodded his head. "Yeah, bad timing for him. Another person's been attacked at the museum. In fact, I want to talk to you about that."

"What? You don't think he'd be so stupid as to go back there and push somebody else off a cliff! He's not a serial killer, just a mixed-up kid."

"Nah, actually I don't." He tapped the steering wheel with his index finger.

"But there's some weird stuff still going on down at the museum. Hey, by the way, I scored tickets to the latest show. Wanna go?"

Her eyes lit up, and she did a cute shuffle thing with her feet. "Words on a Plate? You know I love that sort of thing, yes. Now, what happened to the attack victim. Did he die?" She was like a terrier on a bone with a new case.

Charlie turned the wheel and looked puzzled. "Not yet. The vic's in a coma. The person who found him—the new board guy—swears Damien was on the ground when he got there, but I talked to him shortly before and could swear he was up to something. He was in trouble as a kid, so there's some history. Then there's this vandalism thing with flowers. I'm ready to go talk to him—guy named Richland Bruce. Wanna come?"

"You know it." They were silent as each lit up a cigarette. "Any theories yet?"

"Maybe this Bruce caught Damien destroying the exhibit, and a fight ensued. I'm not sure Damien should have been in there at that hour, need to talk to that curator—Juniper Gooden. Or could be Richland Bruce did find Damien on the floor, but then we're back to what happened? I haven't connected the dots yet."

Alex tapped her index finger on her chin. "Unless this attack victim wakes up, it's a hard case to prove either way." They were silent for a moment, watching the familiar scenery go by.

"Hey, the flower thing? Your old pals Valerie and Juniper Gooden were threatened. Somebody broke in their house and destroyed some really rare flowers. Left them a note saying the same thing could happen to them."

Alex snapped to attention from her reverie. "Why didn't you tell me this sooner! Do you think it's related to the man, what's his name, that got attacked?"

"Damien Simpson, but he never uses his last name, it's just Damien." He said Damien with a mincing accent. "Artists!"

"You say that the same way you say, Women." Alexandra laughed heartily and pulled his ear playfully. "Let's go solve a crime, Sherlock."

Charley Potts gave her a sidelong glance and smiled as he blew smoke out his nose.

❧

Janet sat in her living room with Richland, and the mood was not as festive as when he arrived for tea the first time. "I was so embarrassed, Richland. You couldn't even call? The Mavens were looking at me, like, he's *your* brother, Janet."

"I was so upset, Janet. You weren't there. Damien looked dead, his blood everywhere. I—I couldn't deal. I went to the hospital with him and stayed."

"You stayed?" She laced her fingers around her knee, an old habit, and cleared her throat. "Do you need me to call that therapist from Ohio?"

Richland's head snapped up. "No. Don't be ridiculous. Your precious Horticultural Society will get over it. They should understand a medical emergency, for God's sake."

"Don't be so touchy. That's not what I'm talking about. I can make up an excuse." Janet moved to the chair next to him. "You've been at the hospital all this time?"

"Yes! I told you that!"

"Is he going to make it?"

Richland bit his knuckle. "I don't know."

"Isn't Damien the one you used to—"

Richland stood up so fast his chair hit the floor. "That was before, Janet, you shut up!" He put his face in his hands and started crying. "I never should have come back here."

❧

"What happened to Damien?" Juniper asked as she walked into the museum's administrative offices.

"No one knows," Maribel said. "Apparently, he was here quite late working on the exhibit. Richland Bruce called the police. He said he found him in the Words on a Plate exhibit hall on the floor, knocked out."

"Great. This is my fault," Juniper said. "I never should have pushed him to make those changes." She turned to go. "I need to go see him. What hospital?"

"Mercy General, but Juniper—"

A shrieking voice cut Maribel off and they both turned toward the sound.

"Not so fast! What is it with you and your exhibits?" Linda glared at Juniper as she approached. "Last time Dick Mortimer died, now one of our artists?"

"Excuse me? No one's dead, and you can't possibly think I had anything to do with this."

"Oh, really? Because Penelope told me you called a secret meeting with her and Damien and you're the reason Damien was here last night!"

Penelope, dressed in her purple caftan, came out of the lobby area talking and laughing with one of her helpers. She stopped cold when she saw Juniper. "Oops."

"*Et Tu* Penelope?" Juniper shook her head and then turned back to Linda. "I want to talk about the exhibit, but first, I need to see Damien."

"Well, you don't need to talk to Penelope. We're shutting the exhibit down. I've called an emergency board meeting for this evening at eight p.m. At this point, it's a matter of public safety." She paused dramatically. "I've called Mrs. Windingle."

"Public safety?" Juniper let out a mirthless laugh. "Fine, call your meeting, but last time I noticed, you're only a member at large." She turned back to Penelope, "are you with her on this?"

"Leave me out of it! I only told Linda that Garcia got released."

Typical. Penelope tented her fingers on her chest in a parody of innocence.

Juniper said to Linda in a measured voice, "Oh, you're afraid Garcia made a bee line for the museum to conk Damien on the head." Now she really laughed. "By the way, when I come back, Richland had better be out of my parking space!"

Linda's lower lip quivered. "That's what bothers you most? A parking space? Richland was handed quite a shock. He found Damien. And it's a damn good thing he came by to find out what you've been doing. Really, an elephant head?"

Juniper was upset, but she'd be damned if she let Linda see it. "I need to get to the hospital."

Maribel watched her go back to her Citroen. She walked within a foot of Linda and said in a low voice, "This museum needs her. If she goes, I go."

Linda snorted and said, "That's not hard. We'll find Richland a new assistant." Penelope shrugged as if this all had nothing to do with her and headed into Origins.

Hortense was angry and wanted someone to blame, so she called Sylvia. "Well, that meeting we tried to have was a shamble."

"It wasn't so bad. The tour was a brilliant save. I went on the bus ride and got to know our new member, Denise."

"Sylvia, our keynote speaker didn't show up, the club members didn't get to see the Rothschild's Slipper Orchids, and I understand the thistles, while cut back considerably, appeared amateurish and, well, trashy."

"And you're telling me this why?"

"You put Valerie Gooden up for membership. I'm thinking she hasn't kept her side of the bargain. At our next meeting, I'm moving that her provisional membership be terminated."

"That's not fair. She'll be crushed!"

"I'm not the one who tried to pass off ordinary orchids as Rothschilds. I knew there was something fishy."

"But they were real! We all saw them."

"Sylvia, why on earth would they die so conveniently? Well, we'll give her a fair hearing. See you Tuesday at two p.m. at the old MacGregor mansion. Since you put her up, I wanted to give you the courtesy of advance notice."

"Gee thanks. You know that's when I play tennis."

"Oh, is it? Well, you don't have to go to every meeting."

"See you Tuesday."

❧

Pizza arrived at the Fowler's, and everyone ate quietly. Mitzi relented and had one piece, which she took back into her travel room. After dinner, I knocked on her door. "Mitz?"

"Yes, I'm ready. Bring everyone in."

I rounded up the elves and my brother and sister. Twyla said she had something to do. Brutus invited himself. He was underfoot more than usual. We crammed into the crowded room as Mitzi took the floor.

Elsa and Ekk had showered, and I got the sense they already knew what was coming. A slight fragrance of lavender floated in the room.

Brooke rested against the edge of a table full of exotic tchotchkes. "What's this all about, Mitzi? No offense, but I'm really tired of this whole experience. I want to sleep and go home."

Puddle was a bit grumpy too. "It's happening, Bro, deal."

We were all tired. Puddle looked particularly frazzled. Her un-beaded hair was now back to full ginger afro.

The maps of Peru were still up, but now an X was drawn over a section in Lima. "Hear me out." Mitzi pointed at the cross. We all got quiet. I had a lump in my throat and already felt like crying. Again, that feeling that something of great importance was about to happen descended upon me.

Mitzi took a deep breath and said, "Panda, Puddle, Brooke, your parents are dead." My head jerked up from my reverie. Mitzi got down on her knee in front of me, squeezed my hands and locked her gaze with mine. "I am so sorry." She stood and surveyed all our shocked faces.

"How could you know that?" Brooke was always the Doubting Thomas.

"A lot went on when we were at the portal," Mitzi continued in a soft voice.

"To say the least." Brooke added somberly. This was the first time he'd not been on the move since leaving New York. I'd wondered what he would be like when the dust settled.

Mitzi got serious. "Panda, you asked me who I was talking to when I was, well, flying." This took a different direction than I'd anticipated. Would she tell me she was joining some celestial group? Was she going to be like Wonder Woman and leave me to save the world?

"When I flew, I was able to see things in the swirling and meshing of the worlds."

"That happened to me in our first ritual! I saw Suzie," I turned to the elves, "our old family Collie dog. I hoped it meant she was still alive in some parallel universe."

Ekk finally spoke. "No, Panda, what you saw was only an echo. Wolfrum can pull things from your mind to distract you."

Puddle was fully rapt and motioned Ekk to be quiet. "Tell us what you saw!"

"Okay, I've seen pictures of your folks, and the couple I saw was like that, but maybe a few years older? They were kind of floating there, and your dad was holding your mom's hand. With the other hand your dad showed me a place. It felt like he was trying really hard to speak, and he gave coordinates 12.0464 South and 77.0428 West. Then he said, 'We're gone.' "

"That's it?" was all I could say. "What does that even mean?"

"The coordinates are this place on the map." She pointed like a teacher to the X. "I've been trying all evening to pinpoint it." She turned to me. "That's why I wouldn't answer you, Panda. I was trying to process what happened and to remember those numbers. To make sure I remembered exactly where he said."

"But that's the city," Brooke said. "Lima."

"I know, Brooke. I've talked to both Juju and Sister Lucia."

Brooke said, "Lucia? How is she?"

A tear trickled down Puddle's cheek.

I said to Mitzi, "When did you have time to talk to Juju?"

"He has a phone," she said. "I called from the airport and have been in my office since then talking with both of them." Mitzi turned to Puddle. "Sister Lucia called a friend at the Lima city archives with the approximate date and the coordinates. They found the incident. Your parents died in a bus crash, in Lima, listed as Does, until now. They never even made it to the jungle."

"So this has all been for nothing." Brooke's quick flicker of interest at hearing Lucia's name turned to dismay.

"Not for nothing," Mitzi said. "Paititi is real, but your mom and dad never made it there."

"And we kept Wolfrum from getting into Paititi and finding whatever it is he was seeking," Elsa said, on a brighter note.

Puddle finally spoke. "So, Mitzi, you talked to my dad's ghost?"

Our conversation was stopped short by Ekk declaring, "I don't believe in ghosts."

An unexpected laugh burbled up from my belly. Puddle caught it, and then Brooke grabbed his stomach and bent over in an explosive laugh.

"What?" Ekk said. "I don't believe in ghosts!"

"You're an elf, for God's sake!" Brooke sputtered. "From a magic garden in the Black Forest!" Even Mitzi started a titter.

"There's a fairy right now wandering around our house!" I screamed with laughter. The tension had been so thick, we were helpless.

"It is kinda funny," Elsa said and batted her eyes at her embarrassed mate.

"We don't know everything, Ekkhard." She rarely called him by his full name and had a smile herself.

Mitzi let out a big sigh. "Well, this isn't how I thought it would go, but okay. I'm sorry, guys."

Puddle wiped her eyes. "Did he say anything else?"

"Yes. He said to take care of our family."

At that, Brooke stopped laughing. "You? Why you?"

Mitzi got that fierce look she does sometimes and was very precise in her pronunciation. I hoped Brooke could read women. He was on thin ice. "Because, Brooke, this is my family, too. You're my brother-in-law. I married your sister."

He stood and lifted his eyebrows but didn't seem angry. "I've had enough for one day, or maybe a lifetime. Goodnight." Brooke went upstairs to bed.

Puddle had questions, but Elsa, oh so sensitive, said, "Come on Puddle, I made your special brownies." Ekk and Elsa helped Puddle off the floor. "To me she said, we're going to our apartment soon. We'll be back tomorrow." I was finally alone with my wife.

"Come here." I sat on the loveseat we'd moved into the room after our bean bag chair exploded. She sat. We held each other for the longest time, gazing at the map. A tear rolled down my face. "I had a feeling they were gone." There was so much to say, but I had no energy.

She looked tired, but her eyes were clear. "I'm so sorry, babe." She put her head on my shoulder. Brutus came in and stretched himself across both our laps, and we petted him. Eventually, the three of us fell asleep in front of the map.

❧

At eight o'clock, Juniper strode with purpose to the boardroom at the museum. No moon was up, and light from inside the old craftsman made rectangles of gold on the grass as she walked from the exhibit tent to the main building. Bonnie walked next to her, arms full of the phony trifold brochures.

Inside, around the conference table sat Lucas Windingle, Richland, Maribel, and Linda. "*Déjà vu*," she said under her breath and took her seat. Louder, she said, "It doesn't appear you have a quorum."

Richland leaned forward, tenting his fingers. "Well, not in person. It was short notice. Thank you, Lucas, for coming. I know you had an event." Juniper hated how Richland looked so in charge.

Lucas was Charlotte's nephew, and his place on the board was kind of a family seat. He was nice, but not much of a mover and shaker. It was hard to tell how he would vote on any given topic. Tonight, he wore a strange steampunk outfit and was quite handsome in it.

"Let's cut to the chase," Richland said. He had deep circles under his eyes, but otherwise was primped and overdressed as usual. "Juniper, I don't think it's appropriate to go forward with Damien's work since he's—"

"I know how he is. I spent all afternoon at the hospital. It'll be a miracle if he wakes up." Juniper's voice was sharp. "Linda, I think you and Richland here have a little explaining to do first. You've been trying to sabotage this exhibit since the beginning. Why?"

"That's preposterous!" Linda's face was red she was so amped up. "All I've ever tried to do is keep you from running this museum into a ditch! Need I remind you your assistant, Garcia killed our Board chair? We're still dealing with the fallout from that. And before that you brought that Floodlight exhibit. Shall I go on? Your stint here has hardly been stellar."

Maribel spoke up. "Actually, Linda, I went over to membership today. There's more interest in the museum now than ever."

"Well, it's the wrong kind of interest!" Linda shouted. "People are waiting for the next body to drop!" Linda was rising from her chair, and her voice was shrill.

"Which brings us full circle." Richland motioned for Linda to sit. "We can do this like adults or put more strain on our limited resources. And actually, Juniper, this whole thing is rather moot. Penelope is pulling her artwork from the show. There is no show."

Juniper silently cursed the purple narcissist. "Fine. Get her plates out of there. All we need is Damien's work."

Richland was smug and shared a glance with Linda. "About that, Juniper. I'm pulling Damien's work. I have a Durable Power of Attorney from when he was my, ah, roommate."

"You mean boyfriend, don't you, Uncle Ricky?" Bonnie was at the door with an armful of trifolds.

"Bonnie! What are you doing here! Go home!"

"Oh, I will, but not until I deliver these for Juniper Gooden, your Curator." With that she opened her arms and the trifold brochures spilled out on the table.

Juniper said, "Thank you, Bonnie. You probably should be getting home. It's late."

Bonnie nodded and quickly left.

"See? This is what I mean. Now you're trying to turn my niece gay? Do you get a toaster oven?" Richland looked at Lucas for support. Linda nodded her head, firmly in his camp.

"I gave up Comicon for this? Sounds like a soap opera." Lucas stood. "Here's the deal. My aunt funds half this museum. Get your shit together and put on a show people want to see. What are these?" He picked up one of the trifolds on the table.

"They're Linda and Richland's dirty trick to make Words on a Plate a laughing stock." She picked one up. "They changed all the meanings of the conversations on the plates to be watered down and not what the artists intended."

Lucas turned to Richland, "Did you do this?"

Richland said, "Of course not! I don't know what she's talking about!" He looked at Linda for support.

Linda's face was red, "The bottom line is that we have the proxies. We don't need everyone physically here to shut this thing down." Linda held up a neatly stacked pile of papers. "It was short notice, and the other board members are at various functions tonight. Most of them don't like the exhibit."

Juniper was tired, scratched from removing the thistles in Panda and Mitzi's yard, sad about Damien and furious with Linda. "How do we know the proxies aren't fake? Let me see those."

"Actually, give them to me." Lucas put his glasses on and made two piles. Everyone waited while he counted. "Huh."

"What?" Juniper was on her last nerve. She glared at Richland and Linda.

"It seems the board is evenly divided." He drummed his fingers on the table, thinking. "I guess that makes me the tiebreaker vote. I'm taking the night to talk to my aunt. Read these proxies again and call Penelope. Now if you'll excuse me, Wonder Woman awaits!"

Juniper, Maribel, Richland, and Linda were all speechless. Lucas was growing up, sort of.

Twyla came in the sliding glass door and found Ekk and Elsa in the kitchen. Puddle had eaten some of her *special* brownies and gone to bed. "What happened to you?" Elsa asked. Twyla was quite dirty, but still pretty cute with her tool belt.

"I know you guys don't like your apartment, so I made you a new one!"

"What?" Elsa let herself be pulled into the backyard. Ekk grunted. She knew what he thought of fairies.

Twyla pointed, "Look up!"

The old oak tree was majestic, the treehouse nestled in its limbs. A green, fibrous ladder hung down to the ground.

"That's not *grünzueg*, is it?" Ekk inquired.

"No, no!" Twyla reddened. "Green rope." Twyla, buzzing with happiness, began to float.

Elsa pulled her down like a balloon. "Fairies first, but no magic, all right?"

The three of them climbed to the old cat condo that was now secured firmly to the sturdy limbs by regular old nails, twine and other non-magical substances. When she tried, Twyla really was a pretty good carpenter, and she'd added a small bedroom off the main area. It was cozy, to be sure, but quite charming and mostly concealed from prying eyes by the foliage. Panda's old yoga mat made a soft flooring, and Twyla had bought more to carpet the entire tree house.

"Oh, Twyla, it's beautiful!" Elsa walked to the playhouse-sized window, which was her size.

Ekk jumped up and down on the floor and declared it solid.

"I wanted to show you I could do this, you know, take care of people in spite of all that's happened." Her smile was meltingly sincere.

Elsa put her hand over Twyla's. "You have a good heart. It takes time to learn to live here in this world, that's all."

Twyla bowed her head. "I'm so ashamed. What's Uncle Ehren going to say when I go back to the garden and tell him about the *grünzueg* disasters?"

Ekk looked at Elsa, then back at Twyla. "Nothing. Because you're not going to the garden. You're going to New York."

Twyla appeared puzzled. Elsa said, "Show her, Ekk."

Ekk pulled his dagger out and put a tiny gem in it. Ehren himself appeared in a short hologram. "Twyla, you have been given a good report by Ekk and Elsa. Well done. The counsel at the Hercynian Garden, headed by me, of course, has decided to give you a longer mission, guarding Brooke Fowler. Congratulations." The hologram faded.

After a tiny beat of silence, Twyla hugged them so hard she knocked them down. With tears in her eyes she said, "I won't screw up, I promise!" The three sat on pillows and talked into the night before the elves took their leave.

As Ekk started the car, Elsa said, "Thank you, sweetheart. She'll do fine."

Ekk smiled and mumbled under his breath, "*Gott helfen Brooke.*"

∽

CHAPTER TWENTY-ONE
MERRYVILLE MUSEUM OFFICES

Lucas was as good as his word. Juniper sat across from his big antique desk.

"Okay, Penelope is out. Do you have enough words and plates to do a show?

She started to speak, but he interjected. "This is not a full endorsement. Understand, the advertisement was costly, but Mona at the front desk is getting lots of calls."

"Yes, it'll be a bit smaller, but yes!" Juniper exuded happiness.

"Do it. Don't let me and the Windingle Foundation down. If we can get through this, we'll figure out how best to move forward."

"What about Richland's Durable Power of Attorney?"

"That's smoke. He's bluffing."

"You might make a good Board Chair, Lucas," the beaming curator said.

"Just make sure the show isn't a flop." He smiled and reached for his ringing cell phone.

Juniper grabbed Valerie, Bonnie, Maribel and went to the exhibition tent with her other artists and set to work. They had until seven p.m. that night to work miracles. Words on a Plate was going forward!

∽

I woke up Saturday in the wee hours of the morning and walked a somnambulant Mitzi up to our bed. Mitzi curled up against my back and in minutes was sound asleep. I hoped we could fix whatever was going off the rails in our relationship. My parents were dead. I guess I'd known it in my heart of hearts, but it still made me sad.

It was strange, and kind of wonderful, to have my family all under one roof, as I pondered when we would take our separate ways. My eyes grew heavy and again I slept with Mitzi's warm breath on my neck.

A few hours later I awoke to the wondrous sounds of laughter downstairs. The sun was shining hot and bright through my window. Mitzi was gone. The digital clock said 8:56 a.m. Almost nine! What was I missing! As if to punctuate the point, Brutus jumped on the bed. He walked up to my face, nuzzling me with his whiskers. "Okay, boy, I'm up."

Mitzi usually brings me coffee. I felt the cup by my bed. It was cold. Wow, I really overslept. I ran a quick brush through my hair, pulled on shorts and a t-shirt and went downstairs. Elsa was in the kitchen and said I should go outside to the back yard where I found my family. Mitzi and Brooke were digging, together, trying to fill in pot holes in the yard. Twyla came around the corner with a trash bag full of thistles. The oversized gardening gloves were hilarious on her slender arms.

Ekk set the picnic table with dishes while all this work was going on. "Where's Puddle, sleeping?"

"Nope." Ekk smiled and pointed up.

I saw Puddle's hair poking out a window before I heard her say, "Up here! Come on up, sis, this is so cool."

I looked around, and they all tittered like munchkins. Ekk said, "Twyla built us a new home." By us, I knew he meant he and Elsa.

"That's awesome! I know you're not really happy at the apartment. It'll be great to have you nearby." I truly meant it. I went to the rope ladder and worried my weight might pull it off the tree.

At that moment Elsa came out with fragrant *soyriso* and the reliable Panda stomach went into overdrive. "Breakfast, Puddle. The treehouse tour will have to wait until after we eat. Come on down." Elsa went back into the house for more food. Mitzi and Brooke laughed at me.

"Me and my sister-in-law here," he nodded at Mitzi, "figured if these guys are going to live in the tree, we should at least clean up the backyard." Brooke would never apologize for avoiding our wedding but referring to Mitzi as his sister-in-law was pretty close. As Puddle descended, Elsa returned again with a bowl of scrambled eggs. Ekk followed behind with mounds of toast and yelled, "Let's eat!"

Valerie stopped by as we were finishing breakfast. She admired the new treehouse and said to Mitzi, "I bet you're glad that thing isn't taking up space in the backyard anymore."

"Ya think?" Mitzi was in a pretty good mood. Sleep does wonders. "Still needs a good coat of paint."

Valerie accepted a cup of coffee from Ekk. "I stopped by because Juniper's big opening for Words on a Plate is tonight. Are all of you coming?"

"Oh, my God, I forgot about that! Of course, we'll be there." I looked at Mitzi who nodded. Normally, this wasn't my favorite thing, but I was on best behavior.

"No worries, you sound like you've been pretty busy." Valerie helped herself to a piece of toast. "Juniper could really use the support. We've had more drama down at the museum. The main artist for the exhibit is in a medically induced coma."

"What? What happened?" Several of us spoke at once.

Valerie told us what she knew and headed back to the museum to help with whatever was needed. After breakfast, Brooke made his apologies. He had to fly back to New York that afternoon to see if he could pick up the threads of his life. There might be more to that story, but he wasn't talking about it. Twyla was going with him to make sure all was well. Brooke didn't seem to mind. I think he was reluctant to leave us. Our little group was dwindling fast.

Janet was determined to make sure that Valerie was never accepted into the Merryville Mavens. She knocked on the door of the old McGreggor mansion and waited for it to open. She had invited Hortense, but the older woman was resting after the botched meeting the day before. First, they let in Sylvia—a Mexican! Now, if she didn't act fast, they would have a lesbian! It was too much to bear. The ornate door opened, and Merryville's prodigal daughter, Denise McGreggor, said, "Yes?" She looked gorgeous in a denim pencil skirt and off-the-shoulder blouse.

"Good afternoon. I met you yesterday. Janet Bruce. So sorry to come by without calling. Hortense Miller asked me to stop by for a favor."

"Sure, would you like to come in?"

"I would love to see your house, but, ah, I'm on my way to the hospital—old family friend," she stammered.

"Oh, I'm so sorry. What can I help with?"

"Well, we have a bit of a problem and need a place to hold an emergency executive committee meeting. The Horticulture building is being tented, and we were hoping you would let us meet here. Your mom always let us use the gorgeous gazebo in the back. Hortense is in an uproar with that crazy meeting yesterday and, well, it would be nice. We're dying to see your garden and want to get to know you now that you've returned from the Continent."

"I'd be honored. What time?"

"Tuesday at two p.m. Would that work? There will be five of us."

"I think Mother would have liked that. See you then."

JUDGE AND FLORENCE DINWITTER'S HOME

Hortense rang the doorbell at the Dinwitter home and glanced at her companion. He was wearing a navy blazer with gold buttons and a pale blue shirt. His tie was purposefully loose, and it looked like he was ready to go yachting.

"This better work," Richland said.

"Don't worry, it will. Flo's a good friend."

Florence opened the door and frowned when she saw Richland.

"Can we see the Judge?" Hortense asked.

Florence appeared shocked. "On a Saturday? Why are you doing this for him?" She nodded at Richland.

"Richland is Bill's nephew, Flo."

Richland spoke up, "We have an important legal question that cannot wait. He is a lawyer, isn't he?"

"Of course." She addressed her friend, "Hortense, really, this is quite unusual. And you, Mister Bruce! Where were you yesterday? Our meeting was ruined by your failure to show up."

"Mrs. Dinwitter, I respect your husband immensely, and you. I am terribly sorry for that." He looked at Hortense then back at Florence with big sad eyes. "There was an emergency I had to take care of and now," he gave full warm puppy eyes at Hortense, "the Merryville Horticultural Society flower exhibit is being eclipsed by that woman, Juniper Gooden."

At her name, Florence stiffened. "Ever since her, uh, wife came into the picture. Well, what can the Judge do?"

"Ask him to review this document. One of our artists, Damien, named me his Durable Power of Attorney years ago and, well, I want to know if I can speak for him and withdraw his art. If I can, there will be no show." Richland proffered said document.

"All right. Give me a minute." Florence took the three sheets, stapled together, and disappeared behind paneled doors. Raised voices floated out, but Hortense and Richland couldn't hear what was being said. The polished mahogany door burst open and Judge Dinwitter himself stood in its frame. He was a large man, dressed in a smoking jacket as if it were the 1930s. He nodded, "Hortense."

"Your honor." Hortense loved titles.

"You must be Richland Bruce." The men shook hands. "I've met your sister, Janet, of course, fine woman. You realize I don't take on private clients. That being said, as a general matter, you can do something if the document says so, you can't if it doesn't. I don't see anywhere here where you get to act as this Damien artist's agent."

"Thank you for looking at it," Hortense said to Richland. "We tried." She then turned to her old friend. "While we're here, Flo, there's an emergency meeting at Denise McGreggor's next Tuesday to discuss matters at the Society. Can you be there? Two p.m."

Florence nodded. "With bells on."

Outside, Phillip from the Merryville Bee watched Richland Bruce and Hortense Miller leave the Judge's house. He made a note in his book before driving off.

Back at the museum, Juniper, Valerie, Maribel, Bonnie, and some of the other artists were hard at work. This was a show no one would soon forget. Juniper well knew it could be her swan song. Penelope came by in purple jeans and tried to make nice. Her purpleness adopted an innocent affect. "Actually, you can leave my stuff up if it will help."

Juniper was having none of it. "Such a helper! Oh nooo, you can find some other museum to show your specialized portraits. Oh wait, we're the only one in Merryville. Bonnie, help Penelope get her stuff out of here."

The removal of Penelope's pieces reduced the size of the exhibit but didn't change the overall message. In fact, the toned-down version was actually a bit better. Valerie put her arm around Juniper's waist as they surveyed the final result. "Can I be honest?"

"I wouldn't have it any other way." Juniper was surprised. Valerie ordinarily would never assume her opinion of art should be considered above her curator wife.

"You don't always need to be so, in your face."

Juniper looked at Valerie with surprise. "Go on."

"Lose the decapitated elephant and its head. Dead animals, even papier-mâché, bother me."

Maribel joined them and looked up. "Juniper, I'm pretty sure you added it to piss off Rick and Linda, didn't you?"

Juniper clapped her hands and two workers came forward. "Take that down." She laughed out loud. "Put the head in Richland's office." She put her arms around Valerie and Maribel's shoulders. "Thank you, it's good not to be surrounded by yes people. Let's not go for shock value. Let's let the art literally speak for itself."

"Juniper?" Valerie had a playful warning tone in her voice.

"Okay," She addressed her worker, "Trash the elephant behind the building."

Maribel walked off, shaking her head but smiling.

After Richland dropped off Hortense, he wasn't done trying to ruin Juniper Gooden's Words on a Plate show. He drove straight to the park and found the head of the "New Spirit Revival," Maurice Perkins, backstage and gave him a manly handshake.

"Reverend Morry! I knew you were in town but hadn't had a chance to get over here. How are you?"

"Things are good. Marriage is great, Richland. Me and Doreen are heading up the ex-gay ministry in Colorado Springs. I hear you're doing really well with the museum. Good on you. This is a tough crowd."

He watched a girl walk by in short shorts and halter top. "Merryville, California is sin city."

"Oh, you don't know the half of it. There's an exhibit straight from hell opening at the museum tonight. I've been trying to stop it, but, well, Satan's alive and kicking."

"Tell me about it."

"How about this for starters? There's a bloody elephant head hung upside down from the ceiling. There's also religious blasphemy."

"Really? What time does this start? Don't give up, Richland. There's more than one way to skin a cat." The two men grinned and sat down to talk more.

At seven p.m. I was downstairs trying not to let Brutus get his hair all over me. Mitzi was still in the shower, and Puddle had disappeared. "Come on you guys! We need to be there now!" Ekk came in the front door with a couple of suitcases. He and Elsa were moving into the treehouse and would not be joining us. I was tired but knew how important this show was to Valerie and Juniper. After Peru, I was ready to do something normal. "Mitz!"

I turned to see her descending the stairs. She was dressed in black pants with a silk floral blouse that flowed like it had been draped on her. It seemed to me she walked taller these days, probably because she knew she had a super power. I couldn't help but smile. "Babe."

"Are you done yelling?"

"Yes, sorry. Are you ready?"

Puddle drove us to the museum, so we didn't have to park. Once it was in view, we were stunned to see a full protest complete with signs and chanting, "Boycott the Merryville Museum!" "Gay Art Kills!" "Fire the Curator!" "Put God back into Art!" Among the protestors was—

"Is that Richland Bruce?" Mitzi looked incredulous. "I've only seen him in pictures, but that goatee!" Richland was not carrying a sign but was clearly smiling at the people protesting, even shaking a hand or two here and there.

"What tha?" Puddle pulled over and said, "Man, I'm gonna go home and park the car and walk back. Are you sure you want to stay?"

I sighed. "Yes. These are our best friends. If ever they needed us." Then thinking about her comment. "Be good, Puddle." I put my arm around Mitzi as we approached the oval of walkers with their stupid signs.

"Always, sis," Puddle said as she let us out of the car.

We pushed through the crowd as the leader, wearing a Priest collar and carrying a bull horn, said, "Turn back, don't go in there! Your very soul is at risk! We at New Spirit want to save you!"

Phillip, on Bee business, brought a photographer and was busy texting something on his smartphone. After a quick wave at him, we ran the gauntlet through flashes of camera, bullhorns and bodies.

I had tears in my eyes and held Mitzi's hand tightly as we moved past the twenty-five or so rabid right-wingers until we could see Juniper, Maribel and Valerie standing on the front steps. Juniper had her cell phone plastered to her ear and her hand on her hip. Valerie came forward to gently guide us up to where they stood. The *Words on a Plate* Banner behind them rustled in the wind.

Before I could speak, Juniper said to us, "The police are on their way. I cannot comprehend why these idiots would sabotage their own show." She noticed Richland and Linda walking toward our group. Juniper clicked off her phone hard and said, "Oh, joy."

"Steady, Juniper, don't give them what they want," Valerie said under her breath. Maribel nodded.

Richland walked to within a few feet of us and opened his arms, gesturing to the protest in front of the Merryville museum. "Happy? I told you, Juniper. Now look at what's happened."

Linda added, "I guess you saw the press? In one year, we now have two major scandals. Nice going, Juniper."

"You remind me of Nero, Richland. You set this fire." She turned dramatically and went into the exhibition tent, and we followed. I craned my neck to see two black and whites pulling up to deal with crowd control. Maribel went out to meet them.

Inside, there were several small clumps of people viewing the art, but most conversations were muted, and people kept looking at the door. Surprisingly, I saw Charlotte alone with a cocktail. I walked up to her and said, "Hi, I'm Panda, we met at Origins." She didn't immediately place me.

"You were with Hortense from the Merryville Mavens?" A light dawned on her. "Oh, yes dear, nice to see you." She didn't seem happy at all.

Mitzi walked up to me and handed me a cranberry and seven up, smiling at the museum's largest patron. I continued, "This is my wife, Mitzi."

"Hello, Mitzi. Well, I must say you two are brave, walking through," she pointed a bejeweled finger at the entrance, "that protest. I never thought I'd see this at my beloved museum."

Juniper spotted us talking to Charlotte and came over with Valerie. "Charlotte, I see you've met our friends. Have you ever met my wife, Valerie?"

Charlotte was on automatic pilot, unfailingly polite. "Of course, I knew who you were, but I don't think we've ever been able to chat. Nice to make your acquaintance formally." She turned to Juniper. "I know all the other spouses. Why haven't I been introduced to Valerie?"

I think Juniper believed she was done at the museum and it really didn't matter, so she answered honestly. "Because I'm queer. No matter how much I tried to make this not about me being a woman who loves women, it apparently is—at least sometimes. Charlotte, when I came to the museum, I tried hard to be only about the art. Unfortunately, some on the board—"

"I know," Charlotte said. "Dick Mortimer was a good friend. I knew him good and bad."

"Dick wasn't a bad man, but he was never comfortable with me having a wife. And not only him. Linda, and now Richland made it clear that they were challenged by having me as Curator. There is fear this will turn into a gay museum."

Charlotte took a sip of her wine and nodded. "I've heard that."

"I usually go by myself to the museum events, not wanting to distract from our work here. My term here should be about the art. Since this is probably my last show, shall we enjoy it? In fact, let's start at the beginning and walk the plates. Would you do that with me?"

In the beat while Charlotte thought, we heard chants outside and police whistles. It seemed the noise was much greater than when we arrived. Charlotte said with a sad smile, "Well, I don't relish walking through that again. Let's appreciate some art."

I could tell the socialite really did love art, and this distraction was timely. Mitzi and I let Juniper, Valerie and Charlotte have a private tour of the pairings of portraits and plates and went back to the front to join Maribel watch the drama outside unfold.

❧

When we reached the door and looked out, my first thought was, "Oh. My. God." The police had pushed the protestors back to an area that allowed people attending the exhibit to enter—not that there were many.

Now there was a counter protest. My chest region warmed as I saw Ekk, Elsa, Puddle, Dougie, the Gooden's neighbor boy, and Bonnie, Richland's niece, carrying signs. They walked in a circle and chanted, "Don't Censor Art!" and "Words on a Plate Tells the Truth!"

The press contingent had increased, with Phillip from the Merryville Bee and now a Channel Seven van was out front, the one with all the satellite dishes on it. Our local TV anchor and minor celebrity, Jessica Walters, talked excitedly into a microphone, saying God knows what to our fellow Merryvillians.

Just when it couldn't get any crazier, Lucas Windingle strode up the path with a stunning blond on his arm. He was born into wealth but usually avoided the trappings of privilege. Not today. He had Charlotte's driver drop him and his date off in her Silver Ghost vintage Rolls Royce. The talking heads gravitated to him naturally. A handsome man in a top hat and tails with a blond woman in a tight dress was a photographer's dream.

∽

By seven-thirty p.m. both protest groups had swelled. Mitzi and I joined our friends even though we didn't have signs. I hugged Puddle and stayed in the moment. The police presence was growing, and people started arriving in droves, probably due to the TV coverage. A Chrysler 300 pulled up and Detective Potts yelled out the window, "I leave you guys alone for ten minutes, and this is what I get?" Alexandra Stephanovsky sat shotgun, smiling her mysterious smile.

The Reverend, or whatever he was, put down his bullhorn and walked up to the main TV news reporter. The smiling blond quickly started to interview him.

"So. You're the head of New Spirit, the group protesting today. What's this all about?"

"My name is Reverend Maurice Perkins, but most call me Rev Morry." He fingered his collar. "New Spirit arrived in Merryville a few weeks ago as part of our traveling tent revival down at the park. I must say, the trouble in Merryville goes deeper than anything we could have anticipated."

"How so?" the anchor looked so sincere.

"Well, first of all, there's something rotten underneath all this pretty façade. Yes, Merryville has a coastline and lots of post WWII housing, but those houses are not filled with families anymore."

The camera zoomed in for a close up of the journalist, "Go on."

Reverend Morry warmed to his topic, his voice going into preacher mode. "There is an infestation of homosexuality here, and this Museum and this particular art show are a perfect example of how innocent museum goers are being indoctrinated to believe it's all normal. It's been revealed to me that that's why we're here, and I will take this moment to announce now we are building a church right here in Merryville!"

The camera man made the wind it up motion with his index finger.

"Thank you." She turned back to the camera, "This has been Jessica Walters with Reverend Morry—"

"Excuse me?" Lucas approached and said loudly, "I'm Lucas Windingle, on the Board at the Museum." He was young and dashing and, with his beautiful girlfriend, impossible to ignore. Photographers snapped pictures, and the TV camera swung around to him. The guy behind the camera made a keep going sign to his anchor. She lifted the microphone.

"Perfect! We at Channel Seven like to give balanced coverage. What do you think of the show?"

"As you may know, the Windingles love art, and for at least four generations we've been heavily involved in the Merryville museum. The exhibits we show not only educate, challenge and inspire our citizens to keep growing and to open their minds we—"

Reverend Morry grabbed the mic, "Not true! Not true! Here is Richland Bruce. He's the actual Chair of the Board. He'll describe the abomination awaiting in that exhibition tent!"

Richland made his way through the crowd and took the microphone from Reverend Morry. "Thank you, Reverend. I am *on* the Board, not official Chair yet, but I'm an official spokesperson for the Merryville Museum. What I'm about to tell you is not for young ears. I'm the one who found the chief artist for this show, Damien, on the ground in that very tent, after he was attacked by some dark force. His life is literally hanging by a thread right now! This *art show,*" he used air quotes, "is straight from the devil." He pointed toward the exhibit tent. "There is a mockery of a normal family at dinner and even a headless elephant suspended upside down from the ceiling!" Those around him gasped.

Phillip interrupted with, "Let's go see this show!" A few folks laughed.

When the laughter died down, the TV anchor asked, "Well, if you're in charge, Mister Bruce, why didn't you stop the show?" Jessica smiled sweetly.

"There's a board, Ms. Walters, and a process, but thank God for free speech." He beamed at the New Spirit crowd, who cheered.

Phillip took out his notepad and got down to work, "Isn't it true you were protested yourself for taking down a Stonewall exhibit at the Ohio Museum of Art? It seems to me you're here to dismantle anything having to do with the LGBT community. Isn't that right?"

"Actually no. Next question."

Reverend Morry was having none of it. "I would expect that from you. Aren't you the one who yelled out: Let's see the show? That's the point. No one should see this show. That's why we're here!" His followers roared in support.

Jessica Walters said, "Well, we appear to be at a standoff. I have an idea. Why don't I take you, Mister Bruce, and you, Mister Windingle, and a cameraman, and we let the folks at home judge for themselves?" Her smile showed perfectly white teeth. Some in the crowd, mob like, chanted "Judge for ourselves, judge for ourselves!" Others chanted "Shut it down! Shut it down!"

Lucas smiled a rakish smile, "Let's do this."

∾

Hortense was at home with her husband, Bill, who was nursing a hangover. Channel Seven was on in the background, and she was commenting as she talked on the phone to Lidia. "And this is another reason why we can't have Valerie Gooden on the board. Look at her! She's all over the news."

"Those lesbians," Lidia said in her papery voice. "Thank God that religious group is going to stop them." Hortense heard talking in the background.

"Lidia, are you watching right now?"

"It's on, yes."

"The group with those handmade signs, the ones against the church? Is that Bonnie Bruce-Pippin?"

"Dear Lord."

"I've got to call Janet."

∾

Bonnie's limbs were fatiguing. Not one for exercise, she was tired of carrying the sign but wasn't going to be the first to stop. Actually, it had finally sunk in how much trouble she was going to be in. Uncle Ricky had seen her and was giving her looks to kill. The real challenge came, however, when April, her New Spirit friend, approached her.

"Bonnie, can I talk to you?" April in all her prettiness, stood off to the side with her sign saying 'No Headless Elephants!" down at her side.

Bonnie said to Puddle, "I'll be right back."

She walked over to April and said, "Hi."

"Why are you doing this, Bonnie? I thought you were interested in God?"

"I-I am April."

"Then how could you support that woman Curator who is doing this? She's against the will of God! She decapitated an animal!"

Bonnie's own spiritual upbringing had been not so much. She tried to think back to what she learned at St. John's Sunday school. "My church didn't tell us art was bad, April."

April appeared frustrated at Bonnie's denseness. "It's not just about art, it's about homosexuality—lesbians! God doesn't want women marrying women and men marrying men. Your own Uncle Richland knows that. He changed! He's a real success story, Bonnie! You should be proud of him. He's trying to save you."

Bonnie was stunned. "From what?" She almost dropped her sign.

April looked up at the clouds, "You know."

"No, I don't know."

"You have tendencies, Bonnie. Everyone can see it. But it's not your fault. It probably runs in your family."

Bonnie's face turned beet red. She threw down her sign and ran away. She didn't know where she was going but felt like she should fling herself off the bluff to the rocks on the beach below.

Fortunately, Maribel was out back behind the exhibition tent, sneaking a cigarette. She saw Bonnie streaking by and clothes-pinned her with her outstretched arm. Bonnie fell to the ground and rolled up in a ball.

"Bonnie, what's going on?" Maribel scrunched down and touched the young woman, who was now sobbing.

Bonnie shrugged off her hand, snot running down her face. "Nothing, I want to die."

Maribel crushed out her cigarette, fully sat down on the ground, and held Bonnie while she wept.

❧

Meanwhile, Potts and Alexandra were inside getting drinks. A skinny millennial with a Words on a Plate t-shirt glanced forlornly at his near-empty tip jar. Alex tucked a five in as her date reached for his wallet.

"You bought the tickets. Let me get this." She smiled her radiant smile, and he didn't argue. They stood for a moment taking it all in, milling people, Juniper with Charlotte Windingle. There were not many people inside.

Potts sipped his bourbon. "Did you miss this crazy town when you were up north?"

Alexandra, in her sartorial splendor with a simple sheath dress and strand of real pearls, took a moment to answer. She was elegant. Her hair was down this evening, and Potts thought she had never been so beautiful.

"Actually, Charles, it was rather dull," she said. "Funny, a small town like this has more going on than San Francisco sometimes. I love a good protest." The couple turned toward the door. "Oh, look, the circus has arrived." She laughed her throaty laugh.

Richland, Lucas, Jessica Walters and a TV cameraman burst through the door, with Richland and Lucas still arguing.

Richland said loudly, "All the important art is religious! The Enlightenment in Florence Italy! The Sistine Chapel, the Pieta."

Lucas retorted, "The Rape of the Sabine Women, Venus on the Half Shell. Tons of Pagan art, too! It's all mythology, Richland! And it's all art!"

Jessica put her mic close to her lips and said, "Gentlemen, stop! Let's walk down the tables and see what we see. Hmmm. Mister Bruce, where is the decapitated elephant?"

"On the ceiling." Richland pointed up, but the only thing on the ceiling was a mirror in the shape of a plate. Everyone saw his look of horror reflected in the mirror.

Juniper walked over with Charlette in tow. "Are you finally seeing yourself, Richland?"

He snapped his head toward her and said, "You taking down that abomination is acknowledgement that it was wrong. Let's see what these plates are about."

"Please, enjoy the show," Juniper said sarcastically, motioning with her hand to the tables.

Richland followed the camera over to where the first pairing was exhibited. It was a portrait of a town, a Google Earth rendering in oil paint. A border of cash framed it. The plate was dirty. On it was a Barbie sized tire. In oil it read: "Dirty Rich." The next pairing was a picture of the bluff by the museum as it was lit up in the previous Floodlight exhibit. The painting had already been on display and was actually getting quite famous. The plate below was a chipped porcelain cat dish with one word, Feral.

The next portrait was of the outside of Chez Merida, the most upscale Mexican restaurant in town. It showed a poor family with brown skin peering in through the window at a white couple enjoying the native food. A hand thrown piece of pottery had the words, The Border Crossed Us. And on it went. The work was all Damien's and a poster-sized picture of him dominated the wall by the exhibit. A bio described him as one of the most important LGBT voices in art today.

As the TV showed a picture of two men in overalls with one holding a pitchfork, paired with a piece of pewter with the words in seeds, New American Gothic, Richland exploded. "This is all about Juniper Gooden's Gay Agenda!"

Lucas tucked in his chin and looked a whole lot like his Aunt Charlotte when he said in patrician tone, "Really? We've seen depictions about sexism, greed, racism, pollution and that's the only thing you find to comment about?" Richland stormed off with Lucas opening his hands in a gesture denoting theatrical confusion.

When they reached the end, Jessica said into the camera. "Well, I guess we need to let the art known as—Words on a Plate—literally speak for itself. Expect to hear more about this exhibit." That's a wrap.

Ms. Walters thanked Lucas, handed him her card, and then hurried toward the door smiling, probably dreaming about her Cronkite Award.

☙

Juniper watched the whole thing with Charlotte at her side. When it was over, Lucas brought his girlfriend toward them. I nudged Mitzi to make sure she didn't miss anything.

Lucas was tall and walked with purpose. "Aunt Charlotte, this is Bunny, Bunny, Charlotte Windingle." The young woman smiled nervously, and her white wine tipped dangerously. "Pleased to meet you. Aren't you so proud of Lucas?" She turned toward him, beaming.

Charlotte gave Bunny a social shake of the hand, then smiled at Lucas. "Actually, I am."

∾

CHAPTER TWENTY-TWO

Meanwhile, Richland was dragged back outside by Reverend Morry. "Richland, I'm afraid it's worse than we feared. Come with me." Rev Morry grabbed Richland's arm and led him to a young, blond woman. "Richland Bruce, I'd like you to meet April, a real go-getter for God."

"Nice to meet you, Mister Bruce." She flicked her hair and looked sad. "Um, it's about Bonnie."

Words were exchanged, and April pointed toward the direction Bonnie had fled. Richland said, "Thank you, April" and then, after giving Rev Morry's back a pat, he angrily took off toward the back of the exhibit hall.

Maribel helped Bonnie to her feet and gently brushed her hair from her eyes when Richland came skidding around the corner.

"I can't believe it! You, Maribel? What's going on here? Although I can see pretty well!"

"What? I'm not gay, but I know what you are. You're an asshole. Bonnie is having a really hard time. Don't you care about that?"

Richland went to Bonnie and grabbed her hand, which Bonnie snatched away. He glanced at Maribel and said, "This is a family matter, no concern of yours!" He grabbed Bonnie's arm again to drag her away. "You come home right now, young lady! Your mother's coming and you're embarrassing the family."

Bonnie broke away and went to Maribel and hung onto her for dear life. "Don't make me go!"

This put Maribel in a bad situation. "Richland, she's really upset. Let her stay for the rest of the show."

"Not on your life. This place is a hell hole." He yanked Bonnie's arm again and led her toward the parking lot. He spied his sister, Janet, pulling in with her car.

"Janet! Keep better control of my niece! She's jeopardized everything at the museum. Did you see her protesting out in front?"

"On TV, I'm afraid." Then to Bonnie, "You were not supposed to leave your room. I've got this, Richland." Janet appeared annoyed at both Bonnie and Richland.

Richland pulled himself up to his full five-foot eight-inches and brushed off the front of his clothes. "That's not all. She's showing lesbian tendencies."

"What?" Janet clutched her pearls.

"Some girl named April with New Spirit has been praying for her."

Bonnie's eyes grew wide. "Oh, God! Shut up!" She started crying again.

"We'll talk about this later. Bonnie, get in the car."

Bonnie was outgunned and walked to the car and sat in the back seat.

Janet gave a heavy sigh and got behind the wheel.

❧

Once the TV news crews packed up and left, the protest wound down quickly. Reverend Morry gave Richland a hearty man pat/hug and told him to keep doing the Lord's work. Richland nodded solemnly and went back into the exhibit to find Linda and anyone else on his side. He had meant to take Words on a Plate down but now wasn't sure how things were being perceived by the general public.

Maribel caught him going up the stairs. "Richland, what you did to Bonnie was horrible. She needs love—not your brand of religion."

His expression was menacing. "I supposed you mean gay love. I see you've signed on to Juniper's agenda."

Maribel looked disgusted and said, "You need therapy and I'm tempted to call Social Services. What you're doing to her with all this," she circled her hand around where the church protest had been, "is wrong. If she is gay, and who the hell knows, it's only going to hurt her worse."

Richland poked her chest. "Like I said before, it's not your concern."

Maribel stood there in disbelief, watching Richland go into the exhibit hall. She went to find Juniper.

❧

Puddle took Ekk, Elsa, and Dougie home. I waved them goodbye and turned to survey the wreckage. The Words on a Plate banner was partially torn down, and the lawn was littered with plastic cups, flyers and other junk. I picked up the fallen protest signs and took them to the trash bin, when Juniper ran over and stopped me before I could drop them in.

"Don't throw those away! We can use them for the next exhibit."

I held them up. "These?" I loved my friend, but she saw art in everything, and sometimes I didn't get it.

Mitzi walked up carrying an *Art is Dangerous* sign she'd picked up.

Juniper squealed, "That one's awesome, I may put it in my office." How could she be so chipper? She seemed positively inspired.

"Do you think there will be a next exhibit, Juniper?" Mitzi asked, voicing what I'd been thinking.

"Why yes, she does." These words were said by no less than the cultured voice of Charlotte Windingle, making her regal exit.

Juniper, Mitzi and I turned and smiled as Charlotte's crew descended the stairs. Charlotte's disposition had changed from depressed at the beginning of the exhibit to quite boisterous and happy by the end. She'd been interviewed by the Merryville Bee and said she honestly loved the show. Mitzi, Juniper and Valerie gave her a hug and smiled as she, Lucas and Bunny, said their goodbyes. I kept picking up signs and trash and shook my head in astonishment and relief.

"It's never dull around here," Maribel said as the Windingle Rolls pulled from the curb.

Juniper glanced at Maribel and asked, "Where have you been?"

"Actually, looking for you," she said. "I was assaulted by the Chairman of the Board."

We all crowded around her. "What happened?"

"I was comforting Bonnie—she had an incident with a friend, and Richland comes flying around the corner screaming at us about me," she took a deep shaky breath, "maybe taking advantage of her."

"Oh, God." Juniper's carefully painted nails covered her mouth.

"But you're not gay." I said, in my typically blunt fashion.

"Or a pedophile," Maribel added dryly.

Mitzi waved me quiet, "Then what happened?"

"He dragged Bonnie off to the parking lot. I went to find you." She glanced at Juniper, who shook with rage.

"I thought you said he assaulted you?" Mitzi asked.

"Yes. I ran into him again on the top of the stairs. Panda, I hoped you saw us, but you were looking down picking up trash. Anyway, he told me you and I, Juniper, have a gay agenda and then poked me in the chest three times!"

Valerie grabbed Maribel's arm. "Where are we going?"

"Let's see if Detective Potts is still here."

About this time, Phillip wandered over. "Hey, ladies, great show. Any comment for the Bee?"

Mitzi and I walked toward home, and I put her arm in mine. "Why would we want to travel anywhere else when all the action's here in Merryville?"

She pulled her arm out from mine and said, "Because I love to travel." Uh oh.

My alarm bells went off, and I felt I was walking on eggshells. "Hey, hey, I'm sorry, didn't want to change the mood. Can we talk? I mean really talk about things?"

We were still near the beach, so she sat on a bench facing the ocean and said, "Sure. Talk."

I was about to speak, but she beat me to it.

"You going to yell at me for being late all the time?"

This was a surprise, "No, I—"

"I really don't like that."

"I'm sorry." I was. In the grand scheme of things what did it matter? We sat in silence for a while.

"So'kay." She had forgiven me, again. Another beat as a chill breeze ruffled her hair. "Panda, do you think we're still in danger?"

"I don't know. Let me check." I clownishly studied her shoulders, where wings would sprout if needed. "Nope. We're good."

She smiled in spite of herself. "Panda, I need to admit something. When the first Twyla came along, I felt like she *got me* and you didn't." Seeing my crestfallen face, she added. "Not that you didn't want to understand, you couldn't, ya know?"

My heart sank. "I know. You said she was a magical creature. I felt like since I wasn't magic, you two shared something I couldn't. That made me jealous, and I'm sorry for that." The evening air blew over us, and I stared out at the ocean.

"Oh, honey," she hugged me tight, and we were silent for a few minutes. Below the waves lapped gently against the shore. "When you went missing— got kidnapped—I realized you are my magic. I didn't really care about yoga Twyla. I love you. I would be lost without you."

"Good to hear." A few people walked by with dogs and a jogger zoomed past. "It doesn't hurt that my family is magical too, right? Super Intuiter! But that doesn't sound nearly as sexy as *flying girl*." I put my head on her shoulder. "I know the feeling, Mitz. When I was on a plane flying to Germany to try and get you back, the loss was unbearable to think about."

"See? You fly, too. You just do it in an airplane. Magic Smajick. We need to keep an eye on each other. Who's next to be kidnapped, Brutus?" She held one of my hands in both of hers and scanned the horizon. "That was really something tonight, Puddle gathering everyone to protest." She gave a soft laugh.

"Oh, yeah, I need to tell you, Puddle's taking off again. She won't be there when we get home." Mitzi gave me a frown.

"She said she needed time to process, whatever that means."

Mitzi shook her head and her beads swung. "Where to this time?"

"She said she'll call me when she gets there."

Mitzi made an O with her mouth.

"It's okay. This is her M.O. She's fine."

"Without even saying good bye?" Mitzi was irritated. I stroked her arm soothingly and met her eyes. "You know how she is. We've got a family, Mitzi. A crazy weird Merryville family with fairies and elves, and pot smokers who move across the globe at a moment's notice, and even a beautiful half griffin, but I love it." I kissed her forehead.

"Don't forget a homophobic stock broker," she added.

I let that pass.

"She's going to find Dieter, isn't she?"

"That's my guess." I overheard her talking to him on the phone. At least I think it was him, who knows? The tension that hovered between us seemed to vanish.

Mitzi squeezed my hand. "I've been really mad at myself."

"Why?"

"Because when I was talking to Sister Lucia, I realized that I've been taking you for granted."

Wow, like my brother could be stubborn, Mitzi never admits when she's wrong. I quietly snugged her up closer and thanked my lucky stars she'd met that nun on the plane.

Headlines the next day were mixed but mostly supportive of the Words on a Plate exhibit and Juniper Gooden. An inset by Phillip gave an update on Damien, still in a coma, and the search for his assailant. By Monday's edition, the Letters to the Editor were flying.

"Did you see this?" Linda Chicolet was holding up the paper as she sat in Richland's office. She read, "Richland Bruce, formerly of the Cleveland Museum of Art, doesn't understand California. He should go back to the Midwest."

Here's another, "Juniper Gooden has once again turned our Museum into a public spectacle. She needs to go, now!" Then there's, "We are not a Caliphate! Get Religion out of our parks and art shows!" She put the paper down, "Are you listening?"

Richland sat, stroking his goatee. He looked dangerous. "I'll handle this."

At the Gooden's house, Valerie read the same paper out loud. "There was no mention of the assault, as Phillip said he needed more background." Valerie only read Juniper the things against Richland, and they howled in laughter over morning coffee. The crashing sound of breaking glass came from the living room. Layla jumped up, barking like crazy. Valerie raced ahead of Juniper to see that a rock, wrapped in paper, had been thrown through the picture window.

"Call 9-1-1!" Juniper called to Valerie, who stood stock still, as though paralyzed. With a shiver, Valerie came to her senses and picked up the vintage land line to dial, but there was no tone.

"Oh, my God, Juni—the phone line's been cut!"

"Get the cell phone!"

"It's upstairs charging!" They ran around like Keystone cops, which made the dog bark more. Juniper was part way up the stairs when Valerie, who patted her pockets, said, "Wait, it's in my robe pocket with the keys." At that, as if with one mind, they ran outside to the car.

"Grab the rock!" Valerie went back inside and returned with another bulging pocket.

❧

AT THE FOWLERS

Though the morning started peacefully, something in my gut was tingling. Strange. I was enjoying my second cup of coffee in the kitchen and reading the paper when I heard our unmistakable door-bell ring out Scotland the Brave. Elsa came in the room at the same time, and our eyes locked. We were getting better at this intuition thing.

I raced to open the front door and Valerie, Juniper, and Layla the dog pushed their way inside. Being the youngest child, I always go to humor. "Hello, Pajama party? Did I lose my invitation?"

Juniper's eyes were wide. "Somebody threw a rock through our picture window and cut our phone line. Someone's after us!"

I slammed the door and shot the bolt. Layla lay down on the floor in front of the door as if to keep intruders out.

Brutus gave the dog the evil eye as Valerie, Juniper and I instinctively looked through the window curtins as if expecting another rock, while Elsa said, "I'll get Ekk."

"Who, what?" Mitzi came down the stairs at the commotion, rubbing her eyes.

Valerie turned, "This morning we were reading the paper, and someone threw a rock though our window!" Her robe was open, and Valerie's bright yellow nightgown, covered in cheerful ducks, did not comport with this information. This was so wrong.

"Gay haters?" Mitzi offered. "We've seen the paper."

"Don't know. But somebody hates us." Juniper didn't have her make up on, and I saw the stress in her face. That's not all. Valerie picked up our landline. Somebody must have cut that, too."

Elsa came in with Ekk, who had obviously only just woken up. He was really sleeping well in his new treehouse. "Ladies, tell me everything."

We all started talking at once. Ekk's pale blue eyes went from one to the other under his worried brow.

The doorbell played Scotland the Brave again and I peered through the peep hole and saw it was Alexandra Stephanovsky. My house felt like a set on a play. I deadpanned, "Valerie, your defense attorney's here."

Always the good hostess, Elsa said, "Let's all sit down. I'll get us some tea and coffee."

Alexandra came in and shut the door behind her. The woman always floored me. Here it was before nine a.m., and she had on matching shorts and top and not a hair out of place. "I came to help with the investigation."

"We called for Potts, not defense counsel." This was from Valerie. I don't think she had yet recovered from the shock and was not connecting the dots.

Alex blushed. "I was there when you called him."

I raised my eyebrows a bit. We knew they were a thing, but this was juicy. Good for them. Alexandra turned to Juniper. "Charlie is going to your house first. Any coffee? And I can't believe you guys touched the rock—Charlie told me you have it. It may have had evidence on it!"

Elsa came back in the room with a full tray and Mitzi jumped up to help her. We all sat down to try to figure out what was going on. Valerie smiled and from inside her bathrobe pulled out said rock, which was in a baggie. "No worries, I always keep baggies for Layla. Nobody's touched it since it was chucked through our window."

"Well done," we all chorused.

∾

Potts brought patrol officers to the Gooden house with him and parked down the street. He and the two officers silently walked down the street when he ran into Dougie. "Get inside, young man."

The boy's eyes were wide. "You gonna go all SWAT on the old lady at Juniper and Val's house?"

Potts grabbed the twelve-year-old. "Who are you kid? You know anything, see anything? Otherwise get lost, it could get dangerous." This came out brisker than Detective Potts intended, but his adrenaline was pumping.

"I'm Dougie, Doug. I live over there." He pointed and started to cry. "I saw a lady go in the back this morning." Dougie was twisting away.

Potts let go and softened his voice. "It's okay." He brushed off the kid's shirt where he had grabbed it. "Could you identify her if you saw her again?"

"Maybe. She was wearing a big hat with flowers on it."

"That's good, kid, real good. Do the Goodens know how to find you?"

The young man nodded silently, sniffling.

"Good. Now go inside." He watched Dougie run off toward a house a couple of doors down from the Goodens. The boy flew over the curb with a great leap in the way children do and went inside.

"A little old lady? From Pasadena, I suppose." Potts said under his breath. Let's go see.

Damien opened his eyes. The iconic artist blinked, and his large brown eyes took in the scene. Maribel sat in the corner, reading a book, her blue hair spilling over her forehead. He was hooked to bottles on an IV rack and a monitor beeped softly by his bed. His head hurt like a son-of-a-bitch.

"I like your hair," he croaked.

Maribel, startled, dropped her book and stood. "Damien! Oh my God! Let me get someone." She moved closer to the bed. "We've been taking turns watching you. I need to call—"

He grabbed her arm. "Blue Hair. Maribel. Stop." He coughed. "Give me some water."

She did, holding the straw close to his cracked lips.

"Where's Richland?"

"Who? Richland?"

Damien coughed, then spoke. "Yes Richland. He's out of his mind, Maribel. Sit back down and let me tell you a few things that happened back in Ohio."

CHAPTER TWENTY-THREE

Potts edged up to the Gooden's house and indicated with two fingers that he would go around to the back while the uniforms covered the front. It had been eons since he took part in action like this, and it felt good.

Easing down the side of the old craftsman, he tried to flatten his rather large frame against the clapboard siding. It didn't work like in the movies as his gut stuck out. He wheezed and wished he could quit his smoking habit. Ironically, he would have killed at that moment for a cigarette. All these thoughts flashed by in a nano-second as he turned the corner and was hit in the head by a frying pan. The last thing he saw before blacking out was a big hat with feathers on it that seemed vaguely familiar.

Alexandra got a call, and I saw her expression change.

"Is he going to be okay? Which ER? I'll be right there."

"What happened?" I asked as she ended the call.

"Charlie is nursing a large goose egg on his head from a frying pan, and the assailant got away. The uniformed officers searched your house and found nothing disturbed except in the backyard area by the fence."

"Oh, my God!" Juniper said. "That's where I planted what was left of the bulbs from the Rothschild Orchids. Who could have known that?" She and Valerie exchanged a look.

Alex went on. "Someone took a shovel to it. There were also several man-sized footprints in the dirt outside, which leads them to believe it may not have actually been a woman who broke in." She laughed. "They told me Charlie didn't think it was a woman. He said that pan was swung like a baseball bat."

"Like women don't play ball," Mitzi said.

"Our frying pan?" Valerie interrupted, visibly upset. "That means—"

"Yes." Alexandra nodded. "Whoever did it was in your house, A frying pan is a weapon of chance not choice. What would they be after?"

The color drained from Valerie's face. "Us."

I walked Alexandra to the front door. "Let us know what we can do." I didn't know what, but it seemed like the thing to say.

She turned around briefly before exiting. "You can start by keeping those two here." Alex pointed to Juniper and Valerie. "I'll ask Charlie if the Merryville PD can spare a black and white parked in front of your house for protection. Oh, and you can give me the rock. I'll turn it over to the police lab." Valerie handed over the rock and Alexandra hurriedly left to go to her man.

Valerie called after her, "Please tell Detective Potts thank you and I hope he's better soon."

Juniper, Mitzi, Valerie and I followed Alexandra to her car, the other three still in their jammies.

As the attorney pulled out of the drive, Mitzi declared. "That's it, you're staying here 'til this is sorted out. Puddle left us last night, so we have plenty of room."

"Did she? Everything okay? I need to hear all about what everyone's doing. In the meantime, I can hardly wear this out on the street." Juniper spread her arms indicating her silky pajamas.

"Um, that's exactly what you're doing, putting it out on the street." I laughed. "Let's go inside."

Ekk was waiting by the fireplace. Elsa had leftover quiche and lemonade, as well as coffee and tea on the living room table.

I commented, "Our numbers are dwindling. Twyla went to New York with Brooke, and we're pretty sure Puddle left for South America after the museum protest. She must have bought tickets when we arrived two days ago at the airport."

"That was sudden. When did you find out?" Juniper picked up a coffee.

"She told me at the museum she was leaving, but she didn't want a big thing made about it."

Ekk cleared his throat. "She actually told me first. I let Panda know a few more details when she and Mitzi got home last night. That's why Elsa and I didn't go to the museum at first. We were helping Puddle get organized."

Valerie plated a small slice of quiche. "Do you know where in South America?"

"Nope. She'll let us know when she gets there, unless Ekk cares to divulge that, too?" I realized he knew a lot more than he was telling.

"Be patient with your sister, trust her." Ekk, the wise.

Mitzi jumped in. "Panda and I are pretty sure she's going to meet Dieter, a guy we met while we were in Peru." Mitzi looked worried. "Panda thinks it's fine, but I don't know about that guy. He worked for Wolfrum back in Germany."

"What?" Valerie put her plate down so fast it clattered. "I would so want to know who's with her. Is she alone?"

Ekk had been silent. "Not exactly."

All our heads swiveled toward him simultaneously. I said, "Time to spit it out, Ekk. What's going on?"

"Please don't take offense, Panda. Juju's her guardian. It's like being in the presidency. Once you leave, you still have the Secret Service keeping you safe."

Mitzi was gobsmacked.

He went on. "All of you will have someone watching over you. They may not be as obvious as Elsa and I, but they'll be there. You're all part magic." He looked at Juniper, "or at least know way too much about it."

We stopped talking and thought about it for a moment. In all the nonstop action, tiredness and day to day life, I think this was the first time the idea fully dawned on me. "Juju?"

Ekk nodded. "He really likes Puddle. She'll be safe. If she's not, we'll all hear about it *tout de suite*."

I cracked up. "I heard an elf say toot sweet."

A giggle rippled through the room, and Mitzi added, "Yeah, and Brooke's in New York with Twyla, the fuckup fairy." At that we all howled, momentarily forgetting the danger our friends were in.

Juniper said, "She's probably lost him his job by now. Can you imagine her showing up at the stock market?"

Even Ekk had to laugh.

"Now, now, give her a chance." Elsa reminded me of my grandmother, always willing to give someone the benefit of the doubt.

When the hysterical laughter subsided, Ekk said, "Ladies, I'll go with one of you to your house to get some personal things. The coast, as they say, seems to be clear. You shouldn't be alone there right now."

"We changed the locks. How could she get in?" Valerie played with her ponytail, sleek and black. "We had Lulu." She turned to me, "Panda, she's going to be a cop, right?"

I cleared my throat and thought of her saving my hide when I was under attack at the strip mall and said, "She's one of the bravest people I know, and she'll make a great cop someday. Speaking of the strip mall, I do need to show up tomorrow for work. What do you all have going on this week?"

Juniper answered first. "I need to go see Damien this morning. The poor darling still hasn't woken up. Maribel took the first shift and I told her I'd go at ten. The museum's closed today, anyway."

"I'll go with you, Juniper. It's best if we stick together." Mitzi had such confidence now that she could fly. I was liking this. "What about you, Val?"

Valerie said, "My week is pretty open. I'm between clients for the moment. I was going to work on our garden. She turned to me, "But if we're staying here, let me see what I can do with those Scottish Thistles that have been the bane of Hortense's existence." We all laughed, and Mitzi punched me.

"You don't have to ask me twice. That would be great. Let's go in the yard and plot and plan. I would love to show you Ekk and Elsa's new digs." I got up and carried my coffee toward the door.

"*Ja*, we love our new home, don't we, Ekk?" Elsa smiled sweetly.

Ekk added, "It's great except for a gossipy squirrel." We all laughed, and I realized we were a pretty happy bunch when together.

Valerie brightened. "Did I tell you about Twyla re-constituting the orchids? It was an amazing thing to try to do." She covered her mouth and smiled, shaking her head, her shiny black hair swinging loose. Layla got up with a grunt and followed Valerie outside. Brutus followed him protectively. I guess even the animals had a security detail.

"Valerie, I still need to fill you in on Peru. There's so much to tell. Mitzi has a *nun* therapist now. But Twyla, yeah, she meant well." We laughed again. I loved being with my friends.

Ekk threw up his hands. "I warned you about fairies, Panda."

The house was finally quiet as Mitzi took Juniper upstairs to find her an outfit to wear outside. Actually, some of my clothes fit her better than Mitzi's.

When Juniper came back, I burst out laughing. The woman ordinarily wouldn't be caught dead in jeans and a Pussy Riot t-shirt with the lead singer making the double eagle sign, but somehow she rocked it.

"How come I don't look like that when I wear those clothes?"

She made a dramatic pose and patted her hair like a 1920s star, "It's all in how you present it, darling."

I heard a cell phone ringing, "You light up my life," a reference to her previous show. "That's got to be for you, Juniper."

She picked it up and said, "Hello, Maribel, I—oh, that's good actually! I'm on my way as soon as I can go home and change. What? No, never mind. I'll see you in a minute."

"What's happened?"

"Damien woke up. He said Richland is crazy."

"We knew that." I tossed pillows around trying to find my phone.

"No, like Batshit crazy."

Mitzi stood next to her, my darling wife the protector, car keys in hand.

"I'll tell you on the way. Will you dial Phillip while I drive? Damien is asking for him."

Alexandra arrived at the hospital as Detective Potts was being released from the Emergency room.

"I never saw him coming, Alex."

"Oh, Charlie, are you sure it was a man?"

"I don't know. It happened so fast. I sound like one of those witnesses I always complain about." He mimicked himself, "I saw the big hat with a feather. Did you get the rock? I bet those girls got their finger prints all over it."

"Of course, and no, they didn't." She produced the rock in its baggie. "We can drop it off at the PD while I take you home." A hospital receptionist came in the room with a clipboard. "I think we're all set, Mister Potts. Your credit card went through. You can go now. "She turned to Alexandra. "Are you here to drive him?"

"I am."

"Good, he's got quite a concussion."

The couple headed toward the glass and chrome exit.

Alex touched Charlie's arm. "Hey, there's Juniper and Mitzi."

Charlie walked up to them as they strode purposefully through the ER.

"Wow, you got here quick," Mitzi said. "Or have you not left yet? I guess it doesn't matter. We left a message telling you Damien woke up!"

"Thank you for going to our house," Juniper said. "So sorry about that." She pointed to the rather large bandage on his head.

"Only a flesh wound, part of the job."

Alexandra joined them as they moved to the elevator. "Come on, John Wayne, let's see what Damien has to say."

Hortense was preparing for the emergency meeting the next day. She made her last notification call to Sally. Sally was last on her list because, well, she was so easy. Her husband Jack had approached Hortense years ago and asked her to take Sally under her wing. She was, as society folk say, a bit distracted. The rich are eccentric while the poor are considered crazy. This thought made Hortense giggle.

"Hello?" Jack answered on the fourth ring.

"Hortense here, Jack. Will you tell Sally we have an emergency meeting Tuesday at two p.m.? It's at the McGreggor Mansion."

"Sure, what's the emergency?"

"Oh, um, some membership business. I don't want to bore you with it."

"Sally's been agitated lately after the meetings. Is there anything I should know about?"

Hortense cleared her throat. "If you saw the news, you saw that protest at the museum. We have that big project coming up there soon. Sally is very involved. Maybe that's it."

"Well, please figure it out. I don't need my Sally upset. I've already ordered the roses."

"Don't worry, Jack, I'm taking care of the Merryville Mavens. Once we take care of a little hitch in our git-along, as you Americans say, we should have a return to our golden era. Denise McGreggor is back, and she's got a friend to put up for membership. The cavalry is on the way!"

Jack smiled at that. "I've driven by that mansion many times and always wanted to see the inside." His voice warmed. After all, these women did love gardens, houses, and beautiful things. How dangerous could that be?

"Oh, Jack, wait 'til you see the gardens! Agnes, Denise's mother, put her heart and soul into it. I'll see if we can have a garden party there next Spring."

"I'll make sure she's there."

"Thank you, Jack. Bye now." Hortense hung up, probably the last person in Merryville with a dial up phone.

Damien was sitting up taking nourishment. Detective Potts, with a large bandage on his head, sat at his bedside. "Mister Simpson. Looks like we have matching noggins."

"Noggin. What a quaint term, and I go by Damien."

Potts opened his wallet to show his badge. "Listen, Damien, if you know something, tell me. Otherwise we won't be able to find out who did this to you."

Juniper and Mitzi were in the corner, trying to be unobtrusive. Alex sat on the windowsill.

Damien asked Juniper, "Where did you find Detective Dragnet?" He appeared to be making up his mind about something. "By the way, love the tee."

Juniper looked down at her t-shirt and rolled her eyes. "You can trust him."

Phillip knocked on the door and poked his head in. "I got here as fast as I could."

Juniper said to Potts, "Damien asked me to call him."

The room was crowded, and Potts said, "We need to clear the room. Girls?"

Damien shook his head. "I'm not talking without Juniper and the press here."

The expression on Alex's face said she would deal with being called *girl* later. "Come on, Mitzi, I hear the coffee downstairs is divine."

Damien was the center of the universe and seemed to like it.

He was surrounded by flowers and had three yogurts on his tray in front of him. He loved drama and gave a meaningful pause. Juniper stood on the other side of the bed from Detective Potts. After a moment, Juniper prompted him. "Well, we're all ears, dying to know what happened?"

Damien sighed. "Richland didn't tell you?"

Phillip and Potts said simultaneously. "Richland Bruce?"

Potts said over his shoulder to the reporter, "You're only here because my witness wants you here. Don't interrupt. Report, write—or whatever it is you do."

When he turned back around to Damien, Phillip saluted to Potts's back.

Juniper said, "You may not remember, but you told Maribel Richland was crazy. What did you mean?"

"I mean," he grabbed at Juniper's hand, "he came to the tent that night to sabotage your exhibit, my art. I surprised him."

Potts said, "Go on."

Damien made a face and said, "I'm very allergic to cigarette smoke. Do you bathe in it?"

Juniper poked the artist. "Suck it up, Damien. He's the law and he's actually on our side, so spill what you remember. The quicker you tell us, the quicker he can get out of here and do some justice."

"Wow, too much caffeine? You sound so *noir*. Okay, but it has to stay between us girls. Pull up your chair for a bedtime story."

Charlie Potts turned to Juniper. "Maybe he got hit harder than we thought."

❧

ON THISTLE DRIVE

The rest of Sunday was rather uneventful, and it felt good to be home. Brooke called and said he was getting ready for his first day back at work and that Twyla had already cleaned out his refrigerator. The apartment was small, and he was worried New York was going to be hard for her. They were going to need to work out some sort of routine.

We talked a few more minutes, and he said, "Has Mitzi heard from that nun we met in Peru?"

"Sister Lucia? Not that I know of, why?"

"I keep thinking about her, them, and the work they do. That's all. Can I have her, their number?"

My wheels were turning. "Maybe you can help them with your financial wizardry."

"Maybe I can, and, sis, check in every now and then, okay?"

"Absolutely." It was nice to have my brother back in my life.

Valerie was as good as her word, and the two of us finally put the front yard in the shape it should have been. To tell the truth, sweat and sunshine and putting my hands in dirt was good therapy.

❧

BACK TO WORK

Monday was interesting. Babs, my one and only employee, had done everything she could to keep things running, but there are some things people have hired me alone to do. The tax season was over for now, but the Jiu Jitzu place a few doors down wanted me to do their books, and a month of receipts needed organizing.

Ekk was with us, we all got busy, and it was quiet for a time. After going through the mail, all the things that have happened this year hit me. I thought about being in the jungles of Peru only a few days before. Puddle may be back there now.

I sat and stared through the glass front door and pondered the parking lot and street beyond, with its busy traffic, and sighed. Could I readjust to this?

Ekk threw a balled-up piece of paper at me. "Earth to Panda."

I stared back insolently, "What?"

"You're not getting much done." He stuck a pencil behind his ear and restacked some papers in front of him.

"I'm thinking of where we were a week ago. You know?" I said. "It's surreal now to be here. At least I know I'm not crazy when I see you."

He laughed. "Juju told me Remy thought you were crazy when you put your hand in the Amazon river."

"Who knew there were piranhas in there?" I started giggling.

Babs looked up from her desk. "I don't know how your vacations get so screwed up, Panda." She laughed, and it broke the spell I was in.

Around noontime I opened the door to let in a breeze and saw a strip mall security guard, but it wasn't Lulu.

"Hi, I'm Panda, and you are?"

"Pete." He tipped is head. "I'm new."

"Hey, did Lulu start the academy?" I missed her watching over us in her ill-fitting uniform, with her big ol' heart and funny way of talking.

Pete gave an evasive answer, "Don't know. She was gone before they hired me, I think she quit."

Babs batted her eyelashes at Pete and chimed in, "With all the strange goings on, I guess our landlord is finally taking security seriously. He even had the light bulbs in the parking lot changed."

"Yes, ma'am, darkness is the highway of criminals."

I turned and rolled my eyes as Mitzi showed up at the door. "Panda, I just left the hospital. The cops are after Richland Bruce!"

"That's an APB, All Points Bulletin." We all ignored Pete.

"For what?" All pretense of work was gone. Mitzi had all our ears. Pete put his hand on his belt like an arrest was imminent.

I explained to our new guard. "You read in the papers about that artist, Damien, down at the Merryville museum?" He nodded.

Mitzi went on, "Well, Richland is the one who pushed Damien. The police want him for questioning."

"Wow." Babs pulled her chair closer. "Please fill me in. Last thing I know you're all in Peru, and then I see you on TV protesting the museum. That Richland Bruce guy works there, right?"

Pete ambled off with a friendly wave.

Ekk said to Babs, who was still following Pete with her eyes, "Richland Bruce may end up the new Chairman of the Board. Yes, you could say he works there." Nobody likes a snarky elf.

"Well, anyway, now they're wondering if he wasn't the one at Juniper and Valerie's house, dressed in that floppy hat." Mitzi was fully engaged. She loved community gossip. "Imagine, not only will that stop all this fear and damage, he can't work at the museum after this."

"I tidied my piles of paper. Where's Juniper now? Wanna go home?"

"She stayed with Damien at the hospital. And yes, I walked here. You can drive me." She grinned, and my heart did a flip flop. I looked guiltily at Ekk, who sat in my chair and waved me off. "Go Home. Go."

I felt better than I had in a month.

We got in my Smart car and drove the few blocks home. I stopped before pulling in the driveway, noting the previously sloppy mess that passed for our yard now could be an example from Home and Garden magazine. Brutus sat on our small porch and had probably been supervising the activity. My jaw dropped. Mitzi exuded mischievous energy. "Valerie swore me to secrecy. I couldn't wait to see the look on your face."

I pulled in and parked, got out and walked through the yard. Not only were the thistles trimmed, Valerie had planted flowers in the beds and thoroughly weeded. She came around the back with her gardening gloves on and Layla in tow.

I ran to her and gave her a big hug, "You're amazing, Valerie! How could you do all this in one day?"

"Well, you and I did a lot of clean up yesterday. This was the fun part."

While we stood there admiring Valerie's work, I heard a beep. I turned to see a lovely brunette pull up and park behind my car in her Mercedes.

Valerie pulled off a glove and waved. "Hey, Sylvia, check this out." The well- dressed woman got out and va-va-voomed to where we were standing.

"Sylvia, these are two of my best friends, Panda and Mitzi Fowler. Panda and Mitzi, this is Sylvia Arviso. Without her, I wouldn't be a Merryville Maven."

Sylvia was gracious, "It's so nice meeting you, and kudos for such a beautiful yard." Then to Val, "Can I talk to you for a minute?" While they talked privately, Mitzi and I went into our home. Baking smells emanated from the kitchen.

I put my arm around Mitzi. "It doesn't get better than this." The moment was quickly over when we heard Valerie scream in frustration. She marched into our house and slammed the door. "That bitch!"

"Who? Sylvia?" Now I was curious.

"No, Hortense Miller. She's scheduled an emergency meeting of the executive board tomorrow to try to get me kicked out!"

"Why?" The soft scent of roses now mixed with the aroma of baked goods. I was sure Elsa was calming things down in her elf magic way.

Mitzi said, "Come here. Sit on the couch and tell us all about the dynamics of this group. If they're mean girls, they all act the same whether it's horticulture or high school."

She stood there, so I pulled her toward the couch and took her gardening gloves. She had a thistle in her hair and I fished it out. "You've been working hard. We really need a snack."

Mitzi gave me the look, *any excuse for a snack.*

"Tea anyone?" Elsa entered the living room with a tray laden with scones, clotted cream and Lady Gray. The woman was positively psychic.

"I have half a mind to drive over there and quit!" Valerie said. "She had her hands on her hips, a sign of defiance for the usually gentle woman. "She put *provisional* next to my name at our last meeting. She didn't do that for the other new member." She ran out of steam and sat down.

Elsa said, "I have a feeling it's going to be fine," and smiled mysteriously, pouring our friend a cup of lavender tea.

❧

CHAPTER TWENTY-FOUR

THE MCGREGGOR MANSION

Tuesday at two o'clock came and the leadership of the Merryville Mavens parked their cars on the crushed stone, curved drive of the old McGreggor Mansion. Hortense inhaled deeply as she closed the door on Janet's Audi. "Smell those roses, Janet. Drink this all in!"

Janet, busy with retrieving her purse from the back seat, did as she was told. It was obvious consistent and expensive work had been done on the grand front yard. Neat rows of rose bushes lined the drive and cleverly patterned brick walkways drew the eye toward other bits of well-placed greenery, secret alcoves and other focus points. It was absolutely stunning.

"This," Hortense said, "is what the Merryville Horticultural Society is all about." She beamed and waved at Lidia and Sally, who had arrived moments before and were walking up to join their leader. Florence got out of her small Mercedes, which was almost a twin to the one Sylvia had. They laughed a bit at that. The six women were soon on the front porch. Lidia rang the doorbell after getting the nod from Hortense.

Denise's man, Fergus, opened the door and greeted the women. "Ladies? May I take your wraps? Right this way, please." Hortense almost shivered. It had been years since her old friend Agnes held similar meetings in the mansion. She didn't realize it until now how much she missed it. Finally, things were being put right again. She said to Sylvia, "I'm so sorry you never got to meet Agnes McGreggor. What a dear, wonderful patron of horticulture."

Florence added, "Yes indeed, we're going to restore some of the former glory of the group. Why, I remember when Denise was a young girl, so pretty in those plaid dresses her mother brought from Scotland."

Sylvia smiled and followed the women into an elaborately posh parlor. Denise, who sat on a butter colored sofa, stood to greet them. A shining tea set was laid out on the table in front of a marvelous fireplace flanked by two floor to ceiling windows overlooking the garden.

"Denise, so lovely to see you!" Hortense gave her an air kiss, followed by

Florence. It was as if some protocol had been decided but never spoken. The other women followed suit.

"Please ladies! Have a seat."

Sylvia, no stranger to big money, said, "Your French heritage furniture is amazing. Did you redecorate?"

"You have quite an eye. Yes, mother was all Henkel Harris, but having lived in France for a few years, I have to surround myself with Paris! Shall I be mother?" Denise asked, lifting the tea pot.

The comment struck Hortense, who began to think Denise wasn't at all like her mother. "Yes, I remember Agnes wanted furniture made in the United States—quite a traditionalist."

"But the colors are lovely," Florence added, giving Hortense a side glance. Sally silently gravitated to one of the windows overlooking the garden and stood there entranced.

Janet eagerly reached for one of the petit fours. Lidia pulled out her yellow pad and said in her papery voice, "Well, the tea is very nice, very nice, but let's not forget why we're here."

"All in good time, Lidia." Hortense took control, turning toward Denise. "We do have some pressing business. But first, tell us what you've been doing these past few years, dear."

Denise paused a beat, "I went to Europe to find myself. You know, our family has deep roots in Scotland. I decided to take some classes at the University of Edinburgh and ended up falling in love."

"Oh, that's marvelous, dear!" Hortense sipped her tea. She appeared to be enjoying herself enormously. "But how did you end up in France?"

As if on cue, a slender woman who could have been a stand-in for a young Audrey Hepburn entered the room. She was poised, and her gleaming smile was lustrous. In her soft accent she said, "Sorry, darling, the call home took longer. You know how Marcele gets." Bridget kissed Denise on the cheek, then turned to the group and said, "He runs our apartment in Paris."

"Marcele does mean *warring*," Denise added with a throaty laugh.

The energy in the room changed. Hortense, Janet and Flo looked at each other, stunned. Sally said, "You have an apartment in Paris? Jack said he would take me someday."

"What are you telling us, Denise?" Hortense asked.

Denise laughed. "That's what I was about to say. You see, I fell in love with a certain librarian," she squeezed Bridget's hand, "at the University of Edinburgh. We married last fall."

When she told Valerie later, Sylvia said you could have knocked all the women off the couch with a finger they were so brittle.

Since none of them could afford to offend Denise, who they'd already accepted for full membership, the possibility of coming up with reasons why

Valerie's membership should not be approved, while not mentioning the real reason, was priceless and impossible. But Hortense tried.

"Well, it's her close relationship with those girls. She doesn't really want them to get rid of that scourge in the yard. They're ground zero."

"The Fowlers? I hope you're not going to talk about thistles again. I heard you're trying to eradicate them." Denise smiled, but it wasn't warm.

"Denise, they're weeds!" Florence said. "Do we want weeds choking Merryville?"

Lidia sputtered, "That Valerie lied. She said they cleaned up their yard, but when we took a busload by, it was still unsightly. We can't have that. We need to trust our members."

The doorbell rang. Bridget stood and said, "I'll leave this to you, dear. Shall I get the tapestry?"

"Yes." Denise was quiet a moment. "Do you all feel the same way?"

Both Sylvia and, surprisingly, Sally, said, "No."

Sylvia cleared her throat. "Actually, I drove by the Fowler's house yesterday. Valerie helped them with the gardening. She's done a real turn around on their yard. Let me show you pictures on my cell phone."

Fergus announced, "Ms. Beatrice Mortimer."

A few things happened at once. First, Beatrice called from the hall, "Sorry I'm late girls. Bianca had to go gassie."

Fergus jumped as if someone had goosed him and disappeared quickly, probably picturing the pristine lawn with doggy driblets all over it.

Hortense settled back into the couch. "Well, it's not only that thistles are unsightly and pose a threat, we need to trust our members. If your mother was here, she would understand completely."

Janet, attempting to appear fair, said to Sylvia, "Let me see that picture." A scone rolled off her plate and onto the light blue rug. A white pug came flying into the room and snarfed it up almost before it hit the floor. All heads turned as the portly heiress lumbered painfully into the room.

Denise's face lit up. "BeaBea!" Then turning to Hortense said, "Of course you know Bea Vanderhooven-Mortimer. It seemed right to have the old gang back together!"

Once Beatrice got settled, Denise asked, "Now why don't you trust Valerie Gooden?"

Bea popped a scone in her mouth and talked around it. "Oh please, they don't like her cuz she's a lesbian."

After admiring the yard one more time and drinking our lavender tea, I dropped off Valerie to meet Juniper, who was still with Damien. One of Merryville's finest now guarded the door.

"How is he?"

Juniper's outfit was put together, but a tad wilted. She covered a yawn and displayed well- manicured nails over her pink lipstick. Valerie and I yawned in response, and I giggled.

"What?" Juniper looked at me quizzically.

"I've always heard that if you yawn and other people follow that means they're not serial killers or psychopaths."

"Good to know," she said deadpan.

Valerie added, "It's true. Something to do with inability to have compassion."

"So tell!"

Juniper motioned for us to follow and we walked to the scarred, institutional chairs in the waiting room. "Damien says Richland pushed him, but he doesn't think he was trying to hurt him. What he's really worried about is Richland's state of mind. He's a self-hating gay and you know they can be dangerous. Damien and Richland were a thing years ago in Ohio. Then family and religious pressure threatened his job at the museum, and he dropped Damien like a piece of hot coal."

"Internalized homophobia—it's the worst."

Valerie said, "Doctor Panda Fowler."

Juniper continued. "Anyway, Richland was apparently here until the Doctor told him that Damien wasn't going to die. He hasn't been back since."

"Where did he go?" Valerie asked, then to me said, "He didn't show up at our Gardening meeting, and he was to be the keynote speaker."

"Damien's not sure what Richland is going to do, only that he has now focused on me and the museum," Juniper said. "I told him about the protest." She smiled sadly.

I held up my smartphone, showing Facebook. "The good news is you're trending!"

Valerie and Juniper gave me a look I couldn't fathom. I asked, "Do you think he broke into your house?"

"It's pretty likely. The police are investigating him as a *person of interest.* Can you give me a ride back to my house? I think I need a nap."

"You deserve one." Val put her arm around Juniper, and we walked down the hall. I was glued to Facebook and almost missed getting in the elevator with them. A lovely hand with rainbow nails reached out to stop the door, and Valerie said "Panda!" I reddened and joined them as the door closed.

When it opened on the first floor, we came face to face with Lulu, our security guard at the strip mall. "Lulu! What are you doing here?" She stood with a clipboard in her meaty hand. I noticed her hair was combed and she was wearing a Merryville PD uniform.

"I'm da," she corrected carefully, "*the* guard for yer artist friend." She spread out her muscled arms. "Look who got into the academy." She blushed.

"That's why we haven't seen you at the mall. I called, and they said you were on vacation, and then this new guy said you quit. I hoped it wasn't because of what happened at the mall."

"Aahhh, I din't want to tell anybody. You know, jus' in case." She added, "It was helping you guys that showed me I could be a real cop. To serve and protect!"

"Well, congratulations. I can't think of a braver woman I've ever met." Juniper said it, but we all added "True" and "This is awesome." We really meant it.

After hugs, the doors closed on a broadly grinning Lulu. She was truly going up in more ways than one.

❧

THE SHOUTING

A BOLO was out for Richland Bruce, and soon he was picked up. Potts sat across the scarred metal table in the interrogation room.

"I wasn't hiding! You didn't need to arrest me. This is outrageous!" Richland was disheveled, a bit wild-eyed, and his tie was askew.

"What were you doing in a motel by the railroad tracks then? I thought you were staying with your sister Janice?"

"I needed some time to think. It was really upsetting finding Damien like that."

"Except you didn't."

"What?"

"Find him like that. Damien says you were struggling, and it was an accident."

"What? Then why am I here?"

"Broken flowers, rocks through windows. Petty stuff, except for the note you left." He put up a picture of the note that said, People are fragile like flowers

"You're crazy!"

Charley tossed a manila file on the table. "Look who's been arrested for vandalism before."

"Come on, I was a kid." Richland appeared stunned and surprised. He pointed at the note, "I didn't write that!"

"Then what are you trying to hide, Richland Bruce? You didn't hurt Damien intentionally. You didn't threaten Juniper and her wife. So what are you hiding?"

"Nothing! I'm sick of Merryville and am leaving this cursed place, this Sodom and Gomorrah!"

Potts was getting warmed up when a deputy knocked on the door and then opened it. "The DA says you can let Mister Bruce go."

∾

THE MAVENS AT THE McGREGGOR MANSION

Bridgett returned to the parlor. She held a tapestry and walked to the fireplace. "I've been stitching and stitching, hoping to get this done before your meeting. So sorry." Fergus walked in with a step ladder and said, "Allow me."

The ladies all watched as Bridgett climbed the two steps and placed the tapestry on a hanger above the mantle. The picture was beautiful—dark pale blue background upon which a single Scottish thistle had been stitched—the thing that had been at the heart of so much of Hortense's vitriol toward the Fowlers and, by extension, the Goodens.

Her cup clinked on its saucer. "What is the meaning of this?"

Denise answered. "My mother was pure Mayflower. She loved to emphasize her DAR credentials and suppress my father's Scottish roots. While in Scotland, I researched my family history and found my great grandfather received the Order of the Scottish Thistle! Why, its Scotland's national flower."

"I knew it. I knew it had to be special." No one had paid any attention to Sally, who now stood before the tapestry. "From the first time I saw it up close, I knew it was special. That's wonderful, Denise!"

This was the most animated Sylvia, or any of them, had ever seen Sally get. Hortense was mortified.

"I'm sorry, Denise, this is too much to take. Simply too much. I can't believe your mother would have liked this at all." She stood and distractedly searched for her clip board. Lidia followed. Janet then stood, wrapped her scone in a napkin and put it in her purse.

"So, is that the way it is? Sylvia, Sally?" Denise was bold. There was no getting around that. "What ever happened to this club. How did it get so *small*?"

Beatrice helped herself to some tea. Bianca gave a sharp bark. "Oh, I think I want to join this group!"

Hortense wasn't finished. "You don't have the votes! I've been president of this club for many years." Her cell phone rang, a classic tone.

"Janet get that. It must be Bill. We never use that thing except for emergencies. As I was saying, I'm not about to allow thistles, Scottish or not, to ruin Merryville! Ladies?" She looked around for support.

Janet held the cell phone out to Hortense. "It's Bill. He says the Merryville Police are conducting a search of your home."

The next day, the Merryville Bee carried the Whole Sordid Story.

BILL MILLER, HUSBAND OF HORTENSE MILLER, PRESIDENT OF THE MERRYVILLE MAVENS, ARRESTED FOR VANDALISM AND DEATH THREATS AGAINST MUSEUM CURATOR!

No one could believe it when William "Bill" Miller was arrested Tuesday at the bar of the Merryville Country Club. Several uniformed officers arrived to find him "in his cups" and watching tennis with his cronies. It should be noted that Merryville's Mayor Reed and other notables frequent the club.

Mr. Miller is charged with vandalism, allegedly destroying thousands of dollars in rare orchids at the home of Juniper and Valerie Gooden. In addition, he is charged with throwing a rock through their picture glass window and cutting phone lines. Separate charges have been filed for assault and battery of Detective Charles Potts, who was briefly hospitalized.

A search of the Miller's home turned up several hats that belong to Hortense Miller, and are being tested for her husband's DNA. Miller, it seems, said he was "only looking out for" his nephew, whose recent brief stint at the Merryville Museum was marked by protests. It is also believed he was working in concert with his wife, Hortense Miller, to keep Valerie Gooden from being the first open lesbian in the Horticultural Society.

The Merryville Horticultural Society, affectionately known as the "Merryville Mavens," known for their work at City Hall, have enjoyed a stellar reputation. The mayor has not immediately returned calls for comment in the incidents.

In light of this scandal, Sylvia Arviso was elected Acting President to the Merryville Horticultural Society and is making an open call for others to join. The Bee's own investigative reporter, Phillip Penn, has been on this case since before it turned into an arrest. Apparently, there are ties between Hortense Miller, Richland Bruce and even Judge Dinwitter. The police would only say that Mr. Bruce was brought in for questioning and their investigation is ongoing.

"Wow!" I put the paper down. "Did you have anything to do with this?" I asked Ekk, who sat at the kitchen table with me.

"What would make you ask that?" He looked so innocent.

"Elsa was so sure everything would turn out fine. Hey, where is Elsa?"

"Elsa is watching over Valerie and Juniper. She may have seen a few things."

Mitzi came in and joined us, Brutus in her arms.

"What a day! I just got off the phone with Valerie. She said Juniper's at the museum working with Lucas Windingle, the new Board Chair!"

"What's going to happen to Richland Bruce?"

"She said he left town. I doubt we'll hear from him again."

AT THE BRUCE HOUSEHOLD

Bonnie came downstairs and sat next to her mother on the couch. Janet had been depressed since the meeting Tuesday and her brother's departure.

"Hi. Mom. What's for dinner?

"What? Oh, I hadn't even thought of it."

"Are you going to quit your flower thing?"

"The Mavens? I don't know. Everything went so wrong yesterday." Janet finally appeared to actually see her daughter. "How are you doing, Bon Bon?"

"I'm okay. I feel bad about Uncle Ricky."

"I do, too. He'll be okay, in time. He went back to Ohio to see his therapist. He's confused."

"Well, I've gotta go. If we're not having dinner, I'll go to Taco Bell."

"Wait, let's go out to the Yacht Club for dinner. We should probably talk."

"About what? What Uncle Ricky said?" Bonnie shook her head. "'Cause I don't want to."

Janet sighed. "Honey, I want to spend some time together. We haven't done that in a while."

The beautifully appointed living room was tastefully furnished, but cold. "You need to change."

Bonnie's head snapped up. "I mean for dinner. Listen, whatever you turn out to be, and you can't blame me for hoping you're not gay, I love you, Bonnie. Apparently, something strange runs in this family's blood, and I don't understand it, and I really don't want to talk about it either if the truth be told. But. You're my daughter. I lost your dad and I feel like I've lost Richland now. I won't lose one more person." She started to cry.

Bonnie hugged her and said, "It's okay, Maribel says there's plenty of time for me to figure this out. I'll put on a sweater, but can we go to Origins?"

༄

With the house finally quiet, I took my cat and sat alone in the living room. I looked out the picture window at my now tidy lawn, remembering coming home, a few short weeks ago, to find a press conference being held in front of our house. Why? The Merryville PD was sure someone was murdered and buried in our backyard.

Since March, I'd been to Germany and Peru and faced down evil. Mitzi and I were both kidnapped, Brutus was nearly killed, and now I knew for sure my parents were gone. I felt like I was cracking up.

Ekk came and plopped down next to me and picked up the remote. "You mind?"

"No." I was on overload. When you're in the middle of an adventure, there's no time to think. When it stops, it's like a boat when the wake catches up.

Elsa entered wordlessly with a tray with four lemonades and set it down on the coffee table. She sat on the other side of me, and Brutus immediately went to her, nuzzling her pockets which often contained treats. Ekk put on a taped Jeopardy and was soon doing his best to answer questions. The history and political ones were fine, and he was also pretty good with old-timey actors' names. He was offended at the category Mythical Creatures, Head of an Eagle/Body of a Lion.

"But griffins are real, not mythical!"

I cracked a smile.

"Too soon?" Ekk was becoming quite the comic.

Mitzi came in, having heard the sound of Alex Trebek, and picked up a lemonade. After taking a sip, she exclaimed, "Wow, so great, what's in this?"

"Lavender. It's culinary grade." Elsa was becoming very trendy with her food and drink.

"Scoot over." Elsa went to light a fire in the hearth, and Mitzi sat close to me.

As night fell, our family watched TV, petted the cat and talked about anything other than the craziness we'd been through. After a while, Brutus zipped through his cat door, which had a *Platform 9 & ¾* sign over it.

In the dark, Brutus ran straight into a constable of ravens on the front lawn, scattering them, as the wind picked up. A flyer announcing the building of a permanent church for New Spirit blew in the breeze across the lawn and stuck in the fence. Elsa cocked her head, and the smell of flowers filled the room.

༄

ABOUT THE AUTHOR

Reba Birmingham is an award-winning lawyer, poet, folksinger and author. She was recently inducted onto the Harvey Milk Wall in California for her work with the LGBTQ community. Her website is at: www.RebaBirmingham.com

A NOTE FROM THE AUTHOR

Much has been written about Paititi, the lost city of gold, and many expeditions have set out to find the legendary city. For more information about that, here is a resource:

https://www.mnn.com/lifestyle/arts-culture/stories/the-search-for-the-lost-city-of-paititi

CPSIA information can be obtained
at www.ICGtesting.com
Printed in the USA
FSHW022149260719
60447FS